A STARLET'S SECRET TO A SENSATIONAL AFTERLIFE

KENDALL KULPER

HOLIDAY HOUSE   NEW YORK

HOLIDAY HOUSE is registered in the U.S. Patent and Trademark Office.

Printed and bound in March 2023 at Maple Press, York, PA, USA.

www.holidayhouse.com

First Edition

1 3 5 7 9 10 8 6 4 2

Library of Congress Cataloging-in-Publication Data is available.

ISBN: 978-0-8234-5361-0

For Mom and Dad

The biggest believers in my wild dreams

CHAPTER ONE
HENRIETTA

CHICAGO, 1934

Funny thing: when you drop a bomb, there is a moment of *absolute silence* before the explosion. I witnessed it myself—a space all of three seconds long, during which every one of my family members stopped what they were doing to stare at me with identical expressions of *Excuse me??*

Unsurprisingly, my oldest sister was the first to collect herself. Ruby's fork dropped with a clatter as she pinned me with a stare so fierce I half expected to find my rear permanently glued to the seat. "Absolutely not. Ab. So. Lute. Ly. Not."

That seemed to set everyone else off, too.

Papa: Did you say "Hollywood"?

Mama: But darling, that's in California.

Genny: (No comment. But she did roll her eyes and go back to her book, which for her was a State of the Union address.)

"It's ridiculous!" Ruby again, opining, but luckily her opinion didn't matter. "Hollywood is two thousand miles away!"

I gave her a toothy smile. "Exactly."

"That's where they make the pictures, don't they?" my mother asked from the end of the table, her voice, as usual, all airy dreams and perfume. "What will you do there?"

1

"Make the pictures."

"Have you thought this through, Henrietta?" Papa asked. He took off his glasses and cleaned them, meticulously, on his handkerchief: his tell for when one of his daughters was worrying him. Poor Papa. He'd had spotless glasses for a decade now.

"Of course I have," I said, just as Ruby answered, "Of course she hasn't." We snarled at each other for half a second, then we each got to work.

"Mama, it's just the most magical place! Can't you imagine me up on the screen?"

"Well, you know, dear, all my life people told me I should be an actress and you've always favored—"

"...dirty, mean, unfriendly—Papa, the whole city's paved with bad intentions and the dreams of girls like Henny. If she goes, she'll be back here in three months, her savings gone—and that's if we're lucky!"

Normally, I loved Ruby. I even *liked* her, even at her most annoyingly mother-grizzly-bear. Or rather, I liked her better than my twin, Genevieve, who sat opposite me with her nose so deeply buried in a book it was a wonder she didn't fall in. She'd realized my plan to abandon Chicago for sunny Hollywood had nothing to do with her and promptly ignored the rest of the conversation. I could've set the table on fire and she'd only notice when it got too smoky to read.

Papa cleared his throat, and we all settled down like good little hens. His Grand Judgments were rare enough these days to warrant our full attention. "Henrietta," he said in his thoughtful, lawyerly voice, "please explain yourself."

Please explain yourself. I was going to have those words engraved on my tombstone. My entire childhood it was "Henrietta! Are you climbing

2

up the *outside* of the house?! *Please explain yourself!*" and "I saw you get out of that young man's car, *please explain yourself,*" and "WHO USED UP ALL MY ROUGE HENRIETTA EXPLAIN YOURSELF!"

So I'd had plenty of practice. My hands folded neatly in front of me, I regarded the jury.

"Papa. Mama. Ruby. Degenerate." Genevieve looked over the edge of the book with narrowed eyes. "I've decided to go to Hollywood and try to make it in the movies."

"You can't. Henny, *you can't.*" Ruby crossed her arms. "Where are you going to get the money?"

"I have money. Enough for three months' room and board at the Hollywood Studio Club, a clean and wholesome boardinghouse for clean and wholesome girls."

Genevieve, who shared a bedroom with me and had witnessed me using our fire escape to great personal advantage over the last few years, snorted a laugh but said nothing. Probably because she still wanted to live.

"Wait a sec, I *just* read—" Ruby jumped up from her chair and popped back into the dining room a moment later, the sail of an open newspaper crinkling around her. "Look at this! 'Parents Plead for Information About Missing Girl.' Miss Irma Van Pelt, of Evanston, Illinois, left for Hollywood to become an actress a year ago. Now she's missing! Mama, that could be Henny!"

In spite of the stab of pity I felt for Miss Irma Van Pelt, I considered this a low blow from Ruby. She knew that young girls could find danger down sunny side streets in small towns just as easily as in a place like Hollywood. I hardly gave the article a glance before snatching the paper out of Ruby's hands.

"Probably ran off with some millionaire European magnate," I said, balling it up and tossing it into a corner. "Anyway, it said she had a hard time finding any work, and I won't have to worry about that."

Ruby crossed her arms. "Oh, really? I can't imagine the studios let just anyone in off the street."

I sat up straighter. "You are looking at the winner of the Woodbury Facial Soap Citywide Beauty Contest. Prize: one one-way ticket to Hollywood and a bona fide screen test." Ruby went white as I reached into my pocket and pulled out my trump card: the ticket, a folded-up certificate, and a letter of congratulations from the president of Woodbury Facial Soap, instructing me when and where to go for my screen test.

"Let me see that," Ruby said, pulling the bundle from between my fingers.

"Oh, a beauty contest!" Mama said, clapping her hands together. "Darling, was it very crowded?"

"Two hundred girls." It was actually closer to twenty, but my family didn't need to know that.

"Did they climb out of Lake Michigan?" Genevieve asked, and I flicked a pea at her.

"How do you know this isn't a con?" Ruby asked, peering down at the letter in search of fine print—which was practically her job, busy as she was these days trying to break barriers and become some fine, sword-swinging lady lawyer. She had a few more months of school before her professors unleashed her on an unwitting public, and then everybody'd better watch out. I was actually quite proud of her, when she wasn't swinging that sword of justice in my direction. "I'm going to call this Mr. Woodbury."

She got up from the table right then, although it was Sunday night and I doubted even the hardworking people at the Woodbury Facial Soap Company would be in the office.

"A beauty contest?" Papa's face screwed up in a frown, and he removed his spectacles for another thorough cleaning.

"No answer!" Ruby called from the hallway. She appeared a minute later in the doorway, hands on her hips. "What happens if you get out there and the whole thing was just some publicity stunt so Mr. Woodbury can sell a few more bars of soap? Have any of these past winners ever gone on to anything?"

"Who cares about them? I'm me. And I'm going to do it."

"Men are going to try to take advantage of you." Ruby tossed the letter onto the table.

"Men already try to take advantage of me." I gave a wave with my hand. "Maybe now I can get something out of it."

"Henrietta!" Mama said, trying to sound scandalized. "You're only eighteen!"

"And getting older every second."

"That's another thing." Ruby gave me a hard look. "You look cute now with your blond hair and blue eyes and rosy cheeks, but pretty soon you'll turn thirty years old and no one will hire you again."

"Oh, pish. By then I'll be retired to a mansion with my lovable cocker spaniels and third husband."

"No, not *dogs*, dear," said Mama. "They shed everywhere."

"You've all lost your minds!" Ruby said, her cheeks flushed and eyes glittering and jaw clenched. She had her hands in fists at her side but she took a deep breath and looked me in the eyes. "Henny. Hollywood is nothing but a fantasy, and you are too smart to chase fame and glamor. *What on earth* do you want to do with any of it?"

She said it like the words tasted bad, like she couldn't imagine anyone wanting to muck around in all that filth, and it was the first time I felt a flash of real anger. She didn't get it, my sweet sister, my brilliant sister, six years older, who'd had her wild flapper years, her years of parties in Gold Coast mansions and drinking bathtub booze and sneaking off to the backseats of expensive cars. That was gone now. Ruby's friends thought they were building towers made out of dreams and in the end, that was exactly what they were: nothing concrete or real or solid, skyscrapers of Champagne flutes and feathers. By the time it was my turn for that delicious gin-soaked-black-silk-long-pearls-sweaty-curls debauchery, the party'd ended and the bill came due.

The markets collapsed, the jobs disappeared, and Ruby had disappeared into her safe, secluded university and left us holding the bag. Left *me* holding the bag, thank you very much, what with Papa growing frailer and Mama absolutely hopeless and Genevieve as ungrateful as the cat. I was the one who had to let the housekeeper go, to encourage Mama to turn her gorgeous exotic hothouse into a vegetable garden, to arrange the budget and penny-pinch for groceries and barter and sell and trade and squabble over every little thing that came into or left this house.

Now the ship had made it through the storm, more or less, with everyone blinking into the sunlight, not noticing I'd almost snapped in half from the sheer weight of it—but didn't, thanks to one thing.

You know that moment, when you're sitting in a theater, when it smells like popcorn and taffy and too many children, and the lights have gone all the way out, so you're alone in the warm dark with a hundred strangers... that moment just before the organ blares to life, before the screen explodes with light, when everyone goes still and silent and waiting?

The movies saved me. I couldn't afford the thirty-cent ticket but I could bat my eyes at the ticket man and bring over a basket of Mama's vegetables and take one of the half-price seats at the back. In the darkness, in the light, I could feel my body dissolve. I wasn't Henrietta Newhouse who scrubbed the washrooms and clutched at every saved penny and re-remade my sister's winter coat—I was just a pair of eyes and a pair of ears, taking it all in. Taking in *them*. The *actors*.

I was going to Hollywood, cliché be damned, because I wanted to be a star.

Not the kind that wore mink coats and drank gin and stumbled into every leading man's arms—although that didn't sound too bad, frankly. I wanted to be a literal star, something huge and bright and fierce and burning, something no one could stop staring at, something that turned everyone who came close to it warm and glowing.

You couldn't do that in a place like Chicago, I didn't care how much Ruby chirped on about the theater companies. I knew this city and all its sharp, icy points, the way the cold of the surrounding prairie and the cold off the lake combined into something otherworldly arctic. Someday, that cold would seep into my bones and freeze me to this place forever. I'd meet a nice mechanic or a friendly shop owner or a pharmacist with good teeth and his name would be Harry or Bill or Fred and he'd take me out and in six months we'd be married and I'd have to live forever in a tidy house in a sensible suburb and then you might as well just throw the coffin lid SHUT.

But I couldn't say that to my family over the picked-apart Sunday chicken, so I just shrugged and said, "It's too cold in Chicago. I want a tan."

Ruby stared at me. She stared for so long I thought she might not be breathing, and then she let out a deep sigh.

"What will you do if you fail?"

I had an answer to that, too. "I'll come back." I felt the sting of the words but kept on marching. "And go to college and get married and have babies and do whatever I'm supposed to do, knowing that at least I gave my wild dream a shot."

Mama looked at Papa, who looked at Ruby, and Ruby said nothing, her mouth set in a hard line, and that was that. I'd done it.

"When can we move your bed out of my room?" Genny asked, and I threw another pea at her.

CHAPTER TWO

DECLAN

HOLLYWOOD

A breeze ruffled my hair. My shoes scraped along the edge of the roof, toes pointed toward miles of empty air. Five stories up, the city looked different, the department stores and hotels jutting up like jagged teeth beside dusty one-story buildings. The light shimmered with heat, the mountains just a faraway olive smudge, hazy on the horizon. Sweat slid down my neck as I dug a finger into the collar of my costume—a three-piece suit wrapped around what had to be thirty pounds of cotton batting. How did anybody breathe in this city? Even in January, the air felt yellow and thick, sticking to my lungs.

Down at street level, the cops jockeyed to push back a crowd of tourists so excited by an *actual movie shoot* they'd whipped up into a frenzied mob. They hadn't realized they were being used, that no one would shoot on top of one of the most stylish buildings on Hollywood Boulevard— where the hucksters, grifters, con men, and fools outnumbered the stars ten to one—unless they were after spectacle.

"The longest drop in Hollywood history!" The director made sure everyone in that crowd knew it. They'd put out a call to newspapers, reporters: *Come witness it, a* real *stunt.* Moviegoers had gotten wise to camera tricks and quick editing, taking the shock out of stunts, but everyone knew you couldn't fake a sixty-foot fall: a real body, real distance, real danger. That jolt of reality was what audiences wanted, which made it what the director wanted, and that was why production spent a week calling up, and getting laughed at by, every stunt man in the city, until they had no choice but to put out an open call. And the only person dumb enough to respond to the ad was...me. "Great opportunity for you! Will lead to lots more work!" I'd been hearing it all day, and then there'd be an uncomfortable silence, the kind that said... *if you survive.*

"C-Collins? You set?" They'd sent an assistant director up to the roof with me, but mostly he'd been clutching at the parapets, his face some shade between *I'm going to throw up* and *I'm going to pass out.*

I pulled my eyes away from the ugly horizon and glanced over at him.

"If I said no, would you just give me a push?"

It was a joke, but he blanched, his legs trembling like he could no longer rely on them, as though, this high up, gravity transformed into something you couldn't trust, a loyal pet that suddenly bared its teeth.

"One minute!" Sixty feet below, someone shouted up at me with a bullhorn, and the assistant director, needing to feel useful, echoed back, "That's one minute, Collins."

I looked down. Far below, there was a messy sandwich of cardboard and feather mattresses and plywood that would catch me. At least, that was what I'd been told. I'd never actually done anything like this before. The only stunts Pep had managed to find for me in the last eight months involved background bar fights or twelve hours getting drenched with fake rain on fake ships.

All right. Maybe this was a mistake. Maybe whatever blacklist waited for me on the other end of "Nope, I'll pass, actually," was better than staying in an industry that dropped desperate nobodies sixty feet onto

Hollywood Boulevard with nothing more than a hundred dollars and some crossed fingers. Pep could find me another job...once he started speaking to me again. Or even better, we could get out of this stupid, hot city, where you didn't matter unless you had a list of screen credits or a million dollars, and go back home to the crowded house on Valencia Street—

"Action! Stunts! Go!"

"*Go!*" the assistant director repeated, but before he'd gotten the word out, my body reacted, doing the thing it was meant to do before my mind could say, "Now, wait a sec."

My toes flexed, springing me into the air, high in an arc over absolutely nothing, and for a fraction of a fraction of a second, a moment that felt like a hundred years, I hung suspended, arms outstretched, toes pointed, body free, hot wind in my face like a hiss of breath, and then—the fall.

Just three seconds.

One—head down, air rushing past, flickering flashes of windows, wide-eyed staring faces

Two—flip and twist, face up, cottony clouds, deep blue sky

Three—screaming wind, gasping from the crowd—

FWOOSH!

Wood splintered in sharp cracks, feathers swirled in the air like snow, and for a second all I could do was lie in a pit of debris, breathing hard and blinking up at the bright California sun. Then: "Cut!" and pandemonium broke out; faces looming over me, hands reaching, a thousand voices asking, "Is he alive?"

"Did he make it?"

"I can't believe he did it!"

The relief that broke out on everyone's faces was so desperate that I knew right away no one had expected to pull a warm, breathing, unbroken kid from that mess. They set me down, patting me like they weren't sure I was real, as I blinked out at the roaring crowd.

"Good boy! Good boy!" A flushed face appeared, a hand clapping my shoulder, and I realized it was the director when he turned around and shouted to the spectators, "Sixty feet, ladies and gentlemen! The longest drop ever! And you can see it again on the big screen in *Falling for Thieves,* out this April from Silver Wing Studios!"

I looked back up at the building, the neon KRESS sign far away and pale in the sunlight, my heart pounding fast like I'd gotten away with something. They'd set up a makeshift dressing room for me, a canvas tent on the wide sidewalk, but when I tried to move, one crew member clutched at me, eyes wild. He was shouting about a doctor, getting a doctor, and even though I kept telling him I was *fine,* his fingers gripped my arm like he worried I might explode into a million pieces.

"DUKE!"

The crowd parted—no easy feat, because even at eighteen, Pep barely came up to most men's shoulders. But what he lacked in height he made up in volume, running off the anxious crew member like a sharp-taloned rooster before throwing an arm around me.

"Hey, that looked pretty good." He leaned in with a raised eyebrow. "Think you got another one in you? I could slip the cameraman a fiver, say there was a glare, get you double pay."

What he meant was get *us* double pay. Pep was my oldest friend, but in a city like Hollywood, friendship usually came with some sort of business transaction, which was another way to say he worked as my manager.

"Hello*ooooo!*"

Before I could respond to him, a woman popped into our path, holding a notepad and wriggling her fingers. "Say, that was some swan dive! Think you've got a tick to chat? The *Reel Picture* readers would love to hear what it takes to be a real-life stunt man!"

She gave me a look like she was dangling a juicy bone in front of a starving dog; any extra in this city would kill—truly, *kill*—for a feature in *Reel Picture*.

"Nope," I said, giving my tie a hard yank, and Pep, laughing nervously, slid between us.

"Josepe Perez! Mr. Collins's manager, nice to make your acquaintance!" He had his hand out and his hat off, and, figuring I wasn't needed anymore, I pushed past him into the tent.

In the dim, gold-colored light under the canopy, I struggled to shuck off my costume while I listened to Pep diving into the latest version of his pitch. He'd been perfecting it for close to a decade now, walking the fine line between talking me up and selling me out. Before "Declan Collins, stunting sensation," there'd been "Kid Duke, teenaged prizefighter," and before that he'd tried pitching me to carnivals as the "Incredible, Unbreakable Boy." Even as kids together in the Mission, no bigger than pair of puppies, he'd tell anyone who'd listen, "My friend Declan is SO STRONG he could take on any one of you!"

But then, that was Pep, always pushing, always trying to get me to do just a little more than I'd agreed to.

"Where would you be without me, Duke?" he liked to ask, with a grin and a punch on the shoulder. I knew exactly where I'd be: like the other kids we grew up with, a job at one of the factories or tanneries, the occasional ball game at Seal Stadium, my days spent within the boundaries of our neighborhood. Pep made it sound like prison, but I wasn't so sure.

You knew who you were in a place like the Mission. People knew you, your reputation, and judged you for your character instead of what you could do for them. If five folks like that existed in Hollywood, I'd jump off a building twice as high.

I'd only managed to slip off my tie and unbutton my shirt before I heard Pep's voice rise.

"...not just stunts, but act, too! I've got him set up with a screen test—"

Screen test? I pushed open the flap, startling the reporter.

"Uh, 'scuse me, Mr. Perez, sir, but you are talking out your ass," I said, trying to pull off my jacket. "You know I don't act. You know I don't want to act. You know I only agreed to even *come here* because you said I wouldn't— What's the matter with this damn thing?" The jacket was stuck on something, and I finally gave it a hard tug free, taking my shirt with it. I looked up to see the reporter staring at me—my torso bare except for the roll of padding around my stomach—with wide eyes.

"*What* is *that?*"

"Come on, like you've never seen—" My words broke off as she lifted a trembling finger, and I glanced down...

A piece of wood, three or four inches thick, stuck out from the cotton batting, somewhere in the area of my left kidney. Without thinking, I yanked it free, the reporter letting out a gasp so sharp I thought she might pass out, but instead of bloody, jagged edges, the end of the wood had turned blunt, like someone had tried to hammer it into concrete. I suddenly remembered the white-faced crew member, the one anxious to get me to a doctor.

"It's...It's, uh..."

"You should be *dead!*" The color had drained from her face, her eyes as big as dinner plates, but before I could say anything else, Pep had whisked the wood out of my hand and out of sight, then clapped me on my shoulder.

"Hey, looks like it's a good day to play the lottery, huh? Declan Collins, the luckiest stunt man in Hollywood!" He all but shoved me back into the tent, shouting over his shoulder, "Now remember: it's *Collins* with two *l*'s, and I'm Josepe Perez!"

A second later he'd joined me under the canopy, a loopy grin on his face like a speeding train had missed him by an inch.

"That was close. Think she'll write about you?"

"She better not." I held up the jacket and wriggled a finger through the hole the wood had made. "Look at this! I told you this job was a bad idea."

"You worry too much. And anyway, this job was a GREAT idea! After today, I'm going to need a secretary to handle your offers. Just picture it!" He stretched out his arms, like he was building some grand marquee in the sky. " 'Declan Collins, stunt man, leading man!' "

I unwound the sweaty rolls of cotton and tossed them right at Pep's face. "You promised we'd stick around this city for a year, tops. You've only got five more months—"

"Plenty of time! Now polish your awards speech, Duke, 'cause we're going to the moon!" He had that grin I'd seen a million times before, full of dreams about everything we were going to do, together, all the doors that would open, the money and the fame and the power.

Pep fit right in here, where it seemed like everyone from our landlady to the corner grocer believed they were one good day away from stardom, if they just stuck around, tried harder, met the right person.

But the whole thing left me cold. Hollywood made me think of quicksand, a whirlpool, sucking people in. How many washed-up actors spent their days panhandling on the corner of Wilcox and Hollywood

Boulevard? The lines for the soup kitchens south of Sunset stretched around the block. It was a two-city town: a dream world of glittering parties and expensive clothing and elegant restaurants, and a nightmare of desperate hopefuls and the monsters who preyed on them.

Pep was a good salesman, but he hadn't sold me. I wasn't going to stay. What would the prize be? Money? Fame? Who *really* wanted fame? Crowds of strangers desperate for a piece of you, reporters looking to rip you up, would-be "friends" always after a few favors.

The truth was I came here because there were only so many places in the world that would pay you to survive stupid things, and Hollywood was the closest.

Pep launched into his arguments, but I was ready for him.

"Acting pays more!"

Not after today. I'd earned a hundred dollars to jump off that building and, more importantly, a reputation for doing the kind of stunts no one else would. I was on my way to a steady stream of work. I could get maybe a couple hundred dollars a week, and that was enough to satisfy any decent fella.

"Lots of pretty girls on movie sets!"

I'd already gotten onto enough movie sets to know those girls didn't give a hoot about a lowly stunt man. If they only cared about me once my name had moved up the call sheet, I didn't want to meet them.

"It's safer!"

As soon as he said that, we both burst out laughing. True, I didn't know any stunt men with gray hairs—but getting hurt was one thing I didn't have to worry about.

Shove me down a set of stairs, set me on fire, drag me from a galloping horse, throw me from a runaway train: I'd live. I'd survive, pop up without a broken bone, without a bruise, without a scratch. I couldn't even catch a cold. Couldn't explain it. Didn't know why. Pep was the only person in the world who had any idea what I could really do, and I figured he was also the only person in the world to see it as an opportunity.

That alone made it worthwhile to be his friend, to follow him through his craziest schemes, even all the way to Hollywood. But I had to draw the line somewhere.

"Come on. I did the fall. It's gonna lead to more work, I know it. Let's just make our money, then we can get out of here and go back home."

"Home?" He sounded disappointed. "Duke, don't you want to be famous?"

"Didn't you hear that crowd?" I asked with a grin. "I'm already a star."

"Yeah, sure." He snorted out a laugh. "A falling star."

CHAPTER THREE
HENRIETTA

Well. I had some *strong* words regarding the hospitality of the Woodbury Facial Soap Company. A "grand send-off" consisting of a single bored photographer and a hurried handshake from "Mr. Woodbury," a man who looked like he couldn't even spell *s-o-a-p*, let alone sell it. A one-way rail ticket that made it clear I'd get to Hollywood but failed to mention I'd have to switch trains in St. Louis, Oklahoma City, *and* Albuquerque, or that my every accommodation would get successively smaller, until when I finally arrived, I had to carefully unfold each of my limbs from the cramped compartment. I suppose I couldn't blame Woodbury Soap for the weather—far from California sunshine, I emerged into a storm that seemed to legally obligate every resident of Los Angeles to comment, "There hasn't been rain like this in years!"

Undeterred, I hauled off to the Hollywood Studio Club, which I quickly learned was an entirely different place from the "Studio Club of Hollywood," because one of them existed, with a six-month waiting list, and the other was an elaborate swindle I'd unfortunately fallen for.

"Oh dear. You didn't mail them a deposit, did you?" the girl at the front desk asked me.

"First month's rent," I answered, feeling a bit sick.

"Oh dear," the girl repeated. "Not another one."

Instead of spending my first night in Hollywood dreaming peacefully in a clean bed, I sat up for hours in a string of dingy tea rooms, dozing over cups of cooling orange pekoe and dodging friendly male customers.

But still. I was here, *in Hollywood,* and once the rain cleared out the next morning, the sunshine rolled in so warm and glowing that I barely made it two blocks before I stopped, pulled every pair of woolen stockings from my suitcases, and gleefully tossed them in the trash. Already, I could feel the heat of the city on my skin, warming up the parts of me that had gone cold those last few white-knuckle years in Chicago.

The Woodbury Soap winner's letter came with scant information about my screen test: just the date and time, along with directions to "A. F. Chilton Studios." I'd never heard of them before, although that didn't mean much— there were plenty of independent studios. So A. F. Chilton wasn't Silver Wing Studios, the perennial first place when it came to box office standings, but there was no shame in getting one's start in a small pond.

After ditching my bags in a shabby little boardinghouse, I trekked out to A. F. Chilton Studios, located so far south in the city I kept wondering when I'd hit the ocean. Most of Los Angeles below Santa Monica Boulevard seemed to be industrial graveyards or wide, fenced-in lots with broken-down construction equipment. I passed several old movie studios, names I didn't recognize: Cheshire Films and Actors Amalgamated, their warehouse windows boarded up, their exterior sets of English gardens and Spanish villages sun-bleached and rotting.

Sweating through my best dress, I finally made it to a run-down building barely bigger than my home in Chicago. Outside the front door, a skinny boy in dingy clothing leaned against the stoop, smoking a harsh-smelling cigarette and giving me a long look.

"Lost?"

"Is this A. F. Chilton Studios?"

The boy blinked and then said, "Oh yeah. Yeah, sure."

"I have a screen test," I said, my voice bright in spite of a funny kick in my stomach. I held up my letter to show him. He squinted at it and then dropped his cigarette.

"Someone'll get you in a sec."

He pushed open the door to the building, and I was wondering if I should follow him when out of the corner of my eye, a girl just... *appeared*—there really wasn't any other word for it—as though she'd popped right into existence, startling the hell out of me.

"Oh!" I said, grabbing my chest, and then I laughed. She looked my age, dressed neatly in a forest-green suit, dark-copper hair pulled into an elegant chignon under a hat. "Excuse me! Are you here for a screen test, too?"

She stared up at the squat building. "Don't go in there."

"What do you mean? I've my test in just a minute."

"No." She shook her head, glaring at the building as though she could will it to burst into flames. "No, I would not suggest you go in there. They're not what they say they are."

The little hairs on the back of my neck went up. I looked over at the building and turned to ask the girl what she was talking about, but she had vanished, the long sidewalk empty in both directions.

"Oh, miss! Miss, hello!" A man burst through the front door, pulling me from my thoughts. He wore clothes that showed stains, the edges frayed, his hair colorless, slicked with grease or cheap pomade. "You're, ah, my new girl?" The way he stared at me made me feel like a plate of sausages set in front of a slathering dog—he literally *licked his lips* in a way that made my stomach turn.

"No," I said, the word popping out of me, pure animal instinct. Surprised at myself, I tried to recover with a polite smile, but it wilted immediately. "No, my mistake." And I turned tail and ran.

Later, back at my temporary boardinghouse digs, crammed into the crowded bunkroom, I rubbed my blistered feet and told the story to one of my new roommates, a woman who'd been in and out of extra work for years.

"You threw away a screen test?" Her face scrunched up in disappointment. "A real screen test? For nothing!"

"It didn't feel right," I said with a shrug, although as I sat cozy and safe on my bed, embarrassment set in.

"From Chicago to here, and now what? Your one chance! I think you should go back there and apologize and you better pray they—"

"No." From across the room, an older woman sitting on her bunk set down the laundry she was folding and looked me right in the face. "Did you say A. F. Chilton? They've got a bad name around here. I don't know what they do with young girls, but they don't make them into movie stars."

A chill went through me. "What do you mean?"

My bunkmate let out a scoff. "Oh, don't listen to her." She threw her hands in the air, shaking her head. "Honestly! Some gals got all the luck and none of the brains." She stomped off to the washroom, leaving me wondering what dumb thing I'd done, when the older woman sidled up to me and patted my shoulder.

"You did right. Only a fool'd go into a building you don't know what they do inside'a it."

"You don't think I threw away my good luck?"

She shrugged. "Better no job than a bad job, eh? You keep it up, you'll find something. Luck—luck was that girl findin' you when she did."

"Oh, sure." I let out a dry laugh. "My guardian angel."

The woman didn't smile back. "Maybe she was," she said, her deep voice thoughtful. "I'll tell you this, miss. You come across any other guardian angels in this city—listen to them."

CHAPTER FOUR
DECLAN

Swinging from chandeliers, throwing myself off trains, stepping in to take punches meant for more famous jaws—Pep had me everywhere. The phone hadn't quit ringing since I'd stepped off the Kress building's roof. Productions only had to say, "D'you think he could—" before Pep would jump in with YES, HE CAN. If I ever complained he'd respond, "You're the one who only wants to stay in Hollywood a year. Gotta make the most of it, Duke!"

"Making the most of it" turned out to mean booking jobs at Silver Wing Studios, the biggest outfit in the city, with the highest pay, the best opportunities, and the greatest commissary I'd ever had the pleasure of tucking in at. Set far to the west end of the city, a quiet neighborhood of empty lots and dumpy stores, the studio itself wasn't much to look at: acres of concrete roads, boxy soundstages like looming warehouses, squat offices with stenciled signs. Sunbaked and sterile, the lot felt as lifeless as the surface of the moon, the occasional halfhearted bush gasping in the heat and wondering where all the orange trees went.

Pep exploded with excitement anytime we made it through Silver Wing's famous colonnade. He couldn't stop pointing out the stars, the producers—I had to tackle him when he spotted Irving Reynolds, Silver

Wing's legendary president, strolling the lot with three secretaries trailing behind like devoted dogs. I barely noticed any of them.

My eyes kept catching on the faces of the women on the lot. Not the starlets, not the dancers with their long legs, but the script supervisors, the seamstresses, the assistants: women pushing their thirties, cloche hats pulled over short hair, worry lines at the edges of their mouths.

"Distracted?"

Sitting in the commissary, my hair still wet from that night's pirate ship brawl, I pulled my attention from a group of chatting women at the bar across the room and looked back at Pep.

"What's that?" I asked, taking a sip of water. "You said…there's a war movie?"

Pep gave me a flat look and then turned back to glance at the women, his mouth pulling into a sly smile. "Lookin' for company?"

"Wh-What?" Coughing, I set my glass down, and then I realized he wasn't looking across the room but at the table next to us, a trio of giggling mermaids with metallic paint dusted over shoulders and cheeks, making them glow purple and pink.

Pep's smile spread into a grin. "Let's see what kind of Champagne mermaids like."

I knew what Pep had in mind, and I didn't want to spend my evening at the Embassy Club, trying to convince the bartender I was old enough to drink. Even though we hadn't eaten yet, I stood up and patted Pep on the shoulder.

"Don't spend too much of our money."

The sun had set, the temperature outside finally low enough that I could slip on my jacket as I walked from the commissary to the Main Gate, but the air…A cinematographer on one of my jobs had explained to me that Los Angeles sat in a bowl created by the mountains, and it trapped all manner of heat, fumes, smoke. The air tasted wrong. Choking. Sour. It was the opposite of the Mission, high on a hill, the green of Mission Park warmed by a perfect circle of blue sky while the rest of the city hid behind murky fog. Whenever I pointed this out to Pep, he accused me of dramatics, but I couldn't help feeling like we'd left paradise for a city that wanted to poison us.

"Declan Collins?"

As I passed through the Main Gate, a middle-aged man stepped in front of me, a gray felt fedora obscuring his face.

"If you want to book me," I said, "you need to go through my manager."

The man smiled and set his fists on his hips, pulling his coat open. My eyes went right to his side, to the gun holstered at his belt.

"Actually, Declan, I wanted to talk to you." In spite of his smile, I felt wariness prickle at the back of my neck.

Was he a cop? A thug? A man waiting outside the studio gates *with a gun* wasn't someone I cared to meet. Pep would've been able to talk us out of this situation, but Pep wasn't here.

"Yeah, I don't think—" I started, and when the man took a step closer to me, I turned and hurried down the sidewalk.

"Hey! Hold on—"

The Silver Wing studio sat in a triangle between broad streets—not many places to lose a man with a gun. I made the first turn I could and spotted a small parking lot with about a dozen cars. Crouching, I ducked behind a forest-green Ford and was listening for the sound of footsteps when I felt a hand grab me from behind and push me up against the car.

"Gotcha!"

I kicked and struggled, shouting at him to let me go while he shook me like a puppy.

"Kid—*kid!* Damn it, kid, quit fighting!" He pulled back, tilting my face into the beam of a streetlamp. "Declan Collins, right? Stunt man?"

"No, whatever you heard—"

"*Quiet.* I'm not police, and I'm not gonna hurt you. I want to hire you. Not for a stunt."

His words made me go still, and carefully, he took a step back, hands raised like I was a wild animal.

"Let's just talk. You wanna eat something? Lemme get you dinner, I'll explain the whole thing." He cocked his head at me and pointed down the street. "There's a diner, end of the block. You gotta eat, right? Dinner, for ten minutes of your time. Deal?"

Without waiting for a response, he looped his arm around my shoulders and led me along beside him while my mind spun.

Hire me? For *what*? *Who was he*? I wasn't sure what to say, what to do—Pep had spoken for me for so long, I felt a little lost, and before I could figure out how to get away, the man said with a smile, "Here we are."

The "diner" didn't look like much: a cramped kitchen set back from the street in shadows, hardly big enough to hold customers. But the windows glowed with warm light, and the smell of food made my stomach growl. The man started up the front stairs, which groaned in protest, and as he pushed through the door, the waiter sang out a hello to him.

"How you do, Sam? Usual?"

"Yeah. And a burger for the kid." He looked at me. "You drink cola? Pop? Get the kid a soda, Johnny, would you?" The place didn't have any tables or booths—or other customers—just a line of stools set along a counter. The man eased his large frame onto one, tucking his arms in like wings. "Come on. Sit."

I could run, but curiosity and hunger won out, so I slumped down to a stool. In the grimy light of the diner, I could get a better look at his face. He seemed to be in his thirties, with a stiff brush of gray shadow covering his cheeks. He'd set his hat on the stool next to him, and his dark-blond hair, longish but slicked back, still showed the crease of his hatband. He wore a faint smile, his skin sallow and slack like he didn't get much sleep, shadows under his eyes, which were trained on my hands, shaking on the narrow counter.

Quick, I jerked them away.

"Take a picture," I said, and he laughed.

"Just admiring them. Good hands. Strong, you know. Anyway." He leaned forward. "I saw you, jumping from the Kress Five and Ten last month. Wanted to say hello but you slipped away too quick. Sam Cranston." He shifted on the stool, stuck out his hand, but I didn't move. "You know, that was a helluva thing. Couldn't get it out of my mind. How'd you do it, kid?"

My throat felt dry. "Practice."

"Bullshit. There's years of experience, and there's whatever the hell you are. It's the kinda thing that sticks in a person's head, you know? Hey, let me tell you a story." He smiled, laced his hands together on the counter. "My pop, God rest, loved boxing. A few years back he tells me I gotta come out and see this kid. *Unbelievable.* I expected Dad to say he had smooth feet, quick hands, but no. The kid's skills were weak, couldn't hardly throw a punch. But *take* a punch? The way Dad went on about it, it was like watching a speed bag up there, like he couldn't even feel the hits."

As he spoke, a damp cold worked up the back of my neck, every nerve in my body screaming at me to get up and *go.*

"So Dad dragged me out there. It was incredible. The kid just stood and *took it.* Knock him down and he'd pop right up again. A regular jack-in-the-box, till the other guy plumb wore himself out. Craziest thing.

But then he disappeared from the circuit, never did hear about him again. You know what they called him?" He smiled at me while I stared back at him. "Kid Duke."

His words brought back the day of the sixty-foot jump. Pep shouting for me, calling out the boxing name he'd picked years before.

"What do you want?" I asked, my voice quiet.

"Just answer a question, all right? I saw you take punches strong enough to split a full-grown man in half. A few weeks ago, you jumped off a building and landed on a piece of wood that would've skewered a pig. And don't start about padding or lucky breaks," he said when I opened my mouth. "I'm looking at you, and I don't see a scar, scrape, or scab on you. Kid." His voice dropped and he leaned in close.

"I've got my thirty-eight on my hip. What I want to know is: If I put a bullet right between your eyes, would it even break the skin? Hey, Johnny, that looks great! Just set 'em both there, thanks much."

He leaned back as two plates slid onto the counter. The colors of the food looked too bright, the shapes swirling together, the smell of grease turning my stomach. I looked up at Sam, busy tucking a napkin into the collar of his shirt.

"You... don't know what you're talking about."

He reached for one of his French fries and dragged it through a puddle of ketchup. "Let me tell you something, and I hope it sets you at ease." With the fry raised in the air, he paused. "You're not in any trouble, all right? I don't understand it, I don't want to. I mean, you stick a knife in my gut, I'm done, but if I try it out on you? What happens? The knife breaks? Hey, eat something. Don't let that bun get soggy."

He nudged my plate before turning to his own meal, a sandwich sliced into neat triangles.

"Go on. You look like you're about to slide onto the floor."

I picked up the burger and took a bite.

"See? It's good. My cousin's brother-in-law owns the place. That means I get the family discount."

While I chewed, the food like sand in my mouth, Sam leaned forward again. "It's okay to smile, kid."

"You haven't told me what you want." I set the burger down, and he sat up straight again.

"All right," he said. "I'm a P.I. Private investigator. Before that, it was fifteen years at the L.A.P.D., and you know what my days looked like? Phone calls. Phone calls from parents in Missouri and Michigan. Little towns from sea to shining sea. They tell me their girls got on trains or hopped into cars with slick-haired strangers and came here, Hollywood, to chase their dreams. Maybe they called home once or twice, maybe they wrote letters. Some found work. Most—nothing. And their families never heard from them again."

As he spoke, I felt my nerves go tight as piano wire. I knew all this.

"Girls go missing in Hollywood for the same reasons girls go missing anywhere else. Usually, if you do a little digging, you can find them. Some of these girls, though, it's like they disappear." Shifting awkwardly on the stool, he reached into his jacket pocket and placed on the counter—

A magazine? A glassy-eyed actress smiled from the cover. Sam raised his sandwich again and in between bites said, "Page twenty-three."

When I flipped through I found a photo of a row of smiling young women. Someone had drawn a red circle in pencil around the one all the way on the left, a pretty girl with a dimple in her right cheek.

"What am I looking at?"

"Irma Van Pelt. Arrived in Hollywood a year ago. Couple background parts, bit roles, had a contract with Silver Wing. Whispers around the studio were that she was a little too friendly with some of the fellas on the lot. More interested in socializing than making it to set on time, and her contract didn't get renewed. People thought she left the city in a huff, but then last fall, her parents rang up the precinct where I worked. They hadn't heard from her in weeks, and they said the last time she called, she'd sounded scared. Kept repeating that the movie business wasn't what she thought it'd be." Sam tapped a finger right on Irma Van Pelt's dimpled cheek. "I looked into it, and you know what I found? More Irmas. Some going back years. Girls knock on doors, sign contracts, maybe make a few pictures, and then disappear. Not home to Idaho or Poughkeepsie. Just... gone."

Irma Van Pelt stared up at me from the page, her eyes sparkling, her mouth pulled into a smile so pure it practically shot sunbeams into this dingy diner...

Quickly, I closed the magazine.

"Silver Wing runs this city," Sam continued, "including the police. When I started sniffing around, my C.O. told me to knock it off. When I didn't quit, I got canned." He shrugged. "I gave the Van Pelts the bad news the case would get buried, and they decided to hire me themselves. They've got money. What they needed was someone on the ground in California to find out what happened to their daughter. Now they have me."

"Then why do you need *me*?"

Sam paused. "This doesn't leave the room, all right, kid?" He gave me a level look and reached into his jacket again, pulling out a press clipping, a shot of two men. Right away, I recognized the round glasses and mild expression of Irving Reynolds, president of Silver Wing Studios, but I had no clue about the other man, brick-faced with a haircut so even you could use it to draft architectural plans.

"Irving Reynolds is the most powerful man in Los Angeles," Sam said, his voice hushed, and he tapped a finger on the mystery man's face, "and that's how he does it. Richard Mulvey. On paper, he's Silver Wing's general manager. He gets the electricity bills paid and the grass cut, but the real reason Reynolds hired him is to make all Silver Wing's problems disappear."

"What kind of problems?"

"Oh, you know. The kind clean-cut studios don't want the public to know about. Like maybe one of their wholesome leading ladies has some photos floating around that only her husband should see. Or a cowboy's got a reputation for taking young fellas home with him. With committees of concerned citizens harping on about the Sodom and Gomorrah of Hollywood, Reynolds knows he's gotta run a clean studio, on-screen and off, so he sends Mulvey out to hide, bribe, or disappear the mess. If there are bodies buried—figurative or...y'know—Mulvey would know. But he's a tough character, kid. Reynolds imported him straight from Jersey. He's got mob connections and he's not afraid to use them, or even get his hands dirty himself." Sam tucked the photo back into his jacket. "I hired a couple men to get close to him. The first died in a movie stunt gone wrong."

"What about the second?"

Sam set down his sandwich. "Suicide, according to the studio, but pretty unusual for someone to kill himself with five bullets." He shrugged. "I can't prove what happened, but I'm guessing Mulvey had a hand in it. I quit hiring people after that—too risky. Then I remembered the kid who had no fear."

I blinked, not understanding what he was saying until it hit me in a rush: he wanted me to be a spy inside Silver Wing Studios. The biggest studio—the biggest *anything*—in the city, and he wanted *me* to go against them.

"No, I don't— That's not—" I shook my head. "I'm a stunt man. Barely. I'm a nobody. I don't have a contract with Silver Wing. I don't even have a studio pass!"

"You don't—" Sam put a hand on my arm, but I pulled away quick, knocking into the counter and sending the plates rattling.

"You're asking me to go up against *Irving Reynolds*. You said it yourself—he owns everything in this city. The police, the politicians, the hospitals. Sure, he can't send this Mulvey guy to break my kneecaps, but there are other ways to ruin somebody. I have a friend counting on me, a good person. He believes in me, he got me this work, I owe him, and I'm only here to make us money. That's it! I'm leaving soon, all right? I can't chase down missing girls, that's not— Did you ever think maybe those girls aren't missing? Maybe they just didn't *want* to go back to their families."

Sam stared at me like I'd started speaking in German.

"You think someone would do that? Cut their family off without a word?"

I had my chin raised. "This city changes people. Maybe the Van Pelts don't know their daughter as well as they think."

"Hey—" Sam started, but I was gone. Out the door, onto the street, the winter air cool on my flushed cheeks, my heart beating so fast my head spun. I'd only just reached the end of the corner when I felt a hand on my shoulder, pulling me back.

"Kid, come on..." Sam held out a card before pushing it into my pocket. "Think about it. Think about what it means. These girls...I don't know what's happened to them, but I can tell you right now if no one ever looks into it, if no one does anything about it, it'll happen again and again. You know that. Think about the Van Pelts, think about those other parents, sweethearts, friends, worrying about their girls. You ever lost someone, kid? Wouldn't you do anything to find them again?"

A knot pushed up into my throat, and I shook off Sam's hand.

"I can't help you. I'm sorry, I just—I'm the wrong person."

And before he could grab me again, I turned around, walking quickly into the dark.

CHAPTER FIVE
HENRIETTA

"Howdy, pardner, step right on into the roooooodeo!" Heel, toe, step, kick, swivel, and pose, over and over until I was sure my hips would go on strike, but it was a job, and possibly the only one I'd ever get in this city.

After A. F. Chilton, I'd vowed to only get work from respectable, established outfits, not realizing that "respect" was scarce in this city.

First, I tried the major studios, but none of them would even let me past their front gates, and when I called up Central Casting from the boardinghouse, a girl just trilled at me, *"Tra-la!"* and hung straight up.

Confused, I rang them again and got the same thing—*"Tra-la!"* Click. I stared at the phone until a girl watching nearby broke into peals of laughter and explained that the only thing the Central Casting operators did all day was answer the phone calls of hopeful extras, who would call over and over, a hundred times a day, asking for work. *Tra-la* was industry-speak for "Try later." In other words: Go away.

The so-called agencies weren't any better, and it didn't take me long to learn why the men with flashy offices off Hollywood Boulevard were known as the Cahuenga Casanovas. I'd explain my beauty contest win, my screen test, my career aspirations, only to be answered with a sly "And what are you doing tonight?"

Everywhere I turned—at bus stops, in department stores, outside casting agencies—I found slick-talking men making promises designed to divest me of my money, clothing, or dignity. I could have a part, a job, a role, some glamorous printed portraits, if only I went out to dinner, had a drink, came inside for a bit, paid a hundred dollars up front. When I asked if maybe they might like to see me act first, the jerks laughed; the "nice" ones looked at me as though I didn't know what city I had landed in.

Which was why, a month in and my once-proud nest egg looking very shabby indeed, I practically EXPLODED when a girl at the boarding-house had to call in sick and offered me her evening gig. As the sun set a gorgeous burnt orange over the hills a few miles southwest of Hollywood, I hopped out of a hired car, dressed in a tight-fitting vest, black leather boots, and a cow-patterned suede skirt short enough to make my mother pass out: the newest cowgirl at Silver Wing Studios' annual Night at the Rodeo.

Seven-fifty (plus dinner!) to smile, two-step, and direct people from the handsome barn at the top of the hill to the open-air barbecue out back, but at least it got me on the same square acre as actual, real-life movie people, most of whom, it turned out, saw me as part of the set dressing.

"Hello, sir! Would you like a taste?" Smiling, I raised a tray heavy with corn fritters toward a middle-aged man in a loud blue suit talking with another fellow. He paused midconversation and gave me an up-and-down.

"Sure! Oh, did you mean the fritters? No, thanks."

Hot prickles of embarrassment crept over me as the two men wandered off laughing, unfortunately before I could smack my tray up the sides of their heads. My first Hollywood party and I couldn't say I was impressed. It'd started out tame enough: pork ribs and punch inside the large, overdecorated barn, the floor gritty with sawdust and the air full of the cheerful squawking of a country band. But that'd been before stewards started uncorking miles of bottles of every liquor imaginable and the whole place had taken on a sloppy tilt.

The dour matron who'd supplied my costume promised me more work, next time as an extra and not a dolled-up waitress, so long as I kept my smile plastered to my face. No easy task with these monkey-minded middle managers three sheets to the wind, looking at the ladies in attendance like they wanted to sink their teeth in us.

It was about when three full-grown men cornered me in the barn, asking if this cowgirl might like a ride, that I decided enough was enough—I'd risk the matron's anger over getting out of that rodeo in one piece.

"Lemme just grab my saddle!" I said with a tight smile, slipping past them before they knew what'd happened, and I scooted through the crowd and out the door, my cheap boots skidding in the mud outside. The roar of the party behind me, I stared out at the night sky, my heart beating fast. A bus was due to pick up the cowgirls at midnight, but that had to be at least another hour away. Just when I'd resigned myself to walking the seven miles back to the city, I heard, from far too close: "—you don't have to act so shy!"

My nerves already bowstring-tight, I practically jumped right out of my boots until my eyes adjusted enough to see a couple, half hidden in the shadows behind a parked car. A woman's voice murmured something back, her shoes scuffling on gravel, and the man answered, "That wasn't what you said earlier tonight..." There was a thump of body against metal, a sharp gasp from the woman, and without thinking, I rushed over.

"Oh, *there* you are, I've been looking for you everywhere!" I shouted, nearly running into the man and woman—no, *girl,* she couldn't be more than two or three years older than I was. They both stared at me with wide eyes, the girl's face so pale and bloodless it shone in the darkness, and then the man's mouth lifted up in a sneer.

"Scram, kid." He turned back to the girl, but before he could put his hands on her, I grabbed her by the arm and gave her such a yank she almost lost her balance, toppling into me.

"Sorry, you're gonna have to say good night to your friend, we promised the boys we'd meet them half an hour ago!" Honestly, I didn't even know what I was saying, but she seemed to go along as I tugged at her.

"Hey!" the man protested, and I drowned him out with my stupid babbling: "The car's waiting, we've got to go, so glad I found you, don't want to be late!"

She stumbled, stiff-legged, along next to me as we hightailed it down the dirt path that led through the ranch's makeshift parking lot, her cold hand wrapped tight around mine. It wasn't until we reached the road that she finally stopped and twisted to look over her shoulder.

"He's not following us, is he?" I asked, my voice high, and she shook her head, then turned back and seemed to look at me properly for the first time.

"How—Who—" When she tried to speak, her teeth chattered together, and I put my arm around her. She had to be an actress; she had that kind of look to her, pretty features, clear voice. And I couldn't tell the color of her dress in the dark, but I could feel that it was expensive, well made, fashionable. The collar had come open, and when she saw me glance at it, she let out an angry "Oh."

"It's all right," I said. She shook her head.

"No, it's not." Her fingers trembled as she did up her buttons, and she gave another worried glance over her shoulder. "Come on, before he figures out where we've gone."

I was about to ask her where exactly she planned *coming on* to, when she headed straight for a handsome roadster and pulled open the door.

"You are trying to get out of here, aren't you?" she asked me.

"Absolutely!"

"Then for goodness' sake, *get in*."

I threw one last look at the rowdy ruckus up the hill and jumped for the car.

It was another minute or two, the girl carefully weaving her way down country roads, before she spoke again.

"Thank you." Her voice was soft but clear, her eyes on the road.

"Don't mention it. My sister taught me to look out, never leave a gal stranded." I smoothed down my skirt, my fingertips brushing the suede. "Are you all right?"

She let out a bitter laugh. "I might've just lost my next role, but I'll survive. I'm Midge, by the way." Her gaze fluttered over to me and back to the road, and in that moment—the lashes, the soft voice, the dark hair—it hit me.

"You're Miriam Powell!" I clapped my hands together in absolute delight. "Ohh, I *loved* you in *The Man Who Wore Red*!"

"Did you notice me? I think you might have been the only one."

I waved that away. "Only because everyone is an idiot. You got the short end with the magazines all moony over Franklin Busby's divorce. I couldn't believe they didn't pay you any attention!"

"Frank does have a way of sucking up the air in the room," she said mildly, her fingers drumming the steering wheel. "But enough about me—I don't even know your name."

"Henrietta. Henny to my friends, which includes damsels in distress."

"And what are you doing in Hollywood, Henny, when you're not prying leering producers off poor actresses?"

"Oh. *That.* Trying desperately to get into pictures. Can't you tell?" I stretched out my feet, knocking the heels of my boots together with a sad *clonk.* "*Howdy, pardner* was supposed to be step one to an extra gig."

Midge laughed, but not unkindly. "It sounds like both of us were sold a bill of goods tonight. I'm up for a lead role, and my manager suggested I show I'm capable by stopping by the rodeo—because a movie set on a train has everything to do with barbecue and horse-riding," she finished, her voice dry. "Anyway, you won't get a job as an extra working these kinds of things, and even if you did, I hardly know any actors who started out as extras."

"Sure, but what else am I supposed to do? They pay those studio guards too well for me to waltz in without an invitation."

"Then we'll get you an invitation." Midge's smile grew, her eyes sparkling. Honestly, *how* did those idiot critics miss her in *The Man Who Wore Red*?! "I can't offer you a screen test, but I can get you on the lot. Come visit me on set, I'll take you to lunch at the commissary, and maybe you'll catch someone's eye."

"Do you MEAN IT?" I jumped so high in the seat it was a miracle Midge didn't crash the car. "I wouldn't be bothering you? Never mind, forget I said anything, you offered and I'm showing up!"

"I mean it! You'd be doing me a favor. Chillier than Antarctica, a Hollywood studio lot. Folks would line up for miles if I offered a kiss, but I still haven't made a single friend."

She glanced over at me, her smile now shy, and I felt such a rush of warmth I wanted to absolutely smother her in a hug. I'd been in Hollywood a month now but hadn't appreciated until she'd said it just how *lonely* this city could be. The women at the boardinghouse were kind enough but mostly kept to themselves, and my reduced funds meant I couldn't even ring up home—a pay telephone would probably outright laugh at me if I considered a long-distance call to Chicago. I had to make do with semi-regular letters, where at least I could rosy up my circumstances enough to put my family at ease.

But—a friend.

It made me tingly all over just to think about it.

"How about twelve? Stage 29. I'll give the fella at the gate your name. Would you like that?"

Would I like it? It was as though rays of light suddenly shot out of Midge Powell's pin-straight black hair, framing her like an angel. I'd swear an actual heavenly chorus descended, singing about the virtues of studio tours.

"I'll have to think about it," I said. Midge threw her head back and laughed, and that was the start of our love affair.

"...to Culver City, and then...Are you even listening? Duke? Declan!"

I snapped to the present to see Pep frowning at me, waiting to get into the new car—new to us, at least—so we could drive to the desert for today's shoot.

"You awake?"

I smiled and slid onto the seat. "Yeah, yeah, I heard you." Pep climbed in behind the steering wheel.

"Really? What'd I say?"

"Does it matter? You'll just tell me again in fifteen minutes."

He sighed and the car's engine turned over with a bang that made a passerby leap out of the way. "What gives? Opening Day's still two months away, you can't already be worried about the Seals."

"Hey, we're taking the pennant this year," I mumbled, staring out the window, but Pep didn't push it. It'd been nearly a week since Sam tracked me down, and I felt our conversation burrowing into my brain, rattling at doors I'd thought were long closed. I found his card when I got home that night and nearly tore it into confetti, but something stopped me, made me slip it back into my pocket. It stayed there every day, the edges of the paper softened and worn by my fingertips.

A hundred times I'd opened my mouth to talk it over with Pep, only I couldn't get up the nerve. I knew what he'd say: I was an idiot for even thinking about going up against the studio and ruining the first good thing that had come into our lives. And...I couldn't really say he was wrong, either.

"...visited this bungalow in Beverly Hills, and I think that should be our next place when the lease on the apartment—"

"Next place?" I asked, jolting out of my thoughts. "What next place? We move in May. Back home."

Pep fiddled with the steering wheel, frowning at the city traffic. "About that. You gotta hear the things people are saying about your stunts, Duke. People are calling you the best-kept secret in Hollywood, and you want to know why? Because stunt men don't show up in the credits! You're doing all this work and not getting any glory!"

"I don't want glory. Paycheck's fine."

"But that's just it!" Pep gave the steering wheel a smack. "You know how much you'd make as a leading man?"

"Josepe Perez," I said, my voice even, "I am not a leading man."

"Not yet! But I've been talking around, and guess what's gonna be the next big thing: actors who *do their own stunts*! Think of it! A new kind of star. He acts! He takes punches! And you can be the very first one! Duke, it's a gold mine."

Irritation peppered my skin like buckshot.

"Who wants a gold mine?" I asked, picking at a loose flap of leather on the seat. "All that upkeep, you gotta hire a bunch of miners..."

"Come on. You can't really want to go back to the Mission. A job working the brewery on Howard Street? Where you could get canned any minute just because the owner makes a bad bet? Saving up weeks for a

42

dinner out at North Beach? A house so full of cousins and aunts you don't even bother learning everyone's names?"

"I know my Spanish is excellent, Pep, but those weren't my cousins and aunts."

"Ay, baboso, and you never would've gotten into that house without me, just like I know I can't get through the Silver Wing gate without some-one like you. We owe each other, old pal."

He broke off to swear at another driver who honked at him when he shifted lanes, and then we turned onto the highway, the jalopy buzzing loudly, the wind whipping past. I wrapped my arms around myself and kept my eyes on the landscape, Hollywood's small-town history showing around the edges: lemon trees, dusty plots, abandoned fruit groves rolling out to the horizon.

I'd argue with him, only...he was right. I did owe him everything. I was a weedy nine-year-old stuck in the Saint Francis Home for Boys when Pep pulled me from the wolf's jaws—literally, after he'd found me down an alley underneath a mean cur that was probably wondering why his dinner was giving him such a hard time. Pep swatted the dog away with his stickball bat, dusted me off, got a good look at my tattered clothes, my smooth, unbroken skin—and gasped.

He looked as shocked as I felt. I knew I'd never skinned my knee or had a runny nose, but this was something different, that dog's teeth slid-ing across my body like I was made of marble.

"Santa Maria!" he'd said, crossing himself, and the thought seemed to hit us both at once: I *couldn't* be hurt. We stared at each other, me won-dering what this boy would do with that information, when Pep's face broke out in a grin. Anyone else might've turned and run, but he threw an arm around my shoulders and brought me home to his mama, who all but shrugged at the idea of an extra mouth to feed—Pep was one of nine.

I'd been in the Home long enough to hate it, to dream about a place where I belonged, where people knew me, asked me how I was, and Pep gave that to me in the busy house on Valencia Street. It burst with cousins, siblings, aunts who laughed kindly at my bad Spanish and called me Dito. And it was a big enough gift that I was happy to repay it however Pep asked: the boxing, the carnival side shows, the stunts. I'd never argued with him. Never said no. Never threatened his plans.

But that was before Pep started talking about screen tests and new apartments in ritzy Beverly Hills. Before I met Sam and his words began rattling in my brain like marbles:

Some of these girls, though—it's like they just disappear... You ever lost someone, kid? Wouldn't you do anything to find them again?

"We're here."

The jalopy bumped to a stop, and I blinked at a long, dusty stretch of desert, the horizon shimmering in the distance under a pale afternoon sky.

Pep launched into another rundown of today's stunt, something I really should have paid attention to because it involved a wagon chase, a team of four horses, a tricky bit of maneuvering that would see me jump from driver's seat to right rear horse to left front horse, which I'd untether from the team and ride off into the sunset.

I should have told Pep no. Horses made me nervous: the speed of cars and the power of trains inside a thousand-pound animal with a mind of its own. These stunts belonged to expert horsemen with decades of experience, but they'd all passed on the job, and so the director had called the guy who could make any stunt happen.

"You're gonna be fine," Pep told me an hour later, the costumer adjusting a bandana around my neck.

"How?" I asked, but he just wandered away, and I shouted after him, "I don't recall any rodeo nights at the Roozie!"

"Oh!" The costumer, a deeply tanned woman with short blond hair, looked up at me with a smile. "A San Francisco boy!"

I stared at her like I'd just discovered a long-lost twin.

"You're from the neighborhood!" I said, amazed, because who else would know our nickname for the Roosevelt, the theater that practically raised us? But the woman shook her head.

"Oakland. Had a roommate when I first came here, and she was out of the Mission; told me all about it. Chorus girls," she added, with a laugh. "Oh, that was a long time ago." She went up on tiptoe to set a hat on my head.

"You...knew a girl from the Mission?" My heart skipped a beat and then the questions spilled out of me, fast: "How long ago? What was her name?"

"Gosh, hon!" She raised her eyebrows. "I'm not sure, it must've been... ten years now? Phew, was it that long?"

"Duke!" Pep called to me from the camera car, rigged to run parallel to the wagon. "They're ready for you!"

"You're all set," the woman said, smiling as she turned away, but I grabbed her arm.

"The girl—what was her name?"

She glanced at my hand, then back at my face, the smile faltering. "Wh-What?"

"Her name?" My voice came out strained, desperate.

"Oh, well, I...I'm not...You know, it was a long time ago, and I've had more roommates than I could—"

"Duke!" Pep barked.

45

"Please."

The woman let out a yelp, and I dropped her arm, heat rushing to my cheeks. "I'm sorry, I'm sorry! It's just—it's important."

"Declan! Come on!"

The woman squinted out at the desert, frowning. "I don't... Maybe... Arianna? Ar... Arlene?"

"Orla?" I almost choked on it. "Orla Collins?"

"You hear me, Declan? Helloooo!"

"Hon, you better go, it's not good to keep the horses—"

"What happened to her? Do you know?" I could guess based on the woman's expression how I must look, but I didn't care. I felt like I'd been wandering the desert for forty years and this woman had just appeared in front of me with a frosty pitcher of lemonade. She shook her head, her eyes pained, her hands making helpless gestures in the air.

"I—I'm sorry, hon. I don't know. I really don't. She never came home one night. Never packed a bag, nothing. Left all her things—I gave them away after a few months, never could track her down. Figured she went back home. I don't..."

A hand clamped on my shoulder, Pep spinning me around, annoyance writ into his heavy eyebrows.

"What are you doing?" he whispered to me, leaning in close. "You're at work! Act professional!" But then he pulled back, got a better look at my expression, and the irritation slipped away. "Everything square? You feeling nervous? Need me to call it off?"

I was so rattled by the woman's words that I didn't even appreciate that Pep had offered to cancel a job for me. I brushed him off and made for the waiting wagon.

"I'm fine." I clenched my hands into fists. "I'm ready."

"Duke—" Pep started, but the director called us to our places, and by the time I made it to the wagon, the driver fingering the reins and sniffing about the delays—"Makes the horses nervous"—Pep had climbed onto the camera car along with the director and camera operator.

The director was shouting something, but I could hardly hear him, a white rush of sound filling my ears. I dropped my face into my hands, kneading my temples, and the moment I closed my eyes a woman's face appeared in my mind: young and pretty, big eyes rimmed in black, wavy hair bobbed short. Startled, I sat up, blinking at the desert, golden in the afternoon light. The wagon jolted forward and a horse let out a whinny, the driver swearing as we steadily picked up speed. About fifty feet away, the camera car kept pace until my costume billowed around me, dust and pebbles spitting through the air.

"STUNTS! GO!"

My legs shook as I stood up in the driver's box, the wagon swaying, the wind pushing my body back so that I had to lean forward. The horses were so close—it felt like I hadn't really looked at them yet, four powerful, spot-dappled beasts, mouths open, manes streaming. The right rear horse, steel-colored and broad, threw up clods of dirt, body pounding with every step.

Focus.

Focus.

I unclenched my fists, trying to imagine the jump, but all I could picture was...

Late night, sequins flashing, splinters flying into the air, the soft wood of the apartment floor turned to pulp under her sharp tap shoes...

"What the hell you doin' standing there, kid?" the driver shouted, his voice a growl. "Move!"

His words worked on me like a whip crack, and I threw myself forward, slamming against the horse's neck with a jolt that nearly knocked the air out of my chest. The horse let out a sharp scream, rocking in its harness, and I only barely managed to hold on. Behind me, the driver shouted something I couldn't make out over the roar of the wind.

You'll be okay here, Dee-Dee, and it'll just be for a little while. I have to go.

The memories buzzed in my brain, and I shook my head, my hands sweaty, my legs numb. Somehow, I pulled myself to my feet, standing on the horse's bare back in a half crouch, feeling the horse's steady rhythm underneath me. I had to jump again, this time a diagonal leap to the front left horse, and I knew I had to use this horse's momentum to propel me forward, get me flying through the air—

flying, flying, dancing, flying

greasepaint, theatrical smoke, dusty curtains, sticky theater floors, the heat of the lights, the cold of the apartment, her hand on my cheek, her back as she walked away...

Another jerk, and I grabbed at the horse's mane to keep from slipping off its back. I had to time it just right, waiting for the horse to lurch forward, and then I threw myself up, over, arms pinwheeling, feet kicking like I could really fly.

It's like flying, Dee-Dee, like flying...

Time stretched out again, an eternity of me suspended over panting horses, shining muscles, webs of harnesses, reins, ropes, ground moving in a blur, the bounce and groan and rumble of the wagon, the unending thunder of galloping hooves.

I saw the horse, waiting for me, its neck stretched out, and my stomach jerked, because it knew what my arms, still reaching, and my legs, still kicking, didn't understand yet. Too short, I was too short and the angle was wrong, and instead of landing neatly onto the horse's back I crashed against its side.

Time sped up now, so all I saw was hair—harness—hooves—dirt— dirt against my shoulder, in my mouth, in my eyes, and horse legs, wagon wheels, bright, startling crashing pounding into and around me and me spinning, spinning, thrown across the ground.

CHAPTER SEVEN
HENRIETTA

Silver Wing Studios.

The biggest, most famous, most successful studio in the world.

And I liked it even better on the opposite side of the gates.

I'd read enough flick magazines to know what a studio lot looked like, but somehow, being there, my patent leather hitting the concrete, my eyes wide open, felt like tipping over into a dream. A cowboy walked past, spurs jingling, his cologne spicy and sweet, while from across the path, a door burst open, letting out a giggling gaggle of blue-spangled showgirls and a blare of jazzy trumpet music. I watched a nun put out a cigarette, spitting swears at the short man who came to fetch her from her break, and stepped aside to avoid crossing paths with *a real, live, honest-to-god CAMEL*.

"Watch your toes, Peggy Sue!" a voice shouted right before I tripped over a mess of cables on the ground, landing in an inelegant heap. I'd started to dust myself off when a tanned hand appeared before me.

"Need some help?"

I followed the hand to an arm, a shoulder, and a smiling face. No. *The* smiling face. Jack Huxley—as in "Jack Huxley, actor," or "Jack Huxley, star," or "Henrietta, who do you love more, your sister or Jack Huxley?" He bent over me, his hand still held out.

For me. Was it possible to perish from pure astonishment?

When it was clear I was unable to put words together, Jack Huxley laughed, presumably because he was used to having this effect on people, and gently lifted me to my feet by my elbow.

"I...I..." Of all the unbelievable things to have happened to me since arriving in Hollywood, I knew this one—being rendered speechless—would be the most difficult for my family to swallow.

He started to say something, and the thrill of watching those lips in motion distracted me so much that it took a second to figure out he was asking me where I was headed.

"St-Stage 29!" I blurted out. "I'm meeting someone there, at noon."

"Stage 29!" How did he manage to speak while maintaining such a perfect smile? "Well, that's clear across the lot. It'll take you ages to get there. Here, come on—let me help." He slid his hand around mine, and every atom in my body burst into stardust. Before I realized what was happening, he pulled me over to a purring motorbike, slid me onto the seat behind him, and took off, my arms wrapped around what felt like the world's most perfect waist.

I was going to pass out. I was going to float into the sky. Somehow, I, Henrietta Newhouse, had made it from Chicago, Illinois, to the back of Jack Huxley's motorbike, spinning around Silver Wing Studios with the wind whipping through my hair and the scent of expensive cologne in my nose. I could've been booted back home that second and still counted this trip a roaring success.

Oh, damn. Jack Huxley was saying something to me, and by the sound of his laughter, it wasn't his first attempt.

"What—what was that?"

"What's your name, sweetheart? I'm Jack!"

I wanted to reply OF COURSE YOU ARE. The whole WORLD knew who he was, ever since he'd tumbled onto the screen three years ago as a lonesome seventeen-year-old soldier boy in *The Drums of War*.

"Hen-Henrietta!" I squeaked.

"Well, Hen-Henrietta," he said, and I could hear the smile in his voice, "here we are."

He'd come to a stop, far too soon, outside a huge, boxy, windowless barn of a building with a giant black *29* painted on one end. I tumbled off the motorbike, my knees like jelly, and my hands immediately flew to my hair, probably whipped into a tornado after that whirlwind trip (one million percent worth it). Jack turned and gave me another megawatt smile.

"Don't worry—you look great." And then he was off, like some modern-day knight in shining armor, and I wasn't entirely sure I hadn't hallucinated the whole thing.

Jack Huxley.

Jack.

Huxley.

"All right," I said to myself. "Enough of this funny business. Next time you see Jack Huxley, his stomach's going to be doing backflips over *you*." But I couldn't help the tiny, shrieking voice in my brain absolutely going haywire: *Jack Huxley said you look GREAT!!!!!*

I walked over to the building, paused to double-check that the light (DO NOT ENTER ON RED) wasn't lit, and shoved open the door.

My heels clicked against the concrete floor of the soundstage, and I was Alice in Wonderland, shrinking down to the size of a mouse, the ceiling a million miles above my head, the building somehow ten times bigger on the inside than it looked on the outside. None of my movie magazines had prepared me for this. The soundstage was home to an entire city, absolutely perfect down to the tiniest detail, from the shining paper moon high above the skyline to the weather-worn cobblestone sidewalks. The scene stood empty, but dozens of people swarmed nearby in the darkness, pulling cables, rushing with costumes, ferrying papers or mechanical bits or spare shoes. No one seemed to notice me, everyone focused on their tasks like a hundred ants working together in perfect harmony. But as I neared the stage I heard a bright "Henny!" and whirled around to see Midge, done up in finger waves and smoky Cleopatra eyes.

"You found it!" She stepped forward to dust a kiss on my cheek. She looked so perfect I didn't want to touch her, her costume a spangly gunnysack that would have fit right in among my sister Ruby's wardrobe.

"I keep wondering when I'll wake up." I gazed over our heads, where a canopy of rigging held up lights, cables, props.

"It is wonderful, isn't it?" she sighed, and then she reached over and looped her arm around mine. "We have to shoot a bit more, and then we'll get some lunch, all right? And then—" Her smile grew even bigger. "I've maybe got some incredible news."

"Ooohh, what is it?!"

"Well…" She leaned in as she glanced around, eyes dancing. "I'm not supposed to—" But before she got anything else out, a bell rang, and the mass of people turned even more frantic, rushing to positions around the stage.

"Stick around and watch!" Midge squeezed my arm and whirled off to the set, which was filling with actors, makeup people, crew members checking angles, meters, measurements…actually, I didn't have the foggiest what they were doing.

53

"Ready now!" The director—at least I guessed he was the director, based on how everyone hopped to at his orders—stood near the edge of the set, hovering at the shoulder of a man behind a huge steel-gray camera. "Speed!"

Another man popped in front of the camera, snapping a clapboard.

"Clear the scene!" A small crowd of folks in regular clothes scattered, leaving behind about a dozen actors—my eyes kept goggling as I recognized another famous face—dressed like they were on their way to a speakeasy. "Camera! Action!"

The scene was a meeting of gangsters (from CHICAGO! How did I travel two thousand miles only to end up back on my own block?), the heroes and the villains and their lieutenants and ladies. Midge was one of the ladies, a black-haired beauty on the arm of the hero. She didn't have many lines, but every time she opened her mouth, she drew attention like a damned magnet.

"She's wonderful, isn't she?" I whispered to the person standing beside me as the director called "Cut." On the set, Midge stepped aside so a girl could run a pouf of powder over her cheeks. "Did you notice how she laughs when the tough with the blue fedora threatens her date? She came up with that all on her own. Just brilliant."

The man at my side glanced at me. "Are you her agent?"

"Just a fan," I said with a sigh. "Oh, watch the girl in the red dress, in the back. She keeps edging in between the men talking, but it throws off the whole balance of the scene. She should stick to stage left."

"Hm," said the man, who was probably thinking what I had just realized: that out of every single person in this stage, on this lot—hell—in this *city*, I probably had the least moviemaking experience. I expected him to roll his eyes, or maybe politely find somewhere else to stand and watch; instead, he caught the attention of one of the crew members scurrying around and murmured something into his ear. The scurrier went to the director, the director went to the lady in red, and a moment later, she'd moved two feet stage left.

"You're right," the man said. "It does look better."

He sounded pleased with himself, and out of the corner of my eye, I gave him a subtle once-over, trying to figure out who he might be. Anyone with the power to walk onto a set and move actors like chess pieces had to have some sway. But he looked completely unremarkable: a man in his fifties in a nice but not ostentatious suit. For all I knew, he was someone's brother-in-law who needed an excuse to get out of the house and pester chorus girls.

Our eyes met, and I realized he'd been studying me just as closely. Quickly, I looked away, hoping he didn't get the wrong idea, as he cleared his throat.

"So. Are you in the business?"

Oof, here it came.

"Not yet," I said, my voice bright, my eyes darting in search of escape, because I knew what would happen. An offer to help, hiding an attempt to trap me into a date, or worse. "Oh, I think my friend—"

It'd started as an excuse, but my words broke off when Midge's face tightened into a grimace, and I realized her costar, the hero gangster played by an aging star named Lloyd Rodger, had turned on her, hissing something I couldn't hear.

"'Not yet,'" the man said, turning to me. "But you'd like to be? Are you hoping to act? May I ask your name, miss?" I couldn't tear my eyes away from Midge, who stared back at Lloyd Rodger with a kind of pinched determination even as he began gesturing wildly, pointing to her feet, his feet, a spot on the floor.

"Miss? Your name?" the man beside me asked.

"What? I—Henrietta. Henrietta Newhouse. And yes, I'm an actress. I mean, I'm trying to be. Someday."

"Ah. Well, in that case, I'd like—"

"—you GET IT?"

I jumped as Lloyd Rodger's voice burst into a shout. Midge, her lips pressed into a straight line, held his gaze while he continued ranting: "Is that really TOO HARD for you to see? How can I be expected to do everything I need to do, when YOU—"

"Excuse me," I said to the man beside me, but he held up a card and, quick as a magic trick, slipped it into my jacket pocket. Ugh, the *cad*. Movie executives' phone numbers were easier to catch than the measles.

"Why don't we take a break, Lloyd?" The director had stepped between him and Midge, who looked ready to snap in half. "Everyone? Fifteen minutes."

As Lloyd Rodger stomped off, I slipped an arm around Midge's waist. "Are you all right?" I asked.

"Did you hear all that?" Midge let out a high-pitched laugh.

"What was he wound up about?"

"Oh, this time he thought I'd stepped on the back of his foot." Midge and I walked to the edge of the set, and she collapsed into a chair. "Next time, it'll be because I'm wearing the wrong perfume, or I said my line too soon, or I didn't give him the right cue. Just another day at the office with Lloyd." She sounded breezy, but underneath, she looked bone-rattled. "Anyway, I'm sorry you had to see it. How was it up to then?"

Even though I would have happily spent the fifteen minutes of her break skewering Lloyd Rodger, Midge had made it clear she was done with him, so instead I dropped onto the chair next to her with a sigh.

"Wonderful. Incredible. *You* were incredible. Everything was just… better than I could have imagined! Oh, until some stuffed suit tried to make a pass at me. Could've done without that."

"Professional hazard." Midge shrugged.

"Here." I reached into my pocket and fished out his card. "He gave me his number."

I passed it to Midge, who took it with a smile—and then blanched.

"Did you look at this?"

My stomach dropped. "Oh, lord, he didn't write something filthy on it, did he? Just throw it in the trash."

"No—Henny!" She jumped to her feet, and I took the card from her hand. Bracing myself for the worst, I ventured a peek, but all I saw was a date for next week scribbled beside *Casting Department, 10 a.m.*

"Oh," I said, letting out a disappointed breath. "I'm sure they won't even let me through the door."

"You think? Flip it over. And *look*." She grabbed my shoulders and turned me around, pointing to a corner of the stage. There the man in the nice suit stood, the sun in a constellation of admirers and hangers-on, shaking hands like he was Santa Claus. Confused, I looked down at the card. On the front, in bold, black, Gothic print, I read *Irving Reynolds, President—Silver Wing Studios.*

IRVING REYNOLDS!!!! I'd never pick him out of a lineup, but BOY HOWDY did I know that name! You couldn't open a movie magazine without seeing it on every other page: *The new picture out from Irving Reynolds's Silver Wing Studios.* This was the man who held Hollywood in his hands, the most powerful man in the picture industry, the man who decided the fate of anyone who wanted to make movies. I felt like I was about to throw up. Or pass out. Or both.

"Th-That's *Irving Reynolds*?"

"Yes!" Midge laughed, squeezing my arm. "And Henny, he wants *you!*"

CHAPTER EIGHT
 DECLAN

Flash of blue sky, gray and gritty dust...I tumbled along the ground a long time, and when I fell still, it was as though the world kept spinning. Sky, dirt, clouds, rocks. My body felt fine—I could've been rolling over feather beds. But panic flared through me like a fireball.

I'd felt hooves. The bump-jump of the wagon wheels. Even just falling off a horse at that speed would have turned any normal man into hamburger meat.

A shadow blotted out the light, a person, and I braced myself for the gasp, the scream—until I felt a hand on my shoulder.

"Stay down. Close your eyes."

It was Pep, his voice tight and afraid.

"Help!" he shouted. "He's unconscious! Needs a doc!"

Everything inside me buzzed, but I kept my eyes closed, my body limp, and a moment later there were footsteps, questions silenced by Pep's bark. "Get him into the car! Now!" Hands, lifting me up, bouncing me along the desert, to the camera car, to Pep's backseat, and I didn't open my eyes again until the jalopy had roared off with Pep behind the wheel, a look on his face like he'd just robbed a bank.

"You all right?" He let out a bark of a laugh. "Who'm I kidding? Of course you're all right! Almost gave *me* a heart attack, never mind the rest of the crew…"

My hands shook as I reached over the back of Pep's seat. "Did anyone see, or— Pep, I'm sorry. I—"

"I'll come up with some story. Anyway, we're still getting paid. And I don't think anybody got a good look at you, you're covered in dust!"

I looked down at my arms, painted gray and grimy yellow, and let out a long, shaky breath.

"What happened out there?" he asked, and I settled back in my seat.

"I told you: I'm not a cowboy."

"Oh, we're blaming the horses now? Sure this wasn't because of those dreamy thoughts of yours?"

I didn't know how to answer him, so I turned my attention to the wide, flat desert. Pep was my friend. My oldest, best friend, but we had an unspoken agreement not to bring up anything that had happened before we met, as if I'd sprung into the world as a skinny nine-year-old trapped under a mean cur. He knew about Saint Francis, he knew there wasn't anyone to complain when I moved into the house on Valencia Street, and he knew what I told Mamá Perez when she asked where my people were: "I had a mam, but she left to be an actress in Hollywood."

He must've wondered, but why talk about those things when we could dream about our futures as millionaires or settle once and for all who was the best player on the Seals?

"We'll have to lay off the stunts." A grin popped onto Pep's face. "You know what that means, don't you?"

"If you mention a screen test," I muttered, "I'm pulling you out of this car and socking you in the eye."

"Just think it over," he said, snorting a laugh and drumming his fingers on the steering wheel.

What would she have thought, to see me here, throwing away a screen test? When she traded away everything just for a chance?

I was quiet the whole ride back to the apartment. As soon as we got in, I told Pep I needed a bath, and when he had his back turned I grabbed the small shoe box I kept tucked under my cot and made my way to the washroom down the hall. There, with the water running, I sat at the edge of the tub, sifting through scraps of old school papers, pressed flowers from Pep's sisters' quinceañeras, until I found it: a small photo, a girl, a woman, big-eyed, the details so gauzy it looked like a snapshot from a dream, all shadows and smoke.

"Mam."

I held the photograph up to the light, trying to remember when it had been taken. She wore an elaborate headdress, dripping with beads, her doe eyes painted black and gazing upward. Scrolling script in the corner read *The Majestic Theater*, which meant this must've been a calling card from…"*Egyptian Air?*" "*Egyptian Dreams?*"

I hadn't thought about those years in so long, I expected the memories to feel faded. Instead they rushed into my brain in sharp detail: the smell of oily greasepaint; the taste of sour, watered-down beer and stale crackers fished from her purse; brightly colored feather boas filling the air with soft snow. I could hear the clack of dozens of heels on creaking, worn floorboards, the bell-like tinkle of beaded costumes, the chatter of girls working with and bickering at and loving and encouraging each other. Men weren't allowed in the dressing rooms, but then I wasn't even a sniff of a man yet, barely more than a baby. The other girls would coo over me, petting me, painting a thick black mustache across my upper lip and hiding my eyes under a too-big top hat, teaching me to turkey-trot.

Home. A world with a hundred aunts, and late nights asleep under piles of costumes, and hard-faced bosses, men who wore the dancers out thin and limping, or who would give me sideways looks and ask Mam where her wedding ring was.

What had made her leave?

It'd been ten years now, and I couldn't answer that question. Had it been a girlfriend, telling her to come out to Hollywood? Had it been the promise of a glamorous billboard? Too many magazine stories about out-of-luck chorus girls transforming into movie stars?

If I had known the last time I saw her was going to be the last time I would ever see her, I would've paid closer attention. I could remember the color of the leaves against the sky, the softness of the fur stole she wore—one of her few nice things. She'd brought me to Saint Francis, where I blinked at the other boys, watching me in their uniforms. She spoke to someone, and then when she came back...

She said goodbye, I remembered that. She said she would be back soon. She told me to be good.

And then she left.

The days at the boys' home swirled together, gray and confused. I didn't spend much time there. Within six months, I'd met Pep and moved into the busy house on Valencia Street, and he got started figuring out how to use my ability to change our lives. When Pep and I were twelve, he had his first idea: come see the Incredible, Unbreakable Boy! But not even the wildest carnival owners would sanction an act that was, essentially, one kid trying to pummel the crap out of another, and so Pep turned to prizefighting, nights and weekends, telling the organizers I could fight longer than anyone else in the world. We did a little better there, except no one made a career out of *long* boxing matches. Besides which, my unexplained ability meant I could take a punch; it didn't do a thing to improve my fighting skills.

By the time my boxing career had all but dried up, we only had a few weeks left of high school and nothing waiting on the other side. Pep's father worked ten hours a day, six days a week, rolling cigars at a long table with two dozen other men. Every day, the men would pool their money to hire a lector to come read to them in Spanish: newspapers, poetry, classic novels. It was an education as fine as anything offered in fancy colleges or universities, the discussions over the long rolling tables thoughtful and well reasoned, but whenever the torcedores tried to use their intellect outside the walls of the factory, they found closed doors, grim faces.

Pep was smart, he worked hard, and he could sell just about anything to anybody, so long as they looked past his name and his skin color long enough to listen, but he knew that wouldn't happen in the Mission, and it wouldn't happen rolling cigars ten hours a day, even to a musical background of Cervantes and Dickens.

We were at the movies one night, not long after my eighteenth birthday, when Pep watched a man tumble down a ravine and sat up so fast I thought someone had stuck him with a pin.

Hollywood needed dummies who could stand up and take anything directors dreamed of, and Pep had one of those. Had he remembered what I'd once said about my mother? If he had, he didn't say anything about it, even in the weeks it took to convince me to make the move, even when I made him promise it was only for a year. I was coming back to the Mission. I wouldn't get stuck in Hollywood quicksand.

When we got to the city, I thought I would find her easily, but the number of people overwhelmed me. I searched the phone book for her name. I looked for her picture outside theaters, inside vaudevilles. Any time I ended up on a picture set, which wasn't often since it turned out the people hiring stunt men weren't looking for beanpoles like me, I'd ask chorus girls, choreographers, costumers: "Did you know a woman named Orla Collins? Dark hair just like mine? Green eyes just like mine?"

No. No. No, never, and eventually, I quit asking.

Standing in the washroom, the light falling on Mam's photo, I twirled it between my fingers, studying her face.

No one knew her, no one had heard of her—until today.

She never came home one night. Never even packed a bag, nothing. She just disappeared.

A missing girl. Maybe just one of many.

There was a knock at the door, another tenant wanting the washroom, and I stood up, turned off the tap, and slid Mam's photo into my pocket, right next to Sam's card.

CHAPTER NINE
HENRIETTA

I'd never been in one of Mr. Ford's famous automobile factories, and I'd definitely never in my life imagined what it would feel like to be assembled on a conveyor belt, but getting ready for a screen test had to come close. As soon as I stepped inside Stage 19, I was swallowed by a swarm of busy bees: a short girl in a pencil skirt with a hairbrush held up like a club and a tall man eyeing my cardigan—"I think we can do better than that." As they poked and prodded, they hustled me toward a spot of light that glowed like a lighthouse-topped island in a storm: the set.

Midge's set had all the delicate attention of a finely wrought clock, each detail perfect and precise, but the set in front of me stood bare. A back wall done up in deep, muted browns, a side wall with nothing but a door, set at a slight angle to better show on camera. One plain, solid chair and a table just big enough to hold a vase made up the rest of the scenery.

I sighed—just as someone came at me with a puffball of makeup, filling my mouth with the sweet-sharp taste of talc.

"Oops. Mouth closed, hon." Obediently, I pressed my lips together as a small man in a canvas apron loaded with a whole department store's worth of makeup held up a lipstick so perfectly, sinfully red I could feel my heart sing. Tugs at my hair and a sky-blue sweater slung over my shoulders, and the crowd dispersed as quickly as they had arrived, leaving me alone in a spotlight so bright I wondered if I'd get a sunburn.

"Miss Newhouse?" The words came from the ring of darkness surrounding the set. As I squinted, a smiling man appeared, dressed in a khaki suit and silk neckerchief—the uniform of a director. "I'm Mr. Fitch. I'll be directing your screen test. I understand Mr. Reynolds requested you personally."

"I'm still trying to understand that myself," I said, tugging at the sweater. "But here I am!"

Mr. Fitch chuckled, and the knot of nerves in my stomach loosened just a bit. "I'm sure you'll do fine. We're going to start out with some tests of your photographic quality. Just do as I say."

Just do as I say was not a request I usually followed, but for this, I'd try my best. As Mr. Fitch disappeared back toward the camera, I took a deep breath. Two thousand miles and endless years of dreaming and now here I was, in Hollywood, on a stage, in front of a camera, a dozen judgmental strangers watching, my future hanging in the balance.

No problem.

"Are we ready?"

Honestly, *we* were mostly trying to hold it together, but I smiled.

"Roll camera. Roll sound."

A man popped in front of me, snapping a clapboard—a clapboard! A dumb, dazzled thought ran through my mind: *Wow! Just like in the movies!*

Mr. Fitch called out to me. "Miss Newhouse, I'd like you to walk over to that door, as though you've heard something. Now. There are voices on the other side of the door. Listen for them. Ah, you recognize one! Can you make it out? It is the voice of someone you like, very much. Maybe even someone you love. You melt, it is your heart's own darling, but what is this?! He's saying something terrible, something shocking! You feel hurt, disgusted! No, more than that, you feel betrayed! You consider stepping through the door to confront him, oh, but it's too terrible! You can't even face him, you must— Yes! Very good, Miss Newhouse!"

I'd thrown myself onto the chair, my face buried in my hands, my whole body fizzing with excitement because this

was

incredible.

Here was a truth I hadn't let myself admit until just that moment. I'd convinced my family to let me go to Hollywood, I'd laid aside their hopes and plans for my future, I'd traveled thousands of miles and spent most of my money, and for days, weeks, months, years, absolutely countless hours, I'd imagined this, right here, a camera and a silent stage and at the center of it all, me. But.

But.

All along, a very tiny thought had nagged at me: *I'd never actually...acted.*

Not a high school play, not a Christmas pantomime, nothing more than me alone in my bedroom when I knew I had a few hours to myself to look into my mirror and repeat lines from my favorite movies and *dream.*

What if...I wasn't any good?

What if...I hated it?

What if...they hated *me*?

Typical Henny, putting every one of my eggs into such a precarious basket.

But then the camera whirred to life and the director spoke and I felt a million eyes on me at once and—magic.

Henny slipped away—my sad little boardinghouse room, my sisters, the excess of space in my purse—because I'd transformed, and it wasn't scary and it wasn't overwhelming and it wasn't hard. It was so easy. Like letting out a breath. Like falling in love.

I felt two things so sharply and so suddenly that everything else in the world disappeared:

1. I was not only not terrible at this, I was *excellent,* and

2. It was all I wanted to do for the rest of my life.

"And...cut! Very good, very nice. Now, I have a scene for you to film, but we're supposed to have another—"

There was a metallic clang and a burst of sunshine as the soundstage door opened up, silhouetting a figure in the distance, toward whom the mob of makeup and costume and hair people rushed. Another actor? Did he have a test after me?

He waved the mob away and made his way to the stage where I stood.

"Ah!" the director said, turning around. "Here he is! Now we can get started!" He ushered the man onto the stage, and as he stepped into the light I saw he was just a boy, my age, give or take a bit, with perfect, not-quite-polished movie star looks: dark hair that fell just so into *smoldering* green eyes, lips to make my insides fluttery, and cheekbones that should probably be outlawed.

"Miss Newhouse? Meet your screen partner, Declan Collins."

CHAPTER TEN

DECLAN

"*Screen* partner?" I twisted around, looking at the director with a frown. "I'm the stunt man, here for a stage fight. Broken bottle, lovers' spat, Pep said it would—" The truth of what I'd just walked into hit me and I winced. "Never mind. See you round."

I started for the door but made it all of two inches before I felt something chomp onto my arm. That girl, the pretty blonde in the blue sweater that exactly matched her eyes, clung to me like she was drowning.

"Wait, we have a screen test!"

"You have a screen test." I shook my arm free. "I have a man to hunt down. Good luck."

"What's this?" The director inserted himself between us, which was a good thing because it looked like that girl might launch herself at me again. "It says right here: 'Screen test, Henrietta Newhouse and Declan Collins.'"

"There's been a mistake. I'm not interested in a screen test. I don't want to be an actor. I do stunts."

"Well, I came halfway across the country for this," the girl said, her nose in the air.

"I'm not stopping you. Go ahead and film a solo spot."

She opened her mouth to argue, and then seemed to consider what I'd said—no sharing the spotlight—and brightened considerably. Good lord, these starlets. Heartless mercenaries, every one.

"Now hold on," the director continued. "We've prepared a scene between two actors. I can't film her alone."

"See?" the girl said, grabbing my hand again. "You *have* to do it." She looked up at me with the hopeful innocence of a lost waif, the expression on her face pure beguiling plea, but with an edge to it, like she knew how effective those baby blues really were.

"No," I said, disentangling myself. "I don't." I gave her a pat on the shoulder and drew my hand back quick when she bared her teeth at me in a snarl. I added "stuck me in a room with a rabid starlet" to my list of complaints for Pep.

"Excuse me, young man!" the director shouted. "I will not be disre-spected on my set!"

He had a look in his eye like he'd happily go out of his way to ruin me, and I bit my cheek to keep from swearing. If I walked out of here today, this trumped-up dictator would run off to the closest producer and make sure no one ever hired Declan Collins again, not to act, not to stunt, not even to pick up a loop of cable from the ground. This wasn't the time for me to be choosy. That Pep had managed to bury what happened on the wagon chase felt like a miracle, but he hadn't booked anything for me in a week. I'd been hoping this "fight scene" meant things had gone back to normal.

No such luck.

The girl was muttering something at me, part plea, part curse, I couldn't really make out the details.

"All right! All right," I said, yanking off my jacket. The starlet *squealed* with delight, her hands clasped over her heart, and I gave her a sideways smile. Pep might want me on film, but I was going to make damned sure anyone who saw this test knew one thing: Declan Collins had a promising future as a very silent, very anonymous stunt man.

A script woman popped out of nowhere, handing me two sheets of paper, which I rolled up and shoved into my pocket. The starlet raised an eyebrow, the smile on her face faltering.

"Aren't you…going to…look at that?"

"Nah," I said, walking back to the set. "I like to keep it fresh."

The look on her face almost made me laugh, but then her eyes narrowed sharp enough to kill. Good thing I didn't have to worry about any knives in my back.

"Can we get started? Miss Newhouse, stage right, by the chair, there. Mr. Collins, when you're ready. Roll film. Roll sound."

A man popped in front of us. "Take one," he said, snapping a slate before the camera. I glanced over at the girl, thinking she'd be one of those overeager shouters who couldn't tear her eyes from the camera lens. To her credit, she stood calm and still, her face tilted instinctively to catch the light.

"Aaaand…action!"

I pulled out my script. For some reason, I had most of the lines in this scene, and I spat out the first one—"Haven't you been. In love before?"— with all the emotion of a doctor asking for a medical history.

For a fraction of a second, I could see the starlet stiffen, and then something seemed to settle within her. She turned her face to mine. She didn't hold her script—not that impressive as she didn't have many lines— and gave me a saucy, confident look.

"Who? Me?"

"Yes. You. Isn't there. Someone. Who lights up—"

"Cut!"

Everything ground to a halt as the director waved a hand to get my attention. "Young man! Let's put some more feeling into that reading. And go again!"

The whole process restarted, only this time there was a hint of a smile at the starlet's lips, like she knew what I was up to. So...why the smile?

"Isn't there someone. Who lights up your days?"

"Of course." She seemed to consider it for a moment. "Dozens."

My eyes went from her to the script and back. That was an improvisation, but when no one stopped us, I kept barreling along.

"No. I don't think you know. What is—what it means to be. In love. Love is whispers. And kisses. At midnight. And hot breath on your neck."

"In that case, I hope it's mouthwash and toothpaste, too."

Another improvisation, and under her carefully bored expression I could see a glint in her eye: *You like to keep it fresh, huh?*

Why didn't the director call "Cut"? I'd seen bigger actresses bawled out for playing around with the script, and this girl was ruining the whole thing—we were performing a drama, not a screwball comedy. But when no one stopped us again, I gritted my teeth.

"Love is a beast, pawing and pacing—"

"Down, boy," she said, lifting an eyebrow.

I stepped away, turning to the director. "She's not saying any of the right lines!"

"Well, you're not saying any of the lines right," she said, crossing her arms over her chest.

"Okay, okay, that's a cut!" the director said, but he had a smile on his face. "I appreciate your wit, my dear. But it's no good to show up your scene partner."

72

"A fancy mop could show up my scene partner," she muttered.

"Let's skip the rest and jump right to the end. The embrace...and the kiss."

At that point, I'd be happy to kiss the fancy mop, but when I saw the girl straighten her spine, I knew I couldn't let her beat me.

"Now, these will be close-ups, tightly framed, shoulders and faces only, no sound. Play to the camera, move slowly, and when the moment is right—the kiss. Let's get Miss Newhouse a box to stand on, yes? Places!"

As a stagehand set a crate at my feet, I tossed the script to the ground and held out my arms. "What's the matter?" I asked, when the girl didn't move. "First time?"

"No," she replied with a sigh. "Unfortunately, plenty of louts have tried to kiss me."

"Roll film!"

She stepped onto the crate and slid into my arms.

"Aaand...action!"

As awkward as I'd felt with a script in my hands, reading lines had nothing on this. I tried to think about what I'd do with a girl I actually liked, only...my experiences were limited. Pep might've enjoyed sweet-talking giggling mermaids, but I was holding out for a girl who cared about me beyond what I could do to make her famous.

So I stood there, the starlet pressing her cheek up against my shoulder, and hoped I didn't look like a complete idiot. Just as I wondered what the hell I should do next, she shifted position, lifted her face slowly...

Her eyes met mine, and I felt a kick of surprise in my belly.

It was weird, looking into someone's eyes, not to mention the eyes of a girl who'd seemed ready to throttle me five seconds ago. She was a lot closer than I expected, which shouldn't have surprised me except I'd never been so near another person. With the box to even out our heights, I could make out all the tiny details of her face: the curl of her lashes, the muscles around her eyes. I expected her to give me a simpering smile, flirt for the cameras, but her expression was still. Honest.

She shifted her weight and the movement made her face tilt toward me, her nose brushing mine, and I jerked back in surprise. Her mouth twitched into a nervous smile, and without thinking, and—maybe just because it was awkward to stare into a perfect stranger's eyes, and pretty ridiculous to have to do it in front of a camera, and, okay, sort of funny, too—I smiled back.

Her eyebrows rose slightly, she glanced down, and when she looked up again her cheeks were flushed. Her hands tightened on my back, and I could feel how warm they were, right through the fabric of my shirt. I'd never had a girl's hands on my body like that. My body had had chairs broken on it and survived fires, floods, crashed through false walls, but as I slipped my hands tighter around the starlet's waist and her breath caught in her throat with a soft whispery noise, my invincible body burst into butterflies.

The stage had gone silent, and with my vision crowded by her face, it was easy to feel like it was just the two of us, alone. My heart started beating faster, so fast I was absolutely sure she had to feel it, and maybe she did, because when she looked at me again her eyes flashed with excitement, like she'd just realized she'd spent her whole life getting to this moment, and now here we were.

I knew she wanted me to kiss her, and, incredibly, *I* wanted to kiss her. This strange, demanding, impossible starlet. Henrietta Newhouse.

Thinking seemed like the wrong move here, so I leaned in, brushing my lips against hers. She didn't move at first, and then she swayed, like her knees were about to give way, and caught herself on me, her mouth on mine, her hands creeping up my back until I felt waves of shivers breaking across my skin.

She was warm. And soft. She tasted like mint, and something else. Something that was just her, and I couldn't figure out what but it made my pulse race. I pressed against her, kissing her deeper, my eyes closed, my head swimming in the darkness, and it was only me, and her, and our kiss.

"And—cut!"

She pulled away so quickly I almost lost my footing, catching myself at the last second.

"Very nice, very nice!"

While I tried to remember how to breathe again, I glanced over at her. Henrietta. She had a smile on her face like the last five minutes had gone better than she could have ever imagined.

"That was...," I started, not knowing how to finish that sentence, and she laughed.

"I know." She shook her head. "The best performance of my life, probably, pretending to fall for you."

I felt the words hit me square in my chest, the air *whoosh*ing from my body. I couldn't move. I just stood, staring at her, while the makeup man rushed in to fix her lipstick.

Oh.

Right.

I was a complete...idiot.

The makeup man said something, and she laughed, while everything inside me shattered to pieces. I turned my face away from the lights, trying to put myself back together, trying to face reality. She was an actress. She was *acting*. Of course.

"Once more, from the top!"

"Wh-What?" I couldn't do that again, but the director didn't seem to care. He only had eyes for Henrietta, his gaze full of all the sparkles I'd felt a few minutes ago. Seemed like she hadn't just gotten me to fall in love with her.

"This time, Miss Newhouse, we'd, ah, like to see you wearing this." He nodded for the wardrobe man, who rushed out carrying...something. Scraps of lace, it looked like.

Henrietta's eyebrows shot up. "On...my..." She paused for a moment. "Head?"

The director gave her a smile. "No, dear. Just this."

Another long pause, and then Henrietta threw her head back, laughing.

"Sure!" she said, making my heart leap. She jerked a hand at me. "I will when he does."

"Now, Miss Newhouse—"

"Didn't you say it was only shoulders and faces?"

"Miss *Newhouse*—"

"Seems like a fella could just use his imagination."

"You're not understanding the nature of the scene! It's a romance, you see, and—"

"It felt pretty romantic to me." She glanced over at me. "Why don't you ask him? Do you think I need to be practically naked to sell the romance?"

Was she poking fun? I couldn't tell, but I kept my mouth shut—and her face fell with disappointment.

Meanwhile the director's was turning red. "Now, you may have arrived in this city all of five minutes ago, from whatever little town you call home—"

"Chicago," Henrietta answered, eyes flashing. "Heard of it?"

"Miss Newhouse! If you want to work in Hollywood, let this be your first lesson: you do as you're told." The director's voice dropped dangerously low and he snatched the costume from its hanger.

"I came here to act." She'd raised her chin like she had when we met, although this time she looked less like a spoiled brat and more like a soldier, steeling herself for battle. "If you want to see me do it in my underwear, you'd better convince me instead of barking an order."

It felt like everyone sucked in a breath and held it. The director stared at Henrietta, his face getting redder and redder, until he finally threw the costume on the ground.

"Get yourself off my stage!" he roared, and Henrietta glanced at me with a look that was…pleading? But what did she expect me to say that wouldn't just get me blackballed, too? I looked away not quite fast enough to miss the anger crashing to her face, and she turned to the wardrobe man, snatching her own sweater and trading it for the blue one.

"Thanks for your support," she said to me, her voice flat. "And you're welcome. Seems like I just guaranteed no one'll be watching *that* film anytime soon."

She pushed past me, and the only noises in the soundstage were the hollow clip of her heels, followed by the thud of the door slamming shut behind her.

CHAPTER ELEVEN
HENRIETTA

My blood fizzed like a bottle of cola all shook up. I could hardly see straight, and every atom in my body screamed to stomp back into that soundstage and tear that creepy director to PIECES.

Honestly, what on earth was *that*? Lingerie! That color wasn't even the right shade for me! Oooh, I'd like to see him with that lace wrapped around his throat.

At the same time, I could only imagine what I'd hear if I tried to complain. "Why didn't you just keep your mouth shut?" How many times had someone said that to me? *Smile. Say nothing. Go along.* My mother had even given me a dainty embroidered pillow that read *A woman is beautiful with her mouth closed in a smile* (it made a truly excellent pincushion), and my oldest sister used to scold me constantly, not for talking back but for rushing in without a plan: "If you're going to make a fool out of someone, at least be smart about it!"

Now I'd gone and blown up my chances before I'd started. I just wanted to find Midge, moan out my sorrows, and maybe track down Mr. Fitch's car to pop the tires.

Last week, Midge'd told me to find her *the very second* I'd finished my screen test—"We'll both have something to celebrate!" she'd said, giving me a big squeeze. I didn't relish the thought of telling her: nope, no cele-brations. Not for me, at least.

But when I arrived at Stage 29, a crew member said *Lucky Hand* had gone on hold. Something about Lloyd Rodger not showing up for work. The crew member doubted Midge was anywhere on the lot.

Despondent and a bit adrift, I stepped back outside, the air warm and fragrant with the scent of bougainvillea, the sky above a deep clear blue, the wide streets between the soundstages filled with the enchanted creatures of my dreams: women in wide-hipped gowns and men in sharp tuxedos, walls of flowers carted off to a perfect French village at the back of the lot, and every few seconds another famous face I'd grown up watch-ing, a thrill of recognition zipping through me like an electric shock. As I made my way to the gate, I heard music floating on the breeze, mixing with the warm-pillow scent of baking bread from the commissary, and I looked up to see a plain gray building, the windows thrown open, and inside: piano, violin, horn, their songs lapping up against each other as beautiful as waves.

I quit walking, a lump in my throat. How could I ever leave this mag-ical place? What would happen when I stepped through those gates and they closed forever behind me? I half expected the whole studio lot to melt away, disappear into sand and fog and leave me to my gray little life: a rumpled boardinghouse room, handsy managers, my money steadily dwindling until all I could afford was a ticket back home.

I wouldn't. I *couldn't*.

If acting wasn't an option, I'd find another job on the lot. They needed script girls, didn't they? Or someone to answer the fan mail, or maybe I could put those hours I'd spent raiding Ruby's makeup collection to good use?

Could I just...wander onto a set and act like I belonged? How long could I camp out at the lot before someone realized there was a woebegone starlet skulking around the soundstages?

"'Scuse me! What do you think you're doing?"

Oh. Apparently, the answer was "about two minutes."

When I turned around, it wasn't a security guard but a man in a smart suit, on the older side of middle-aged and tall. Weeks of encounters with Hollywood men in smart suits had taught me to be wary, but he had a look about him that I liked right away, an air like he didn't care a whit for chasing starlets and a Southern drawl that reminded me of my mama's own Louisiana coo.

He had his hands on his hips, eyebrow raised, and I realized that I had stopped to ponder my future right in front of a small bungalow; I was blocking the door.

"Do you need an assistant?" I asked—why the hell not? He blinked at me, dropping his hands to his sides.

"I'm an editor!" he said, as though this answered my question.

"I can edit!" Which was, of course, not true, but I could learn. Once I figured out whether he meant *words* or *film*.

"You know how to work a Moviola?" He sounded suspicious.

No.

"Absolutely!"

He snorted out a laugh and slipped past me to pull open the door. "This I have to see."

I'd been about to follow him inside when I grasped how incredibly, idiotically dangerous it would be to throw myself at the feet of a strange man, in Hollywood, when not a soul knew where I was.

"Well? Are you coming?"

80

I gave him an appraising look. "As soon as you get me alone in your editing room, you're not going to ravish me, are you?"

For a moment, he stared at me, and then he burst out in gales of laughter so huge they would've been insulting if I hadn't felt so relieved.

"If that's what you're after, sugar," he said, wiping actual tears from his eyes, "you're in the wrong place. Come on. Your virtue is safe with me." And, still hiccoughing with laughter, he disappeared inside.

It turned out a Moviola was a wonderful machine that projected film onto a monitor about the size of my hands held together, like a miniature movie theater set deep into the maw of a great steel monster. You flicked a switch and the soundtrack came on with a *wom-BLAHT*, the talking and music and effects all tinny and metallic over a background of endless whirring clicks.

The editor—"Name of Jerome Calhoun"—showed me how he fed the raw film into the Moviola, snipping and pasting different takes together into one beautiful, smooth final version.

"Like a chef, mixing together a *gour*-met meal," Jerome drawled.

"Huh. Neat."

"Neat! This generation doesn't have any appreciation for the craft, you kids moony over talkies or color, but where would movies be without solid fundamentals? The greats?! I'm not talking about the stars, you know—I mean the *real* greats, Adam De Longpré, Alaina Wright, FAY FAIRFAX! You know, I've been around here since Silver Wing was just a dusty warehouse called Argent Studios, and it's a true shame no one these days—"

He was off, spilling out another history lesson while his long fingers expertly danced along the film. By the end of the afternoon, Jerome had decided he didn't need an assistant, but he did enjoy having someone who sat patiently and listened to him while he worked.

"I'm not going to hire you," he told me, "but if you clean up these scraps, you're welcome to come back tomorrow."

"You're throwing these away?" I reached down to the floor, littered with snips of film like a carpet of leaves, and picked up a short length. In my hand, it looked like dull, amber shadows, but when I held it to the lamp on Jerome's desk, the whole thing sprang to life: a couple in evening clothes, dancing together and caught midkick, their eyes locked on each other's smiling faces. I turned to him, the film pressed to my heart. "Can I keep it?"

Jerome laughed, shaking his head. "You wanna be an editor, sugar, you're gonna have to be more ruthless."

<hr />

I didn't want to be an editor, but as long as Jerome kept my name on the studio visitors' list, I'd happily do whatever he asked, even though I should have been finding another job to buy myself more time in Hollywood. But a week later and my savings desperately low, I was only more certain I'd made the right choice: better broke on the Silver Wing lot than getting paid pennies for more cowgirl gigs, especially if it meant one-on-one moviemaking lessons from someone like Jerome.

"... now, back then, we used nitrate film. You gotta handle it delicately, not many these days understand that. I was working on this picture with Marvin Hubert—"

"Oh, I *love* him! He was my favorite actor as a kid—even named our old cat after him!" I said fondly, and Jerome gave me a look. "They had the same ginger hair."

"As I was saying," Jerome said, rolling his eyes, but there was a knock at the door and he let out a sharp breath. That would be the projectionist, who came around this time to fetch the day's reels, which he'd play for the Silver Wing bigwigs in the executive screening room. Today's picture was one of Silver Wing's more important features, and Jerome wanted to take especially good care with it. But he hadn't quite finished yet, and at another, sharper knock, he jerked his head at the door.

"Go see if you can distract him for a few minutes, would you, sugar?"

The projectionist was young and smiley, and I slid off the stool, wondering if I could get him to buy me an ice cream at the commissary, but when I threw open the door, my heart stopped.

"M-M-Mister—Reynolds?"

There was a clatter as Jerome jumped to his feet, all but knocking me out of the way. Behind Mr. Reynolds, a beaky-nosed assistant with rolled-up shirtsleeves hovered like a bumblebee.

"Good—good afternoon, Mr. Reynolds!" Jerome stuttered. "What can I do for you?"

"I'm scheduled to view *Phantom Rider*," he said, his voice polite but authoritative. "I understand you're preparing the first reel."

"Yes, sir." Jerome cleared his throat. "But it's not quite done yet."

My attention flicked back to Mr. Reynolds. How would the King of Hollywood take to bad news? I'd seen enough grown men in this city throw hissy fits over smudges on their Mercedes and prepared myself for the worst, but Mr. Reynolds smiled.

"I'm early. I was looking for an excuse to stretch my legs. Take your time, this is an important picture."

The atmosphere in the room relaxed, Jerome returning Mr. Reynolds's smile. I realized this important, powerful man reminded me, more than anything, of my own papa, who'd been a lawyer for years and managed to make even a request to take out the garbage into a quietly intelligent, confidently delivered master class in strength and restraint.

"Yes, sir."

Mr. Reynolds glanced over at me, for the first time, it felt like.

"Red dress? Remind me of your name again, miss?"

"Oh! I, um, Newhouse, sir. Henrietta Newhouse."

Mr. Reynolds frowned, and I felt my stomach drop. "Didn't we have you scheduled for a screen test last week?"

"Um. Yes, sir."

"I didn't see that film," he said, and his assistant looked ready to jump to the moon for it, but Mr. Reynolds turned to Jerome. "Could you locate Miss Newhouse's screen test for me?"

"Of course, sir," he said, shooting me a raised eyebrow—I'd, ah, neglected to mention the screen test to him. Mr. Reynolds smiled and folded his hands.

"Excellent. I'll wait here."

I might've made the tiniest, strangled noise; Jerome, just as he disappeared through the door, threw me a look that seemed to say *Don't touch anything don't say anything DEAR LORD don't even DO anything!!!* Immediately, sweat prickled under my arms.

I wondered if Mr. Reynolds would try to make conversation, and what I'd say if he did. Me speaking would probably not help my situation, and also I didn't know what would happen when Jerome came back to say, "Well, I tried to find Miss Newhouse's film but apparently Mr. Fitch used it as dental floss," and then I'd have to explain why my screen test only had value for its hygienic properties. But it turned out not to matter: Mr. Reynolds's assistant handed him some papers to review, which completely absorbed him for the ten minutes Jerome was gone.

"Is that it?"

The moment Jerome entered the room, a canister in his hand, my tremulous heartbeat immediately rocketed into a tarantella pace.

"Yes, sir."

"Play it for me, please."

RIGHT NOW? IN FRONT OF ME??

Jerome, carefully avoiding my eye, fed the reel into the Moviola and stepped aside for Mr. Reynolds to take a look.

Silence, darkness, then a loud *POP* and there I was, the hopeful girl from last week. It all came back, those emotions unspooling with the *tick-tick* of the film: excitement, nerves, the absolutely magical moment when the scene began and I felt myself falling into a different world where I transformed into something new.

I *was* good. It wasn't just my imagination. From his position beside Mr. Reynolds, Jerome glanced over his shoulder at me, the compliment of his admiration only slightly tempered by his obvious surprise.

For just a moment, I let myself remember that *oh, yesss* feeling, because I knew what was coming next.

The scene flickered, and my wooden stiff of a screen partner appeared beside me. I winced as he choked out his dialogue, and the scene crashed to an end with his complaint to the director.

"Hold there, please."

The Moviola went dark as the whole thing spun still, and Mr. Reynolds turned around.

"You were funny," he said, and a smile popped onto my face.

"Thank you, sir!"

"That character wasn't supposed to be funny."

"Oh," I said, and Mr. Reynolds's mouth pulled into a small smile.

"It's all right. You did well. I liked it."

Behind his back, Jerome gave me a huge grin—double thumbs up—and I let out a burst of nervous laughter.

"Thank you, sir."

Instead of responding, Mr. Reynolds put his attention back on the Moviola, giving Jerome a small nod to restart the film. The monitor filled with our faces—mine and Declan Collins's. Right. The *kiss*. In my memory, the whole thing had been quick and chaste, a peck from a Sunday school sweetheart, but played back...

My mouth went dry, because I could see now on the monitor what I hadn't noticed one inch from that boy's face: the feeling between us, the look he gave me, awed but mostly just helpless, his eyes tracing over my face like...like he'd never seen anything like it.

We didn't look like a movie star couple. We looked like two people hopelessly in love. *Real* love, not something for a scene; honest and messy and scary and—

Only that didn't make any sense. I knew it wasn't real, I was the damned actress! But when he bent his face toward mine, his eyes open until the last second as though he couldn't bear to close them, when he finally touched me in the lightest kiss, I felt a swoop in my chest I hadn't even experienced there in his arms. The kiss deepened, and a blush worked onto my cheeks—my actual cheeks, the ones attached to the person standing in a dim room with three adult men.

Pull yourself together, Henny!

The camera closed in on our faces just as the screen went black, and Mr. Reynolds turned around to his assistant handing him a sheet of paper.

"The report from Burton Fitch," he said, and my heart sank.

Shoot.

So long, Silver Wing. It'd been a nice ride.

Three times, Mr. Reynolds's eyes swept down and up the paper.

"Would you care to explain what happened on set, Miss Newhouse?"

No, thanks much, actually I would not, but I glanced at Jerome, who gave me another warning look. *This is not a man you lie to.*

"Um. The director, Mr. Fitch, had a...costume recommendation I disagreed with," I said, and when Mr. Reynolds stared at me, I added: "He wanted me to do the scene again in lingerie."

"Ah. Well. We do that around here, sometimes, you know."

"Yes, sir. Only it's just a simple kiss, isn't it? A first kiss. I don't know about you, but I haven't had too many first kisses in my underwear. Second kisses, sure, but—"

In the corner, Jerome was making pointed expressions: *TOO FAR!*

"I see."

Well, any excuse to get out of Chicago in the winter was good, I suppose. Maybe I could get a lovely tan before I made it home.

"As it is...," Mr. Reynolds continued, "I would agree with you. That was an error on Mr. Fitch's part—and someone will need to have a word with him. I've seen too many errors like that in his screen tests lately." At this, the assistant immediately flipped over a sheet on his notepad and scrawled something down.

Oooh, excellent! I hoped that creep got nailed to the wall.

"In fact, there are a number of Mr. Fitch's judgments I'd have to disagree with," Mr. Reynolds said quietly, rereading the paper. "You have a natural ability, Miss Newhouse, that's very appealing. And the boy has some charm to him as well."

"Him?" I said, too fast. Mr. Reynolds glanced back at me, smiling, and I wiped the disbelief off my face. "I mean—"

"Miss Newhouse, I'll expect you to treat everyone with courtesy if you'd like to stay at my studio."

"Yes, of course, sir, I— Stay at your studio?"

"I'd like to offer you a starting contract, Miss Newhouse. Let's say six months, at one hundred and fifty dollars a week. Would that be—"

"YES!" I said, and I could practically hear Ruby, back in law school, screaming at me, *You dummy! Don't you dare agree to any contract you haven't read yet!!!* "Um, what I mean is, I'll have to look over all the details, but thank you so much, Mr. Reynolds, sir, really!"

He nodded. "Come back tomorrow and we'll have the papers ready for you. Welcome aboard, Miss Newhouse."

And then they were gone, me hardly daring to breathe, Jerome staring at me like I'd just transformed into Cinderella right before his eyes.

"Pinch me," I said, sticking out my arm, and he shook his head, stunned.

"Can't. You're Silver Wing property now."

I was so excited, I *screamed.*

CHAPTER TWELVE
DECLAN

"You want the good news or the bad news?"

Pep strolled up to me, riffling through the magazines at the Silver Wing newsstand. He'd asked me to meet him on the lot this afternoon but hadn't said what it would be about. We hadn't spoken much, honestly, since his trick with the screen test two weeks ago.

"Bad," I said, pushing a copy of *Reel Picture* into its stand, and, squinting in the bright sunshine, Pep jerked his head to walk down Main Street, the wide concrete road that cut through the studio from the main gate to the backlot sets.

"I heard from a producer on that Western. They got the footage back." He glanced over at me. "Doesn't look good."

"Doesn't look good *how*?" I asked, and Pep shrugged.

"Like you should've died about nine different ways. I got him to give me the reel and to keep his mouth shut, but it cost us two thousand dollars."

The words hit me so hard I stopped walking. *Two thousand dollars.* If you added up all the money I'd made in my life, it still wouldn't come close to two thousand dollars. To lose that, in minutes...

"Where...where did you even get the money?" I asked, confused about how Pep, who regarded money as something like his own personal religion, was still breathing.

"I gave him our savings. The rest I got on loan."

"On loan? What bank would give you money to pay for blackmail?"

"Which brings me to the good news." He paused, a smile on his face. We stood not far from the main gate, surrounded by tall administrative buildings populated by the unglamorous people who made Silver Wing possible: the accountants, the lawyers, the executives. Pep reached into his jacket and, with a flourish, held out a piece of paper.

"Congratulations, Duke. You're Silver Wing's newest supporting player."

I reached for the paper, but Pep, probably figuring I'd rip it to pieces, pulled it away.

"I told you I don't want to act! No acting, no contracts. *Stunts,* Pep. Put me in stunts."

But he didn't seem to be listening, his eyes on the air somewhere above my head.

"You're not getting it. Stunting is done. Too risky. How long before what happened on that Western happens again?" He gave me a hard look, but when I glared back at him, silent, his expression softened. "Come on, Dec. A hundred dollars a week, guaranteed, every week. This is a good thing, all right? Can't you trust me?" He held out the paper and reached into his pocket for a pen. "Just sign the damn contract."

But I could only stare at it. I didn't know much about studio contracts, but what I did know I didn't like. *Indentured servitude,* some people called it, because the contracts controlled your life and always favored the studios. And they lasted *seven* years. I'd just turned nineteen a few days ago; Silver Wing could end up owning me until my twenty-sixth birthday.

Plus, a hundred-dollar-a-week contract meant even if you hit it big, the studios didn't have to pay you a single dollar more. And if you went bust? The studios had options every six months to can you. They decided where you worked and what movies you filmed—anywhere, anytime, and you couldn't say no or you'd get suspended with no pay.

Didn't like it? Get sued.

And the contract didn't just cover what happened in front of the camera. The studio could change my identity, my face, my story. They'd give me a new person to be, and I had to become that person, every second of my life; not just on movie sets or during publicity events, but on the street, at a restaurant, alone in my apartment.

"I...can't. I just can't. You told me, one year. You promised. Pep, I wanna go home."

The paper shook as Pep held it up higher.

"It's not a request, Dec. I know what I promised, but I couldn't get my hands on the kind of dough we needed. Silver Wing gave you a six-month advance, and that money's gone. What do you think would happen if you backed out now? They're gonna want their money, and if we can't pay... they'll find some other way to get it out of us." His voice was quiet, but I could hear the tremble in his words, and I remembered Sam, the private investigator, sliding me the photo of Silver Wing's general manager, Richard Mulvey. Mob connections. Broken kneecaps.

"Six more months," Pep said. "Then, you want to go? Go."

I didn't know if I believed him, but what choice did I have? I signed the damn contract.

"Good." Pep patted my shoulder and jerked his head to a snowy-white building on the corner, guarded by a pair of life-sized marble swans. "They want to see you. Third floor. Remember to look happy."

I trudged toward the entrance, feeling like I was walking to my own execution. What had I just signed up for? What had I just signed away?

"Ah, you must be Mr. Collins—welcome!" On the third floor, inside a room marked PUBLICITY, a tall man with a pencil-thin mustache jumped up from behind a desk. It was a corner office, floor-to-ceiling windows letting in generous sunlight and a sweeping view. Unfortunately, we were so far out of the city that it mostly showed the surrounding empty lots and faceless warehouses. Opposite the windows, black fabric draped one wall and a tripod pointed suspiciously at empty air.

"I'm Mr. Baxter, and I'll be working with you to develop your image here at Silver Wing."

"My image?"

"Haircut, clothing, a bit of polishing. We'll get you into dancing lessons and elocution, along with—"

"I don't dance," I said, yanking at my shirt collar. Had it gotten real hot in here?

"Well, not yet." Baxter ushered me to a chair. "That's what the lessons are for! Now, let's go over your role here at the studio."

"My role? It's not just...saying lines?"

Baxter let out a cheery laugh that made my blood run cold. "Oh, no! It's more than that. You see, here at Silver Wing, we like to support each other. Occasionally, we match up stars together, in a personal capacity. It helps drum up public interest, and that never hurts at the box office!"

The dancing Baxter did around the issue made it clear that he, at least, had had a few lessons, and I crossed my arms over my chest. "What are you asking me to do?"

"A real trial!" Baxter said, but he smiled as though he'd just made a witty joke. "We'd like to pair you with one of our most promising young starlets."

Ten minutes they'd had me and already with this?

"I don't really—"

"I have to be perfectly clear about this, Mr. Collins." Baxter's smile stiffened. "This came directly from Mr. Reynolds. Your positioning in future pictures is yet to be determined; for the moment, your main task is to support one of our actresses as we build her image."

"You hired me to be...a boyfriend?" How was it possible this kept getting worse?

"A pleasant task, I assure you! I've heard from everyone that this young lady is an absolute delight! You'll be charmed as well, I'm sure, and—oh! Here she is!"

A knock at the door and I turned around to see *her*. The starlet. Henrietta something. Somehow, she'd survived that screen test and made it here to ruin my life. She looked different, shining with some of that Hollywood polish: blond hair brighter, shorter, expertly curled; makeup applied with a careful hand; clothes straight from the wardrobe department. I choked on my groan.

"Hello, Mr. Baxter! Janet said I should come by for some photos?"

"Yes, of course, welcome! Let me introduce you to—"

"*You*." The sweetness dropped from her expression as her eyes fixed on me.

"Oh, lovely! You remember each other! Miss Newhouse, Mr. Collins here will be accompanying you to various engagements, dinners, premieres, parties, that sort of thing. We thought we'd start with some photos, yes? Just test shots. Now hold on a moment! I'll fetch the photographer." Like a well-intentioned matchmaker, Baxter smiled at me and the starlet before gliding out of the room and leaving us alone.

"Looks like you got what you wanted," I said.

"No thanks to you, Mr. 'I Only Do Stunts.' How did they even drag you in here? Blink twice if you're being held hostage."

I stood up and tugged one of her curls. "New hair? What was the matter with the way it was?"

"Platinum shows up better on film," she said, sweeping her hair out of reach. "I'm guessing they haven't gotten to you yet?"

"You look like one of them. Those actresses who swan around this city like they own it."

"Since I came here to *be* them," she said through gritted teeth, "I'll take that as a compliment."

"Funny. I would've figured you came here to be yourself."

"Miss Newhouse, Mr. Collins!" Baxter reappeared with the photographer just as the starlet spun on me, murder in her eyes. "Let's get you in front of that curtain there, please, yes, thank you."

Henrietta marched to her place like an obedient show dog, and I let out a sigh. Better get this over with.

"All right now," Baxter said, but he was frowning. "We'll need you to actually...touch each other. Mr. Collins? Put your arm around Miss Newhouse, please."

I took her shoulders with all the romance of a drunk man clutching a streetlamp. Baxter's frown deepened.

"The idea here is to...look...happy," he said, uncertain. "People looking at this photo need to believe you two care for each other!"

I wondered if Henrietta would be shocked by this, that we weren't just taking a few test shots but selling a sham romance. Instead, she gave Baxter a tight smile and snuggled in closer. I could smell the fresh peroxide in her hair, the fake floral perfume of powder—not exactly inspiring romance.

"And this way, please!"

Snap! went the camera. I felt like I was posing for my mug shot.

"So," the girl said as the photographer switched out the flash bulb. "Stunting. Anything I would have seen?"

"Oh, I'm not allowed to tell you that. Stunt man's honor," I said, and when she rolled her eyes, I couldn't help adding, "Did you see *Wings of Gold*? You know the shot where the guy leaps from the train into the river?"

"That was you?" She gave me a dubious look, as Mr. Baxter shouted, "And—pose!"

Another flash, a few excruciating seconds of holding still, and the photographer pulled his camera away to pop in a new bulb.

"Can't prove it's not me."

"Can I sign up to throw you off a moving train," the starlet asked, "or do they set up some kind of lottery?"

"Mr. Collins?" Baxter hovered at the photographer's shoulder. "Why don't you try standing behind Miss Newhouse and putting your arm around her waist?"

Henrietta dutifully nestled her back against my chest, and when I was too slow with my hand, she picked it up herself and held it. I didn't know what to do with my fingers—loose? Spread out? Cupped?—and finally Henrietta whispered at me, "What are you doing? Quit twitching!"

Pose. *Flash!* And then Henrietta held up my hand.

"Are you really a stunt man? Look how smooth your skin is—not a mark on you! What kind of beauty cream do you use?"

I jerked away.

"Everyone's got scars. See?" She held up her own hands. "That one on my little finger I got from our cat, when I was nine, and this one is where I broke my wrist after my sister shoved me off the front steps."

"A hero," I muttered, and when she raised an eyebrow at me, I shrugged. "No breaks, no scars."

"I can't believe that. What kind of stunt man has no scars?"

I leaned in with a grin. "A very, very good one."

"No…no…" We both turned to see Baxter frowning at us. "Ah, just a moment…"

The girl let out a huff of frustration. "Will you hurry up and smile? There's somewhere I need to be."

"Are they giving you a new nose?"

"Don't be an idiot, my nose is perfect. I should be studying my lines right about now."

"Booked a role already? Whose neck did you step on?"

"I haven't booked anything yet. I have an audition. They're still looking for the lead in *One Night in a Train Car.*"

She said it like I should have known what it was, but I stared at her, unimpressed. "Don't tell me you think you're gonna star. Since when does Silver Wing stick newcomers into lead roles?"

"Probably when they see me. Or more accurately, when Jack Huxley sees me. Word is he's got final say on his costar." A sly smile spread across her face while I tried not to gag.

"But first, I need to practice." She batted her eyelashes. "So can you please unclench and give the camera a smile so I can get out of here?"

"You're fine with all this?" I swept my hand across the setup. "You don't care that your boss decides who you're sweet on?"

She looked at me as though I'd just told her I believed in little green men.

"It's not *real*. It's smart business. I'm eighteen years old, which is too old to go everywhere with my mother and too young to be an independent woman on her own. A steady beau tells the bad boys to keep their hands off and lets the world know somebody's in love with me so maybe they should give it a try, too."

"I'm not in love with you."

"It's. Not. *Real*," she repeated.

"Mr. Collins?" Baxter gestured me over, and I gave one last look at Henrietta, checking her makeup in the reflection of her compact, before stepping over to him.

"You're looking a bit ... stiff."

"Stiff?"

"To be frank, young man, you seem as though you're in the middle of a painful medical procedure. Mr. Reynolds said you had wonderful chemistry with Miss Newhouse in your screen test, but I can't say I see much of that here now."

I shrugged. "Oh well. Guess I'm not the right guy for the job. Good luck." I'd started to head for the door when Baxter stopped me.

"You don't seem to understand, Mr. Collins. She is Silver Wing's newest star. *You* only have one job here, and that is to make her look cherished and adored. If you'd like to continue with this studio, you'll do that."

He gestured to the set, and I swallowed the screeeeeeam of despair in my throat. One foot at a time, I made it back to her side. I could do this. I jumped off a damn building! I could smile for a camera.

"Indigestion?" Henrietta asked, and I grimaced.

"Just ingenues."

"Mr. Collins, you know what will happen to me if this photo shoot is a disaster?"

"What?" I asked, and she gave me a beautiful smile.

"Absolutely nothing."

I scowled. Damned starlets.

"You know," I said as the photographer fumbled with his camera, "I don't know much about moviemaking—"

"No kidding," she muttered.

"But I would guess it doesn't look great to the higher-ups if their fresh new starlet can't pull off a simple photo shoot. Not a terrific message to send just before your audition for *One Night on a Steamboat*—"

"*Train Car*," she ground out, but I could tell I'd rattled her. The look of determination I'd spotted during our screen test flashed across her face, then she turned to me and *melted*.

Shock kicked through me, just for a second. *Not real!* But she shifted her body against mine, and that felt very real. Her hands, which she inched up my waist, my back, felt real, too. At the screen test, she'd looked so deeply into my eyes that I felt turned inside out, but now, a smile slid onto her lips, which parted just so, her lipstick as freshly red as a candy apple. One eyebrow arched, her cheek tilted in a suggestion that made my heart stop. If our screen test had captured two people realizing their feelings for each other, this photo shoot was more like a boy and a girl about to sneak off somewhere private.

"Ah-*ha!*" Baxter murmured. "Yes, very nice!"

Henrietta glanced at the photographer and a lock of hair fell across her face. Without thinking, I reached up to brush it away. Her skin felt soft, impossibly soft, and warm, and as my hand curled around her chin, her jaw, a blush came across her cheeks, delicate and pink.

Flash! "Hold it!" Baxter warned, and we both went still, her pulse kicking gently under my fingertips. "There! We've got it. Yes. Yes, I think that should work."

I thought she would jump away like last time, but she stayed in my arms, her eyes on mine.

"You're getting better at this."

A wiggle of warmth wormed its way through my stomach. "What?"

"Pretending to care about me."

"Beautiful, just beautiful!" Baxter came over, looking ready to jump in and join the embrace, and the girl let me go, rubbing her hands along her arms. "Absolutely magnetic—a thrill!" Baxter threw his arms around our shoulders, looking at us as though we were made of gold. "Keep it up, and you could convince even *me*!"

CHAPTER THIRTEEN

HENRIETTA

I was so tired my hair hurt. Literally—these white-blond curls looked smashing but I bet all that peroxide shaved years off my life.

I'd always thought I was cute enough, but after a month tumbling through the Silver Wing Studio publicity machine, I'd learned my:

> ears stuck out a bit too much
> nose pushed in a little too round
> cheekbones hid under too much baby fat
> knees knocked slightly with every step and
> hair was perfectly fine, for pig farming

"That's what they do in Chicago, right?" the stylist had asked, holding out a lock.

"Who knows?" I'd replied wearily. "Mostly my hobbies back home involved the high school football team."

"Well, they won't recognize you when I'm through," he said, which had to be true, since I hardly recognized myself—not even, in the end, my own name. The triumphant phone call to my family about my success took an awkward turn when I told Mama and Papa the studio had tossed *Henrietta Newhouse* like a worn-down shoe that no longer fit.

"I need you to focus on the *steadily employed by the finest studio in the world* bit," I told my papa, while I could hear Mama in the background wailing about *"The family! The family!"* There was a long pause, during which I imagined Papa had removed his spectacles. "Anyhoo," I continued, "you have to admit, *Etta Hart* is easier to spell in lights!"

It was all worth it, every sting, every hoop to jump through:

I had it.

The role.

One Night in a Train Car.

I GOT IT.

The whole thing felt like a dream, and I kept waiting for someone to knock on the door and tell me they'd made a horrible mistake. Until then, though, I planned to enjoy every single second, *and I did,* from the costume fittings to the camera tests to my first day on set last week with Jack Huxley, who grinned at me in a way that made my knees tremble and whispered, "Well, Hen-Henrietta, here we are! Don't be nervous. I'll keep an eye on you."

"Only an eye?" I asked, my mouth doing that thing where it shot off without proper clearance from my brain. Before he could answer, my on-set publicist/chaperone cleared her throat and made loud gestures that read, *Young lady, you are supposed to be wholesome and TAKEN!*

Sigh.

In spite of what I'd told Declan, I highly suspected they'd saddled me with him partly as a threat: be good and don't fool around with any of the male stars, or risk being branded a high-class floozy by the tabloids. Here I was, surrounded by some of the best-looking fellas in the world, unable to even accept an invitation for a stroll around the lot without some publicist looking daggers at me, while the only boy I was allowed to kiss had to be threatened with *immediate termination* to put his hands on me.

But in spite of our offscreen feelings for each other, our photos had been a roaring success. Now they had us posing together practically every day: me and Declan sunning ourselves on the fake beaches of Stage 12, a cozy carriage ride through the French village set, moony-eyed sundae dates at the commissary, where I could look at but not touch my ice cream (per the idiotic pamphlet pushed on me by my publicist, "DON'T LET AN EXPANDED WAISTLINE SHRINK YOUR PAYCHECK!").

While I'd never complained about snuggling up with a cute boy, Declan proved there was a first time for everything. It was an honest-to-god crime that a person who looked the way he did could inspire such frustration. He would have done fabulously in the silent pictures—close-ups on those full lips, his perfect *I did nothing to make it look this adorable* hair, muscled forearms that would inspire poetry, and *no one able to hear him.*

But I refused to let Declan Collins's handsome frown ruin my lucky streak. I managed to bump my contract up to three hundred a week, thanks to my future-lawyer sister, who ignored my smug gloating that I hadn't ended up penniless in a ditch and offered me useful advice: *Are you worth it? Then ask for it. And for god's sake, don't apologize for a thing.* I had a wonderful role in a sure-to-be-a-smash film and the attention of every reporter, photographer, and gossip columnist in the city. I had a team of assistants, managers, and general errand-runners whose main responsibility seemed to be getting me whatever I wanted, even if it was getting me out of trouble. ("Anything bad happens," the studio's gruff and mildly terrifying general manager, Mr. Mulvey, said to me, "you don't call your mama, you don't call the police, you call me.") And I had Jack Huxley filling my new dressing room with flowers, along with a note suggesting some private rehearsal time.

Yes, everything was perfect, except—

I opened the door to my suite—a three-room knockout in the Knickerbocker Hotel, just off Hollywood Boulevard and paid for by the studio—still buzzing from another day of filming and dropped my purse on the floor, where it landed with an echoing thud that popped my lovely bubble of happiness.

What did all this success mean if I had not a single soul to celebrate with?

Everyone seemed to forget, amid the hairdos, the makeup, the grown-up clothing, and the fancy new contract...I was eighteen years old, barely out of high school, used to a full house and family dinners.

My studio schedule kept me too busy to make friends on the lot. There wasn't even time enough to visit Jerome in his editing room, and in spite of my new long-distance calling privileges, getting my family on the phone proved such a headache I gave up. Other than Mama, who in the right frame of mind could keep up a cheerful conversation with a streetlamp, my family wasn't much for gabbing. Once Papa had confirmed I was fed, sheltered, paid, and avoiding jazz bars, he'd invariably say, "Well, I'd better let you go," and as for Ruby, she famously hated the telephone. Unless I called with a specific question, I could practically hear her counting down the minutes. I'd even gotten desperate enough to ask for Genevieve, but she never seemed to be around the house. Mostly, I'd curl up listening to Mama's chatter about her social club or gardening woes like a program on the radio, until she'd exclaim she was late for something or other, had to run, lots of kisses, have fun, darling! And I was alone, again, somehow even more alone than before.

I should've been palling around with Midge, of course, patron saint of hopeful cowgirls. Everything I had I owed to her and her invitation to the lot, but that had turned out to be our last hurrah. Production on *Lucky Hand* remained shut down after Lloyd Rodger "got the flu" (industry-speak for recovering from a twenty-four-hour bender). The Los Angeles number Midge had given me just rang and rang, and her publicist shooed away my questions with "What? Are you working for *Photoplay* now?"

Imagine my surprise when, a few days after moving into the Knicker-bocker, I opened up my morning paper and read a line in the daily "Hollywood Doings" column that reported that Silver Wing Studios had by mutual agreement dissolved its contract with Miss Miriam Powell after the latter decided to return to private life with her family in New York.

"She didn't even say goodbye," I said later to *One Night in a Train Car*'s costumer, who let out a disapproving sniff.

"Typical. Some girls just can't hack it. She was an odd bird, you know, always by herself. I'm surprised to hear you call her a friend. Didn't think she had any. Thought that was why she hightailed it home."

It stung to consider that Midge hadn't counted me as a friend, but I had to admit the costumer probably had it right: we hardly knew each other.

Sighing, I kicked off my heels and let my jacket fall to the floor. Hollywood Boulevard seemed to rock night and day with an energy that would rattle a skeleton to life. I could hear music now, several stories below, and cars honking, voices rising in shouts and laughter. Neon glow came in through the blinds, falling in tiger stripes on the floor, so I didn't bother turning on the lights and instead padded in the semidarkness to my bedroom. I pushed open the door—and gasped.

There was someone sitting on my bed.

"Who—" I started, and then the words froze in my throat because I knew that dark hair, falling down her back in a sheet of black. I knew the fine tilt of her head. I knew the delicate way she sat upright.

"Midge?" My voice came out in a whisper. "Midge, is it... Is it you?"

She was silhouetted against the window, facing away from me, one hand in a tight fist at her side. I wanted to take a step closer to her, but I couldn't move. The air felt cold, even though my skin was still dewy with the heat of a California evening.

"Henny?" She sounded a million miles away, like she was speaking from the bottom of a deep canyon. "Henny, is it you?"

"Midge!" I ran to her side, dropping to the floor so that I could look up into her face, pale and indistinct in the dim light. I wanted to take her hand, throw my arms around her in a hug, but she pulled away when I got close. I could see the outlines of her fine cheekbones, her nose, her forehead, her mouth set in a grim line. "Where have you been?"

"I'm..." She began to talk and then sounded confused. "Where... am I?"

My heart gave a strange start. "You're in my hotel suite. It's me. It's Henny. You're here with me. You're safe, Midge," I added, because it was clear to me that *Something* had happened to her, and my thoughts raced with all sorts of wild, terrible possibilities.

"*Safe?*" she asked, an edge to her voice, as though I was poking fun.

"Do you know how you got here? Do you remember anything?"

"Why do you sound so... far away?" She lifted a hand as though to touch my face, but missed me in a way that felt strange and wrong, like she couldn't properly control her body.

"I'm right here."

Her attention shifted from me to the window, the noise and revelry below, and she'd gone so still, unreal still, as though I was looking at one of Jerome's film snips, a frozen image held up to the light. Somehow, this unnerved me more than anything. Was she even breathing?

"Hold on," I said, not sure if I was speaking to Midge or myself. "Let me turn on the light." I wobbled to my feet and groped for the switch, jabbering nonstop, because that awful silence, the silence of aloneness, had returned: "Are you hungry? I'm a mess at cooking but even I can't ruin tea. Or do you want coffee? Honestly, I might have some trouble with coffee, I never could—"

I flicked on the light.

I turned.

I gasped.

Empty bed. Empty room. Sheets smooth, neat, not even a wrinkle.

Midge had simply disappeared.

CHAPTER FOURTEEN
DECLAN

Photo shoots, makeovers, lessons in something called the Swan Walk: suck in your stomach, square your shoulders, take a deep breath, and step off on the right—"RIGHT FOOT, MR. COLLINS!"—and I started looking at the concrete walls surrounding the Silver Wing lot the way an inmate dreams of freedom.

"Why can't we go to an actual baseball game?" I'd asked that morning, blinking up at the glare of lights on Stage 19. Behind us, yards of artificial grass stretched to a painted backdrop of stadium seating. "The Seals are at Wrigley Field next week."

"Because then," Henriet—no, *Etta Hart* said, leaning on her bat, which she held with the knob in the fake dirt, "you'd have to act like you enjoy being around me for more than the time it takes to stand still for a photo."

The thought made me grimace, and Henrietta gave her curls an absent fluff.

"Anyway," she added, "even I know Wrigley Field is in Chicago."

"Hey, Babe Ruth." I pulled the bat out from under her and flipped it end-cap down. "The Los Angeles ballpark is also Wrigley Field. And here's some trivia for you: the Wrigley Field here in L.A. is actually older than the one in—"

Henrietta let out a dramatic snore and then jerked awake. "Oh! Sorry, nodded off for a second there. Did I miss anything interesting? No. I didn't. Because we're talking about *baseball*."

"All right, kiddos!" The art director for the shot clapped his hands together, grinning at us. "Let's get Miss Hart with the bat and Mr. Collins behind her, very good, thank you, now *smile!*"

I'd never get used to being moved like a pawn, but I had figured out the quickest way through these photo shoots: give them exactly what they wanted. When Henrietta got into a hitter's stance, I cozied up behind her, wrapping my hands around hers.

"Your grip is all wrong," I muttered, eyes on the camera, cheek close to Henrietta's temple. "Your elbows are drooping—line up your knuckles and—"

"Keep talking," Henrietta sang back through her smile, "and you'll see just how good I am with this bat."

Less than an hour later, I was back out in the sunshine, released from the publicists' clutches for lunch. Playing the part of Etta Hart's sweetheart had one perk: the famous Silver Wing commissary. Done up in chrome and green, the commissary served breakfast, lunch, dinner, afternoon tea, midmorning snacks, and more kinds of dessert than I'd even known existed, all for rock-bottom prices.

Inside, I spotted Pep, holding court. Since signing me over to Silver Wing—and since my pay for the next six months had already been spent—Pep had stuck around the studio lot filling in on whatever odd job people needed. He might pass the day in the studio woodshop, coming home covered in a fine fuzz of sawdust, or help pack out massive painted flats to the back corner of the lot, but he had his eyes on white-collar work. He usually haunted the executives' long central table at the commissary, trying to look especially employable.

He gave me a wave but didn't come near—he'd spent too many lunch hours listening to me complain about publicity-hungry starlets—and I took a seat at a booth with the best thing on the menu: a steamy bowl of Mrs. Reynolds's famous chicken dumpling soup, thick with pillowy matzoh balls and a steal at thirty-five cents a pop. I'd just dug in when I heard a sharp *"Oh!"* and looked up to see a woman, the blond costumer from the Western shoot, the one who had been roommates with my mother.

"Oh!" she said again, stopped in her tracks. "You're—you're all right! Oh my goodness, thank heavens! We all thought you'd *died!*"

The taste of the soup turned sour as I stared at her. Ever since she'd told me about my mother, pieces of our conversation kept drifting into my thoughts. I'd tried to track the costumer down, but I didn't even know her name. When I brought it up with Pep he shook the whole thing off with a frown: "I don't want to hear any more about that Western, all right? And I *don't* want you talking to anyone from that set!"

But here she was, staring at me like I was a ghost.

I cleared my throat. "Just, um. Lucky. I guess."

"Lucky!" She laughed. "I'll say. You must have an *army* of guardian angels…"

"Declan. Declan Collins."

Her eyebrows rose a centimeter, and then she put out her hand. "Wendy Harris. Can I sit?"

I took her hand with a nod, and she slid across from me, studying me. "I see it now. You're her boy? I remember, she mentioned you." There was a stack of paper napkins on the table, and she picked one up, idly shredding it with her fingers. "She didn't come back to you, did she?"

I shook my head, and Wendy let out a sigh. "You know, after we talked…I went home, dug up my old diaries from those days. Orla

Collins..." Another sigh. "All right. Do you have questions? I'll tell you what I can."

"Why did you come here, to Hollywood?" I felt as surprised as she looked by what I'd asked, but the question had been in my head, on my tongue, for so long, it seemed to appear on its own.

"What girl doesn't dream of life in the chorus?" She shrugged. "You could make money, get pretty clothes, meet people. Anyway, it was this or secretarial school."

"And my mother? How did you meet her?"

"A friend, another girl in the chorus. It was 1924. I'd just arrived and found a flat. I needed a roommate, and this friend suggested Orla. When I met her, I thought she was young, like me. Eighteen, nineteen. I couldn't believe she was twenty-four already, and with a little boy back home! But she didn't talk much about that—we didn't have the time! If you weren't auditioning, you were rehearsing, usually until three or four in the morning, and then you had to be back on set, in full makeup, at six on the dot. The directors swore at us like mules, but that was just the way they were. They treated us like machines, and if we broke down, so what?

"It could be a hard life. You had to have friends to survive, and Orla... She was my friend, for that little while, at least. It made it easier, having a girlfriend to laugh with. Sometimes, when we had the odd afternoon off, we'd fill a big washtub full of salt water, stick our feet in, and just *talk*. Nothing important, just anything. And we laughed, too. Even when it didn't seem like much fun, sweating away in our apartment, every single muscle aching, we managed to have a good time. It was exciting! You never knew what would happen next: maybe you'd get fired and not work for fifty days in a row, or maybe the biggest star in the world would spot you coming out of rehearsal and whisk you away." She let out a laugh, her gaze drifting up to the commissary's ceiling.

"Orla...," she said, and her voice was fond. "She was sweet. But quiet. Serious. I think she'd been around for too long. She worked hard— probably harder than anyone, but she didn't have the stamina. And she took it rough when the directors picked on her. You had to learn how to shake those things off, but Orla...it bothered her." Carefully, she clasped her hands and studied them.

"You know, since I talked to you, I've been thinking about when she ran off. I was too young back then to really worry about her—I am ashamed to say that what bothered me the most was having to find another girl to help with the rent. But now I think about it, it was so strange. She left everything behind. *Everything.* Her clothes, makeup. Even her dancing shoes. I gave those to a friend of mine. The shoes...that was what made me think she'd given up. If she meant to dance again, she would have taken her heels.

"I would have written, sent her things back, if I'd known her family. But like I said, she didn't talk much about her past. I just figured she didn't have anybody. Except you." She got a troubled look on her face. "She never went back to you? Really?"

She'd already asked me this, and when I didn't say anything, the expression on her face tightened. "But you had a good life, didn't you? You're so handsome and grown! And here! Going to be in the pictures, are you? So you must have had a good life."

"You don't know what could have happened to her? What was she doing before she disappeared?"

"Well, we were working, here at Silver Wing. A picture called...shoot. What was it? *A Gentleman's Pact*? I think that was it. It was 'twenty-six.

Lloyd Rodger in the lead, back when he could remember his cues," she added, with a disapproving sniff. "He had eyes for Orla, but that wasn't unusual. She was pretty, and so *different* from the rest of us. She never took up with anyone. None of us had cars or bus fare—you needed a boyfriend to get around the city! But Orla wasn't like that. She had her eyes on her career, and she wanted to get to stardom on her own, not because some producer wanted to take her out to dinner."

"She turned Lloyd down?"

"She turned everyone down," Wendy said with a laugh. "Lloyd was a big name. When she told me he'd been hanging around her, I told her to give him a shot! Ah, well, I was young back then, and silly. And Lloyd wasn't any kind of gentleman, no matter what his pictures were called. Looking back, I don't know. He could be a handful. I think he scared her a little. Maybe that was just the last straw, you know? Soured her on the whole thing."

"Why didn't you do something when she disappeared?" I tried to keep the accusation out of my voice, but she could hear it, the muscles around her eyes going tight.

"Like what?"

"Talk to the police. The studio. Ask around. She could've—"

"The police had more important things to worry about than a girl who didn't come home one night, and the studio— Didn't you hear what I said? They didn't see us as people. We were pretty lights glowing in their pictures, and if one of us burned out, they got a new one. Who would listen?" She shook her head, and then she glanced up at the large clock on the wall opposite us. "I'm sorry, hon. I've got to get back to the set. She'd be proud to see you here, you know?" Wendy stood up and reached over, touching a hand to my arm. "Don't be a stranger." And then she was gone.

For a few minutes, I couldn't move, the soup in front of me going cool. My mother... I couldn't believe that she had actually been here, in Hollywood, on this lot. Maybe she had even sat in the commissary, in this very booth, laughing with friends over ice cream.

She abandoned me. She went away and forgot about me. That was the story I'd told myself, for almost a decade. How could it be wrong? But now I felt a door opening up. A different story. Something had happened to her, and maybe there were people who knew, who kept it secret, people I now worked for.

What was the truth? Which story was the right one?

He was waiting for me, a block from the studio, the light from the streetlamp casting him in a faint glow.

"Can't say I expected to hear from you again." Sam stepped closer, until I could see his smile underneath the shadow of his hat. "Does this mean—"

"I'm still thinking it over." It wasn't far from the truth. I'd called him from the bank of public phones in the commissary, probably before Wendy Harris even made it back to set, and I'd been sure, decided, but now...

I couldn't stop thinking about Pep. He could've hung me out to dry when that Western producer came asking for two thousand dollars, but he didn't. He covered for me. Plus, he kept talking about his future here, in Hollywood. Even if I went home, it was clear enough: Pep had found a place where he could carve out the life he wanted. How could I risk that after everything he'd done for me?

"I... I'm sorry. I can't. Sorry I wasted your time."

I pushed past him on the sidewalk, and he called out, "It happened again."

The words hit me like ice water; I turned around to see a pained look on Sam's face. "Just a few weeks ago. Girl named Miriam Powell."

"Actress?" I tried to sound uninterested but my voice cracked.

"Nothing big, not yet, but she had a good reputation. Rising star. Then one day, she was in the middle of a movie, and she never showed up to work."

"Maybe she was fired."

"If she was, no one told the director. Official word is she quit. Couldn't hack it, gave up her contract, moved back home to her family in Manhattan."

"What's suspicious about that?"

"I wanted to hear it from Miss Powell herself. Got her real name—Miriam Perlman—and found her parents in New York City. When I called, a girl answered, said she hadn't heard from her sister in weeks. Then a man gets on, all upset. Tells me sure, his daughter's home, just arrived from Hollywood, and no, she can't talk, but everything's dandy, don't call back ever again."

"You believe the kid," I said, and Sam gave me a wry smile.

"Let's just say Miriam Powell didn't get her acting chops from her pop."

I went quiet, thinking it over. "The studio knows you're looking into Irma Van Pelt, don't they? They got to Miriam Powell's family first, paid them off to not make a fuss."

The smile spread across Sam's face. "You're figuring it out. Good for you." When I didn't say anything, he took a step forward. "Look, kid. I'm desperate here. I can't get near the studio. Production on Miriam Powell's last picture is starting up again soon, and someone on that set knows something. I need you."

He watched me, waiting for an answer.

"What are you going to give me for it?" I asked, and he frowned.

"The Van Pelts have funds if that's what you're after. We can work out—"

"I don't want money." I reached into my pocket, and my fingers closed around Mam's photo, held it out. "You say you're looking for missing girls? She's missing. You help me find her, I'll help you."

This time, the P.I. went quiet. He reached for the photo, paused, checked to make sure that was all right with me. Then he took it gently by the edges, his eyes roaming over my mother's face, like he was searching for clues, but when he looked up at me, I didn't see a hard investigator. Just a very tired, very determined man.

"Who's this?"

"My mother. Orla Collins. She came here ten years ago. Did some acting in the chorus line. Haven't heard from her since. Roommate said she disappeared."

Sam looked for a moment like his expression might turn pitying, but he thought better of it. "I'll see what I can do." He held the photo out to me, but I shook my head.

"Keep it."

"Thank you." Carefully, he slid it inside his jacket pocket before glancing up at me. "Does that mean you'll do it?"

I looked away from him, in the direction of the studio. The Silver Wing sign glowed bright white, illuminating the clouds above it, turning the sky a pale, silvery purple.

"What exactly do you think we can do? A lot of people make a lot of money because of Silver Wing's clean reputation—regular, honest people, studio employees, laundries, restaurants, hotels. You think the district attorney will do anything to threaten that? The mayor? The papers?"

Sam nodded, like he'd been waiting for the question. "We go bigger. Outside Hollywood, outside California, straight to Washington. You know about the Motion Picture Review Board, right?"

"The censors? They don't care about what the studios do in real life. They nag about hemlines and on-screen kisses."

"They're more than censors. They're federal agents. The government installed the MPRB to satisfy all the housewives and church groups worried that the youth of America's getting corrupted—what do you think they'll do when it gets out that Silver Wing's not just putting criminal activity in their pictures but covering up crimes on their studio lot? The Van Pelts have connections," Sam continued. "If we can get proof Silver Wing's covering up crimes? Believe me, kid. The feds will care, and they'll make Silver Wing pay."

"But if that's true... the studio's got everything riding on keeping this secret. They're going to do anything they can to stop us."

Sam gave me a grim smile. "That's why I'm hiring a bulletproof assistant."

But there were other ways to get at a person. What would Reynolds do if he found out I was trying to destroy his empire? What would he have Mulvey do *to* me?

Would they go after Pep? Take away everything he wanted? If I worked with Sam, I couldn't let Pep know anything. I couldn't let Reynolds think he had anything to do with it. To protect Pep, I'd have to keep secrets, tell lies, and even then, I'd be putting him in danger.

Was it worth it? Risking my friend's future to find the truth of what had happened to Mam?

Why did she leave? Why didn't she come back? Those questions buzzed through me, tiny electric shocks that distracted me from everything else. I'd never know peace until I had the answers.

"All right," I said, fast, before I could regret it. "I'm in. What's first?"

Sam nodded and reached into a pocket for another magazine, which he flipped open to a double-page spread. The light on the sidewalk wasn't great, but I could make out a familiar face, coy and clever.

Get to Know One Night in a Train Car*'s Leading Lady: Etta Hart!* Photos of Henrietta decorated every square inch: leaning into a microphone, a smile on her face; dancing in a rehearsal hall, miles-long legs stretched out in a pair of black shorts; peering down at a script, chin resting against her hand. And then…

They'd said those pictures we took in Baxter's office were only test shots, but there we were. Henrietta and me. Since then, I'd gotten used to Etta Hart touching me and kissing me and gazing dreamily into my eyes. I'd figured out it was all an act and learned to smile dutifully, the perfect studio-appointed boyfriend, supportive and chaste and feeling absolutely nothing for the starlet in my arms. There were hundreds of those photos they could have chosen. Instead, they went with…this.

Printed for the enjoyment of thousands of movie fans, Henrietta watched me out of the corner of her eye, a smile full of wonder on her lips, her cheek flushed under my hand, while I stared down at her like I'd never wanted anything so bad in my entire life. The feeling of her heartbeat under my fingertips, the pounding in my own chest, came back to me in such a rush I felt dizzy. I thought our screen test had been the first and last time I'd let myself get tricked into thinking anything this starlet did to me was real, but looking down at the photo, my throat went tight.

Underneath, a caption: *Gentlemen dream of a kiss from Miss Hart, but*

steady beau and stunt man-turned-actor Declan Collins might have some-
thing to say about that!

I snapped the magazine shut. "What's this have to do with any of it?"

"I managed to get ahold of the list of studio guests for Miriam Powell's last days on set. Turns out she had a visitor. Miss Hart. I told you I
needed you to ask around about Miss Powell. Start with Etta Hart."

I stared at him. "You think she's covering for the studios?" Heartless
and conniving, sure, but could she really be involved in something like
that? Sam gave me a grim look.

"I don't know, kid. But if she's not involved, maybe she's next."

CHAPTER FIFTEEN
HENRIETTA

I'd never get tired of this. Never, ever.

The set sprawled out in front of me, a massive train station with amber-tinted skylights drenching everything in a golden glow. I could smell the sweat of the electricians, high in the rigging, stripped down to the waist to better wrangle the lamps, burning big and hot as suns. Cables snaked along the floor, dense jungle tree roots minded by the grips who pinned everything in place with miles of tape, looped around their arms like clunky bracelets.

Fully transformed by the makeup man, the dresser, the hairstylist, the prop master, I should be in my place, thinking about the scene, but I had to stop and take it all in and remind myself for the millionth time it was REAL.

I needed the reminder. I couldn't begin to guess what wires had tangled in my brain to make me imagine Midge in my bedroom. Probably some mix of star-powered exhaustion and hollowed-out loneliness, concocting a friend just when I wanted her most.

In any case, I had to push her from my mind. The first weeks had gone better than anyone had expected, but I still had a set full of people wondering if bubbly Etta Hart would fall flat.

"Places, Miss Hart!" The director, Mr. Zuckerman, waved me over, and as I walked onto the set, I saw, like a knight in shining armor, Jack.

My skin tingled as he gave me a warm smile and a wave. He wasn't scheduled to shoot until this afternoon, and there were a million places he was needed right now—the studio paid its stars handsomely but it expected to get every penny's worth. He'd come to set just for *me*. I could have floated into the air, only I glanced to his side and came crashing down to earth: there was Declan, glowering at me from a director's chair.

Ugh.

Thankfully, bright lights and an open camera lens worked better than anesthetics on my brain. Filming began and my problems disappeared so completely that when Mr. Zuckerman called a break for lunch, I thought there had to be some mistake—surely we'd just started?

"Not bad, Hen-Henrietta," Jack said to me as I stepped off set.

"What poor assistant is getting fired because you decided to play hooky?" I asked him with a smile. "Unemployment is still a problem in this country, Jack."

He laughed and leaned in. "Say, what're you doing tonight? Let me take you out, so you don't starve."

The flutter in my chest grew wings, but—

"Can't," I said, glancing over at my angry little shadow. "The studio's saddled me with a ball and chain."

Jack looked Declan up and down, unimpressed. "I think I could take him."

"Don't bother. They already said I can't go anywhere in public without him."

"Even better," Jack said, in a tone of voice that fairly *tore* my attention from Declan and back onto him, leaning in so close I caught the scent of his aftershave and the heartbeat warmth of his skin. "We'll meet in private."

He pulled back with a smile. "See you later," he said, walking backward so I could appreciate his perfectly symmetrical features for as long as possible. I wasn't naïve. I'd read enough movie magazines to know Jack was a "fling of the month" type, but come on: Who on this planet would turn down attention from anyone who looked like *that*?

Drifting happily to the bank of directors' chairs, I retrieved my purse as Declan gave me a sour look.

"All done?"

"Lunchtime. Feel free to abandon your post whenever you want."

"Right now, the only job I have is you."

The thought made me wrinkle my nose. "Then you could do better selling it. I know this isn't the front table at the Brown Derby, but people on movie sets *do* talk. Why don't you ask me how my scene went? Or compliment my performance? Or give me—"

"Are you the only possible topic of conversation?"

I bit my tongue and plastered my pleasant smile back on my face. "Gee, Declan, you're welcome to spill your deepest, darkest secrets, but since you don't seem to be in a forthright mood, I figured I'd make it easier."

He stared at me, stone-faced, and I sighed.

"Just give me a kiss and go get some lunch," I said, and he froze for a moment before pecking me on the lips like a distant nephew greeting an aged aunt. "Excellent, very convincing."

I started to wander off, but he stopped me.

"Wait! Um. I . . ." He stared off into the space above my head, as though performing complicated long division. "I read something interesting in the paper the other day."

"Oh?" I said airily, and I shifted the purse strap on my shoulder, craning to get a look at Jack. "Reading. Quite the accomplishment."

He ignored me, adding, "It was an item about Miriam Powell."

"Midge?" Of all things!

"You knew her?"

"Did *you*?"

"I, um…" Oh dear. There came the mental arithmetic again. "I'd seen her around. Anyway, sounds like you were friends with her."

"I believe I still am," I said with a frown, and I thought about the night before, Midge appearing to me like a dream…I didn't care what that suit in personnel said about "privacy" and "studio policy"—I was going to wring Midge's number out of him. Probably she'd think I was a loon. "Hello, Midge, darling, just double-checking to make sure you're snug at home with your family and not magically teleporting across the country…"

Declan was staring at me as though I had something on my face, and I stared back.

"What?"

"Don't you think it was strange that she left? I thought our contracts meant we'd be sued if we did that."

What on earth? "Are *you* thinking of leaving?"

Declan blinked at me. "Leaving? No."

"Hmph. Pity. Anyhoo, charming as this conversation is, I've got an hour for lunch, and—"

"Wait!"

He darted in front of me, and I let out an aggrieved sigh. Honestly! Maybe I could bill conversations with Declan as hazard pay.

"*Yes?*"

"Um." He shuffled for a second. "Why don't we meet up tonight? We've got that interview tomorrow. With *Picture Perfect*. We could...get to know each other better."

I might've accused him of working on his pickup game, but Declan had an expression on his face like he'd rather clean the extras' dressing room with his tongue. I gave his arm a pat.

"Stand down, soldier. I think we know each other plenty. Anyway, I can't tonight," I said, and finally, I caught Jack's eye. When his face broke into a smile, my whole body felt dipped into warm honey, and I grinned back, not even caring that Declan could see. "I've got rehearsals."

CHAPTER SIXTEEN

DECLAN

Filming on Miriam Powell's last picture should have ended weeks ago, but when I asked around, I learned they were still at it, thanks to endless production delays so that lead actor Lloyd Rodger could dry out.

Hearing the name Lloyd Rodger set my nerves on edge. He was a Silver Wing marquee star from the silent pictures, and he'd been riding the wave of that good favor through years of nasty rumors. When I'd told Sam over the phone a few days back that Lloyd Rodger had also worked on my mother's last movie, had tried to take her out just before she disappeared, he went so quiet that I figured we'd lost the connection. Then I heard him, carefully, clear his throat.

"Maybe you better leave him to me."

"I can handle him," I'd replied, and Sam let out a whistle of a breath.

"That's what I'm worried about."

If he'd had more to say, I didn't catch it. Pep had come home to see me standing at the telephone and immediately put his hand out. He wouldn't trust me to broker a deal with our laundry man. I turned and said quickly into the receiver, "No, no está aquí ahora...Está bien, Mamá Perez, yo le dire...Sí, y usted también." The phone hit its cradle with a clatter, and I glanced over my shoulder at Pep. "Your mama wants you to call her."

Those Silver Wing acting lessons must've paid off, because Pep rolled his eyes but didn't question it—or maybe he didn't like the reminder that he'd been dodging his mother's calls for weeks now, while she lit candles for us and prayed for our safe return to the Mission.

Sam knew not to call me at home, and I didn't ring him back, too worried he'd call me off Lloyd Rodger, which meant I set out toward Stage 3 with the uncomfortable feeling that I didn't know what the hell I was doing. Between Pep dragging me around and, now, Sam pushing me to investigate what he needed, I was better at following directions than coming up with my own plans. But how much could I mess this up?

Compared to the expensive and complicated sets for Henrietta's *One Night in a Train Car*, *Lucky Hand* looked puny: a grubby speakeasy, shot at an angle to cheat how small it really was. They were in the middle of filming, and it wasn't going well. Lloyd Rodger barely made it through a single line before drifting off to blink at nothing with unfocused eyes.

I headed for the back of the soundstage, to a long counter set up with two bulb-framed mirrors. A mousy-haired woman with a tape measure around her neck sat in a canvas chair, looking so bored I thought she might slide to the floor.

Lloyd, with an unexpected burst of energy, tried shouting his lines next. He rushed for his scene partner but missed the mark; instead of catching the man's lapels, he collided off-balance with one of the treelike lighting rigs. Half a dozen technicians dashed to steady it, but it was too late, and it crashed to the ground with a finality that I could see on everybody's faces.

The director, looking about ready to burst into tears, called, "Cut!" and as people sprang into action to clean up the mess—and Lloyd— another girl joined the mousy-haired woman, collapsing into a chair with a deep sigh.

"There he goes again! My feet are killing me." She fanned herself when she noticed me. "You lost, cowboy?"

Okay, I told myself. *Acting!*

"Well, hello!" I said, pulling on a big smile. "I was wondering if either of you happened to know Miriam Powell!"

The women looked at me like I was a dog that had just figured out human speech. I cleared my throat.

"I mean, um—"

"What's it to *you*?" the mousy-haired girl asked. "You some friend of hers?"

"You'd be the only one," the other girl said, smirking. "Put on airs with everyone, stuck-up Miss Too-Good-to-Speak-to-Us."

"Oh, be kind, Ethel, she wasn't bad, just quiet. Shy, I always thought. Anyway, didn't she leave pictures?"

"Typical actress," Ethel said with a wave of her hand. "Probably heard some bad press or got turned down for a job or—"

"No, she'd just booked a lead." The other woman jumped in. "*One Night in a Train Car,* remember? Came in buzzing."

Miriam Powell had been cast as the lead in *One Night in a Train Car*? Did Henrietta know? I hadn't given much thought to Sam's suspicion that Henrietta might've had something to do with Miss Powell's disappearance, but I knew how badly she'd wanted that job...

"*Ohhhh,* that's right!" Ethel added. "I remember when she told us. Whistling like a little bird and Lloyd, the lout, told her to shut her mouth or he'd shut it for her." She rolled her eyes while mine shot to Lloyd, breathing heavily in a chair at the edge of the set.

"He said that to her?" I asked, trying to keep my voice steady. "They didn't get along?"

"Oh, Lloyd doesn't get along with anybody. Nasty temper. I think all that booze he stews in pickles his heart."

A young woman—a girl, a teenager—rushed toward Lloyd with a glass of some fizzy, clear liquid and held it out to him. While the two women beside me chattered on, I watched him reach out, take hold of the girl's wrist. The director was talking to Lloyd, although he wasn't listening, pulling the girl closer, a smile on his face. She was smiling back at him, but it was strained, her eyes so wide I could see the whites from across the stage. He said something that made her laugh, her eyes darting to the director, to the other crew members around her; she kept trying to ease away, but I could see him, still smiling, his grip so tight on her arm it had to hurt, and Wendy's voice filled my head: *I think he scared her a little.*

I didn't know what I meant to do, but in a moment, I heard the glass crash to the floor, spraying my shoes with seltzer as I pushed the girl behind me. Lloyd, his pant hems wet, jumped to his feet.

"Of all the CLUMSY, IRRESPON—"

"*Orla Collins,*" I said, hissing her name between my teeth, my hand grabbing tight to Lloyd Rodger's shirt front. He had to have nearly twice the weight on me but I had height, looking down into his sputtering, red face, so close I could smell something sour on his skin, could see the veins of red in his once-famous blue eyes.

"Wh-What? Who are—"

"Nineteen twenty-six. *Gentleman's Pact.* She was in the chorus. *Orla Collins. What did you do to her?*" My hand tightened around his shirt, and he clawed at me, but I felt nothing, rage turning me so hot I thought I might burst into flames. Only a second later, hands grabbed my shoulders, my arms, yanked me away. One of my arms cranked backward, but I was too fired up to pretend to be in pain. I couldn't stop staring at Lloyd, who couldn't stop staring at *me,* his face turning a mottled reddish gray. The shock only lasted a moment before he remembered just what size a star he was—or had been. He let out a bellow of anger, shouting questions, demands—"Who let him in here?! Get him out!"—while I felt myself dragged out of the soundstage, into the sunshine.

"Hey!" I tried to wrench myself free. "Hey, let me go!"

But the two crew members on either side of me had iron grips on my arms, frog-marching me with determination, while I stumbled to keep up.

"Where are you taking me?" I asked, and one of the crew members gave a laugh that sounded like a grunt.

"You threaten a Silver Wing star, there's only one place for you."

How would Sam take it when I called him from jail? Would he give up on our deal? Leave me to find out what had happened to Mam? And then my stomach lurched as another, even more unpleasant thought entered my head: How would *Pep* take this?

But they didn't take me through the main gate, or even to the security department. The two men turned with purpose toward the stately Swan Building, home of executives and publicists, and marched me inside. *Why here?* I wondered as they pushed me down a first-floor hallway to a humble office door, and then I looked up at the silver nameplate hanging from it and my stomach dropped to my shoelaces.

Not police, not security—why bother with any of that? By jumping on Lloyd Rodger I'd become a problem, and now I'd come before the man who made Silver Wing's problems disappear: Richard Mulvey.

CHAPTER SEVENTEEN
HENRIETTA

Hours later, another day of shooting done, I pushed open the door of my dressing room. Silver Wing corralled the actors into a hundred-foot-long, two-story skinny row of rooms connected by a covered verandah and nicknamed, with a wink, the bordello. Any time of day you could see berobed actors padding down the outer walkway to the bathrooms or hanging in each other's doorways, chatting away. Right now, things were quiet, only a few lights on behind drawn blinds, the low hum of a radio floating through the air.

A set of outdoor stairs, stamped with NO MEN ALLOWED—twice, just in case the fella hadn't gotten it the first time—led to the second floor, and as I climbed, I slipped off my shoes, my toes wriggling with relief. In thirty minutes, I would meet Jack in one of the rehearsal rooms—"rehearsal" being the official reason we planned to be alone together—but first, I wanted to wash off my makeup. With a dreamy smile on my face, I pushed open the door of my dressing room.

There, on my sofa, sat Midge.

"M-Midge!" My shoes slipped to the floor as I clutched at the doorjamb, and she turned her head. I blinked, screwing my eyelids shut, but when I looked again, she hadn't moved, that same stillness etched into her as the night before.

"Midge, I thought you went back home to New York!" I ran over to her, the door slamming shut. "You're supposed to have left!"

She looked confused, worried. She opened her mouth, but the door flew open with a *BANG*. A woman walked in, heavy makeup, blond hair wild, a satin dress slipping off one shoulder.

"Excuse me?" I said to her. She was talking to herself, mumbling, and when she saw me, her eyes went wide with fury.

"You!" She had a husky voice, a deep, unsettling growl. "What are you doing in my dressing room?!"

I glanced at Midge, watching with concern. "You must be mistaken. This is my room."

"Howard Abner gave me this room, personally, just last week! He said it was mine! Get out! Get!" She flew at me, fingernails bared like claws, and I let out a shriek and ran, my heart pounding.

When I realized I was alone, I spun back to help Midge—only my room was empty. No Midge. No wild-haired woman. What...had *happened*...?

"You there! I'll need my car prepared in ten minutes, warmed up and gassed!"

A woman marched briskly down the verandah toward me, done up in a trim driving suit of leather and tweed, a huge hat tilted dramatically over one eye. As she neared, she snapped her fingers.

"Well! What are you standing there for? Yes, darling, one moment!" The last part she addressed to some person I couldn't see or hear, but as she turned to call over her shoulder, I got a look at her whole face—or what was left of it, as most appeared to be missing. One side was bloody, gritty with gravel, as though she'd just walked away from a horrible accident.

The floor tilted under my feet, and I reeled away from the woman, down the verandah, my brain absolutely *on fire* with fear. I glanced over my shoulder and nearly collided with a sandy-haired girl, dressed in a thin, clingy white slip, water dripping off her.

"Oh!" I said, and she turned toward me, slowly, her skin gray-blue. The scent of ocean water filled my nose, mixed with sickly-sweet rot. The odor of washed-up dead things. My hand flew to my face as acid swelled up my throat, and I backed up, careened into the railing, kept running.

The stairs were just ahead of me, but as I reached the landing a girl appeared out of nowhere, large doe eyes, Cupid's-bow lips open in an O of surprise. Her arms windmilled through the air, and she reeled backward.

"No!" I gasped, reaching for her, but it was too late. She tumbled down the stairs, her body hitting hard angles with horrible cracks, until she crumpled on the lower landing like a rag doll, her neck bent oddly. I felt all the blood in my body turn cold. She was so still, so still, and I snapped to, and was making my way down to her when—

crAAACKK!

She rose, balanced impossibly on broken legs like a tangled marionette, her head swinging loosely, her eyes wide open but sunken into deep pits.

"Who...who *pushed* me?" she asked, her voice high and reedy. My stomach roiling, I turned and made for the stairs farther down the verandah. As I ran, I heard doors open up, felt something tug at my dress. I didn't look back, just wrenched free, catching my balance on the railing, running as fast as my bare feet could carry me.

"Wait—wait! Don't LEAVE me!" a voice screamed. I ignored it, focusing on the stairs just ahead, where I could see Midge, waiting at the bottom, no longer a frozen shell but reaching for me, just as terrified.

"Henny! Henny, run!"

I jumped for the stairs and took them two at a time, stretching out my hand. I meant to drag her with me, away from the dressing rooms and off the studio lot, but the moment my skin touched her, a cold went through me, cold so shocking that at first I thought I'd burned myself and I yanked my hand away.

"Henny?" she said again, my name coming out strange and echoey. I'd reached the bottom of the stairs, the studio path, and I wanted to run, but something...something was happening to Midge...Her eyes grew dull, cheekbones stretching, fingers shedding fat, muscle. "Henny...What...is wrong...with me...?"

Before I could answer, a keening noise erupted, a moaning groan of what sounded like a thousand female voices harmonizing together a song of pain and fear and fury. I clapped my hands over my ears and *screamed*.

The cold pressing against me released, so fast that I let out a gasp of surprise to feel the warm night air on my sweaty skin. A door on the first floor flew open and I jumped, but it was only a man in a striped robe, frowning at me.

"Was that you screaming?" he asked. Panting, shivering, barefoot, I could only stare at him, and after a moment he let out an annoyed huff. "Keep it down! Some people are trying to *rest*!" The door slammed shut behind him, and I gazed up at the dressing rooms, so utterly calm that the quiet of the night set my ears ringing.

No Midge. No women. Nothing odd.

What had happened?

I was losing my mind. The thought terrified me, but it had to be true, because even just considering the other possibility sent a fresh shiver of fear through me.

Girls, dead girls, brought back from wherever they'd been sent—and only I could see them.

CHAPTER EIGHTEEN
DECLAN

"I'm sorry—it was a misunderstanding, you don't have to—"

Outside Mulvey's office, the men pushed me into a chair like I was a naughty schoolkid waiting to see the principal. "Didn't you see Lloyd Rodger grabbing that girl? I just wanted to—"

"I'm gonna tell you again," one of the men said, arms crossed. "I don't care what happened: you don't threaten one of Mr. Reynolds's stars, not on this lot, not anywhere."

I ran a hand over my face, but when I looked up, I could see something like pity, like they couldn't blame me for going after Lloyd, sort of wished they'd done it themselves a long time ago. Leaning forward, I dropped my voice. "What'll he do to me?"

The men exchanged glances and then the one wearing a flat-top cap said with a shrug, "Kick you off the lot? Fire you? Depends on how much clout you've got. What do you do here, kid?"

"I'm a fake boyfriend for one of the starlets."

"Oof," Flat-Top said, while the other gave my shoulder a friendly pat.

"Tough break."

I dropped my head into my hands. There was nothing to do but sit and wait; Mulvey was in another meeting. My escorts stood patiently while I tried to figure out how in the hell I'd get out of this.

What if he guessed I was looking into the missing girls?

What if he found out I was *related* to one of them?

What if—

The door swung open and a tall, beautiful woman I knew from magazine covers and marquees stepped out, and then Mulvey's rough voice called us in.

Given what Sam had told me about Mulvey—tough mobster straight out of Jersey—I expected an office full of gaudy glitz, a shrine to everything Mulvey had done for Reynolds and Silver Wing. I was surprised to walk into such a humble room: rough, wheat-colored carpeting stretched across the floor, setting off a pair of solid wooden chairs upholstered in dark green and a simple desk decorated with a row of framed photos featuring the same brunette woman and rosy-cheeked children. Not a single autographed picture or newspaper headline.

The man himself sat at his desk, scratching something out across a sheet of paper. I recognized him immediately from Sam's picture and, I realized, from the lot, where I hadn't seen him so much as felt his presence, a sharp undercurrent of wariness that filled the two men from Stage 3, even though Mulvey hadn't even looked up at us. Reynolds must've hired Mulvey for his discretion. Who better to make things disappear than someone who hated the spotlight?

"All right," he finally said, looking up while folding the paper. "You've got two minutes before I need to call Washington. What happened?"

He had a voice that came right out of a gravel pit, deep and rough, and a look on his face like maybe he'd rather just kill us than have to go to the trouble of solving whatever problem we'd brought to him. I had *no trouble* believing what Sam had said about his dirty hands.

"Ju-ust a dust-up, with, uh, L-Lloyd Rodger," Flat-Top said. I'd never seen a man that big look nervous. He nudged me forward. "Kid here went after him."

Mulvey's cool gaze jumped from the man to me. "Went after how?"

"Got in his face, grabbed his shirt. Lloyd's fine," the man added quickly. "Little shook up. You'll probably be hearing from his—"

As if on cue, the door flew open, but it wasn't Lloyd, or his manager, or his assistant. Instead, a familiar-looking man in a coffee-colored suit, scarf around his neck, strode in, already midcomplaint.

"Dogs?! You have me filming *shorts* about *dogs* now?" His voice had a shrill, desperate quality that rang a bell.

"Mr. Fitch," Mulvey began, and the name made my eyebrows rise: it was the director on my own screen test. "You can step outside, and—"

"EIGHT YEARS I've been a faithful employee here at Silver Wing, EIGHT YEARS! I have directed Baker, Leach, LeSueur—now you have me filming trash with filthy mongrels, and I demand to know why!"

Mulvey's eyes narrowed—another problem he didn't have the energy for—and the temperature in the room dropped twenty degrees, but Fitch didn't seem to notice. He leaned forward and put his hands on Mulvey's desk, voice low and furious: "I know what this is about! You don't think I see her on the lot? That haughty blonde flouncing around like she owns the place!"

I blinked in surprise. Was he talking about Henrietta?

"If you have a problem with one of the actresses—"

"You better believe I have *a problem* with her," Fitch said through clenched teeth. "Telling lies about me to Mr. Reynolds! Oh—I tried to *make her* wear a revealing costume? Ridiculous! I am a gentleman, Mr. Mulvey, I would never!"

Was that what this was all about? Henrietta had told the truth about why she'd been thrown out of the screen test, and Fitch got caught being a letch?

"She's dragging my name through the mud!" Fitch continued. "And what is she but some little chippie who thinks she's too fine to follow directions? When I catch her alone, I'll—"

"That's enough, Mr. Fitch," Mulvey said, rising to his feet so quickly that Fitch flinched. He pointed at the door, but before Fitch could move, it flew open again.

"Pep?"

He was breathing fast, tie askew, glossy dark hair falling across his forehead.

"It was a misunderstanding!" he said, practically throwing himself at Mulvey, who towered a full head above him and looked down at Pep like he was an overly aggressive beetle. "Declan would never—"

"Who"—the word dropped out of Mulvey's mouth heavily enough to hear the *thud*—"are *you*?"

"Josepe Perez!" Pep, incredibly, stuck out his hand, and Mulvey gave it a pained look. "I'm Declan—ah, Mr. Collins's manager!"

I noticed the two crew members glancing at each other, and my stomach sank. Had they just connected me with the name I'd hissed at Lloyd Rodger?

The buzz of an intercom broke the silence and a secretary's fuzzy voice called out, "Mr. Mulvey, the senator is on the line for you."

Mulvey glanced at the phone and then looked from Pep's showman smile to Fitch's simmering rage to me, slouching in the middle of the room like a nabbed thief.

"Lloyd isn't hurt?"

"Just his pride, I think," Flat-Top said.

"All right. Everyone *out*." Mulvey pointed at the door again. The crew members left at once, Pep throwing me a glance before following them reluctantly, but as I moved to the exit, Fitch jumped into my way.

"What about me? It's absurd, allowing that girl to sully my name, and I won't—"

"Mr. Fitch, you might've shot stars," Mulvey rasped, "but that don't make *you* a star. You want to keep working in this city? Turn around and keep working, and next time you come into my office it better be to say *Thank you*."

Fitch's mouth snapped shut so fast I could hear his teeth click together. He spun around without another word, and for a moment, I wondered if I should say something to Mulvey about the screen test. I knew Henrietta hadn't lied, and if it got Fitch demoted, well. Good for Henrietta.

Then I glanced over at Mulvey and realized he'd been studying me this whole time, his gray eyes narrowed on my face, and my good intentions shriveled up. I wanted out of that office, but at my first step to the door, Mulvey took hold of my arm.

"Declan Collins." He said my name like he was committing it to memory. Whatever invisibility I'd had on this lot was gone now.

"You get one strike here, and you just blew it. Next time won't be so easy."

He let me go, and I hurried out, feeling his eyes on the back of my neck until the door closed behind me. The crew members had gone, but Fitch was still there, eyes wild, muttering under his breath: "*...dogs...lies...*

loyalty" before spitting out, with sharp, angry consonants, *"Etta Hart!"* A look of purpose came over his face; he spun around and stalked down the hallway. Just what did he have planned for Henrietta when he caught her alone? Frowning, I'd started after him when Pep grabbed me.

"What happened? Someone told me you socked Lloyd Rodger!"

"Socked? No, um…" Distracted, I watched as Fitch disappeared down the hall. "Where do you think he's going? Do you think Henrietta—"

"Henrietta? *Etta Hart?* You're thinking about Etta Hart right now?"

"No—only, Fitch says she lied about what he did in that screen test, but—"

"Probably she did lie, or she overreacted. Sounds like something a spoiled starlet would do."

I winced. "That's not—"

"Enough about her. You *attacked Hollywood royalty*! If this is some ploy of yours to get fired or something—"

"No, no, it's not like that! I, he was…" How did I explain this without mentioning my investigation with Sam?

"I…was supposed to meet a dialect coach on Stage 3, and I saw Lloyd Rodger there, between scenes. This girl came up to him, and…he grabbed her."

Pep stared at me. "And?"

"She kept trying to get away! And no one was doing anything to stop him!"

Pep gave a wave of his hand. "If no one did anything, they must've known it wasn't anything to worry about."

"No—she was scared, and she was laughing but—"

"If she was laughing, she couldn't've been too scared."

"You're not listening! Lloyd Rodger has a nasty reputation, and years ago he—" I stopped myself before I could say any more. I didn't like how he'd treated that girl today, but to be honest, I wasn't thinking about her when I went after him.

"No, *you're* not listening." Pep took a step closer, glancing from my face to Mulvey's closed door. "Do you have any idea how bad this could've gone for you just now? Do you know what Mulvey's capable of? What he's done?"

I stared at him. "Do *you*?"

"Of course! Dec—everyone knows. Reynolds is the brains around here, but Mulvey's the one who runs everything. You know he personally vets every full-time employee? I've been trying to introduce myself, but—"

"You want to work for Mulvey? When you know what he does? Pep—how?! How can you follow a man like that?"

Pep gave me a hard, confused look, like a rift the size of a canyon had opened up between what he thought we were doing here in Hollywood and what I thought.

"Declan," he said, shaking his head, "how can you think to go *against* him?"

CHAPTER NINETEEN
HENRIETTA

All right.

I took a breath.

What now?

I couldn't return to my dressing room. Not yet, and not alone. I wanted to go back to the hotel, but I had no purse, no *shoes*. And also... I wanted someone to hold me, very tightly, because I was afraid I might actually fly apart, like a tiny bomb was ticking, ticking away in the center of my chest.

Five minutes later, I knocked at the door of the rehearsal room, shivering like mad even though the air hung heavy with warmth. Jack opened the door, but I didn't return his smile. I felt about half an inch away from complete collapse.

"Etta? Are you all right? Here, come in."

He put a hand on my shoulder, pulling me inside, and he felt so warm and solid that I almost burst into tears.

"What's the matter?" he asked, his voice gentle. "Are you hurt? You're white as a sheet!"

I tried to talk, only my teeth wouldn't stop chattering, and Jack slipped his arms around me, pressing me to his chest.

I could feel his heartbeat, the muscles under his shirt, I could smell his cologne, and now I really did start crying. I looked like a sniveling, snotty, miserable mess, but I didn't care and neither did Jack, holding me tight and mopping my face with his handkerchief, a huge, white thing so deliriously soft I wished I could wrap myself up in it.

"What's happened?"

I tried to catch my breath and hiccoughed. His hand on my back helped, and I gulped out, "You're—you're going to think I've lost my mind."

He smiled. "Doubtful."

I shook my head. "I saw…" Where would I even start? I saw girls with broken bodies stand up and speak to me? Women appear and disappear? "I saw…Midge. Miriam Powell."

He stared at me, his face blank, and I added, "You might not remember her. She was in *The Man Who Wore Red*? Pretty girl, black hair, she left Hollywood—"

"*Oh,*" he said quickly. "Yeah, sure, I heard about her." He gave me an odd look. "What do you mean, you saw her?"

"Tonight. I saw her in my dressing room."

I expected him to ask me what I meant, or to wonder if Midge had returned to Hollywood. Instead, he let out a laugh.

"Your dressing room! No, you must've seen wrong. There are plenty of actresses that look like her. You're just confused."

"No, no. It was definitely—"

"Or it could've even been a fan, someone sneaking in! Probably gave you a fright! Is that why you ran in here so scared? Next time just ring up security, they'll sort it out."

"*No,*" I said, my fear spilling over into annoyance. "It was Midge, I saw her, I—"

Another laugh, and this time the noise prickled across my skin like hot sparks. "You poor thing! Come here, I'll help you feel better." He held out his arms to me, but I could only stare at him, my body stiff. After another moment, he dropped his arms to his sides and said, "What's the matter?"

I JUST SAW A DOZEN GRUESOMELY INJURED GIRLS APPEAR OUT OF THIN AIR, I thought, but I couldn't imagine how Jack would respond to that—either he'd think I was joking or he'd try to send me straight to a sanatorium. The look on his face suggested he wondered when we might get to the canoodling portion of the evening, but for the first time in my life, his handsome features inspired absolutely nothing in me.

Jack leaned in with a smile. "Come on. Let's forget all that. Why don't we get to rehearsal?"

Oh, right. Rehearsing. But before I could wonder if it might do me some good to get my mind off things, those girls' faces popped back into my head. I could hear Midge's frightened gasps, see her body melting away to nothing, and I wrapped my arms around myself, shuddering.

"No. No, I think I just want to—"

"Come on, it'll be fun! Why don't we start with the scene at the end?" He raised his eyebrows, mouth pulled into a sideways smile. "The very end."

It took me a second to get it. The last scene of the picture was always going to be tricky: a moment of drama, when my character, dreamy shoe salesgirl turned train car stowaway Virginia Leigh, laid out everything she wanted from life, from love. Honestly, it scared the hell out of me, figuring out how to balance Virginia's sweet lightness with how afraid she was, the open vulnerability of her loneliness. I'd been so nervous about it

I didn't even want to rehearse in front of Mr. Zuckerman, and he'd promised me we'd save it for the end of the shoot. From that perspective, Jack's offer made sense, but I somehow doubted he had my nerves in mind. The final scene also ended with our grand, intense, and only kiss.

I had to admit, thinking about *that kiss* had given me more butterflies than Virginia's tricky monologue, but in spite of the years I'd spent imagining myself on the receiving end of Jack Huxley's attentions, the idea now made me feel cold.

"No. I . . . I'm exhausted. I should go home. Could you help—"

"Home? But you just got here!" He reached out for me again. Instead of falling into his arms, I took a step back.

"I know, but I don't feel very—"

"Well, then, you need to let me help you feel better." His smile widening with every word, he stepped closer to me, arms still out. I backed up—right into a wall—and he moved in, his hands on my elbows. "Come on, doll. I stayed late for you."

"Sorry." The word popped out of me even though I wasn't sure what I was apologizing for. Maybe on another night I could quip my way out of this situation, but I felt as if I'd just gone over Niagara in a barrel. "My head's in a thousand places right now, and—"

"Let's keep your head right here." He reached one hand up to the back of my neck. It could've felt nice, comforting, but as his fingers stretched to cradle my skull, I heard again the dull, sickening, *CRACK* of the dark-eyed girl's body falling down the stairs, and this time I couldn't help but let out a jolt of revulsion.

"Gee, a fella could start to feel insulted." Even though Jack had a smile on his face, his voice turned chilly.

"It's not— I don't—" I tried to step away, but he only held me tighter.

"Aw, just relax, doll! We're having fun here, aren't we?"

"No." My voice sounded firmer than I felt. "Let go of me, please. I want. To go. *Home*."

He actually rolled his eyes, the hand on my elbow slipping around my waist, the one at the back of my head tightening into my hair.

"Come on—are you worried about what people will think? I won't tell." He leaned in, smiling, and here was the moment when I thanked every one of my lucky stars that I had an older sister who'd made sure her girls knew what to do if a fella turned fresh: I pushed out with my hands, right in his gut, and lifted my knee smoothly into his groin—not enough to really hurt him, but enough that he wheeled backward with a grunt, letting me get to the door.

Which was locked.

"What's the matter with you!" He'd doubled over, staring at me as though I'd transformed into a completely different creature. "You lead me on—and then you *attack* me?!"

I didn't like keeping my back to him, but I couldn't figure out how to unlock this stupid door. The moment I heard it click open, Jack's hand slammed it shut.

"Let me out of here!" I spun around on him, panic exploding through me: "You horrible, petulant ASS!"

Damn it, Henny! It was true, but this wasn't the time to name-call an angry, wounded Jack Huxley—his skin flushed, his blond hair flopped into his face, his eyes small and narrow with rage—talk about *transforming into a completely different creature*. I could hardly believe how many years I'd wasted mooning over this face, now that I knew what hid beneath it.

"Oh, I'm an ass, am I?" he asked, hissing out the words. "And what are you but a stuck-up priss? I thought you understood how things work! You certainly acted that way at your audition."

He had to be talking about my audition for *One Night in a Train Car*, only I couldn't imagine why, but as soon as I opened my mouth to protest, I quickly shut it with a snap. My audition scene had been a straightforward bit of light comedy, but when the camera hadn't been rolling, I'd—okay, yes, it was true—shamelessly flirted as he watched from the sidelines. Some *deal*. I had absolutely no doubt in my mind that I deserved that role as much as any girl in this city, but apparently it hadn't been my talents that had won me the job.

"If I knew what a little friendly banter would cost me," I said, trying hard to keep from shaking, "I would have told you to take this job and *shove it up your rear.*"

He snorted out an angry laugh. "Do you know who you're talking to? One phone call, and you're done. No one will remember you—and that's if you're lucky." He snapped his fingers in my face, and I hoped he'd blown himself out, but it seemed he was just getting started. "You're not special. You'd be nothing if *I* hadn't picked you for that part."

"It's funny," I said, fighting hard to keep my words from shivering with *rage*, "from the moment I've gotten here, I keep running into men who tell me my success as an actress relies on what I can do for them *off* camera. But let me tell you, Jack Huxley: I am a good actress. I'm going to be a star, and when that happens, it's going to be not *because of* but IN SPITE OF YOU!"

Jack gave me an incredulous stare, and then *laughed*, like I'd just tripped and landed face-first in a mud puddle. He looked like a twelve-year-old bully, which was an insult to twelve-year-old bullies, and then the smile dropped from his face so fast that for the second time that night, I felt my blood chill.

It happened all at once: he rushed at me, and my mind scrambled for Ruby's defense lessons as my throat let loose a scream, but before we collided, something threw me off-balance from behind, sending me tumbling to the ground. It was the door, flying open, and a figure bursting in.

"De-Declan!"

Declan whirled around, looking from me to Jack with narrowed eyes.

"What's happening here?" He settled his gaze on Jack, who straightened up, sweeping back the mess of hair on his forehead with one smooth shove.

"Ask her," he said, throwing a hand in my direction. "Out of nowhere, attacks me like a rabid dog!"

My nerves absolutely frayed to pieces, I let out a desperate snort of laughter—if I tried to say anything, I thought I'd burst into tears—and Declan gave me a confused look.

"Oh, we're *fine*," I finally said, my voice high, and I rose to my feet on jelly legs. "Completely *fine*."

"We're not '*fine*,'" Jack said. "She went and threw herself at me, and—"

But it seemed that Declan had heard enough. He grabbed my arm with a muttered "Come on," and pulled me out the door of the rehearsal room, ushering me along like I'd done something wrong. *Oh.*

Of course.

He'd busted in on me and Jack, alone, not on account of my safety but for his job security. Some shining knight.

"I can walk!" I wrenched my arm free, nearly losing my balance. "And I can see myself home, thanks."

"Why are you...barefoot?"

We both looked down at my feet, grimy from my trek across the lot.

"Acting exercise," I mumbled. I kept walking, and a second later Declan jogged to catch up.

"Sure you don't... need some help?"

"Worried I'll run right back to Jack?" I let out a bitter laugh. "I don't need a chaperone."

"Really? You didn't seem very much in control of things back there."

That was it. I'd had one last nerve, and Declan's words had crushed it to dust like a piece of chalk. I wheeled around on him and let my mouth spew out anything it wanted:

"What is it? You'd like me to say *thank you*? Well, then, thanks so much for your help, my hero, good thing you were there to keep a tramp like me out of trouble. Now, if you'd like me to be capable of standing in the same room as you without fantasizing about setting myself *on fire,* you'll bite your tongue on whatever fabulous cutting remark you've got queued up, crawl into your miserable little cave, and LEAVE. ME. *ALONE.*"

I spun around and stomped off as hard as my poor feet would allow, and as I left them all—Jack, Declan, the girls from the dressing rooms—behind, I'd never felt so happy to be alone.

CHAPTER TWENTY
DECLAN

I should've run after her. A gentleman would've chased her down with an apology, handed her his socks for her bare feet, made sure she got home safely. A cad would've shouted back, "Good riddance."

So, if I wasn't a gentleman, at least I wasn't a cad, either. Instead, I waited until she turned down a path that led to the studio gate, then I shoved my hands in my pockets and headed home.

She had it wrong. I'd figured "rehearsing" was the last thing she and Jack Huxley would get up to, but I honestly didn't care, even though I thought she could do better than him. It was hearing Fitch spit out her name, and me not having the guts to tell Mulvey what I knew about it... I got an itch in my conscience that wouldn't be scratched until I knew she was all right. I'd planned to swing by the rehearsal rooms, check she was fine, and go home, but then I heard shouting, and—

That stupid *prat*, Jack Huxley. As I remembered Henrietta's bloodless cheeks, her wide, scared eyes, something blazed up in me fast and fierce, and I wanted to tear Jack Huxley to pieces. Good thing I hadn't. If roughing up Lloyd Rodger earned me a scolding from Mulvey, I didn't want to know what I'd get for busting Silver Wing's masterpiece.

Still: I should've run after her. If not because it was the gentlemanly thing to do, then because Henrietta and I had our first big interview as a pretend couple with *Picture Perfect,* and it had to go well. The only thing keeping me at Silver Wing, where I could help Sam find the missing girls— and Mam—was how well I convinced the world that Declan Collins and Etta Hart were desperately in love. But as I walked through the studio gates the next morning, I wondered if my "girlfriend" was speaking to me.

I found Henrietta waiting alone in a beautiful sitting room in the Swan Building done up with flower-filled vases and delicate paintings. She didn't react when I came in, eyes on the *Train Car* script balanced on one knee. She looked pretty good after last night's drama—although when I got closer I noticed that most of her rosy glow came from liberal use of rouge and powder.

"Mind if I sit here?" I asked, gesturing next to her on a velvet love seat, and she said nothing but gingerly moved to one side.

"Um...How are you?"

"Reading." Eyes down, she snapped her script in her hand.

"Get home okay?"

"No," she said, her voice dull. "I was kidnapped by pirates and made their ocean queen. I'm currently sailing for Tahiti and horribly sunburnt. Send the navy."

"You found your shoes." We both looked down at her feet, her blue high heels, and then she tucked them away and returned to her reading. I could hear every tick of the clock on the wall as I picked at my fingernails, not sure what to say.

Did Jack Huxley hurt you last night?

or

Did you know Fitch blames you for losing his job?

or

Can you tell me what happened to Miriam Powell?

"So…" I started talking before I knew where I was going, hoping something'd come to me. The word hung there, getting dumber every second, until I blurted out, "How's filming going?"

She didn't look up. "You're there every day. You tell me."

"Oh!" I cleared my throat. "It's, um. Good. You're good."

She really was. Most of my time on film sets I spent trying to stay awake—nothing like watching the same thirty-second scene for eight hours in a row to strip all the glamor out of the movies. But Henrietta had a way of making every take feel different. When she acted, the film set and camera and lighting seemed to fade away until there was nothing between you and her, like you could slip into her skin, feel what she was feeling.

But I couldn't say that to her now—she wouldn't even look up at me.

"I mean, um, I don't know, I don't really go to the movies. And if I did, I wouldn't watch something like *Train Car*. You know, that love junk, not my thing, I like gangster movies, car chases, stuff like that."

"Mm-*hmm*," Henrietta said, drawing the noise from the back of her throat. "Any other notes?"

I ran a hand through my hair. I never would've accepted Sam's job offer if I'd known it involved so much talking.

"Hey—funny thing about someone else getting your part. You know. Before you."

Well, that got her attention, although the look she gave me wasn't exactly friendly. "Are you saying I was the *second choice*?"

"No, no, I just meant—I mean, I'd heard—I mean, they offered the role to another actress first. Right?" I thought I did a pretty good job setting that up without mentioning Miss Powell, but Henrietta gave me a panicked look.

"They cast someone else? Where did you hear that?"

Oops. Either Miss Powell hadn't told her, or Henrietta was an even better actress than I thought. I stammered out, "Uh, n-no, must've been my mistake. Sorry."

"You can't just go and tell me someone else had my role! Who was it?"

"I don't—"

"Are you saying this to get under my skin?" She tossed her script down and glared at me. "Don't you have anything better—"

"Oh, good! You're both here!"

Saved by our publicist, a short woman who'd introduced herself to us several times now, but I couldn't for the life of me remember her name. I wondered if she'd comment on the frost between her two lovebirds, until I glanced over at Henrietta and saw she'd swept it all away. Her cheeks glowed with a pleasant smile.

"Now listen: the gal from *Picture Perfect* will be here in five. Have you gone over your briefs?"

Henrietta nodded like a good student, while I stared blankly.

"Briefs?"

The publicist gave me an exasperated look. "I put yours in your mailbox."

"I didn't get any mail from the studio."

"Not *the mail*," Henrietta said, her smile slipping into a scowl. "Your mailbox here, on the lot."

I blinked at her. "I have a mailbox?"

"Are you joking?!" the publicist asked, with a tone that suggested that either a yes or a no was unacceptable. "It had your whole history in there! You were supposed to memorize it! You met in Chicago, in a blizzard, you grew up on a farm, you—"

"Farm? Chicago? I'm from San Francisco. I've never even seen snow!"

"This is why you needed to read the brief! Oh, lord, she's going to be here any second, we'll need to reschedule, we—"

"I'll take care of it," Henrietta said, so firmly that both the publicist and I stared at her.

"Knock, knock!"

I turned to see a heavily made-up woman in a fussy peacock-green dress at the door, smiling brightly, a notebook raised in one hand.

The publicist tripped over her own feet, ushering the reporter to an empty seat, offering up water, coffee, tea, her firstborn child. But the reporter—"Call me June! Let's get cozy and familiar!"—waved it all away. The cramp in my stomach tightened another notch as I recognized her: June St. James, the poison-quilled columnist of Hollywood. The studio must have thought we were ready for the big leagues. I felt fourteen years old again, thrown into the ring with a heavyweight who just wanted to tear me apart.

The publicist watched with horror as June began: "Don't you two look darling! Tell me all about how you met!"

I raised an eyebrow at Henrietta as she smiled at me, but then she took my hand and it became clear we could relax: Henrietta had everything under control.

How'd she think up this junk so quick? In minutes, she and June St. James were laughing together like old chums as Henrietta whipped up the perfect romantic story: we'd met just before high school on her family trip to San Francisco, exchanged addresses, fell in love by letter. I'd invited her out to Hollywood after getting into stunting. What luck that someone happened to spot Henrietta and offer her a screen test!

"Well! Sounds like you have Declan here to thank for your successes!" June St. James beamed at us, and I turned to Henrietta with a wide smile.

"You're welcome, honey."

As June bent over her notepad, Henrietta let out a beautiful laugh and shot me a look like she'd rather cut my throat.

"Now, Declan!" June looked up at me. "You were a stunt man! How exciting! What made you give up?"

The publicist made a sort of choked-cat noise.

"Uh, well..." I yanked at my shirt collar. "I guess, with stunts—"

"Maybe you weren't very good?" June raised her pen like a small, sharp sword. "Two left feet? Don't have the physique?"

"Uhhhmm..."

But Henrietta swooped in again, her laughter ringing. "It's my fault! Those stunts made me *so* nervous, and I asked him to try out acting. And as for his physique"—she leaned in with a wicked smile—"just between you and me and the drapes, I could sell tickets to a shirtless Declan Collins and retire a wealthy woman."

June let out a roaring laugh and scribbled in her notebook while I gave Henrietta a *look* that said, *Noticing my physique, are you?*

"Let's hear about San Francisco, then! Tell me all about your childhood! What do your parents do?"

The smile slid from my face. "My...parents?"

"Do you have a favorite family tradition? A cherished memory? Something special your father taught you?"

The only thing I'd learned from the man who fathered me was that you could disappear as soon as a girl told you she was pregnant, and you'd never have to worry about her or the baby ever again.

"Or, how about a favorite food? Don't you miss anything your mother makes you?"

"My—mother..." My voice came out broken, small, and I caught a look of alarm on Henrietta's face. Mamá Perez's kitchen was a wonder palace, turning out meals to feed a small army every day. While she always had a plate for me, she didn't have the time for special requests. Besides, the food on Valencia Street felt like a miracle after the grim sameness of the Home, or even Mam's own cooking, which hardly ventured beyond ham sandwiches.

But the reporter's question kicked free memories so long buried that they burst into my mind fully formed: Boxing Day, cold air, warm smells, my mother's hand on my cheek, waking me up, a cake still steaming hot, "Take some," her whisper in the darkness, full of excitement, and sleepy-eyed me, feeling for a slice, the soft sweetness like something I'd dreamed, sugar and gummy-bright fruit. One year, a bite into something so hard it jolted through my teeth, an electric shock, and I spat the thing out into my hand, confused, until I recognized my mother's ring and she squealed with happiness, "You got the slice with the ring, Dee-Dee! A year of good luck!" Kisses, hugs, the darkest morning of the year made bright with her promises...

I hadn't thought about that cake, that day, in...I couldn't even remember. It had been...A lump rose into my throat, and I swallowed hard, my head swimming. "I...I, um..."

"Oh, it has to be her apple pie!" Henrietta jumped in with a broad smile. "She puts persimmons in there, and it is *incredible*. Persimmons, can you believe! Don't tell Declan, but I really came out from Chicago just for another taste."

June laughed, and that was it, my awkwardness smoothed over by Henrietta's charm. They chattered together while I caught my breath, so focused on clearing my mind that I only realized the tone of the conversation had shifted when I felt Henrietta stiffen beside me.

"Sorry—what rumors do you mean?" she asked, a line of concentration between her eyebrows. June practically licked her lips, her eyes bright.

"Oh, I'm sure it's nothing, I just wanted to give you a chance to refute it. A source claims that you showed up for your screen test in nothing but some lacy knickers."

My eyebrows shot up my forehead while Henrietta let out an explosion of laughter. *"Lacy knickers!"*

"Is it true?"

"No," Henrietta said with a snort, "I actually came in naked riding a horse like Lady Godiva."

"You were naked?" June asked eagerly, and Henrietta gave her a look. *"No.* Obviously."

"Is it obvious? It's hard for young girls to stand out. I've heard crazier gimmicks."

"Anyone who needs a gimmick to get a job doesn't deserve it," Henrietta said, unimpressed. "Where'd you even hear this?"

June gave a self-important sniff. "Oh, I never reveal my sources." Well, I'd bet Silver Wing's annual budget that when Fitch marched out of Mulvey's office the night before, the first thing he did was ring her up. "Do you want to make a comment?"

"Why should she? It's not true." Everyone in the room turned to look at me, Henrietta whipping her head around so fast I thought she might spin off the seat. I could tell she was shocked I'd bothered to open my mouth. Truthfully, it was guilt, not nobleness, that made me say something. Fitch never would have dared spread this rumor if I'd spoken up in Mulvey's office.

"Oh? How would you know?"

I crossed my arms. "I was there. That's where we—"

Interrupted by a choking cough from our publicist, who raised her eyebrows at me with meaning.

"That's where...I got to see her act for the first time. Fully clothed."

"*Really?*" June said, but with interest, like she believed me, which honestly only made me more annoyed.

"Yes, *really*. She already told you." I tossed a hand in Henrietta's direction. "I don't understand why the story's more convincing coming from me. Wouldn't Hen— Etta know if she showed up to a screen test half naked?"

"Well, it is my responsibility to investigate rumors."

"Then why don't you check your sources? Because this one"—I nodded at Henrietta—"is about to be the biggest thing in Hollywood, and the other one just got demoted to dogcatcher."

Henrietta let out a surprised laugh, looking at me with delight, but the smile curdled as she fixed June with a glare.

"Any other facts about my career you need Declan to confirm, or are we all finished?" she asked, and, I had to admit, it was nice watching someone else on the receiving end of Henrietta's acid tongue.

June gave us a tight smile and stood up, and the publicist, white as a sheet, ushered her out of the room before either of us could open our mouth again. The second they'd disappeared into the hallway, Henrietta collapsed back against the sofa, looking ill.

"What a mess," she sighed. "I knew that creep was going to cause problems."

I felt another stab of guilt. "Sorry," I said.

"What do you have to apologize for? You showed June St. James that if she tries to come at me with another ridiculous rumor, she's going to walk away looking like an idiot." Her mouth had a sour twist to it, and she gave me a sideways glance. "Is that true, by the way? That stupid cad Burton Fitch is working with dogs now?"

"Exiled to Barkville," I said, and the corners of her lips twitched. "But you should know... He's not happy about it. He blames you."

"Me! Maybe he should have kept his creative ideas out of the gutter."

"Yeah, well, in any case... Just... watch out for him."

Her eyes narrowed, then quickly widened, like she'd realized she might have a dangerous enemy on the lot and that I, of all people, was the one to warn her.

"Maybe she won't write about it," she said, her voice thoughtful. "We gave her plenty of sunny material."

"You gave her," I corrected. "I mean, when she asked me about my... I froze and... Well. Etta Hart saved the day. Thanks."

Henrietta shrugged. "Anyone could see you didn't want to talk about your family. Stepping in was the decent thing to do."

"Huh. I didn't think you had it in you."

"What?" she asked, looking right at me. I had my response on the edge of my tongue—"Being decent"—but the vulnerability in her expression made my words feel mean.

A flush of embarrassment crept into my cheeks, and I replied, "Caring about me."

She lifted her eyebrows, surprised, and I stood up and shoved my hands into my pockets. "I guess I'll—"

"About last night—" She jumped to her feet. "I didn't know he'd... I didn't go there thinking we'd... Well. I guess I knew what he had in mind, but when I didn't want to anymore, I thought he'd... stop," she finished flatly. "Anyway, you don't need to worry, because I am now fully immune to Jack Huxley's charm. Your job is safe." She said it with a note of sarcasm, not looking at me.

"I didn't go in there because I thought you were...unfaithful to me." I winced, because how could you be unfaithful in a relationship that didn't exist? "I heard shouting, and...I was...worried about you. I thought maybe Fitch had...But even just Jack...Anyway, going in there...I guess you'd call it the decent thing to do."

She blinked at me in surprise, and I didn't know what was more depressing: that I worried about this ridiculous starlet's safety, or that she found the idea of my decency so astonishing.

"Well," she said at last. "Well. Thank you, then."

I nodded, and I was about to escape when she put out a hand.

"Let me ask you something," she said, speaking slowly. "Is there anyone in this entire city who cares about you beyond what you can do for them? Anyone you can be completely honest with?"

Pep popped into my mind, but lately, I wasn't so sure. The last few weeks had shown me how much I'd been hiding from him, and yesterday's dust-up outside Mulvey's office had only made things worse.

When I got home last night, I'd tried to bring it up again, but he wouldn't hear it. While I'd been chasing after Henrietta, he'd landed himself a job in the Silver Wing mailroom. One step closer to Mulvey's office.

"Just..." Pep had let out a sigh. "Do your job, don't make trouble. Please don't mess this up for me."

He'd left early this morning, and I didn't know if it was to make a good impression or because he wanted to avoid me.

"I guess...No. No, I don't," I said to Henrietta.

"Yeah." She nodded. "So. How 'bout a deal?"

"A deal?"

"A truce. You watch out for me, I'll watch out for you. I miss that, especially in this city."

"You had that with Miriam Powell? Until she…left?"

The name seemed to hit her like an arrow, and a strange expression came over her.

"Midge…" She let out a bitter laugh. " '*Left.*'"

"The studio said she went home to New York, right?"

"I know what they said." Her voice was sharp, and I could tell that she didn't believe Silver Wing, that she had no idea about where Miss Powell had gone, and that she was maybe the only person in this entire city, other than me and Sam, who cared to find out.

"Anyway…" She pulled on her smile. "What do you say?"

I watched her carefully.

"All right. But—why? Why me?"

Shrugging, she seemed to consider the question for the first time. "I guess…you seem like you could use a friend. And lord knows I'm desperate for one."

"You'd have to be, to ask me," I said, and even though I hadn't meant it as a joke, she broke into a pure, surprised laugh, the most genuine thing I'd ever seen from her.

CHAPTER TWENTY-ONE
HENRIETTA

My good fortune had run out. Even with the force of the Silver Wing machine, June St. James's story had enough rumors to set off a low-level hum of intrigue. It didn't help that the *Train Car* set had gotten remarkably chilly. Whispers, from Jack's camp, no doubt, hinted that I had a schoolgirl crush, that I'd thrown myself at the movie star and fallen apart at his polite rejection.

The sting over misreading Jack almost bothered me more than what he'd done. I'd always figured he was a smooth talker and a fast worker but generally decent; I'd never imagined he'd considered my kisses his right, instead of a privilege.

And those *girls*. What on earth had happened in my dressing room? Days later and I still hadn't ginned up the courage to go back. They'd had to set up a little curtained-off area for me on set.

It didn't make sense! Just the other day, I'd cut through one of the production buildings and spotted a man's smiling portrait, the name under the frame leaping off its plaque like a slap: HOWARD ABNER. The first woman to appear that night, the one who had thrown open my door and shrieked to get out, said she'd gotten the room from *Howard Abner*. But the plaque showed he'd died eight years ago.

Alone in my hotel suite, I threw myself back on the bed. My body ached, my head buzzed, I spent my days fighting off exhaustion, but when I returned to the Knickerbocker at the end of the day, nodding hello to the bellboy and slipping past wealthy tourists, and the heavy door of my suite closed behind me, my mind went wild, my thoughts like a flock of frightened birds impossible to calm.

I would have given anything for someone to talk to about all this. The makeup girls and dressers and hairstylists were friendly enough, but the last thing I wanted was more gossip about my behavior. Jerome Calhoun, the editor who'd taken me under his wing, might've consoled me over Jack and Fitch; it was too much to hope he'd listen to me go on about *ghosts*. And although Declan had gotten markedly less annoying since our interview with June St. James, I doubted he'd have much sympathy for the problems of a spoiled Hollywood starlet.

My telephone beckoned from the side table. Ruby would listen, and she'd probably even believe that I'd seen something that scared me silly, but if I told her, *Right, so Jack Huxley tried to get his paws on me, and some vile director is telling everyone I'm a harlot, and before that, a dozen horrifically injured girls appeared out of nowhere, and then promptly vanished...* In a matter of minutes Ruby'd show up to drag me back home.

Instead, I paced like a caged animal until I decided to throw all the windows open and catch the late-spring breeze. Down below, Hollywood Boulevard was busy with clumps of tourists, the glamorous descending from their mansions in the Hills to parties and restaurants. The Knickerbocker had a kicky basement club, and my skin itched so bad I nearly considered throwing on a gown and heading downstairs. Etta Hart's presence would set off a flurry of attention big enough to distract me from my own thoughts...

I sighed. What was it Midge had said to me?

Folks would line up for miles if I offered a kiss, but I still haven't made a single friend.

I turned back around to the beautiful, cold, and empty hotel suite.

"Midge?"

As soon as I said her name, I felt like a fool.

"Midge!" I stepped into the center of the room, my bare feet silent on the plush, blood-colored carpeting. "I don't know if you can hear me. I don't know if you're real. But when I saw you, if that really was you, you looked scared. Do you remember what I told you, the night we met? *Never leave a gal stranded.* If you need me, I'm here. Wherever you are, I'm here for you."

I stood still, my senses quivering, waiting for...what? A chill had filled the room, the breeze turning sharp. I pulled my arms around myself, not ready to go to bed, not ready to move, until I let out a breath, and it appeared in a puff of white, as though I'd whirled back to a freezing Chicago winter.

I spun around.

"Midge!"

She stood at the window, her back to me.

"Can you hear me?" My heartbeat thrummed with fear, but I pushed it away. I refused to be afraid of my friend.

A moment of silence, and then: "Henny?"

I reached for her hand, hanging limp at her side, but the moment my fingers touched her, a chill went through me and I pulled away with a shudder. Midge seemed to have noticed; she stared down at her hand like she'd never seen it before.

"Are you all right?" I asked.

"No...No, I don't think so. Henny. Henny, I think...Something happened to me." Her beautiful face, pale in the darkness, crumpled into a frown. "Henny, I think I'm...dead."

NO.

It'd been waiting for me, that truth, and now it crashed into me like a violent, tumbling wave.

"Midge, I— But—*how?* If you're...*d-dead*—" the word dropped out of my mouth, a lead weight. "How...I can *see* you, Midge."

Silence.

"What happened?" It came out in a whisper. "I mean, how did it... happen?"

She blinked, then shook her head. "I don't remember...It feels...so strange...It's like trying to remember...a dream...I felt...I feel..." She closed her eyes. "I'm walking in darkness. Darkness, everywhere...But then...I heard you..." She put out her hand, but when I grasped for her fingers, my hands closed on absolutely nothing, slipping through Midge's as though they were a trick of the light.

"The studio said you went back home. Why would they lie?"

"I don't know. It's all...It's black, Henny, all black..." Her body seemed to be fading at the edges.

"Midge!" I said, and she snapped into being again, but when she spoke, her voice sounded breathless, more air than noise.

"Henny...I think...There are others...More..."

"More...ghosts?" I asked, and as her eyes locked onto mine, something within them lit up, blazing and fierce.

"*Girls.*"

My mind reeled back to the dressing rooms, full of women, hurt women, angry women, scared women. Were they ghosts? But how? And why? Why come to *me*?

"I don't understand," I said, and when the fire in Midge's eyes faded to worry, I continued, "But that's all right. I'm going to figure it out. I'm going to figure out what happened to you. I'm going to figure out what happened to everyone. However I can help—I'm going to do it, I promise! Midge? Midge!"

But she had already gone.

CHAPTER TWENTY-TWO
DECLAN

"What's this thing again?"

The publicist in the front seat spun around with a frown.

"As I already mentioned, Mr. Collins, you are on your way to a banquet in support of the Mayor's Summer Youth Employment Fund! Mr. Reynolds is passionate about assisting the local community, and insists his stars— Miss Hart! Eat those crackers!"

With a stern shake of her finger, she turned to the front again, and Henrietta and I glanced at each other before she gave her digestive biscuits a look of pure loathing.

"It's not fair Declan can tuck in at these things, and I get crackers in the car."

"A proper young lady maintains a refined appetite!" sang the publicist, and Henrietta made a gagging face, dropping her head back against the seat without a care for her elaborate hairstyle.

Thanks to a wave of rumors about Henrietta—fueled by Burton Fitch's and Jack Huxley's bruised egos—Etta Hart's shining reputation had gone brassy. In response, Silver Wing launched the Etta Hart and Declan Collins Tour, only instead of watching Joe DiMaggio lead the Seals to an eight-two victory over the Hollywood Stars at Wrigley Field, they sent us on a whirlwind of industry parties and nights on the town, dancing at the Bamboo Room, a picnic at Cabrillo Beach—just me, Henrietta, a makeup person, a wardrobe consultant, and a photographer shouting, "Put your arm around her waist, *then* lean in for the kiss!"

"I know Etta Hart loves a party, but good lord, *I'm* exhausted." Henrietta let out a sigh before gnawing on the cracker. "Declan, if you see me tug my ear, get me out of there."

She'd said it like a joke, but underneath her heavy makeup, dark rings shadowed her eyes. My own schedule'd been so jam-packed with classes and lessons and events, I barely had time to work on Sam's investigation into the missing girls; when did Henrietta get a chance to sleep? Rather than commenting on that, I leaned over and brushed some crumbs off the lap of her spangly, pale green gown. "Which one of you is the neat eater—Henrietta or Etta?"

"Oh, Etta Hart would never do anything as common as *eat*." Henrietta smacked my hand away before stuffing another cracker into her mouth.

Since the *Picture Perfect* interview, Henrietta and I had become... Well, what did you call it when you spent half your time kissing a girl and the other half bickering like kids? *Friends* seemed like a stretch. Whatever it was, I'd started to realize there were two sides to her: Etta Hart, the polished, charming starlet with the magnetic ability to draw attention, and... Henrietta.

She could switch between them like a magic trick, and at first it made me feel funny, like she put on an act to puff herself up, get some more attention, but during our interview I realized I'd gotten it wrong. Etta Hart was the armor that protected the real girl, the bright, pretty distraction that let Henrietta Newhouse slip by unnoticed.

Just before we stepped out of the car, she took my hand, smiling into my eyes like she hadn't just cursed me for stealing one of her biscuits. She did it so smoothly, so effortlessly, it made me wish I was better at hiding away the real me, too. But no matter how hard my acting teachers drilled me, it seemed like I was forever stuck as myself.

Luckily it didn't matter at an event like tonight's, where no one cared about Declan Collins, real or pretend. The banquet, held in the Blossom Room at the Roosevelt Hotel, would be a half hour of desperate mingling, seated dinner (dry fish or drier chicken), a long speech patting us all on the backs, then dessert and dancing. The End.

My best bet? Stick near Henrietta and go to town on hors d'oeuvres, which was exactly what I did. I rarely bothered paying attention to the conversations—Henrietta seemed born for these surface niceties—but when I glanced over at her a few minutes after we'd arrived, pinned into a chat with one of the powerful producers Pep idolized, I got a surprise. She'd gone rigid, her eyes wide, staring straight ahead. Her fingers were tight around the stem of her glass, so tight I could see the whole thing trembling.

The producer leaned in with a sly smile, his voice quiet, but Henrietta didn't seem to be listening.

She gasped and the glass dropped from her hand, shattering on the tiled floor. Every head in the room turned to see what had happened: Etta Hart, her beautiful gown splashed with soda water, looking around like she had no idea where she was.

Except this wasn't Etta Hart anymore. Her armor had slipped away, showing the real girl blinking like she was coming out of a dream. A ripple of whispers ran through the crowd of actors and movie moguls and reporters, watching Henrietta, small and exposed. As someone let out a snicker, heat flared through me.

"Um. Sorry—I bumped you, darling," I said, loudly enough for people to hear. "Let me help you clean up."

I put my arm around her waist and half dragged her through the crowd, pushing through like a defensive lineman, mumbling something about fresh air. When we'd made it through a small side exit, we emerged in a narrow, dimly lit hallway, rows of doors on either side and a window at the end.

"Where are we going?" Henrietta asked, her voice shaky.

"Here." I walked down to the window and shoved it open before jumping out, and when I heard Henrietta's shocked gasp, I popped back into view. "Fire escape," I said with a grin, and she rolled her eyes and swatted me.

"Idiot. Move out of the way."

Grateful that she sounded like her old self, I immediately stepped aside to let her clamber through, her high heels ringing against the fire escape. I slid the window shut and took a seat on the ledge, wishing I'd grabbed more to eat.

"What happened back there?"

She didn't respond, her back to me, her hands holding the railing. We were only on the second floor, but it was high enough for a breeze eddying past to pull at wisps of Henrietta's blond curls. The front of the hotel bathed in the bright glow of Hollywood Boulevard, but here on the quieter, eastern side of the hotel, we stood in semidarkness, Henrietta caught between the pale light of the moon and the honey glow of the streetlights below.

"Can you tell me something?" she asked, still looking out over the city. "Did you see another girl standing beside us down there in the ballroom? A girl in a long red dress, cape over her shoulders?"

"Just you and that producer."

A muscle in Henrietta's neck twitched. "Hm," she said, while I wondered what that meant. Was she seeing things? Maybe she was more tired than I thought.

She brought her arms up, hugging herself, her shoulders hunched like there was a chill, even though it was a beautiful spring night. Before she could give me a hard time about acting like a gentleman, I pulled off my jacket and held it out to her. She stared at it for a second, then reached for it with a bright smile.

"Gosh, you're long-limbed," she said, flapping the sleeves at me. "You must have to tailor *everything*."

"That belongs to the studio, so be careful, it has to go back tonight."

"This, too." She stared down at her dress. The delicate, shimmering green fabric had dried, but I could see the ghost of a water stain. "I don't know what I'll get in more trouble for—the dress, or abandoning the banquet." She glanced up at me. "If you cover for me, I'll give you Nancy Lake's phone number."

I raised an eyebrow—Nancy Lake had won an Academy Award last year—but shook my head.

"Not my type."

"Oooh, he has a *type*? I'll have to tell publicity what to look for when they go through your fan mail."

She was grinning, but I didn't smile back. I'd gotten enough ribbing from Pep, who'd been working in the mailroom for a few weeks now: "Letters from every state in the union, Duke!"

"Come on," I said, "none of those girls are interested in me. They only want the guy in the magazines, and even then, it's only to get themselves in the magazines."

"That's awfully cynical. Those girls might just like a pretty face."

I grinned. "You think I have a pretty face?"

"Don't be an idiot, I'm trying to expand your perspective." She reached down and hauled me to my feet before dusting off my shoulders like one of the publicists. "Somewhere under that dour frown has to be a boy who wants to go out and have fun."

"I have fun," I said, and she gave me a look.

"Not *baseball game* fun. Make a girl laugh! Neck in the moonlight! You've only got one life on this planet, Declan Collins, and once it's gone, it's *gone*." Her smile dropped away, her eyes taking on the faraway look from the banquet hall, sending uncomfortable prickles over my skin.

"Did you forget we're supposed to be dating?" I asked, and that snapped her back. She let out a laugh and pulled up the collar of my jacket.

"So, neck in some private, hidden moonlight. My point stands. This gig doesn't have many perks—enjoy the ones we've got."

"Just the paycheck is fine."

"Well, not for me." Henrietta turned and looked over the city, her eyes lingering on bright Hollywood Boulevard. Right across the street from the hotel was the famous Chinese theater, the dramatic red columns outside its pagoda-topped entrance lit up like twin flames. "I don't care what rumors those spineless creeps throw at me. I'm not quitting until I'm the biggest star in this whole damn country."

At this, I let out a snort of laughter, and she glanced sharply over her shoulder.

"What did *you* come out to Hollywood for, Mr. High-and-Mighty?"

"Not fame," I said, laughing. "Stunt men don't show up in the credits."

"So—what? You could've gone anywhere to do crazy tricks, but you decided to risk your life in the most glamorous city in the world."

"Hollywood is glamorous?" I waved a hand. Hollywood Boulevard might've been glamorous, once, in the twenties, when it still catered to movie stars. Now it was just the tourists, walking around with vague expressions of disappointment, and the con men hunting for prey.

Everything in this city looked flashy and cheap, neon lights, slapdash construction hidden under tissue-paper-thin gilt, the buildings a jumble of styles like even the architects didn't have original thoughts.

Henrietta wouldn't hear it. She pushed a finger against my chest with a steely look.

"Listen here, you ingrate. You are lucky enough to live inside the *dream* factory. Home to the best writers, writing for the best actors, acting in worlds created by the best visionaries in the history of this species! If you're trying to tell me you didn't come to Hollywood for a taste of that, I'm telling you: you are a terrible liar."

Before I could stop myself, it spilled out. "I didn't come to Hollywood for that."

The way I'd said it—sincere, certain—surprised Henrietta, her hair blowing around her face in delicate feathers.

"Then tell me." There was a challenge in her words.

"I came…" I'd always told myself that I came to Hollywood for Pep, in spite of Mam's history here, but ever since talking to Wendy Harris, since Sam found me, that felt like a lie. I was always going to make my way to this city. I was always going to look for her.

I didn't have to tell Henrietta all that. I could push it away, change the subject like I did with Pep. But Henrietta and I had agreed to be straight with each other. And sure, I usually took that as license to let her know when she had spinach in her teeth or to tone it down when meeting a particularly famous director, but now that I'd gotten into the habit, I realized how much I appreciated not having to hide what I thought.

"I came… to find someone."

She blinked. "Who?"

Aaand that was about as much honesty as I could handle for one evening.

"Not important." I couldn't meet her eyes.

"A *girl*?" she asked, a smile pulling at the corner of her mouth.

"I said it's not important." It came out rougher than I meant, and when the smile vanished from her face, I frowned and took hold of the railing, staring out so I wouldn't have to look at her, kicking myself for opening my mouth.

A moment later, I felt her shoulder brush up against mine. I could smell her perfume, light on the breeze and mixing with the scent of the flowers in the Roosevelt's roof garden above. The bracelets on her wrists clinked together, delicate, like faraway bells.

"Did you ever find her?" Her voice was quiet.

"No."

"You're still looking?" I could feel her studying me, and I glanced over, my eyes catching on hers. I felt like I did back in our screen test, staring into her face, only she wasn't a stranger anymore—I'd kissed her hundreds of times.

But there were no cameras here, and no one watching us. We were alone—truly alone—for the first time.

"Yes," I said, the word coming out like a sigh. Warm prickles crept up my chest, the breeze cool against my cheeks, my head feeling like I was falling, and I pushed it all away. Henrietta had told me how she felt about me. Our relationship was just another role to play.

Her hand nudged closer on the railing, her pinky skimming mine, and I felt it like a lightning bolt, straight down my spine. What was she doing? Her fling with Jack had imploded—was I just the next thing to entertain her? *"It's. Not. Real."* She'd said those words to me.

So why was it so hard to believe?

CHAPTER TWENTY-THREE
HENRIETTA

I looked up into Declan's face—how had I never appreciated how tall he was?—and felt my heartbeat pick up its pace. It'd been so long since I'd properly talked to someone as Henrietta, not *Etta Hart,* and I felt so relieved that I thought any second now I would throw my arms around Declan's neck.

Before I could, he took a step away, clearing his throat, his eyes everywhere but my face.

"What about you?" he asked. "You were trying to find your friend. Miriam Powell. Did you?"

The question nearly knocked me over.

Midge was dead.

It was incredible how that thought would pop into my brain, at any moment, setting off a *gong* of despair. The more I pushed it away, the more it would fight to the center of my attention. *Midge was dead.*

Maybe I'd only known her a few days. Maybe we'd only met a few times. But she was my friend, and, more importantly, she was a bright, beautiful, talented, kind, wonderful girl. She should be lighting up the screen right now. She should be alive. The knowledge that she wasn't set a kind of oily fire in my stomach, roiling and wild.

"No. No," I repeated. "I don't know what happened to Midge." It was the truth. I only knew she was dead, and it was terrible. I felt tears spring to my eyes, and I swiped at them, not in the practiced way I'd learned for the camera, but desperate, like I was a kid again and if I just rubbed fast enough it would keep more from falling. After a moment, a handkerchief appeared in front of me, warm from Declan's pocket, and I took it, wiped clean my ruined makeup.

"It's just—I keep thinking…Midge was *here,* happy, laughing, and then she disappeared and—no one seems to notice! No one *cares!*" The words broke out of me in a sob, and once I started, I couldn't stop. The feelings I'd been pushing down, pushing away with work and parties and late-night worrying, all burst out of me.

I cried for Midge, my friend. I cried for those other girls. I cried for whatever had happened to them, that they should show up in my life as bruised, bloody, broken shadows instead of beautiful, laughing, living girls.

"Hey."

I felt Declan's hand, patting me awkwardly on the shoulder.

"It's…"

If he says "It's all right," I thought to myself, *I am going to scream.*

"It's…terrible. I'm sorry."

It surprised me so much that I hiccoughed, my head snapping up to see Declan looking at me.

"Wh-What?"

He shook his head. "Losing someone, like that…It's terrible."

Stunned, I blinked at him. I hadn't realized how much I'd needed to hear that. It was as though I'd been alone in the dark, alone in worrying, alone in grieving, and someone had turned on a light.

Not just *someone*. Declan had lost a person, too, and now he was standing here, telling me he understood.

I must have scared Declan to pieces when I burst into tears again, and I *knew* I shocked the stuffing out of him when I threw my arms around his neck and buried my face in the hollow of his shoulder. One part of my brain shrieked *Declan?! Of all the people in the world who understand you, it's Declan Collins?!* and another part of my brain told it kindly to SHUT. UP. Declan was here, and he understood, and he was warm and smelled nice and wore a clean white dress shirt that felt incredible pressed up against my cheek.

He'd jerked when I touched him, but a moment later, he put his hands around me, his fingertips barely touching my skin.

The last few weeks had gotten me used to hands all over my body: makeup people brushing and dabbing, wardrobe girls poking and pulling, and then there was Declan himself. He'd kissed me for the cameras, held me on red carpets, spent whole evenings with his hand around my waist, but this... was different.

I felt his words before I really heard them, soft vibrations rumbling against my skin: "I'm sorry, Henrietta. I'm sorry." One of his hands came up to my hair, stroking it gently, so gently that shivers ran through me. I spent every day pretending for people who looked at me and expected Etta Hart, pleasant and unruffled and charming. But the way Declan touched me now... His fingers trailed through my hair, down my neck, across my back, and I knew I didn't have to do or be or feel or act any other way right now than how I actually was.

Which was sad.

And lonely.

And scared.

And confused.

And a remarkable thing happened. The moment Declan made space for me, inside the circle of his arms, those feelings seemed to get a bit...lighter.

I looked up at him, amazed. How had he done that?

He'd bent his face down close, all of three inches away, studying me, and even though I'd seen that face almost every day for weeks, and even though I'd long felt myself inured to the handsomeness that set *Picture Perfect* readers aflame, now I couldn't stop staring into his eyes. Soft and warm and strong and kind. Three inches away felt suddenly too far.

I wanted to know what it would feel like to kiss Declan Collins. The real Declan, not the ex–stunt man actor keeping me company at fancy parties. I wanted to touch him without anyone watching. I wanted to kiss him as myself, just because I wanted to, and I wanted to do it *right now*.

When I leaned in, he whispered my name, a question. He didn't pull away, and I didn't stop. I closed my eyes, felt his warmth on my lips, and I brushed my mouth against his—

The blare of a horn down below made us both jump, Declan leaping back like he'd been shocked. He glanced down at the street, the tourists walking Hollywood Boulevard, and pushed away from the railing.

"Someone could see us."

My bones felt like they'd been replaced with taffy, and my cheeks burned. I worried I might collapse, and then I glanced over at Declan, pressed up against the wall of the hotel like a little boy caught stealing, and I let out a nervous laugh.

"You know, we're *supposed* to be sneaking off together. Maybe they'll give us a bonus." Light-headed, I felt another wave of giggles. "Oh shoot, my lipstick!" I reached over to wipe away a crimson smudge at his neck, and he stepped aside.

"I can handle it." He rubbed hard at the mark, not meeting my eyes. "I should go."

"Go? Worried you're going to miss the speech?"

I had a loopy smile on my face, but he didn't wait for me, shoving open the window and disappearing into the hotel. For a second, I stood on the fire escape, swimming in Declan's jacket, trying to piece together what had happened. Had I really, truly, almost kissed Declan?

And his response was to ... make a break for it?

He'd always acted like romance pained him. His stiffness anytime we had to cozy up, his lack of interest in other girls—almost as though...

Oh.

I felt so stupid, so colossally dense, that my whole face scrunched up in pain. Of course.

He'd followed a girl to Hollywood. Lost her. Never stopped searching for her.

He loved her. Was *in love* with her. No wonder he didn't care about his scores of fans. His heart belonged to another girl.

Declan and me ... we could never be real.

The smack-up-the-head realization that Declan, unlike pretty much any other fella in this city, didn't want to swoop in and save me for some big reward but was happy to simply sit by my side when I needed a friend— it didn't matter.

My fake boyfriend was in love with someone else.

CHAPTER TWENTY-FOUR
DECLAN

I rubbed my skin raw, but I could still feel Henrietta's lips brush up against mine. My mind kept spinning, a darkened theater playing the same loop of film: Henrietta's tears, her arms around me, her weight against my chest, the question in her face when she met my eyes, like she was falling and wanted to know if I'd catch her.

What the hell was that? It felt nothing like the ridiculous photo shoots, the "dates" where we barely spoke, the premieres when reporters would ask for a good shot and Henrietta would dutifully turn to me with a smile, lips raised to mine.

No—I had it wrong—that had been *Etta Hart*. I'd only kissed Henrietta once, just now, and it lit up something inside me I hadn't even known could go electric.

My thoughts tangled me up so much that it was a while before I realized I was lost. I was spinning around, trying to figure out where to go, when a nearby door opened, letting out a blare of music and—shoot—Mulvey, followed by a hotel bellboy.

Quick, I ducked around a corner, and then I heard his gruff voice ask, "You said she's in bad shape?"

Is he talking about Henrietta? After a murmured reply from the bell-boy, I heard Mulvey say, "Roof? I'll take care of it."

Footsteps, going the other way down the hallway, then the sound of the door opening, music blaring, quiet again. Not Henrietta, then, but who was in bad shape? Another girl?

I headed back into the banquet hall, searching for Mulvey. The huge golden chandelier had dimmed since Henrietta and I had left, the ball-room turned over to the band, dancers clustered together on the floor in the center of the room. The few people sitting at tables had their heads bent close to hear over the music, slices of cake set before them. I spotted Mulvey, moving quickly to the exit opposite me, and I made my way after him.

When I got there, I pushed open the door to find another hallway. I looked around, not sure where to go, and spotted a small, ornate sign: BLOSSOM PATIO ROOF GARDEN. The nearby entrance led to a staircase, which I followed up to a landing and a pair of glass French doors, a CLOSED sign hanging on one, the other pushed slightly ajar.

Through the doors, I couldn't see much: lush greenery made up most of the view, delicate flowery vines that wound around awnings, dozens of small round tables, and a large stone fountain. I put my ear to the door, listening.

Was that...crying? A man, letting out burbling sobs, and another voice, sharp in response.

Holding my breath, I eased the door open and slipped onto the roof, hiding behind a table under one of the awnings. I could hear more clearly now, and I crept closer, staying low, until I nearly reached the edge of the roof.

"...didn't even *mean* to!" a man's voice wailed, and in the dim light I could just make him out: middle-aged, his thin, dark hair stuck to his flushed forehead, sitting crumpled on the ground, back against the parapet. Beside him, next to one of the tables, a woman slumped in a chair as Mulvey leaned down, slapping her cheeks.

"Is she all right?" the man asked, his head rolling on his neck. "Irma? Are you all right?"

Irma? The name shocked through me. Irma Van Pelt? But a second later, Mulvey gave the man an irritated look.

"I keep telling you, this isn't Irma." He shook the girl. "Come on, sweetheart, on your feet."

"She's gonna be fine, this time, right? Irma, hon, you're gonna be fine!"

"Keep your voice down," Mulvey snapped, and then the girl moaned, lifting her head from the table. "That's it, come on."

"See? She's all right!" The man tried to get up as Mulvey helped the girl to her feet, but he lost his balance, catching himself before he toppled forward. With the girl swaying unsteadily against him, Mulvey glanced at the man.

"Stay put. I'll deal with you later." Half carrying, half dragging the girl, Mulvey made his way to the French doors, while the man let out another sob.

"Irma! I'm sorry! I'm—" He broke down crying as Mulvey and the girl stumbled away. Before I could follow them, the sobbing man swung out an arm wildly in my direction, and I ducked down quick.

"Irma, Irma...," he mumbled, but he was just reaching for his jacket, slung over a nearby chair, searching the pockets. "Oh, Irma..." Whatever he found only made him cry harder, dramatic, gasping sobs that turned my stomach.

I crept closer. The thing in his hands—small, rectangular—caught a flash of moonlight. A lighter? A card? No—

A *photograph.*

I wanted that photograph. I wanted to know if it was of a sandy-haired girl with a single dimple in her cheek, smiling like sunshine, and I wanted to know how this sobbing letch had ended up with it.

He held it tight, pressing it against his heart, eyes closed. He couldn't quit crying, mumbling Irma's name and snippets of sentences: "…didn't mean…had to…sorry, *sorry*…"

It went on for so long, my muscles began to cramp, but gradually, the sobbing slowed, his ragged breaths coming more evenly. His eyes still squeezed tight, but he held the photo loosely between his fingers now.

I sucked in a breath, easing around the table, and slowly, slowly, held out my hand. The man didn't react. I stretched inch by inch, sweat trickling down my neck, until I was close enough to feel his ragged breath, hot and sour, on the back of my hand. Gently, I gave the photo a tug.

At the far end of the roof, the door banged open again, and I snatched the photo from the man, who jerked awake as I slipped behind the table, my heart pounding.

Had he seen me?

No time to worry—Mulvey was back, making his way toward the man, who was now searching the ground with wide eyes and whimpering panicked noises.

"Where…," he was saying. "Where—where—"

Smoothly, Mulvey lifted up the man by the back of his shirt like he weighed no more than a kitten.

"You listen to me, Anderson," he growled. "I'm sick of cleaning up your messes. You already burned your one shot. Now you're a problem.

You're lucky all that girl's gonna have is a whopping headache and some bad dreams, because—"

My hand tight around the photograph, I'd tried to edge deeper into the darkness and instead pushed against one of the chairs, which let out a *whine* against the stone floor.

Mulvey froze, his eyes snapping right to my hiding place. He dropped the man in a heap, making for the table. I jumped up like a rabbit, clutching the photo, running for the French doors, but Mulvey was faster. He cut me off, his huge frame sliding into my path, and I turned and ran, searching for another exit while Mulvey shouted, "Stop! Who are you?!"

The rooftop wasn't big, maybe only fifty feet end to end, and I was soon back at the far edge, the crying man crumpled on the ground, my hands on the waist-high wall separating the patio from the empty sky.

"You're trapped, kid!" Mulvey shouted to me. I looked three stories down to the street below, not busy Hollywood Boulevard but quieter, darker Orange Drive. I couldn't let go of this photograph—what if it was the clue we needed to find Irma Van Pelt? To prove that something had happened to her and the studio had covered it up?

My breaths felt wild in my lungs, my heartbeat so fast I thought I might collapse.

No people, I realized. The sidewalk down below was empty.

"Gotcha!" Mulvey said, clamping a hand on my shoulder, a second before I wrenched away, threw myself up onto the wall, and leaped out into the air.

CHAPTER TWENTY-FIVE
HENRIETTA

Somehow, we'd made it to the end. The last day of shooting for *One Night in a Train Car,* which also happened to be the last scene of the movie. The dramatic heart-baring, the big, swoony kiss.

I had to pull this off—if only to show up Jack Huxley, pouting around the set like a put-out two-year-old—but as I sat in my makeshift dressing area, my script on my lap, my mind kept filling with thoughts of that *other* big, swoony kiss.

What would I say to Declan next time I saw him? Whenever that would be…Half a dozen reporters had seen me nearly pass out in the Blossom Room, and now they wanted to know if Etta Hart suffered from health problems. The publicists had unanimously agreed that some time out of the spotlight was in order.

My career looked like it might be over before it started, which didn't relieve the pressure to do well today. I needed to stop thinking about Declan!

"Miss Hart? They're ready for you."

I looked up from my script and pulled on a smile for the production assistant. No more worried, anxious, moony Henrietta; it was time for polished, successful Etta Hart.

I made my way over to the set. There was Jack, lounging in a director's chair, flirting with one of the script girls. He paid no attention to me, which was JUST FINE, and I stepped into the crowded luggage room inside Grand Central Station.

As the director, Mr. Zuckerman, called, "Places," Jack sauntered over with a smile.

"Ready for our big scene?" he asked, and I smiled back.

"I had anchovies for breakfast."

"All right! Come on, here we go!" the director called. I closed my eyes, took a breath, ran my first line over in my head.

"Roll film! Roll sound! Aaannnddd...action!"

Jack burst through the door of the luggage room, and I spun around.

"I thought I told you to stay out of New York!" I said, and there was a look of confusion on Jack's face—ooooh, did he forget his line??!!—before Mr. Zuckerman called, "Cut."

"What was that?" he asked, but when Jack didn't answer I realized he meant *me*.

"Sorry?"

"Miss Hart, that's the *old version* of this scene."

"The—what?"

Mr. Zuckerman pointed for one of the script girls to run over to me. The top of the page read *FINAL SCENE – INT – LUGGAGE ROOM,* but the lines—all the lines—were different!

I opened my mouth to protest, but as I looked up I happened to glance at Jack's crooked, smug smile, and my stomach dropped straight to my shoes.

"Something wrong?" he asked. "You don't need to be nervous, Etta. You'll do great."

He said it low enough to sound like he was comforting me, loud enough for everyone to hear—for such a nasty person, he wasn't a half-bad actor. *Oooh,* I wanted to leap over and wring his neck! He did this! He made sure no one got me a new script! He made sure nobody mentioned it to me!

And he knew how important this scene was. We all did. The film built up to this moment, the silly screwball comedy falling away to show something true and complicated. Either the kiss would feel like the perfect conclusion to all Virginia's hopes and longings, or it would feel cheap, tacked-on, unearned, and ruin the movie like a sour dessert. But what would Jack care if this film flopped? He'd made plenty of stinkers and still managed to keep his audience.

Everyone was staring at me. I had two options: 1) accuse Jack of sabotaging me, refuse to do the scene, set production back a day, and be labeled *temperamental,* a kiss of death in this industry, OR 2) jump into the most demanding scene of the film with no preparation, no more than a glance at the lines, and just hope I didn't completely ruin my career.

That disgusting little sneak! Behind Mr. Zuckerman's back, he gave me a warm smile.

"Right!" I said, smiling back at him. My eyes tripped down the page. Could I ask for five minutes? Ten? And there was that grinning idiot, eating up every second. I'd opened my mouth—possibly to ask for a break, possibly to vomit—when one of the makeup girls came over to touch me up, only instead of lightly dusting my nose she tripped, sending her whole container of powder down the front of my costume.

I yelped, and my dresser jumped to my side. I thought she might give the makeup girl a piece of her mind, but she put an arm around my shoulder and declared to the whole set, "This'll need twenty, thirty minutes to clean up!" And before anyone could say anything, both women ushered me back to the dressing area and yanked the curtains shut.

"You get me some wet towels," the costumer said to the makeup girl, "and *you*"—she turned to me—"better read fast."

When I blinked at her in shock, the makeup girl let out a sigh. "He pulled the same stunt on Roxane LeFaire, during *The Devil You Know*. Stuck-up cad. You think you can learn your lines in thirty minutes, or should I get the hairstylist to put something in Jack's pomade?"

I looked at them both—maybe I hadn't been quite so alone in this city as I'd thought—and I felt so surprised and delighted I wasn't sure whether to kiss them or cry. I chose a bit of both.

"Good thing you're here for touch-ups," the costumer said to the makeup girl with a pleased smile, and then she waved a rag at me. "And you better quit blubbering and show that fool what you can do!"

Could I learn a scene in thirty minutes? My mind felt so full of so many different things—Jack and the scene and Declan and Midge and the *ghosts*, good lord—I wasn't sure I could even recite the alphabet.

When I finally stepped out from behind the curtain, Mr. Zuckerman rushed over to me. "Ah! Miss Hart! Are we ready?"

"Washed and pressed," I said smoothly, and he leaned in closer.

"Good, because we've got the big boss on set." Mr. Zuckerman glanced over his shoulder, and there, waiting in the darkness and watching with polite interest, I saw Mr. Reynolds.

My stomach took another tumble, and as Mr. Zuckerman retreated to shake Mr. Reynolds's hand, Jack drifted over to me.

"Hope you don't mind," he said. "Everyone's been raving about your performance, I thought you might like the opportunity to show Mr. Reynolds just what pony he bet on. I told him how unusual your methods are, like no one I've ever worked with. Guess he had to see for himself."

Meaning: *I told Mr. Reynolds you're an inexperienced idiot with no business starring in the biggest film of the year, and now he's wondering if he made a giant mistake believing in you.*

My boss watching. A crew waiting. An ass, hoping I'd fall flat on my face. And my whole future resting on my ability to speed-memorize the most difficult scene of my career. I'd had nightmares along these lines.

"Well then," I said with a smile. "Let's get started."

CHAPTER TWENTY-SIX
DECLAN

The last time we'd talked, Sam had given me an address for emergencies. I wasn't a hundred percent positive, but I thought "just leaped off a three-story building to escape Mulvey with a stolen clue in the case of Irma Van Pelt" counted as an emergency.

After I hit the ground, I rolled a few feet, my fingers closed around the photo. For a second, I panted on the sidewalk, catching my breath, before my jackhammer heart pushed me to my feet and toward the taxis on Hollywood Boulevard. I flagged one down and slid into the backseat, babbling Sam's address.

Even with the cool breeze streaming in through the window, I couldn't relax. Had I just come face-to-face with the man responsible for Irma Van Pelt's disappearance? Had Mulvey recognized me? And—Henrietta! Was she safe? I never should have left her alone, but when she reached for me, when I didn't stop her—it was like something had cracked inside me.

I'd stared down broken-nosed boxers, I'd thrown myself off speeding trains, I'd jumped from crashing cars, but looking into Henrietta's beautiful face was the first time I ever thought *Here's a thing that could break me.*

"This is it." The driver pulled to a stop, and I reached for my wallet. I'd never been to Los Angeles's quieter neighborhoods—Boyle Heights, this one was called, far removed from the shouting dazzle of Hollywood. This late on a weeknight, the sidewalks were mostly empty. I passed a Jewish delicatessen, a dusty dry goods shop, a music store displaying three honey-colored guitarróns, all their windows dark, and stopped in front of an apartment stoop, where two men in neat suits spoke to each other in Chinese. It reminded me of the Mission, where you couldn't go a block without hearing a dozen different languages, where the edges of everyone's family brushed up against each other, and I felt such a wave of homesickness that it made my knees weak. I'd lived in a city of false fronts for so long that I'd almost forgotten what it was like to be somewhere real.

"Declan?"

I turned around to see Sam, walking down the sidewalk with a bag of groceries in his arms. He said nothing, hurrying toward me, jerking his head at the stoop and the two men, who moved aside with accented "G'evening"s when Sam and I came near.

He stayed quiet until he'd gotten me up the stairs, into his apartment, and into a chair at his kitchen table, a glass of water in my shaking hand.

"What happened?"

In response, I slid the photo across the table. His eyebrows lifted and he dropped onto the seat opposite me.

"Is that...?"

There she was. Irma Van Pelt's single-dimple smile beamed from underneath a sun hat, her body tilted toward a man whose long arm stretched to hold the camera. I recognized the crying man's dark hair, beaky nose, dopey smile. They wore beach clothing—a polka-dotted suit for Irma, light-colored short sleeves for the man—and in the background, I could see sand, water, clear sky. Sam picked up the photograph and checked the back.

"Catalina Island, 1933." His eyes snapped to my face. "Explain."

I did the best I could. Sam, somehow, kept his expression still, until I got to the part about the roof, and then he gripped the edge of the table like he was about to slide onto the floor.

"You're all right?" He shook his head. "Of course you're all right. Jeez, kid—that's some armor you've got. Did Mulvey see you?"

"I don't know. It was dark, I was far away, but the moon's out tonight, and...I don't know. Maybe."

Sam thought for a second. "Nothing we can do about that now. More importantly—" He tapped the photo. "You said Mulvey called this guy Anderson? He didn't say anything else about Irma?"

"Just her name. And that he was sorry. When the other girl was passed out, he said this time she was going to be okay. *'This time.'*"

"You think he would talk?"

I saw in my mind the crumpled man, carrying around this photo of Miss Van Pelt, crying out apologies.

"I think he *needs* to talk."

"Anderson...No first name?" He sighed. "I don't know how many Andersons work at Silver Wing, but it's going to take a minute to track him down. The couch is yours, kid."

I was already getting to my feet, shaking my head, when Sam put a hand on my shoulder.

"I know you're made of steel, but you look about to collapse. And I'm not sending you home, where Mulvey might be looking for you. Get some sleep, call in sick for boyfriend duties, and let me track this Anderson down. All right?"

When I opened my mouth to protest, nothing came out, and I let Sam lead me over to his slouchy green couch. My eyes might've closed before my head even hit the pillow.

∽∽∽∽∽∽∽∽∽∽

I expected Silver Wing to kick up a fuss the next day when I told them I couldn't make it in. Instead, they said they'd cleared my and Henrietta's schedules after last night's party. My stomach flipped—had Mulvey said something to them?—and in a panic, I called home, reaching Pep just before he left for his mailroom job.

"No, no one stopped by for you. Why? Why didn't you come home? Don't tell me you had a late night with Miss Hart!"

"I gotta go," I said, quick. "Talk later." Sam came in as I set the phone back in its receiver. "Did you find him?"

In response, Sam held out a piece of paper. "You know how many Andersons there are in the Los Angeles area? I stopped counting at two hundred. Eight work at Silver Wing—two women, six men. We've got a carpenter, a driver, a cook in the commissary, an assistant editor, a janitor, and the head of the Research Department. Which one do you think's big enough to get protection from Silver Wing?" He handed me the paper.

"'Donald Anderson, head of Research. Burbank.'"

"Ready?"

I looked up and realized with surprise that we were going *right now*.

"This is it, isn't it?" I said, my words fast and urgent. "This is what you need. If Anderson talks, not just about what happened to Miss Van Pelt but about Reynolds, Mulvey, Silver Wing covering everything up...if he's willing to confess to federal agents, that's what we need, right? To stop it ever from happening again. We can find out what happened to all of them, to my mother."

191

The smile on Sam's face twitched with pity, just for a second, before he reached out to pat my shoulder.

"Let's just get out there."

Sam had a car, a long, low Buick the color of river mud, and as I slid into the passenger seat, he told me to get comfortable. Burbank sat on the other side of the Hollywood Hills, a long drive from Boyle Heights.

"There's talk of someday putting a highway right here," Sam said, his voice carefully casual as he pointed to the heart of his neighborhood, alive with people. "But they'll have to plow under all these houses first."

I nodded absently, my mind on the task ahead. Anderson would talk. He couldn't *stop* talking last night. He could probably tell us exactly what Mulvey did. Would he give us anything on Reynolds? Or was the head of Silver Wing too smart to handle anything personally? Maybe if we could get to Mulvey, pressure him with the might of the federal government...

"Are you listening?"

"What's that?" I said, snapping my head up. Sam must've moved on from highway construction. Both hands were gripping the steering wheel, his eyes on the road.

"I wanted to tell you. I've been looking into, well, that other thing."

I found it suddenly hard to breathe. I'd stopped asking for updates on Mam. Maybe part of me didn't want to know. Maybe it was better to believe that she was somewhere out there, living her life, instead of... well... another of Silver Wing's missing girls.

"What you told me—I confirmed all that. She worked at Silver Wing. Did a couple of bits in the chorus, and, sure enough, her final film was *A Gentleman's Pact*. I found a production note telling me the last day she worked: May 8, 1926. And I looked into Lloyd Rodger. Four days before your mother didn't show for work, he left for a charity gig in New York City and stayed away for weeks. He's cleared."

I stared at him, silent for so long that my next words came out sharp: "What else?"

Sam's hands tightened on the wheel. "Not much, kid. She'd paid up on the apartment till the end of the month, which makes me think she didn't stay in the city, but if she left, where'd she go? I checked San Francisco. Looked into other cities in California. Vaudeville theaters, traveling shows. Nothing. But she could've changed her name, gone farther."

"If she's alive," I said, my voice flat.

Sam didn't have an answer for that. He took a hand from the wheel and reached into his jacket pocket. I knew what it was before he held it out to me, but I still felt a kick of shock to see Mam's big, dark eyes.

"Take it," Sam said, when I didn't move. "It doesn't mean I'm giving up, all right? But you should have it back. It belongs with you."

Carefully, I held the photo between my fingertips.

"What if Lloyd Rodger—"

"Not him, kid. Not with your mother. I'm not saying he's a saint. You know, he's skipped town again? Not long after you roughed him up. I wanted to ask him more about Miriam Powell." He paused. "You *sure* Etta Hart didn't mention something, because I've been reading in the paper that she's been acting—"

"Henrietta doesn't know anything," I said, quick enough that Sam's eyebrows raised.

"Is that a fact?"

"She's the only one in this city, besides you and me, who actually cares about Miss Powell. And those reporters are worthless. They don't even bother getting to know the real her, they're just out to sell papers."

"Well, well! Has someone changed his tune on Miss Etta Hart?"

"What does that mean?"

Sam, a small smile on his face, shrugged. "I'm just saying. Last time we talked, you didn't seem too happy squiring her around. Nice to see a young man taking interest in his work."

"*You* told me to keep an eye on her. You told me she might be a target, and I'm just—"

"Aw, calm down, I didn't mean anything by it. You're doing good, kid, okay? You did good getting that photograph. If we can get a confession out of Anderson, even if Mulvey and Reynolds deny everything, that's huge. You want to make sure nothing happens to your starlet? This is how. Show Silver Wing they're protecting the wrong people."

I leaned my head against the seat, looking out my window as we wound through the Hollywood Hills. I should've been thinking about Mam, but it was Henrietta who popped into my head. Silver Wing would protect the star, Etta Hart—I was sure of that. But what if she stopped showing star potential? Did they care about the real girl?

"That's it."

The Buick rolled to a stop on a quiet, manicured street, far from the crowded apartment blocks of Boyle Heights and the busy, bustling, light-filled Hollywood Boulevard. It felt like we'd dropped onto another planet: wide, neat lawns like plush carpeting, bungalows painted pastel candy tones, a warm stillness to the air that made me think of playing children, happy families, security.

Sam and I climbed out of the car, our eyes on the house. Robin's-egg blue, empty driveway, dark windows.

"You police?"

We turned to see a man holding a pair of garden shears, standing on the front lawn of the house opposite Anderson's.

"What's that?" Sam asked.

"I called this morning," he said. "The fella on the phone said not to worry, but Don looked in rough shape, and I thought Annie might pass out. Then there was that man with 'em, helping them empty out their house and load it into the car. Big man, mean mug. Yelled at me when I came out to ask what'd happened."

Sam and I exchanged a look, and I turned back to stare at the house. I could see something now, caught on the bushes outside the front door, waving like a flag: a shirt?

"Did he say where they were going?" Sam asked. "When they'd return?"

"No clue. Annie told me to take the cat." He pointed to a window in his house, where a gray tabby sat in the sunshine. "Are you going in there? I didn't like the look of that man, practically pushed Annie into—"

But before he could tell us more, Sam pulled open his door and slid onto the seat. As the car rumbled to life, I got in next to him.

"What are you doing?" I asked. "What about the house?"

"Close the door," Sam said, and the second I did, we roared off, Sam's hands so tight on the wheel his knuckles turned white. "We're too late."

CHAPTER TWENTY-SEVEN
HENRIETTA

"Cut! And...wrap!" Mr. Zuckerman looked like I'd just bought him a pony. "That was wonderful! Excellent job, Miss Hart, truly!" He gave me a round of applause, the rest of the production joining in, and I smiled back, exhausted but buzzing.

I did it.

I didn't have to see the dailies—I'd felt it, all the way down to my stocking feet. Filming had started out rocky, my brain tap dancing to keep up, but then I noticed Jack watching me fumble with so much obvious glee that a tiny bomb exploded inside me. *I was going to nail this damn scene or DIE TRYING.*

Well, he wasn't grinning anymore. After applauding me like the cheering section of a funeral, he shoved his hands into his pockets and stomped off set, snapping at the makeup girl, "Can't you find someone else to bother!" Ooooooohhhh! Better than Christmas.

"Miss Hart?" Mr. Reynolds's owlish assistant appeared, blinking behind his round glasses. "Do you have a moment? Mr. Reynolds would like to speak with you."

Honestly, I'd forgotten he was there. He'd only watched the first few takes before popping back in the afternoon for another peek. By that time, though, I hadn't even noticed; the makeup girl had to point him out to me.

His assistant led me to the Swan Building and up to Mr. Reynolds's office. He was on the telephone at his famous white desk, the curved, clean lines evoking the studio's favorite animal. Quietly, the assistant ushered me to a couch in the corner, and when the door closed behind him, Mr. Reynolds set down the phone and looked over at me with a smile.

"Miss Hart. Welcome. Can I get you a drink?"

"I'm just fine."

He made his way to the bar cart, where he filled a tumbler with brown liquid.

It was early evening, not a ridiculous time for a drink, but the action made my nerves stand on edge as it hit me I was *alone,* in a *closed room,* with *the most powerful man in Hollywood.*

Every studio had its rumors, barely kept secrets about what went on behind closed doors. Sometimes they were laughed about, with eye rolls and good-natured *tsk*ing, secretaries complaining about the constant parade of chorus girls, "Always at three p.m., on the *dot*!" Other times the whispers took on an edge of warning: "If he asks you to meet alone, if he asks you to come to a hotel, if he visits your dressing room—get out."

Mr. Reynolds didn't have that same galaxy of rumors swirling about. He had a wife he famously adored and two doted-upon young daughters, but he also had a reputation for picking favorites, for making things happen, for getting what he wanted out of people.

What did he want out of me?

"Your performance today…" He came closer and my posture went rigid, but instead of sitting beside me, he dropped into a nearby armchair. "You did well."

I let out a breath in one quick rush, relieved.

"Oh! Thank you. I'm glad you liked it."

"You are going to do very well here." He paused to take a sip from his glass. "Now that *Train Car* is done, I'd like to put you in something else. Can you sing?"

"Maybe if I have a charitable audience. I can mouth words along with the best of them, though."

He smiled. "We'll work something out." Another pause, and he examined the beautiful cut glass in his hand. "You know, everywhere I look, I see people talking about 'glamor.' Actresses must be glamorous, films must be expensive, we must give people fantasy. I'm not so sure. This country still feels the pain of the Depression. I think people want humbler things. Kinder things. The fantasy they wish for isn't diamonds and furs but sweetness. Lightness. Joy. You have that, Miss Hart. I noticed it in you immediately. I'd hoped you would bring that same quality to *Train Car,* but what I saw today surprised even me." He set his glass on the table and leaned back in the seat, folding his hands in his lap.

"Miss Hart, I'd like you to see Silver Wing as your home. I believe we can guide your career to tremendous success, and I want you to be very, very happy here." He leaned forward, picking up a folder resting on the coffee table.

"Please take a look at this, and let me know if the terms are satisfactory."

I took the folder, flipped it open—and froze. The contract looked similar to what I'd signed a few weeks back, except for one huge difference: my salary had catapulted to two thousand dollars *a week.*

It was a star contract. A top-billing, featured-actress, all-the-perks *star contract.* This wasn't just "Gee, Henny sure did well in Hollywood," this was my second-grade teacher calling every single person in her address book to say *she KNEW Etta Hart!!!* Oh, lord, I was going to hit the floor.

"I— I don't— Is this *real*?" I clutched the paper just in case Mr. Reynolds said *no*. But he nodded.

"Of course, Miss Hart. I told you, we'd like you to be happy." He held out a pen, expensive-looking, dark wood, gold band. "If you turn to the last page, you'll see where to sign."

I grabbed the pen like a piece of candy, and then stopped, Ruby's voice in my ears—*DON'T SIGN ANYTHING YOU HAVEN'T READ YET!*

"That's a good point."

I blinked. Standing against Mr. Reynolds's chair, a woman in a slinky peach dress played with the strand of pearls around her neck.

"You really don't want to sign anything before you read it," she continued, and she let out a sigh. "Just ask me."

Mr. Reynolds hadn't moved, and I stared down at the paper, my heart beating fast.

"Hel-*lo!* Don't you listen?" The girl spoke again, her voice a gravelly threat. "Don't sign that contract."

"Especially from *him*." Out of the corner of my eye, I saw another girl sitting beside me on the couch. She wore a simple drop-waisted dress in a tea-colored crepe, and she stared at Mr. Reynolds, her face twisted in disgust. "Don't trust anything he says."

"Miss Hart?" Mr. Reynolds leaned forward. "Is anything wrong?"

"Yeah, you're a sneaky, slimy jackass," the girl in peach said, and as she fluffed up her candy-floss-blond hair, I recognized her as the girl from my dressing room, going on about Howard Abner.

"I, um, I'm just…Would it be all right to have a day or two?" I asked. "My sister's a lawyer, and she'd want me to run this past her."

"I don't think that will be necessary," Mr. Reynolds said smoothly. "We design our contracts to be to our stars' benefit—"

"*Li*-ar!" Another girl had appeared, her copper hair formed into perfect finger waves, singing out her words in a braying accent.

"—and there's no reason to assume the terms wouldn't be in your favor. We'd like to take care of you, Miss Hart."

"Like you took care of *me*?" In a sudden gust of wind, another woman blew through the room, rushing at Mr. Reynolds as though she wanted to shred him to pieces, and I jumped, covering it up as best I could with a cough. The woman moved fast, whirling like a tempest, but I could see she wore something red, her short, severe bob whipping in dark twists as she screamed, "Remember how you took care of me?! Remember?!"

"Ah, I think actually I would like something to drink," I said, my voice high, the woman's endless keening like a needle in my ears. "Soda water?"

Mr. Reynolds, after a moment, rose to his feet. "Of course."

As he turned to the bar, the girl in the crepe dress began whispering.

"*You need to get out, you need to run, far away, don't believe a word he says, get away from him, go, go—*"

"Ice?"

The sound of a *splash* made me look up, thinking he'd spilled, but instead I saw another girl, sandy-haired, a single dimple in one cheek, water running in endless rivulets down her body, plastering her clothes to her skin. She was muttering something to him, spitting out words, but they were hard to make out over the endless *drip, splatter, trickle*.

"Miss Hart?"

"Oh! Y-yes, please. Thank you."

With his attention on the ice bucket, I dropped my head into my hands, rubbing hard at my temples, as though that could block out the girls' voices:

"—why don't you just—"

"—remember what you said to me? Back then? I—"

"—never should have trusted—"

"Miss Hart? Your drink."

I looked up—and gasped. At least a dozen other spirits had appeared, filling the room. Blond, brunette, pale, dark, tall, thin, but all of them young women, all of them circling Mr. Reynolds like wolves, their voices a quiet buzz. A woman with beautiful, full cheeks and skin that glowed a rich, deep brown stood in front of Mr. Reynolds, opening her mouth so wide I could see the fine pearls of her teeth, the pink of her tongue, but when I braced myself for her scream, no sound came out, her face clenched in tortured silence.

"Miss Hart? Are you all right?"

"Why didn't you ever ask *me* that! You *threw me away*!" The girl in red reappeared, swirling around Mr. Reynolds, and now I could see I was wrong—she wasn't dressed in red but covered in—my stomach turned—covered in *blood*. Drenching her, washing her, falling over her body in a continual stream so that it looked as though she wore a crimson gown.

The edges of my vision went grainy-gray, and I gripped the corner of the couch.

"I'm so sorry, Mr. Reynolds," I said, wincing—the girl in red seemed to have set off the rest of them, all of them but the round-cheeked girl shouting, screaming, their voices rising in a din of anger. "I don't feel well. I'll have to—" But I couldn't get anything else out, I clutched the file and ran from the room, my head spinning, and didn't stop until I'd made it through the front door, out to the night, where I panted for breath.

"You."

I gasped as the girl in the crepe dress appeared, staring at me with serious eyes, her Cupid's-bow lips pressed in a line.

"You can see us?" She sounded confused, but it was mixed with hope, as though she'd long ago given up on getting anyone's attention. I swallowed my trembling fear and stood up straighter. I nodded.

"Why?"

There was no one around, but I still whispered. "I don't know. Maybe to help you."

The words came out before I knew what I said—Midge had popped into my head, my promise to her—and the girl didn't seem to be expecting this response, either. Her eyebrows lifted and the quiver of air around her took on a heightened thrum. She drifted closer to me, so close I could see her smooth, cool skin, her huge dark eyes.

"Find Fay," she said to me, starting to disappear. "Fay Fairfax. If you want to help, find Fay."

CHAPTER TWENTY-EIGHT
DECLAN

When Sam dropped me off, I wandered up to my apartment in a daze. Inside was quiet, dark, and I lay down on my cot, took out the photo of Mam, and ran my fingertips along the edges.

Where had Anderson gone? What had Mulvey done to him? We'd been so close to getting some answers! Now what could we do?

Hours later, the door opened and Pep walked in, humming, a greasy paper bag in one hand. I stood up, still in the dark, and he jumped and then laughed, turning on the lights.

"Duke! You scared the stuffing out of me! Where've *you* been?" He had his manager face on, but I had eyes only for his leftovers. As if on cue, my stomach let out a grumble, and Pep sighed before tossing the bag onto the table.

"Try to taste the food before you swallow it," he said as I sat down and tore it open. Steak, baked potatoes, even a couple pats of butter. "Cost me three dollars with drinks."

"Must be some girl." I glanced up at him as he slid into the seat across from me.

"Eh, I don't know about that, but she works in the Swan Building. She's got connections—and the best gossip. For instance..." He leaned forward and I paused, looking up at him. "Apparently, last night, Mr. Mulvey got attacked by someone who then jumped off a three-story roof."

The steak went dry in my mouth, and I swallowed it in a thick lump. Pep's expression was unreadable as he watched me carefully.

"Huh," I said.

"Mulvey spent today calling hospitals, asking if anyone came in with broken legs. Told Louise to make a list of working acrobats and stunt men."

"...*Huh.*"

"Duke. You wouldn't happen to know anything about this, would you?"

"Uhhhmm."

"Declan!" Pep threw his arms up in the air, letting out an exasperated sigh. "What the hell were you thinking?! You *attacked* Mulvey?"

"I didn't! I didn't attack anybody!"

"What happened, then? Louise said she'd never seen him so angry, and I gotta believe a man like Mulvey's not afraid to show off his temper."

He was frowning at me with disappointment, and I didn't know what to say. But then he put a hand on my arm and stared into my eyes, the look on his face melting to worry.

"First you go after Lloyd Rodger. Now Mr. Mulvey? This isn't like you, Duke. You must have a good reason. What is it? You can tell me."

For the first time in a long while, I looked across the table and saw Pep. Not my hard-nosed manager, scolding me to behave, but my friend, the kid I'd grown up with. What was I doing thinking I couldn't trust him? Shakily, I let out a sigh.

"Pep...Silver Wing is...covering up crimes. There are girls, actresses, going missing—for years—and instead of looking into it, instead of protecting the girls or making sure it doesn't happen again, Silver

Wing—Reynolds, and Mulvey makes it happen—they're sweeping it under the rug. They're making sure the men responsible get away with it, and last night, I'm pretty sure I found one of those men. I found proof he knew a missing girl, and Mulvey tried to get it away from me. We were on the patio roof at the Roosevelt Hotel, and...I jumped."

Pep stared at me, not blinking, and then he shook his head.

"I don't...You say Mr. Mulvey's involved in this? Mr. Reynolds knows, too?"

"Pep, I'm pretty sure it's all Reynolds's doing. You remember you told me he hired Mulvey to get things done? *These* are the things he's doing."

Stunned, Pep wouldn't quit shaking his head. "No, you must be— Mr. Mulvey wouldn't— And *Mr. Reynolds*? But I don't understand—what does this have to do with you?"

I'd tucked Mam's photo into my pocket when Pep had come home; now I pulled it out. "My mother was one of those missing girls. She worked at Silver Wing. She went to set, disappeared, no one ever heard from her again. Maybe she's dead—" The word got broken up, and I swallowed hard, blinking away tears. "And maybe somebody is responsible. I thought it was Lloyd Rodger, but now...I don't know...And Silver Wing is the reason I don't know."

Pep hadn't stopped staring at the photo of Mam, his thick eyebrows knit together in a frown.

"When'd she disappear?" he asked.

"Nineteen twenty-six. May 8, 1926."

Pep's head snapped up, his expression wild, and then he shook his head again. "No. No, you have it wrong."

"Wrong? What are you—"

"She didn't disappear, not in 1926."

205

"I know what you're thinking," I started, irritation prickling my skin. "It's pathetic, me looking for her, but—"

"That's not what I mean. I don't know where you got this idea from, that she never came back for you because someone did something to her. But Duke. Declan." He bit his lip, seeming to be pulling free something buried deep.

"Years ago, back home, I was in the kitchen when the phone rang. Mamá answered... It was her. Your mother."

I stared at him, the words not coming.

"I don't know how she got our number," Pep continued. "Maybe she wrote to the Home. Mamá had told them she'd take you in. But she called and—Mamá's English, you know, she didn't like speaking to no gringa, especially not over the telephone. She had me do it."

"You talked to her? You talked to my mother?" The shock soured quickly into anger. "You never told me!"

Pep's expression was pained. "It wasn't anything you'd want to hear. She asked me if you were living there. I told her yes. She asked if you were happy. I said yes. She asked if you ever talked about your mother. What was I going to say?" He lifted his hands, helpless. "I told her no. Never. She was quiet for a while after that. Asked again if you were happy, if you had clothes to wear, food to eat, if you went to school. I told her yes, yes, all those things, my mother took good care of you. She asked me who I was, and I told her: *I'm his best friend.* I told her I took care of you, too."

I felt my throat squeeze around a lump, blocking any sound from coming out.

"I asked if she was going to come get you. She said no. She said I shouldn't tell you she called. She said she would send money, and she told me to keep taking care of you. That was it, Duke. I don't know if she sent anything or if she ever called again." His frown tilted as he studied me. "We were twelve. Nineteen twenty-seven. We got the phone that summer, remember?" He paused. "If I knew how much this ate at you, I would've told you a long time ago. You never talked about her. I figured, why bring it up? She left, and she didn't come back. But it wasn't because someone stopped her. And it wasn't because of Silver Wing."

I felt the words hang in the air, like smoke. They wrapped around me, I breathed them in, my head light and empty. Carefully, Pep touched my arm again.

"I'm sorry, Duke," he said, his voice soft. "You had it wrong about Mr. Reynolds and Mr. Mulvey. They're good people, all right? They care about their employees. You saw what Mr. Mulvey almost did to you when you went after Lloyd Rodger. You think they'd let anything happen to a Silver Wing star? I know what they say about Mr. Mulvey, that he's a hard character, and I believe it—but everything he does, everything Mr. Reynolds asks him to do, it's to protect the studio."

Now I was shaking my head. "No, no, it's not just Mam. Pep, there are other girls out there, missing girls, and I'm worried—"

"Did Etta Hart put you up to this?"

I stared at him. "Henrietta? Why would you ask that?"

"I see what they say in the papers about her," Pep said with a shrug. "Acting funny on set, throwing herself at anyone to get a part. And I hear what you say about her, stuck-up, spoiled, coldhearted."

"*No.* Pep, the papers aren't— And I'm not— Why are you even bringing her up?"

"I'm worried. What if she's using you? Filling your head with stories about missing girls to make you worried about her? You got all worked up by that director in Mr. Mulvey's office. She wouldn't be the first actress to

207

cook up some story about being threatened to get sympathy. But I thought you'd be smart enough to see through it."

"What...Threatened? What are you talking about?"

Pep had a look on his face like he wasn't sure how much he wanted to say, but finally, he shrugged.

"I didn't want to tell you when it happened. Seemed like a whole lot of nothing. I heard it from the girls who answer the fan mail. A few days ago, this weird letter comes in for Etta Hart. They were talking about it, and when I asked they said they'd told Mr. Mulvey and he said it wasn't anything to worry about, that it was probably a hoax."

"Pep—you're not making any sense. *What* letter?"

"I told you, it was a letter that came in with Etta Hart's name on it. Some threat. 'Quit acting or...' You know, something like that."

Cold prickles ran down the back of my neck. "Someone threatened Henrietta? Who?"

"That's just what I'm saying, Duke. The letter wasn't signed, but Mr. Reynolds told the girls not to worry about it. The way it was written, it had to be a hoax, and the girls all figured that Etta Hart had written it herself, try to drum up sympathy, distract from her bad news. What I'm saying, Duke, is if she's trying to convince you there's some big conspiracy going on at Silver Wing, if she's the one who's getting you into trouble, then you need to—"

"What did it say?" I asked, my voice brittle, and when Pep blinked at me, I said, "'The way it was written.' Something about it proved it was a hoax? *What did it say?*"

He shook his head, annoyed, it seemed, but his words had made me go cold. A threat to Henrietta, and something about it made Mulvey not want to investigate...

"That was the weirdest thing," Pep said. "It mentioned this actress who was a friend of Etta Hart's—and nothing even happened to her! She just went home to her family! Some threat, really, it's—"

"*Pep.*"

He stared at me. "It said something like…'You better—' No, it was 'Get out of Hollywood, or end up just like Miriam Powell.'"

CHAPTER TWENTY-NINE
HENRIETTA

Fay...Fay...Fay...

The girl's voice echoed in my head, *Fay Fairfax. If you want to help, find Fay...*

I hadn't realized I'd fallen asleep on my sofa, a telephone directory open on my chest, until a bang rocketed through my suite so loud that my scrambled Midwestern brain panicked— *Earthquake!*

BANG! BANG!

"Henrietta!"

I blinked at my front door.

"Henrietta!"

"D-Declan?" Another bang on the door and I jumped to my feet, the telephone directory sliding to the floor. "Hold on!"

I snatched up my robe and threw it over my shoulders as I stumbled in bare feet to the door. There was Declan, eyes wild, sweaty hair hanging across his forehead, gasping for air.

"You're all right!" he said, looking me up and down. "Are you all right?"

"Is the hotel on fire? Yes, I'm all right!" I said, ushering him in and closing the door. "What's the matter with you? Did you run here?"

"Did anyone else try to get in?" He searched around the suite, and I tightened my hold on the neck of my robe.

"It's"—I squinted at the clock on the far wall—"almost three in the morning! How much socializing do you think I *do*?"

For the first time, he seemed to look at me properly, and my annoyance disappeared; he stared at me like something precious just rescued from the edge of disaster.

"What is it?" My words came out in a whisper. "Sit down."

He collapsed onto the sofa, but his nervous energy couldn't stop him from twitching, the muscles in his arms—bare underneath rolled-up shirtsleeves—tense and shimmering with sweat. One foot jangled, bouncing a knee. He looked about ready to jump out of his skin.

"What's wrong?"

He didn't answer at first, rubbing a hand down his face, and then he took a long breath.

"I...I haven't been totally honest."

My heart gave a strangled leap, my thoughts flying to what he might say next—he was secret royalty, an informant for the gossip columnists, his heart belonged to another girl and he needed to end our sham relationship for good.

"I'm working with a private investigator to find out what happened to Miriam Powell."

I stared at him, waiting for the punch line, but he swallowed and kept going.

"There's...more. You might want to sit down."

More? As if on command, my knees went wobbly. Declan tipped a chair toward me, and I grabbed onto it before dropping into the seat.

"Henrietta." Declan leaned forward, his voice quiet. "I think someone hurt Miriam Powell. I think she's dead."

The air seemed to have the charged quality of a lightning storm, white noise rushing in my ears like radio static. When my vision cleared, I saw Midge, standing just behind Declan's shoulder, staring at us both in stony-faced silence.

"I know." It came out before I could stop myself, and now it was Declan's turn to stare at me.

"What do you mean? How do you know?"

Yes, Henny, how? I wondered, and as I searched for some way to explain myself, Midge drifted closer. Declan didn't seem to notice her, not even when she floated to his side, studying him. After a moment, she gave me a nod.

"Because...because she's sitting right next to you," I said, throwing up my hands helplessly. "Look, I know how it sounds! I can't explain it. All I can tell you is I've seen Midge, since she went missing, and she told me she was dead. That's all she knows. She's dead."

While I spoke, Declan's mouth moved soundlessly, as though he'd forgotten the necessary components of speech, but he pulled himself together to stutter out, "Y-you...can see...*ghosts*?" He shook his head. "Henrietta, ghosts aren't real! That's not— What you're saying doesn't make any—" The color drained from his cheeks as Midge laid a hand on his arm. He went so still, I thought he might've forgotten how to breathe.

"That's her. She's touching your right arm now." I made a hesitant move toward him. "Um. Do you need—I know it's a lot—"

He jumped to his feet so fast that I almost lost my balance, and as he paced around the sitting room, he rubbed at the spot where Midge had touched him.

"Henrietta, this doesn't make any— It can't— How can—" He stopped, one hand gripping his forearm, so terribly pale I wondered if I should be ready to catch him, even though he'd probably flatten me. Anxiously, I reached for a pillow. "Ghosts aren't real!"

"I know! I...don't know. I told you, I can't explain it. It started when I got to Los Angeles. At first, I didn't realize what was happening, and then I thought...I thought I was losing my mind, Declan, and honestly, I'm not convinced I'm *not* crazy. All I can tell you," I said, throwing up my hands, "is I see them. Girls. Women. They appear to me, they talk to me...They're like Midge, I think. Actresses, missing. Dead." I hadn't gotten used to saying that word, and my gaze jumped to Midge, sitting on the couch. I didn't think she'd gotten used to it, either.

"What do you mean, you've seen more? Why do you say they're actresses?"

"I'm just guessing. They've appeared to me at the studio, and they say things about the picture business, and they just, I don't know, *look* like actresses! Long glamorous dresses, and there's this one girl, dark eyes, straight out of the silent pictures, and another girl with a dimple in one cheek, she's always— What is it? Are you going to faint?! Sit down!" I said, leaping to my feet, pillow clutched between my hands, because Declan had gotten the oddest look on his face. He reached into his pockets and started turning out coins, keys, bits of paper, until he found a small, square photograph.

"That her?"

I set down the pillow and took the photo between my fingertips. It was too dim to see properly, and as I brought it over to the lamp, a gasp slipped out from between my lips. There she was, the girl with one dimple, young and full of life, laughing with a man who gave her a foolish, smitten smile. I glanced over at Declan, and Midge, and—there she was, of course, the girl in the photo.

Both times I'd seen her, she'd stood in her own never-ending puddle, rivulets streaming down her body, the stink of rot heavy in the air, but right now she looked like the girl in the photo, barefoot in a pretty flower-patterned summer dress, sandy hair gently waving around her face.

"Catalina," the girl said, her voice dull and far away, looking at the photo, and when I peered down at it again I noticed the bathing suit, the distant ocean. "We went out there for my birthday last summer. Me and Donald. An executive. Married, of course, and of course he said exactly what I wanted to hear. 'Oh, we don't live together anymore,' 'Oh, I don't love her, I love *you*, you dummy.' Tack those lies right up next to 'I've got a picture I want you to star in' and 'Baby, you'll be famous.'"

When she went quiet, Midge gave her a small nudge. "Tell her your name."

The girl stared at Midge in angry surprise, like she couldn't imagine why Midge would be so cruel.

"Why bother? I could scream it, and she wouldn't—" We locked eyes, and her shock turned into recognition. "That was *you*—at the dressing rooms, and in Reynolds's office. *You* pulled me there—how? How can you see me?"

Midge quietly repeated: "Your name."

The girl glanced at Midge, then back at me. "It's...Irma. My name's Irma Van Pelt."

The name rang a bell. A memory of Sunday dinner in Chicago, my sister Ruby shaking a newspaper and warning me about a girl gone missing, frantic parents.

"Irma…," I said, surprised to find my eyes welling with tears. I felt Declan by my side, taking back the photo.

"How did you know that?"

I threw my hand vaguely toward the spot where Irma stood and let out a small laugh. "She just told me, of course."

Declan turned and stared at what for him must have been absolutely nothing. I saw Irma Van Pelt glare back, eyes narrowed.

"What does *he* want?" she asked. "Where did he get that picture?"

"I'm not sure," I said.

"Are you…" Declan sounded like he couldn't believe what he was saying. "Are you…talking…to her?"

"Them. Midge and Irma. They're right there." I pointed again at the two girls, holding hands now, and Declan looked down at the floor, shaking his head.

"I don't see anything."

"Of course not," Irma grumbled. "As soon as a fella can't get his hands on us, we're just worthless nothings."

"Hey, be nice," I said to her. "He wants to help." I glanced at him. "You *do* want to help, right? That's why you have Irma's photo?"

Declan's head swiveled around as he tried to make sense, and, letting out a short, exasperated breath, he threw his hands up in the air. "I don't understand this, none of this. But…yeah. I'm trying to help. Irma. Miriam. Anybody else. I want to know what happened to them."

Irma snorted a laugh. "Oh, I can tell you that."

I looked at her in surprise. "You can? Midge can't remember—isn't that right?"

Midge shook her head. "My last memory is from the night before you visited me on the set, Henny. Everything else is…black."

Irma let out a coo of sympathy. "Poor dear. It can take a while, remembering, and it's a terrible shock. I thought it'd tear me in two when it all came back to me."

"What's happening?" Declan asked, trying to look where the girls stood but missing them by a good foot.

"Irma says—I think—that...she can— You *do* remember...? How you—died?" It felt so impolite to ask. Emily Post hadn't prepared me for the proper way to speak with the dead, but Irma didn't seem to mind.

"It was on Donald's boat. He wanted to break things off, gave me too much to drink, and the next thing I know, I'm back on the studio lot with a whopper of a headache, only no one can see me or hear me, even if I screech right into their faces. Took a minute to figure out I was dead."

"Did he...did he do it?" The words came out in a whisper, and Irma gave me a look like *I thought you heard what I just said.*

"We argued. He pushed me away. I slipped. He didn't go in after me." She lifted her shoulders in an impatient shrug. "What a hero, huh?"

"What did she say?" Declan asked, and when I repeated it back to him, he nodded. "Mulvey hustled Anderson and his wife out of town. Can you ask if she has any idea where he might've gone—"

But Irma had started talking over him: "Look at that handsome dum-dum, thinkin' he can help. What does it matter if I tell him anything? Police don't care. Papers don't care. The district attorney's practically on the Silver Wing payroll."

"Henrietta?" Declan asked.

"She, um, she's not sure how you can help her," I said, as delicately as I could. Who would've thought speaking for the dead could get so complicated? "She says no one cares about the truth."

"Well, I care," Declan said, and Irma let out a laugh that I was glad he

216

couldn't hear. "The man I'm working with, the private detective—he cares, too. He got fired from the police for looking into this. And if Irma Van Pelt can hear me," he began, raising his eyes to the ceiling—Irma huffed and said in a singsong, "Over *he-re!*"—"I want her to know that she's the reason we're seeing it through. It's her parents who contacted Sam. They're not giving up. Neither are we."

Irma made a sound of surprise, the bluff and bravado fading away, her features blurring until she appeared years younger, a girl with bright eyes, round cheeks, less the hardened Hollywood actress and more the girl who must've kissed her family goodbye before getting on the train.

Midge put her arm around Irma's shoulder, but Irma seemed to grow fuzzy along the edges. A sharp taste of metal filled the air, and a moment later, she'd disappeared, leaving Midge holding nothing.

"Where did she...," I asked, and Midge shook her head.

"When we think about what happened to us... Or our families... The people we miss the most... They feel so far away..."

A look of sadness came over her as she paused, and I said, alarmed, "Midge? Are *you* all right?"

"It's so...strange," she said at last. "I don't know why I'm still here. It's almost as though... As though you've left home, only you're convinced you forgot to turn off the oven, and you're certain your rooms are filling with gas, and you can't stop thinking about it, wherever you are, whatever you're doing... There's a part of you that just can't let go, because you're afraid something terrible will happen...

"Henny, I feel like I want something. No... *Need* something. That's why I'm stuck here, why I can't let go. I thought maybe it was... to know... But Irma knows, and she's still here, and the other girls are, too. Why are we *stuck* here?"

"I don't know, darling," I said, and when I looked over at Declan, wondering why he hadn't interrupted, I saw him studying me with intensity, careful not to talk over anything I might be hearing.

"I think…," Midge said, more to herself than to me, it seemed, "it's not enough for me to know what happened. I need *everyone* to know. They hid the truth, didn't they, Henny? I just can't let it go. They want everyone to forget about me. Henny, they…buried me."

"Maybe so," I said, and I wished I could hold on to her hand and give it a hard squeeze. "But darling: buried things can grow."

CHAPTER THIRTY
DECLAN

My mind spun:

> Ghosts weren't real
>
> Talking to ghosts was crazy
>
> Henrietta must be losing her mind
>
> But then how did she know about Irma?
>
> None of this was possible

As impossible as... a boy who couldn't be broken?

"Irma's right," Henrietta said, after a moment of silence. "If no one in this city will listen to us, how can we help?"

"The man I'm working with, the private investigator, he has connections to the Motion Picture Review Board."

"Them?" Henrietta wrinkled her nose. "What could they possibly do?"

"They're part of the federal government, which wouldn't be too happy to hear that the picture industry is covering up crimes to stay in business. If Miss Powell could tell me—"

"She says to call her Midge," Henrietta interrupted. "She says only people at the studio ever called her Miss Powell or Miriam."

"All right," I said, feeling…well…pretty weird to be on familiar terms with a ghost. "You said Midge can't remember what happened. But—Midge?"

"She says she can hear you."

I didn't know where to look and just kept my eyes moving, hoping Midge understood. "Midge, did anyone threaten you? Anyone you worked with?"

A pause, and then Henrietta said, "She's not sure. She says Lloyd Rodger was no picnic, lost his temper a bunch, but she doesn't think he hurt her—she was never alone with him. Oh, Midge! What about that man, the night we met, at the ranch?" Her mouth twisted into a frown as she listened before turning to me. "He was a producer, promised to help her with her career and then cornered her at some Silver Wing party, but she says if you want the name of any man who made a pass at her, you're going to need to sit down. I hate to say it, but she's right. I think I could fill a phone book."

Her words made my chest ache. "About that…," I started, and Henrietta's eyes went wide, like she'd just remembered I'd crashed into her apartment, breathless and terrified.

"About…what?" Her voice came out small, scared.

"A letter came in for you. Unsigned. Not really a letter…a threat. And it mentioned Midge, which makes me think the person who sent it to you also knows what happened to her. Is there anyone who might've had a grudge against both of you?"

"I…can't think…" Henrietta turned and locked eyes with nothing, and then a moment later her shoulders slumped. "I don't understand. Who would want to hurt *me*?"

What Pep had told me, about how Mulvey had dismissed the letter so quickly, floated through my mind. If Mulvey ignored the letter because he believed Henrietta had written it herself, not even Silver Wing would protect her right now.

It was hard to look at her. She seemed so fragile, skin that could bruise, bones that could break. I thought of her slipping away, like Midge, like Irma Van Pelt...I wanted to pull her close. I wanted to hold her. I wanted to find the person who meant to hurt her and tear them to pieces.

I cleared my throat and got to my feet. "All right. I'll tell Sam—the P.I.—about all this. Not the ghosts. Sam's a good guy but something tells me he wouldn't be able to swallow that. But I can tell him about Irma, and your letter, Henrietta. Maybe he has some ideas." I shook my head. "I'm sorry. I wish I had more. But we—"

"Fay Fairfax," Henrietta said, and I blinked at her and then looked around.

"Another...ghost?"

"No. One of the girls, the ingenue with the long curls, she told me if I wanted to help, I needed to find Fay Fairfax. Only, I looked in the book, and I can't find her anywhere." She gestured to the telephone directory splayed out on the floor. "I spent all night combing through the *F*'s, just in case I heard wrong. Nothing. It's driving me absolutely crazy. I *know* I've heard her name before, somewhere, only I can't think where!"

"All right," I said with a nod. "I'll ask Sam, and—" I broke off as Henrietta's clock chimed three, and she grimaced.

"I hate to break up the party, but I need to get some sleep—I've got another promotional shoot for *Train Car*, bright and early." She paused, looking over at Midge. "Yes," she said, her voice soft. "I will."

Something in the air shifted, some subtle change in temperature or feeling or electricity, and I looked around.

"Did Midge...go?"

Henrietta gave me an impressed look. "Could you feel that?"

"I'm...not sure. This is..."

"Believe me, I know."

She bent down, sweeping up everything I'd pulled from my pockets, and as I realized she was sending me on my way, I panicked. She was still in danger. There was someone after her. The thought of leaving her alone, right now—

"Is this another girl? I've never seen her before." She'd stood up, frowning at— My heart gave a strangled leap, and I snatched Mam's photo out of her hand.

"No, that's not— She's not—" I shoved it into my pocket, then grabbed my other things from her hands. Immediately, I felt like a jerk, and I braced myself for some of her patented indignation, but when I glanced over at her, I saw her cheeks were pink.

"Sorry," we said, both of us, at the same time, and then there was a second of quiet before we started up again.

"I shouldn't've—"

"I understand, it's private, it's not—"

"—not what you think, I—"

"—don't have to explain—"

"I can—" I began, but I broke off when I heard Henrietta finish, "your girlfriend."

"My—what?"

"It's fine!" Henrietta said. "I mean, this must be uncomfortable, and you've been, well, I can't believe I'm saying this, but you've been a real gentleman, all things considered, and—"

"*What* are you talking about?"

Henrietta fluttered her hands. "Us! I mean, this *thing* the studio forced us into. I knew you weren't a fan, but I didn't realize it was because, well…you're in love with someone else."

After everything I'd heard today, *this* was the thing that made my jaw truly *drop*. What in the hell was the starlet getting at? Before I could say anything, she jumped in.

"I'm not upset about it, of course! It's actually sort of…nice. Romantic, I guess," she said, although she sounded unsure. "That's the girl you were talking about on the fire escape, right?" She gestured to my pocket, Mam's photo. "The girl you're looking for? You love her, don't you?"

I didn't know how to answer. "She…She's…"

"It's fine," Henrietta repeated, and before I could come out and say it—*She's my mother, and I haven't seen her in a decade*—she added, "It's not like she has to worry I'm out to steal her fella!" She let out a laugh while my eyebrows raised.

"I was thinking I should ask them about it, anyway, even before…I mean, it makes sense—"

"Nothing you're saying now makes sense," I said, and Henrietta went pink.

"Well. Ending things."

"Ending…What things?"

"You know. *Us.*"

"Us?"

She wasn't looking at me, her eyes darting from her toes to the walls to the table to the window. "Well, it's crazy, when you think about it, right? You, forced into a relationship when you're in love with someone else. It's not fair, to you, or to her. I know it's not real, and we don't *really* care about each other…"

We don't? I thought, wondering if I would have rushed out in the middle of the night for a girl I didn't really care about.

"Um. Oh."

"I'll go to the studio and I'll tell them we're done. After those rumors about my behavior in the Blossom Room, I've been benched until *Train Car*'s premiere next month. I bet they'll let us call everything off after that. You'll be released," she said with a laugh.

Her words took so many turns that at first, I could only stand in silence, trying to follow along. Henrietta thought the girl I'd come to Hollywood to find, the girl I was looking for, was my long-lost love?

"Just imagine!" She had a smile on her face, and she reached over to cuff me on the shoulder. "No more late nights stuck with me, no more photo shoots, no more interviews. Freedom!" She paused, her smile slipping. "Unless...That is what you want, right?"

What could I say?

No, you had it all wrong. That woman is my mother, I'm not in love with anyone, and I know I've been complaining about you and this fake romance for weeks, but...I was wrong about that, and you, because you're not some spoiled brat—you're smart, and tough, and you care about your friend, and you care about these girls, like no one else in this city seems to. And I'm worried about you, and I'm sort of amazed by you, and I know someday soon everyone is going to realize what a star you really are and you're going to go on to fame and fortune and leave me behind, and you'll never think about me again and...that breaks my heart. But it's clear you don't feel the same way, so...

"Uhhhmm, yeah. Yeah, sure. That...sounds good."

Henrietta gave a nod, her smile growing stiff. "Well. Wherever she is, I hope she knows how lucky she is to have you looking for her."

"Henrietta...," I started, because I'd realized this was ridiculous, she should know there wasn't any other girl, but she cut me off, walking over to her door and throwing it open.

"I'm *so* sorry, I really need to get some rest. We'll see each other soon, all right?"

I didn't know how to turn things around.

"All...right." I walked to the door. How was I going to say goodbye? How could I acknowledge the strangeness of this whole night, how everything seemed to have changed? As usual, Henrietta saved the day.

"Thank you," she said, pulling me in for a hug. We were always touching, and part of me had gotten used to this girl's weight, the smell of her perfume, the tickle of her curls against my neck, but as she pulled away, I realized these touches were numbered, and there was going to be a day, not too far in the future, when I'd never hold her again.

"Thank you for what?"

Her mouth quirked in that smile she only showed off camera, a mix of delight and teasing and scolding.

"For making sure I wasn't dead tonight," she said. "For wanting to help my friend. For caring."

"Doesn't seem like much of an achievement, any of those things," I said, and she shrugged, leaning on the door.

"Then...I guess you've got more to do."

CHAPTER THIRTY-ONE
HENRIETTA

I'd spent so many of the past few weeks fantasizing about a good, long stretch with absolutely nothing to do, and now here I was, climbing the walls of my dreamy hotel suite, no movie to film, no dates with Declan, nowhere to go, nowhere to be, the looming fear that *someone was out to get me,* and no one but a rotating cast of dead girls to keep me company.

It seemed like Silver Wing had put me on ice. After the excitement of Declan's middle-of-the-night visit, I'd completely forgotten I owed Mr. Reynolds an answer about my new contract. He called me into his office the following evening and asked if this was a negotiation tactic. Honestly, every time I thought about that contract, my stomach seemed to fill simultaneously with rainbow bubbles and lead. It was everything I'd ever wanted, but it would tie me to Silver Wing...and whatever they were hiding. Sweating bullets and praying I'd avoid another onslaught of dead actresses, I told him I was so sorry, I just didn't feel right signing anything that big before my first picture premiered.

Mr. Reynolds simply shrugged. "In that case, we'll wait, and we'll see if we need to make any adjustments to our offer. Perhaps we'd better hold off on putting you on another film as well."

It was amazing. His expression hadn't changed, his tone stayed neutral, but I could see a flash of the frighteningly intelligent, determined man who had set off those wronged girls. When he blinked at me, coolly, behind his round glasses, I couldn't get out of there fast enough.

I'd hoped to put my contract out of my mind, only somehow the vultures at the movie magazines had gotten wind of the offer—and my indecision. They tossed around countless theories—I really *had* lost my mind, I was on the verge of a nervous breakdown, I was looking to get an even bigger offer from a rival studio—and even though none of them had a shred of truth, it turned my relationship with Silver Wing downright chilly. No more photo shoots, no interviews, no classes, the bare minimum for promotional events—it seemed Mr. Reynolds wanted to remind me just how empty and dull my life would be without Silver Wing.

Not that I was entirely unhappy to stay away from the lot, now I knew about that threat. Midge and I had compared notes, trying to see if we shared any enemies—Fitch had jumped to mind, and Jack was still acting like a sour prig, but it was no good. She said she couldn't remember meeting either one of them and couldn't think of anyone who'd want her dead.

I'd planned on passing this information to Declan next time I saw him, but the studio had canceled our outings as well, although I was to blame for that. True to my word, I spoke with the publicity department about ending things. Who cared if the studio threw a fit! His heart belonged to someone else. I'd refuse to keep it up, no more fake dates, no more kisses for the camera—but to my shock, they agreed.

Apparently, they felt the whole thing had run its course. Either I would go on to be a huge star, or I would fade away to nothing, and in neither case did I need an ex–stunt man boyfriend without a single acting credit. We'd have one last turn together on the red carpet of my premiere and then announce our breakup and hope that, supernova-like, the dying explosion would generate one final burst of public interest.

Alone in my hotel suite, I spent the days counting down to the premiere, chewing my nails to shreds and trying to help Midge, Irma, anybody, figure out what had happened to them and what to do next.

The dark-eyed silent film star, the girl with the long, soft curls, hadn't reappeared since she'd told me to find Fay Fairfax. Declan had passed the name on to Sam Cranston, the private investigator, who promptly returned a scant report on her: she'd lived in Hollywood twenty years ago, had never worked for Silver Wing, and seemed to have left the city for parts unknown before I'd even been born. Some savior. How could she help us if we couldn't find her?

<hr>

"Maybe you should just bump him off." The girls liked to visit me in my suite, offering a range of advice on what to do next, although some, like Irma, seemed stuck on a particular train of thought.

"Who?" I asked. "Mulvey? Or Reynolds?"

"All of them," Irma said with a sigh. "You could get that adorable do-gooder to help you."

"Murder," I said, "is not an option."

Irma let out another sigh and draped herself over my couch. "Then at least bring back the boy. I haven't seen him in ages."

"We're...winding things down. Anyway, what do you care? It's not as though he can talk to you."

"Henny, I'm dead, not *blind*. Let a girl have her simple pleasures."

I rolled my eyes, and when I looked up, Midge appeared across from me at the table, where I'd spread out stacks of yellowed movie magazines.

"What's this?" She peered down at them, and I fanned a few out for her.

"I rescued them from the publicity archives."

"Doing some light reading?" Another girl had arrived, the dark-bobbed flapper who'd first appeared drenched in a gown of blood. These days she was less terrifying and significantly better dressed. (One of the few perks to the afterlife, apparently: the ability to manifest any outfit you wanted.) Tonight, she was a knockout in golden-squash-blossom velvet, swirling with silver appliqué and cut in a deep V nearly to her waist. Her stage name in the midtwenties had been Georgette Jewell, but she told me to call her Jet. She'd been less forthcoming with the circumstances of her death, which the papers had put down as "complications relating to appendicitis."

"I'm looking for Fay's name. Or the girl who told me to find her, if there's a picture of her." I flipped through the magazine with a frown. "You're *sure* none of you know her?"

"It's not as though there's some heavenly lobby where we all relax together, painting each other's toenails and polishing each other's halos," Irma said with a shrug, and Jet poked her side.

"Bold of you to assume that wherever you're going, there's a halo," she said. "If ghosts could kill..."

"You didn't know me when I was alive," Irma replied, unbothered. "I was *very. Nice.* Excuse me for taking a dim view of humanity after being murdered."

Midge placed a cool hand on mine. It wasn't *quite* like she could touch me, but we both appreciated that, on some level, I could feel her there.

"All of us being able to talk to each other and see each other...that wasn't something we could do before you pulled us together," she said. "Most of the time, we're just..."

"Alone," Jet finished.

Midge nodded. "You make it easier to communicate, Henny. Just you being here, it's like…pulling everything into focus. But there are things that make it go blurry again. Our lives. Our pasts. Remembering our people…It's painful. You don't know how hard it must have been for that girl to give you Fay's name. Maybe that's all she can do, for now."

She was right, as she so often was, and I went back to sifting through the magazines. But hours later, my eyesight blurry and my blood buzzing from too many cups of tea, I'd turned up nothing.

Where was she?

"You looked through *all* of these?" Irma asked, still lounging on my sofa, staring at the pile around me. I sighed.

"All of them. The issues from before 1920 don't have many clear photos—none that looked like that girl, at least—and Fay Fairfax's name wasn't anywhere. Maybe she didn't work in pictures. Sam is positive she never worked for Silver Wing—he went back and combed through the records, everyone from the lowliest script girl up."

I rubbed my aching eyes and when I opened them again, I saw the girl with the liquid black curls sitting across from me. Her mouth was moving, but I'd never heard her speak—it seemed like she couldn't. I'd only been able to get her story in pieces: she came from Harlem, she'd been a singer, her name was Tressie Washington. Now, she pointed to the magazines, her long, painted nails catching the light, her face animated, and mimed pushing the pile away. Obediently, I set each issue aside, until she put out a hand, telling me to stop.

The issue was an old one, from 1915—the oldest magazine I had. There wasn't even a big, beautiful illustration on the cover, just rows of text, a list of *MOTION PICTURE FILMS GUARANTEED TO DELIGHT AUDIENCES!*

"I looked through this one already," I said. "No Fay. And no photos of the girl."

But Tressie shook her head and put a finger to the cover, tapping one of the list headings, *FROM ARGENT STUDIOS.*

"Argent Studios...," I read out loud. "Why does that ring a— OH, Tressie, you're a genius!" I jumped to my feet, the memory coming back to me. Jerome Calhoun, the kind and funny editor who showed me a Moviola on my first day on the Silver Wing lot: *I've been around here since Silver Wing was just a dusty warehouse called Argent Studios.*

"Fay Fairfax never worked for Silver Wing, because it wasn't *called* Silver Wing back then! She worked for Argent Studios! And I know how to find her!"

CHAPTER THIRTY-TWO
— DECLAN —

"Want to take a drive?"

Coming out of my apartment, I jumped a mile to see Henrietta, leaning against the front stoop railing like we had a date. It'd been nearly a month since we'd last seen each other, that night in her hotel suite. Now that Silver Wing had called off our relationship, I didn't have any reason to come to the lot. I'd spent the last few weeks holed up in Sam's apartment, combing through sacks of Etta Hart fan mail in search of clues to who might have sent that letter.

"What are you doing here?" I asked, hurrying down the stairs. "Are you crazy? This is *Hollywood Boulevard*. A star could cause a stampede!"

"But I'm wearing my incognito look. Here—see?" She slid on a pair of sunglasses and adjusted the silk scarf that covered her now-famous blond hair, grinning.

I glanced around, half expecting to see someone looming out of the shadows, but no one even gave her a second glance. It helped that she didn't have on any of her Etta Hart finery, her plain checkered dress something that any high school girl in the country would hang in her closet.

"We need to get you off the street," I muttered, starting to lead her up to my apartment, but she planted her feet firmly.

"Wait! I need a ride, and before I liberate a Buick from the studio's car collection, I thought I'd check with you."

"What for?"

She leaned in, her eyes bright with excitement, and said, simply: "I found her!"

I considered telling her it was too dangerous. She didn't know this Fay Fairfax woman, and how could she blindly follow instructions from a *ghost*? I thought about asking her for the address instead, going over there with Sam, but she had a determination in her expression that put me in mind of the Henrietta I'd met at the screen test. I could probably maroon her on a desert island and she'd still figure out how to get to that woman's house.

"All right," I said, defeated, and I led her upstairs—I couldn't leave her outside on the street. Pep was inside and froze, mouth open, to see Etta Hart materialize in our kitchen.

"Car key?" I asked, putting out a hand, and he leaned in, his voice a whisper.

"Thought you two were done?"

"Uh. Yeah." I glanced over my shoulder at Henrietta, who wriggled her fingers in a wave. "She's found someone who can help prove what Silver Wing's doing."

He raised an eyebrow. "You haven't let that go?" There was an edge of annoyance in his voice that made me give him a second look. He'd been helpful with Henrietta's fan mail, but he continued to doubt that Mulvey—and especially Reynolds—could be involved in covering up the girls' disappearances.

Talking about it just made him anxious, and our friendship felt too fragile these days; it was easier to stick to baseball and his latest dates.

It helped that neither of us was around much. He'd gotten a promotion, from the mailroom to filing clerk, a job that earned him his own desk in the records building. It wasn't much, but it was a long way for a kid from the Mission, especially one with the last name Perez.

"I know what you're going to say, but you don't have to worry," I said, looking back over my shoulder at Henrietta.

"It's my job to worry. You're so concerned about the starlet's reputation—what do you think would happen if it got out she's investigating Silver Wing? You need to *stop*."

"Pep, we're just going to visit an old woman who used to work in the picture business. We'll be fine." I held out my hand again, and Pep stared at me for a second, like he was trying to think of something to say, before fishing in his pocket. He held out the key like he already regretted it.

"Go gentle with her, I think she needs a new transmission."

Or possibly an exorcism. Henrietta slid into the jolting, barking jalopy with the confidence of a new rider facing down a bucking bronco.

"When I said *car*"—she glanced at the wisp of smoke coming from under the hood—"maybe I should've been more specific."

"It'll take you where you need to go." I jerked into first gear. "Which would be...?"

Henrietta looked out the front window, shoulders set and chin raised. "Pasadena."

———————

While I maneuvered the car through Hollywood traffic, Henrietta explained how she'd managed to find Fay Fairfax.

"As soon as I realized she'd worked at Argent Studios—that was Silver Wing's name back in the early days—I remembered that I knew someone at the studio who'd been around since then!"

"You talked about this with someone who works for Silver Wing?" I asked, giving her a sharp look. What if Mulvey connected her to Sam's investigation? Sam was already watching out for tails, had me take back routes to get to his place. But she waved away my concerns.

"Jerome's a good egg. And he and Fay were *friends*! I'd forgotten. She was a writer, apparently, and damned good, too. Anyway, I don't think he believed me when I said I wanted to ask her about character development, but when I mentioned she wasn't in the telephone book he told me she'd changed her name, ages ago, to Francine Fairmont. Sure enough, I found a Francine Fairmont at Seven Dice Road, in Pasadena. What do you think? Maybe if this acting thing doesn't work out, Sam could take me on as a partner."

The Declan of a month ago would've had a field day with a comment like that, but so much had changed between us, teasing her felt impossible.

"Very, uhm, clever," I said. I could feel her giving me a strange look, and I added quickly, "What do you think you're going to get out of her?"

"I...don't know. That girl made it sound like Fay would have the answer. But...What could she do?" The gloom in her voice made me glance at her as we drove east, through the smaller towns surrounding Hollywood like satellites. Henrietta tended to radiate pure confidence, but now she looked small, fingers twisting together. Without thinking, I reached out a hand and covered hers, stilling them. She sighed.

"It's not just a matter of knowing what happened to them," she said. "They've been telling me, in bits and pieces. One girl died in an accident that the director, Howard Abner, should have caught, and another—Mr. Reynolds *forced* her to undergo a medical procedure, and it went horribly wrong. Then there's Tressie—Tressie Washington. You've never heard of her but I guarantee you've heard her voice. She recorded dozens of songs for Silver Wing musicals, must've made men like Mr. Reynolds hundreds of thousands of dollars, but she died poor, alone, penniless...

"And did you know Mulvey had a girlfriend?" Henrietta asked, and I shook my head, thinking of the photographs I'd seen on Mulvey's desk of his wife, his children. "Well, he put her in the hospital with injuries so bad she accidentally took too much pain medication. I sit and I listen and I let them talk as much as they need to, but what does it matter if I can't hold the people who hurt them accountable?"

Her hands felt cold; I gave them a squeeze. "I don't know what Fay Fairfax will tell us." I had my eyes on the road but I could feel her watching me. "And I don't know how to punish those people for what they did. But... It's gotta be a relief for those girls, don't you think? Having someone to talk to. Someone who will finally listen. That's not nothing."

Henrietta let out a ragged breath.

"You might be right. But still... it'd be nice to send some bastards to jail, too."

CHAPTER THIRTY-THREE
HENRIETTA

"I think that's it." Declan pulled the car to a stop, and I looked out at the run-down bungalow. It might've been pink once, but now appeared grayish blush, the color of dead, bloated fish. "Ready?"

We got out and walked through the gate, pushing aside an overgrown curtain of weeds. As we climbed the front steps, they groaned loudly enough for me to wonder if they'd hold us, and Declan gave the front door a brisk knock. The door's large, cut-glass window was impossible to see through, gritty with dust and covered by a dingy curtain, but I noticed a shadow creeping close.

"Miss Fairfax?" I squinted at the edges of the window. "Miss Fairfax, can you hear me? My name is Henrietta. I'm an actress, and I'd like to speak with you. Hello?"

I knocked again, but the shadow had disappeared. After a minute or two of standing on the doorstep, Declan turned to me. "What now? Scale the roof?"

"I'm not breaking into an old woman's house." I rubbed at the dirty window.

"No, spying on her is much better," Declan replied dryly, and my heart gave a funny leap to hear the Declan I knew: smart-mouthed and sharp-tongued and impossible and endearing.

Except that made me feel even stranger, that he could make me giddy with one sarcastic comment, and then I realized I'd been quiet for too long, the silence stretching between us, so I blurted out, "Why don't you, um, check along the back?"

I ducked to peer through the window again, pretending I wasn't focused on the sound of his retreating footsteps.

"Miss Fairfax? Please, can you hear me? Something terrible has happened, and if you don't help, well... You're about all I've got. Hello? Can you hear me?"

"Nothing."

I turned back to Declan—and gasped. There was the girl, the silent film actress with soft pin curls and huge doe eyes.

"Tell her it's about Lola," she said, her voice a faraway echo.

My hand shook slightly as I rapped it against the glass.

"Miss Fairfax? I need to talk to you... about Lola."

Silence. Then the door creaked open, just an inch, enough to see a woman's narrowed eye, sharp and intelligent.

"What did you say?" She spoke in a low, suspicious rasp.

The girl behind me said, "Tell her Lola's come back."

Uncertain, I glanced at her. I really didn't want this door slammed in my face, which was how I expected Fay Fairfax to react as soon as I told her some dead girl had a message for her. The girl, Lola, lifted her chin.

"Tell her Lola's in dreamland."

"*What?*" I whispered, but when Lola gave me an even look, I shook my head and turned back to Fay. "It's... Lola. She, um. She says she's in dreamland."

The color drained from Fay's face so suddenly that I jumped forward, pushing the door open and grabbing her before she could drop to the floor.

"Declan!"

He was there in an instant, scooping Fay into his arms while her eyes rolled like marbles.

"What did you do?!"

"There! The sofa!" I led him to a small sitting room just off the foyer. Papers, books, notes piled high on every surface, but I managed to shove aside a stack of pads on the sofa—and one very offended tabby cat—to make room for Fay. Just beyond the sitting room, I could see a shabby kitchen, and I ran inside, grabbed a glass, filled it with cold water, and rushed back to Fay's side.

"Here," I said, tilting the glass to her lips. "Take a sip. There you go, nice and easy."

She seemed to be coming to, slowly and then all at once. She sat up and I reached for her again, but she pushed away my hand with surprising strength.

"Who said you could come into my house!" Her face was white, other than two red spots high on her cheeks. "Get out! GET OUT!"

"But—"

"Tell her Lola says she's acting like a complete idiot and not holding up her end of the bargain." It was the doe-eyed girl, her voice sharp and her eyes on Fay.

"I don't—"

"*Tell her.*"

I ran a hand over my face, wondering what bomb *that* would set off, but I dutifully mumbled it out. Fay stared at me, wide-eyed, and I winced.

"Don't kill the messenger."

Her head dropped and I worried she'd fainted again, but she seemed to have caught it in her hands and was kneading her temples. When she finally looked up, her eyes were bright with tears.

"Is what you're saying— Is it real?" she whispered. "Lola…"

I knelt at her side, taking one of her hands, gnarled, fragile, the nails bitten down to the quick.

"I know how it sounds. But…yes. She's here. She told me to come here."

Fay's eyes rose and searched around the room, and Lola drifted to her side, reaching for Fay's other hand. Her fingers passed through Fay's skin like a mirage.

"She's sitting right next to you," I said in a quiet voice, and Fay let out a breath, almost a shudder, the hand underneath Lola's twitching.

"It…It was…a promise…A promise…we made to each other." Fay's words came out dreamy, so unlike the sharp rasp I'd heard at the door. "Talking to spirits had been in vogue, once, no party complete without a séance. I told her it was nonsense, I didn't believe, and she said she'd come back, haunt me…" She let out a laugh and then rose to her feet. Declan started, ready to catch her, but she moved steadily to a gramophone in the corner, its huge, flower-shaped horn a beautiful coppery green. After a moment of fussing, there was the pop of a record starting, and then, scratchy and sweet:

> *Meet me tonight in dreamland,*
> *Under the silvery moon,*
> *Meet me tonight in dreamland,*
> *Where love's sweet roses bloom.*
> *Come with the love-light gleaming*

In your dear eyes of blue,

Meet me in dreamland,

Sweet dreamy dreamland,

There let my dreams come true.

"Sentimental slop," Fay said, looking down at the record fondly. "Her favorite song. 'Dreamland' was her secret code. So some heartless, conniving medium couldn't trick me. As if I'd ever sit down at a séance." She turned and gave me a hard look. "Who did you say you are?"

I rose to my feet. "Henrietta Newhouse. This is Declan Collins. We're both actors, at Silver Wing."

"Etta Hart. I've seen you on newsstands." She didn't sound impressed, and I swallowed.

"Erhm. Yes."

"So, what is this? You can communicate with the dead? Or are you a mind reader?"

"Just the dead. It started when I arrived in Hollywood, a few months ago. I began seeing…girls. Women. Actresses. They all had something in common: they died, and their deaths were covered up by the studio."

Fay's eyebrows lifted. "I see now why Lola got involved."

At that, I shot Declan an excited look, my heartbeat picking up. "Does that mean you can help? I want to give those girls justice. My friend, she died, too. No one knows how. I want to stop it from ever happening again."

"My condolences. But I'm sure someone knows how your friend died."

"Then you understand why it's so important I learn the truth. They can't get away with it."

"They already have," Fay said, sounding exhausted. "Years ago, and

241

again, and now with your friend, and in the future, too, with some poor girl who doesn't suspect a thing."

"But—"

"I'm sorry." She turned and pulled the record off the gramophone before pushing it into its sleeve. "I can't help you. I'm sorry for your friend, but there's nothing I can do."

"Wait, I—"

"You're going to have to leave." She nodded at Declan. "You too, Slick."

"You can't! Lola said you could help!"

But she had already started out of the room, making for a narrow hallway leading to the back of the bungalow.

"Close the door on your way out."

"She's leaving?" Declan asked.

"What do I say to her?" I turned to Lola, watching Fay walk away, her expression tugging between pity and anger.

"Tell her…" Lola weighed her words. "Tell her to give you the film. Tell her it's time."

"It's time to give us the film? What film?"

But apparently that was enough. Fay froze, her back to us.

"I don't…" she started, turning around, and then her shoulders slumped, her eyes closed. I heard her take a breath, letting out the air in slow, heavy measures, and when she looked into my face again, she seemed thirty years older.

"All right," she said. "All right. But take a seat. It's a long story."

CHAPTER THIRTY-FOUR
⟩ DECLAN ⟨

The sun had been high when we left the studio, but you wouldn't know it inside Fay Fairfax's house. She led us down a hallway cluttered with faded movie posters, newspaper clippings, dusty photographs where I could make out a younger Fay, dressed in tailored blazers and wide ties, her short, dark hair combed back to accentuate a dramatic widow's peak and shrewd gaze. Now, she stooped as she shuffled in front of us, a long, knitted housecoat dragging on the floor, which was crowded with stacks of books and clusters of cat hair like lonesome prairie tumbleweeds.

She gestured us into a cramped, bookshelf-lined study, and Henrietta reached for my hand. Her skin felt cold, her fingers trembling, and I was glad when Fay pointed us toward a sagging love seat. Everything about this house put me on edge, like Fay was living in a pocket out of time, and I wanted Henrietta at my side, her fingers wrapped around mine.

Fay fumbled with a lamp, its light tinged amber by the shade, and turned around a chair set before a messy writing desk.

"You don't know what it was like back then," she began, settling into the chair like every movement pained her. "Nowadays, it's a factory. They only care about the bottom line. Pictures decided by accountants in offices with lists of expenses. When I started, you had to be half crazy, because there was no money and it was hard work, round-the-clock. You had to be a dreamer. You had to learn quick, because the business changed so fast, what you did in the morning could be outta date by lunch.

"They use those big, ugly warehouses now, but when I started, our stages were glass castles. Like massive greenhouses. Unreal. We lit our scenes with the sun. We shot three, four different pictures at a time, each in a corner. We'd bring in musicians to play music, set the tone. And it was good business for the ladies, too. Today, they think a woman's too dumb to look through a camera. Or set up a shot. Or make her own picture with her own money. But back then, nobody respectable worked those jobs, so the men didn't care if the women took a crack. And we did a damned good job.

"Before Silver Wing was Silver Wing, it was just a shop set up by a man named Daniel Argent. He was an idiot with too much money but at least he was generous with it. I made shorts, nothing fancy, though they had style. I helped put Argent Studios on the map. What I didn't know was I was putting myself out of a job. As soon as the men realized *Oh, there's money in pictures,* they couldn't trust women to handle it anymore. Danny Argent said to me, 'Fay, you've got such good ideas, stick around.' They had me as 'supervisor,' which meant my name didn't show up anywhere in the credits, but I didn't care. Everybody knew: a Fay Fairfax picture was a Fay Fairfax picture, that's it.

"Then, in 1913, I met Lola Rosado. Vaudeville girl, you know. In the pictures, she went by Delores Rose. A beauty. Cameras just ate her up. Here, take a look." She paused to pick up a framed photo from her desk and held it out for me. The grinning girl in the photo looked to be in her twenties, with beautiful round cheeks framed by long curls, the light falling on her so she appeared to be glowing from within.

"Prettiest girl in the world, huh? As soon as I saw her, I wanted her in all my pictures. Then Danny tells me I'm gonna be working with this new kid, a whiz theater director from back east. Irving Reynolds. Yeah. You both know *that* name.

"Everybody in this city thinks Irving Reynolds can do no wrong, but when I met him, he was a gawky beanpole in glasses and a cheap suit, so desperate to make a name for himself, he'd skin his own grandmother. Well, he had this idea for a serial. Fifteen-minute shorts, something to bring audiences in every week. Folks loved seeing a pretty girl get into trouble, fall into scrapes, always having to be rescued by her true love. 'Cliffhangers,' so called because the picture'd end with the girl dangling off the cliff. You gotta come back next week to see if she makes it. In other words, garbage. But Reynolds knew they made lots of money, and he wanted to make lots of money.

"Lola was gonna be *his* star. *Delores in Danger*—that's what he said. By that time, me and Lola were..." She paused, cut me the kind of look that made me wonder what she would've said if it had been just her and Henrietta.

"Well. We were close. She asked me what I thought and I told her: if she wanted to be a real actress, she'd stay away from that trash. It wasn't just the material. Serials got made quick, and they got made messy. I knew a girl who broke both her wrists getting thrown from a horse—she couldn't ride, but the director tossed her up there.

"Reynolds doesn't like hearing no. He waved money at her. Promised if she hacked it for a year or two, she'd star in his features. She asked for some time to think it over, and he brought in another girl, began introducing her to everyone as 'the new Delores.' Well, that settled it. Reynolds got Lola, and he got her for half as much as he first offered her.

"It was bad from the start. Twelve-hour shooting days. No breaks. Real danger. Real stunts. They churned out those serials ahead of schedule and under budget, and things started looking real good for Irving Reynolds. This was going to be his big break. No one cared if he broke Lola first.

"I could see her, run ragged. She couldn't sleep, or else she'd fall asleep in the middle of a conversation. She'd come home black and blue. She wouldn't say how they treated her on set, and I had to get a buddy to tell me straight. He said, 'Fay, they toss her around like a rag doll. You gotta do something.' I tried to get Danny Argent to put me on the set, but Reynolds threw a fit. Said he'd take his shorts to another studio, and that got Danny scared.

"Then I heard they were filming in the mountains. Lola was worried enough she asked me to come out. They were on top of a peak, and right away, I saw Lola, scared to death. I told her quit, walk away, we'll find something else. But she said she had to do it. And she told me to stay. I think she thought if I was there... nothing bad could happen.

"The scene went like this: There's a fight at the edge of the peak, bad versus good, and Lola in the middle. When it's clear the hero's gonna win, the baddie throws Lola over the cliff. It was gonna be this big, dramatic thing, a real cliff, a real drop, Lola rigged up with a harness. Well, they go to film it and Lola's white. She never complains, never, but she asks to find another way to get the shot. Reynolds laughs, says her nerves'll help her get into character, and calls 'Action.'

"First take, fight, the villain pushes Lola, and it looks terrible. She crumples to the ground and rolls over the edge. Reynolds calls 'Cut,' resets, runs it again. And again. And again. Must've been ten times, and now he's getting angry. Lola's not falling right. The villain's not pushing her right. He keeps shouting how they've got to *sell* it, they're ruining his picture, and he goes up to the cliff, hollers that he's gonna show how it's done, and *throws* Lola right off the edge. Like she was garbage. Nothing.

"Maybe he didn't know how hard he pushed her. Maybe that damned harness wasn't supposed to catch her a dozen times in a row. Maybe he was so angry, part of him really wanted to kill her. I don't know. What I do know is that instead of sending Irving Reynolds to prison, *Delores in Danger* became his first big hit. 'Come see Delores Rose's final shots!' He turned her death into an advertisement.

"Argent Studios put out some story that Delores Rose died in an automobile accident. Real sad, such a tragedy. Reynolds paid off the actors and the crew. Tried to give me some money, too, but I threw it in his face. When the carrot didn't work, he took out the stick. Told me if I spoke out about what happened, he'd make sure it was the last thing I ever said.

"Well, in 1916, Danny Argent turned operations over to Reynolds. His first order of business was changing the name to Silver Wing. Second was firing me. Spread rumors so I couldn't get a job writing greeting cards—I was a crank, a hack, a deviant, me and Delores Rose hadn't been roommates but lovers."

My eyebrows lifted, and Fay gave me another sly look, her mouth pulled into a crooked smile. She shrugged. "Broken clocks, and all that. But he still made me unemployable.

"Only he missed something." She turned in her chair and bent down under her desk, reemerging with an iron box, which she set on her knees before drawing a long necklace from under her blouse. There was a silver key hanging on the end, and she fit it into the lock on the box and pushed the lid open. Henrietta let out a gasp.

"Is that…"

"The camera kept rolling when he went after Lola," Fay said. "Reynolds made sure he got his hands on the film, but nobody works quicker in this business than Fay Fairfax. By the time he burned the original, I'd already made a copy." We all stared down at the canister: small, tarnished, nestled in a silk scarf the color of a sunset.

"So here we are. I changed my name. Stayed shut up in this house. I'm living off my picture money, plus whatever work I can do by mail. Reynolds hasn't a clue about the film, I'm sure—otherwise I doubt I'd be here—but I know the truth, and he knows I know the truth."

Henrietta reached out and took Fay's hand.

"And now," she said, "we know, too."

CHAPTER THIRTY-FIVE
HENRIETTA

"Henrietta?"

I'd stopped, frozen, on the steps outside Fay's house, my hands clutching the iron box with Fay's film inside. Our evidence. I'd wondered if it would take some convincing for Fay to hand it over, but she'd just given it to me. "I don't know what good it'll do," she'd said, "but it's not doing anything rotting away in here."

The film felt impossibly heavy, impossibly precious, and I held it against my chest. Declan didn't say anything, just offered his hand. But I couldn't move.

"Mr. Reynolds killed Lola." The words didn't feel real even after I said them out loud.

"I know," Declan replied, his hand still outstretched. I stared at him.

"He killed her. He killed her, and he covered it up. The head of Silver Wing, the smart, kind, older man who reminds me of my papa—he killed a girl. And we have proof." My hands tightened around the box as my eyes filled with tears.

"I know," he said again, his voice patient.

"He *killed* her." That last one did it; I broke down, the sobs rolling free, and before I knew it, Declan had pulled me off the steps, wrapping me up in his arms, the metal box pressed between us. My mind whirled, the tears falling hot and thick, until I felt wrung out, so weak that I didn't even know how I'd make it to the car. Declan must've understood that, since he took me by the shoulders and led me to the street.

Sycamores lined the curb outside Fay's home, their branches thick with early-summer growth that broke the pale purple evening sky into small stained-glass fragments. I could hear the quiet chirps of insects, the air heavy with the smell of dirt and green, growing things. We got into the car, not speaking, and as the engine turned over with a roar, I looked back to the house. It sat silent and dark, but in the front window, Lola watched us, a shadow in reverse, a faded light that would never reach Fay's eyes.

"What if this film isn't enough, Declan?" I whispered as the house slipped out of view. "What if I can't help them? What if they stay trapped as lost spirits, forever? What are we going to *do*?" The tears were back, desperate now, but before they could really start up again Declan held out his handkerchief.

"Figure it out." He had his eyes on the dark, sweeping road before us, but he sounded so certain that a drop of courage slid through me. I took his handkerchief, gulped down a breath. No more crying. Not now.

"Okay."

The road out of Fay's neighborhood took us quickly through Pasadena, and within minutes, we were alone, the sky clinging to the final darts of daylight, the buildings giving way to trees and steep, rocky banks. I kept Declan's handkerchief knotted and damp in my lap, twisting it around my fingers. Surely Sam's federal agents would be interested in film showing the head of Silver Wing pushing a girl to her death. But handing it over to them felt wrong. Any charges Mr. Reynolds faced, he would fight, with his pictures, his stars, his influence, his money. What if he paid off witnesses to lie for him? What if he figured out I got this film from Fay?

"Do you think—" I started, but my words broke off when I caught Declan grimacing, his attention divided between the rearview mirror and the road. "What?"

"The car behind us is too close."

I twisted around to see the snub-nosed silver grille of a great black Buick, nearer than a car length away and inching forward. The road underneath gave a jolt as we drove onto a bridge arched high over a riverbed.

"What's it doing?" I asked, frowning. "This bridge is too narrow to pass anyone."

"I don't think he's trying to pass us..."

Declan urged the car forward, and I could feel it vibrating from the speed, wind whipping through the windows. The Buick kept pace, shrinking the gap between our bumper and that grinning, shining grille to five feet, three feet...

"Hold on!" Declan jerked the car left, into the opposite lane. I barely caught myself on the dashboard as the Buick leaped forward into the space where, seconds before, our car had been. For a moment, we drove parallel to each other, the Buick on our right so that I stared out my window into the unnaturally calm face of—

"Mulvey!"

"Mulvey?!"

I'd heard about him from Declan and Gussy, the girl who'd dated him while alive—if you could call semiregular dinners followed by violent outbursts "dating"—but I realized I recognized him. He roamed the lot, looming over everyone, advising—or warning—me those first few days at Silver Wing to call him if I ever got into trouble.

He'd seemed all hot, bombastic energy when I'd met him, but now, he kept his expression so blank he could've been thinking about his taxes. Then suddenly, he glanced our way, his eyes locking on mine, and the utter blackness in them took my breath away.

He meant for us to die.

I tore my eyes from his face and gasped—just ahead, another car sped right for us.

"Declan...," I started, as the car began to honk furiously, but he kept going straight, hands gripping the steering wheel so tightly I wondered if it would snap in half.

"Hold on...," he muttered, the car's headlights blinding me, its horn wailing a warning, and I put one hand on the dashboard and gripped the back of my seat as our car filled with light.

"*Declan!*" I screamed, just as he threw on the brakes and swerved sideways, skidding behind the Buick. Something snapped off our car, the whining scrape of metal against metal mixing with the indignant yowl of a horn as the other car screamed past. We'd survived, but our car had complaints. The odor of something burning, noxious and oily, made me cover my nose, and the whole thing began to shudder.

Ahead of us, the Buick seemed to consider what had happened, slowing slightly before taking off down the bridge and speeding into the darkness.

"*What* just *happened*?!" I asked, my voice coming out strangled. At the wheel, Declan battled for control, fighting the gearshift while the car ground out its protests. Great quantities of black smoke began pouring from under the hood, and despite Declan's best efforts, it let out a shuddering groan and died, maybe two hundred feet from the end of the bridge. I wasn't sure if I should burst into tears or laughter. Of course the car broke down. OF COURSE.

"Maybe I can fix it," Declan said, shaky and uncertain, but before I could respond I looked up and sucked in a breath. The silver skeleton-grin of the Buick's grille reared out of the darkness.

"Out—*out!*" Declan shouted, but when I slid from the car, Fay's box clutched to my chest, he grabbed my hand and tugged me *toward* the Buick, instead of running away. I spun on him with a confused look, and he shouted, "We can't get penned in!"

My heart flew into my throat; if the Buick got back onto the bridge before we got off, we'd be trapped. I started running, my useless heels kicked off. I felt my stockings shred on the asphalt, tiny bits of gravel digging into my skin with every step, but I didn't slow, holding tight to Fay's box, racing for the end of the bridge even as the Buick roared for us.

We were fifty feet away, twenty, ten, and I could see, a little beyond the bridge, a wide, sloping hill to our right, thick with trees and perfect for hiding. Just before we reached it, there was a horrible *screech* as the Buick swerved sideways, blocking our exit so that Declan nearly lost his balance, and I had to yank him backward to keep him from toppling over.

"Run!" I shouted, turning around, as the Buick's door popped open and Mulvey exited, unfolding himself in one smooth motion, arm already extended.

Arm? My mind felt slow, stupid, but at a sharp *pop!* everything came into focus: HE HAD A GUN.

"Get down!" Declan threw an arm around me as another loud bang sounded. I felt something jolt through Declan and every nerve in my body seized with fright.

"Did he hit you?!" I gasped, momentarily losing my balance, but Declan dragged me to my feet.

"I'm fine, keep moving!"

A grunt, a tug, the two of us jerked backward as Mulvey yanked Declan away, and I tripped and landed hard on my hands and knees, the box clattering to the road. There was a click right at my ear that made me spin around and look up, only to see the cold silver barrel of a gun. Behind it, Mulvey looked at me with a blank face, the kind of expression you wore when putting out the garbage, washing the dishes, scrubbing the toilet.

"Sorry, hon. Nothing personal."

Before I could breathe, a blur rammed into him, Mulvey flying sideways, tipping over the railing of the bridge and dropping away so abruptly it wasn't until I stood up and shouted his name that I realized Declan had gone over with him.

CHAPTER THIRTY-SIX
⟩ DECLAN ⟨

The wind whistled faintly under the bridge, everything still. Somewhere in the dark, Mulvey's body lay broken, but I didn't go looking for it. I'd seen his face as he fell, eyes wide, mouth open in shock—that was enough.

We'd fallen onto the dry path that ran along the riverbed, the stream shallow and trickling a dozen yards away, and at first I didn't move, flat on my back, breathing hard and blinking up at the first pinprick stars. Then I heard a noise from the bridge, a wild screaming that sent me into action.

"Henrietta!" I shouted, bounding to my feet, dusty and worn out but otherwise fine. A nearby hiking path led from the river up a hill to the bridge, and I ran for it, yelling Henrietta's name every few seconds.

It didn't take long to reach the road, but when I saw her face, I knew that to her, it must've felt like a lifetime. She buckled to the ground, face crumpled with sobs.

"No—I'm alive, Henrietta! Here!" I took hold of her arms, pulled her to her feet. Her face was a mess of streaky tears, and I held her cheeks between my hands, wiping them with my thumbs.

"Do you feel that? I'm alive!" I was breathing hard, but that was nothing compared to her—I thought she'd pass out, her eyes wide and searching my face. Tentatively, she touched my chest, my throat, my arms, my cheeks.

"Wh-What is this?" she asked, her voice hoarse. "What— Why— How—?"

I let out a helpless laugh while cradling her face in my hands.

"I told you I was the world's best stunt man."

She stared at me like I'd lost my mind, and then, almost against her will, she laughed. She clapped a hand over her mouth, but she couldn't hold it in, rolling laughter that almost immediately transformed into tears. I pulled her in for a hug, but she pushed away.

"What is— You can't get hurt? You knew nothing would happen to you and you didn't tell me?! I thought you died!"

"It's... not the kind of thing that comes up."

"I told you about the dead girls! Even when I didn't think you'd believe me! I was honest about my crazy thing and you didn't tell me *this*?"

I blinked at her. "You sort of seem like... you're not that happy I survived."

"He shot you, didn't he!" She spun me around and a second later I felt her finger poke through my shirt. "Honestly—look at this! BULLET HOLES! I SHOULD THROW YOU OFF THAT BRIDGE MYSELF!"

"I—" But we both spun around at the sound of an oncoming car, and Henrietta let out a gasp.

"His car is still blocking the bridge! We have to move it before—"

I didn't wait for her to finish, just ran over to Mulvey's Buick, which he'd left idling—guess he hadn't planned on this taking long—and parked it on the shoulder beneath some trees. By the time I'd turned off the engine, Henrietta had appeared at the window. She'd found her shoes and rescued Fay's box, which she cradled against her chest.

"What about that thing?" she asked, giving our car a dubious look. It'd stopped smoking, which was something.

"I'll try to move it. Stay here." We must not've run through our good luck for the night, because after a few desperate minutes fiddling with the ignition, the gearshift, the pedals, the car bucked to life. Or, at least, enough life to cough pitifully off the bridge. The car Henrietta had noticed passed, with nothing more than a glance.

"It's not going to catch fire, is it?" Henrietta asked, standing at the passenger door, which I threw open for her.

"No promises."

She took a breath and slid in, and I hit the gas before she even closed the door.

"What do you have there?" Along with the box, she held a suitcase, fingers worrying the latches.

"One of the girls told me to grab it from his car," she said, and then she shot me a look. "The one who knew Mulvey."

"Where are we taking it?"

Henrietta settled the case on her knees. "Mulvey's office."

※※※※※※※※※※

"He must've followed us to Fay's and heard what I said outside her house," Henrietta said when the lights of the studio appeared on the horizon. She shook her head. "Nice work, Henny. Fay kept that film secret for twenty years and I blabbed about it within twenty seconds. But I don't understand how Mulvey knew to follow us. Jerome wouldn't have ratted me out, I'm sure."

That'd bothered me, too. "Sam thought he had a tail on him. I was careful going to his apartment—or I thought I was." I shot Henrietta a guilty look. "The tail must've spotted me and reported back to Mulvey that I was helping Sam with his investigation. But I don't understand why he went after *you*. Mulvey could've just given us a good scare, stolen the film, and threatened us into silence."

Henrietta let out a bitter laugh. "Oh, I already thought about that. Reynolds offered me a new contract. A star contract," she said, her eyes sliding toward me, and I wasn't sure how to react. Her big break, her ticket into the secluded world of the glittery people.

"I—Congrats." It came out stiffer than I meant. I cleared my throat. "I mean, really. Congratulations. You're going to be great. But—a star contract would only make you more valuable to Silver Wing. Reynolds would never approve of knocking out someone who could make him a lot of money."

Henrietta looked down at her lap, miserable. "I never signed it. I just...couldn't. Not knowing everything Reynolds and Silver Wing are involved in. There were these stupid blind items in the magazines about it, rumors that I turned him down because I wanted a better offer from another studio..."

"You could do that?" I asked, surprised. "Break your contract and work with another studio?"

"I don't know, but my sister's a lawyer, and she was absolutely savage with my first contract. If anyone could find a way out of it, it'd be her. Besides, you heard what Fay said about how badly Reynolds wanted Lola, how he threw a fit when she asked to think over his offer. Reynolds must've given up on me and figured the best thing I could do for Silver Wing is have a splashy, tragic death, right before the premiere of my first big film. If it worked for Lola, why not me, too?"

"But that means just getting rid of Mulvey isn't enough. To keep you safe, we've got to bring Reynolds down, too."

"Don't forget my secret admirer," Henrietta said with a desperate laugh. "We still don't know who sent me that threatening letter."

My skin prickled; it felt like a black cloud had slowly crept up on us, blotting out the sun. How could I protect her?

When we were a block away from the studio, I pulled the car to the curb, where it bucked and wheezed and all but collapsed. Silently, we walked to the studio and through the gate. It was late, although not late enough for the lot to be empty, and I wasn't sure how we'd get into Mulvey's office until Henrietta, with a focused determination that suggested she was getting instructions from someone else, swerved away from the main entrance of the Swan Building to a humble side door. The lock barely slowed her down; apparently, she had pinched Mulvey's keys, too.

The door led straight to a small, cramped storeroom, which opened out onto a dark and deserted hallway. I carried Fay's box and offered to take Mulvey's case, too, but Henrietta declined, glancing sideways at what I could only guess was a ghost with trust issues.

"His office is—" I started, but Henrietta stepped past me, heading right for Mulvey's door. A jingle of his keys, and we were inside.

As I closed the door, Henrietta placed the briefcase on the desk. Another key popped it open, and a moment later she held up a thin stack of paper, cream-colored and embossed at the top with *Richard Mulvey, General Manager, Silver Wing Studios.*

"Letterhead?"

Henrietta brushed her fingers across his name. "He's the only one with access to it. Gussy told me." She glanced somewhere five feet to my left.

"Gussy?"

"Mulvey's...She says she doesn't like the word *girlfriend*. Can you find me a typewriter?"

It took a minute, scouring secretaries' offices, but I tracked one down. When I returned, Henrietta sat at Mulvey's desk, midargument.

"—not a debate, of *course* we can trust him," she was saying, as I settled the typewriter in front of her.

"That about me?"

"Sorry." Henrietta frowned, giving the air to her right a sharp glance. "Gussy's nervous."

"I think I'd be, too, in her position. What's this for?"

She sat up straight and fed a sheet of paper into the typewriter.

"Mulvey's last confession."

⚬⚬⚬⚬⚬⚬⚬⚬⚬⚬⚬⚬

It didn't take long. The room must have been full of girls; Henrietta's gaze flicked to various points in the room, her fingers flying as she transcribed what they told her: their deaths, their killers, Reynolds's instructions, Mulvey's executions. Maybe Gussy had suggested Mulvey wouldn't mess around with flowery description, because the final product was a tight list of horrors that ran three pages and left Henrietta looking pale and worn out.

"Soon enough, the police will find Mulvey's car by the bridge and follow it down to his body. They'll think he jumped, and when they want to know why, they'll find the reason right here on his desk." She tapped the confession, but I shook my head.

"We can't leave it here. The studio will bury it. We have to bring it to Sam's contacts, the Motion Picture Review Board."

Henrietta's head turned to one side, and she listened, wide-eyed, before grimacing.

"Okay," she said to the space on her right. "Okay, okay." She sighed and glanced at me. "Gussy says Mulvey would *never* talk to the feds. Not even a deathbed confession. He came straight out of the mob—he wouldn't hand over information to the federal government. Jersey habits," she added apologetically.

"Fair enough," I said. "No feds. Then what?"

Another girl must have spoken up, because Henrietta turned her head again, nodding thoughtfully.

"That could work. Gussy?" A pause. "Then we'll try that." She looked up at me. "Midge thinks we should send a copy to every major newspaper in the country. Reynolds has pull, but not when papers are competing with each other for a story like this. And Gussy says Mulvey reached out to the papers often, to put out the information he wanted."

I raised an eyebrow, impressed at the girls' ingenuity. "Smart."

Henrietta reached for a blank page and set to typing, pausing only every now and then to rub her eyes or pick up a fresh sheet of paper. When the letterhead finally ran out, she leaned back in the chair, surrounded by eight neat bundles, and stretched her fingers. One of the girls must've said something to her, because she looked up with attention. A moment later, she frowned.

"I...don't know. I've never tried that."

"What?"

Henrietta held up her hands.

"Gussy said she can, well, forge Mulvey's signature. She thinks if she...touches me...she could control me."

"Is that even possible?"

She shrugged.

"Or...safe?" I added, but she was already reaching across Mulvey's desk to his briefcase, where a handsome gold pen was tucked into a strap on the lid. "Henrietta...?"

She picked up one of the bundles and turned to the last page, the pen held loosely in her hand. Her body went still, and then she sucked in a breath so quickly, I jumped around the desk.

"Henrietta!" I grabbed her arm, and the moment my skin touched hers, an electric jolt ran through me, if electricity could be so cold that I felt raw, turned inside out, shivering. My hand felt attached to her like a magnet, I couldn't breathe, I could barely see, my vision blindingly white, but I could just make out Henrietta's face, blank, eyes open and staring dead ahead, while her hand scratched across the page, one quick motion. And then I looked past her hand, and I saw...I saw...

It was *them*. The girls. A girl with a heart-shaped face and orange corkscrew curls had her hand wrapped firmly around Henrietta's, while the rest stood around us in a ring. They were young and beautiful and watching Henrietta with desperation.

One of them turned, tilting her head to study the paper.

"The ink splatter is a nice effect," she said. "Very 'I can't live with myself anymore.'"

I made a choking noise, and she looked my way, her eyebrows sailing up in surprise.

"Well, hel-*lo*!"

"Y-You're all—" The words stuttered out of me, and my attention tore from them as Henrietta slumped in her chair. "Henrietta!"

"What did you do to her?" one of the girls demanded, and it took me a moment to realize she was talking to the girl who had to be Gussy, fluttering around Henrietta like a nervous hen.

"I didn't—! She should be— Oh, look! Here, she's coming round now."

Henrietta's eyelids fluttered, and slowly, she sat up.

"See?" Gussy said, sounding anxious but relieved. "She's fine! Come on, hon, only seven more to go."

"No, she's not doing that again," I said, and the girl who'd talked about the ink splatter—it was Irma Van Pelt, I realized with a jolt—let out a huff.

"Why don't you let *her* decide?"

"It's all right," Henrietta said, her voice faint. "I'm just surprised, I…" She paused, then looked from me to the girls. "Declan…Can you *see* them?"

I looked up, the girls staring at me. Irma grinned and struck a pose.

"Welcome to the party, handsome."

CHAPTER THIRTY-SEVEN
HENRIETTA

"How?" I stared at Declan, but he could only shake his head, his gaze drifting from girl to girl.

"When Gussy was controlling you, I touched you, and it was like...I felt a shock through me. And then they appeared."

"We were always here," Jet said, crossing her arms over her chest. "We didn't *appear* anywhere. You just couldn't see us."

"You're right," Declan said. "But I can see you now."

"For how long?" I asked. "Do I need to be right next to you? Can you see other ghosts, or only these girls?" He shrugged, bewildered, and it wasn't as though the rest of us had answers, either. Where was the manual for communicating with the dead?

"I hate to interrupt here," Gussy said, not very convincingly, "but we gotta keep moving, or people are gonna wonder how Mulvey could've mailed those letters *after* he died."

She was right, although I wasn't excited to hand my body back over to her. The whole thing had felt a bit like I'd been driving happily along only for someone to hop into the driver's seat and throw me into the back with my hands tied.

"Slower this time," I said to Gussy, pulling over another sheet of paper.

It took a few tries before we got the hang of it—Gussy handling me more gently, my nerves not fighting back quite so hard—and by the last page, I fell back into the chair to catch my breath, heart pounding, but confident I could do it again, if I needed to.

"We'll have to move quickly to get this in the mail," Midge said, looking at the piles, and Declan swept one into his hands.

"I have a friend who used to work in the mailroom—someone I trust with my life. He'll help." He tapped the papers on the edge of the desk and set them down. "I'm going to find some envelopes. Hold on."

As he disappeared, I stood up and stretched, feeling my bones pop and creak.

"Oooh, I can't wait to see Reynolds mess his britches when he realizes he's lost his big, mean dog," Irma said, clapping her hands together.

"Don't celebrate too soon," I said. "I'm sure he's got other people to do his dirty work. Besides, we have to figure out what to do with this film." I nodded at the box on the desk. "Declan keeps talking about the federal government, the Motion Picture Review Board, but I don't know…It makes me nervous, sending it off to them and hoping they'll do the right thing."

"Wouldn't that be a peach, though, if the MPRB took this whole thing down?" Gussy asked. She'd taken over the chair at the desk and had her feet up. "Richie was *obsessed* with them. 'Was.' He *was* obsessed. Sounds beautiful, doesn't it? Like music."

"Why was he obsessed?"

"Buncha fools trying to tell the studios what to put in their movies, under threat of *permanent dissolution*. He couldn't manhandle them and it drove him crazy."

"'Permanent dissolution,'" Irma said with a snort. "Fancy way to say

We'll kill your picture, and your theaters, and your studios, and laugh while doing it."

Jet crossed her arms over her chest, the beads on her dress tinkling. "I hate to be on the studio's side about anything, but I was never much of a fan of the MPRB or their silly 'Code of Decency.' Who decided they were the arbiters of good taste? You know, my last film was supposed to be a real humdinger, and then the MPRB people downtown refused to give it their stamp of approval! Can you believe? Had to reshoot half the picture!"

While the girls chattered, I stared hard at Fay's film, thoughts tumbling through my head.

"They have offices in Los Angeles?" I asked, cutting through the conversation. "Do you think I could get them to come to *Train Car*'s premiere?"

"But that's in only a few days. Surely *Train Car* already passed review," Midge said. "Why would they come?"

"Because they're not going to see *Train Car*," I said with a smile. "They're going to see Fay's footage."

For a moment, the girls were silent. Then Gussy barked out a laugh.

"Ohhh, that's brilliant! A big, public screening, full of newspaper people *and* federal agents? Oh-HO! It'll be in every paper and Washington before they roll the credits!" She raised her hands and gave me a round of applause, the bangles on her arms jingling merrily, and a moment later, Irma let out a *whoop* while Tressie jumped into a perfect shimmy. Jet gleefully clapped her hands together, but Midge didn't join them, her face still etched with worry.

"What is it?" I asked her. "What are we missing?"

"It's a good plan," she said. "The Motion Picture Review Board will be sure to investigate an outright murder, especially with reporters holding them accountable. But Henny...If you play that film instead of your own picture, you won't just ruin Reynolds. What about your career?"

The thought had already crossed my mind.

"I know. Who'd stick around to watch the picture, after *that*? And once the news is out about Reynolds, Silver Wing will be cooked. Maybe some part of it will survive—someday, years later, with a new name and new leadership—but by that time, I'll be old news with a name that's poison. I know how it works."

"But you're so...*good,*" Irma said, her smile wilting. "I thought I was getting a front-row seat to stardom."

"We'll find another way," Midge pleaded. "We can't ask you to give up your dreams, Henny..."

They meant well, but if they kept at it, I felt pretty sure I'd burst into tears. Gratefully, I turned to the distraction of an open door, Declan striding in with a bundle held in his hands.

"Sorry that took so long. Had to dig these out of some secretary's desk. I thought you'd need the addresses for the papers, too, so I went to the publicity..." He paused, and I remembered he could see the girls—and their stricken faces. "What's...wrong?"

"Nothing," I said, quickly, before the girls could speak up. I rushed over to take the bundle, a smooth smile plastered to my face. The last thing I felt I could survive right now was an argument with Declan about my career plans.

"Now let's put Mulvey's rotten name to good use."

CHAPTER THIRTY-EIGHT
DECLAN

Forty-eight hours after Mulvey's death, and other than a brief mention in the *Hollywood Citizen-News*—SILVER WING EXECUTIVE DEAD BY SUICIDE—none of the papers had covered it. No mention of the confession.

Maybe it didn't mean anything. It would take time for the letters to get across the country, and we always figured the local papers would be too nervous to run the story—maybe they'd even contacted Reynolds, alerted him about the confession.

When I'd filled Sam in yesterday, I wasn't sure if he'd kiss me or shoot through the roof. We'd met outside, late at night, behind an abandoned hotel construction project a few blocks south of Hollywood Boulevard. Henrietta agreed I shouldn't tell him about the ghosts or Fay's film—Henrietta kept saying Fay had entrusted it to her, and she couldn't hand it over to a stranger—but he didn't for a second buy the story we'd come up with: I'd confronted Mulvey in his office and he'd broken down in remorse, typed up his confession, and jumped off the Colorado Street Bridge. The look on Sam's face when I finished speaking made me wonder if the ghosts might've been more believable.

Finally, I asked, "Do you trust me?"

He studied me so long I worried he might say no, but at last he nodded.

"Then trust me when I say I can't give you the full story. But I can promise that everything I told you about those girls, what Mulvey did under Reynolds's instruction, is all true. The least you can do is let their families know."

"But no Miriam Powell," he'd said, and I shook my head. She'd tried, but Midge still couldn't remember what had happened to her. "And not your mother, either?"

"No."

Sam closed his eyes for a moment, shaking his head. "Reynolds isn't going to let this go. If what you said is true, if he had Mulvey tail you, if he was willing to cut Etta Hart loose—you need to be ready. Just because you got rid of his attack dog doesn't mean he's out of ways to hurt you. Or her."

<hr />

"Where's my tie?"

"This thing?" Pep dug into the cushions of the couch and pulled out a scrap of black silk, and I snatched it out of his hands. "Why aren't you getting ready at the studio?"

I studied my reflection in the tiny mirror we'd tacked to the wall over the sink, trying to remember what the wardrobe assistant had done last time I'd been shoved into a tux. All those weeks of work, planning, prepping, waiting, and we'd made it. Henrietta's premiere. Tonight, the world would see what she could do, but I couldn't stop thinking about the red carpet, the hundreds of fans lined up, the theater full of people who might want to hurt her...Either she'd finish the night a big star, or...

"Henrietta's got a suite at the Knickerbocker," I said, my fingers fumbling with the tie. "That's just a ten-minute walk away. It's easier to meet her from here."

When I yanked at my collar with a groan, Pep pulled himself off the couch.

"Relax," he said, smiling as he rescued my tie. He smoothed it down before looping it around my neck. "Why are you so jumpy? Gonna be a lot of reporters there, lots of people eager to see you. Maybe now you and Etta Hart are calling it quits, you can get some parts for yourself."

While he focused on my tie, I felt my stomach drop. It wasn't just the *lots of people* or even the *you and Etta Hart are calling it quits*—although both those worries flopped through my gut like wriggling fish. Sometime over the last few days, I'd made a decision, and I knew Pep wasn't going to like it.

"Listen," I said as Pep gave my perfectly even tie a final tug. "I need to tell you something. After the premiere—I'm quitting."

The fond smile vanished from Pep's face, and he looked up at me in confusion. "Quitting?"

"I'm breaking my contract. I know it'll cause trouble, and I'm sorry. I'll pay you back, I'll pay whatever fines Silver Wing throws at me, but I can't do it, Pep. I can't work for them, not for another day."

He took a step back. "Is this because of that junk you told me about? The investigation? You said you and Etta Hart never found that person you were trying to meet."

I winced at the lie. "I'm sorry. I knew you didn't want to hear about it, but…well…We did meet her, and what she told us…It was true, everything we suspected about Reynolds and more. Silver Wing has been covering up crimes for years: murders, accidents, problems on sets, and Reynolds…he killed a girl. It might've been an accident, I don't know. But he lied about it. He built his career on it, on the other women that Silver Wing used up and threw away. And when Reynolds suspected Henrietta and I were getting close to the truth, he sent Mulvey after us. We're only alive right now because Mulvey is dead. He pulled a gun on Henrietta and...I took him with me over the Colorado Street Bridge."

The color drained from Pep's face. Mulvey's death had shocked him—had shocked everybody at the studio, setting off a flurry of rumors about why he'd killed himself—but hearing the truth, Pep looked like he might pass out. I jumped forward to grab him, but he pushed me away, sliding to the floor. He drew his knees up to his chest, hands clutching his temples.

"Pep?"

"He wanted to *kill* you? You and...Etta Hart?" His voice came out small, muffled. "I...I didn't know he would..."

I crouched down, trying to see his face, but he kept it hidden.

"Pep...Did you...Did you know he was...coming after me?"

When he lifted his head, his eyes were bright with tears. "He...came to me...a long time ago, Duke. When you...went after Lloyd Rodger. He wanted to know more about you. He asked who Orla Collins was, and I told him, but I didn't know what it meant. I said you were a good kid, you were worried about that girl on set, you didn't mean anything—Mr. Mulvey didn't seem angry. He gave me the job in the mailroom, told me to keep an eye on you—I told him...I always did.

"When you said you jumped off the roof because you thought Silver Wing had something to do with your mother going missing...I knew you were wrong, Duke. You wouldn't listen to me. I was worried—I didn't know what you'd do next! I...I told Mr. Mulvey. I told him it was you, that your years of stunting taught you how to survive a fall like that."

"And he promoted you," I said, my voice flat, but Pep shook his head.

"It wasn't like that, Duke. I thought that starlet was using you! I figured she wrote the letter herself. You kept telling me how desperate she was to get ahead! She knew you wanted answers about your mother and got you hooked on some crazy idea about Silver Wing and Mr. Mulvey and Mr. Reynolds, used you to get attention."

"But Pep, none of that is true! Henrietta doesn't even know about my mother!"

Pep opened his mouth like maybe he meant to argue with me but he couldn't seem to get the words out.

"I'm . . . I'm *sorry*," he finally said, his voice breaking. "I didn't— You brought her by the apartment . . . I called up Mr. Mulvey and said you two were going somewhere together, and I was worried the starlet was setting you up. I just wanted him to look out for you, make sure you didn't embarrass yourself, that the girl didn't . . . He tried to kill you both?"

"You can check the bullet holes in my shirt. Henrietta's lucky she was standing behind a human shield."

Pep dropped his face in his hands again.

"There's . . . There's one more thing," he said, his voice shaking, and as he lifted his face out of his hands, my stomach dropped.

"Our letters . . . Our *proof* . . ."

"I didn't know what they were, but I didn't think . . . Eight letters to different newspapers? No return address? I thought it had to be some scheme from the starlet."

"What did you do with them?" I asked, rising slowly to my feet. Pep shook his head.

"I'm sorry, Duke. I didn't know why you gave them to me. I didn't know he was already dead. I brought them right to Mulvey's office. Slipped them under the door."

CHAPTER THIRTY-NINE
HENRIETTA

Tonight.

Everything was happening tonight, in just a handful of hours.

Months of preparation, countless hours of dreaming, and at last: I'd sit in a dark theater with an audience ready to look up at a flickering screen and watch me sweep away their troubles.

But of course, they wouldn't see me at all.

This morning, I'd visited my friend Jerome in the editing department and spilled my guts. The secrets at the studio, the deaths, the cover-ups, the whole mucky business. I'd debated telling him about the ghosts, except at that point he'd looked a little...gray...and I needed him to stay conscious.

Kind as he was, if I hadn't had Fay's old iron box, he probably would've thrown me right out of his editing room.

I didn't realize until he fed the film gently into the Moviola that his first time watching Lola's death would be my first time, too. Knowing what would come didn't make it any easier: Lola, perched on the edge of the cliff, eyes wide, the whole thing playing out against the *tick-tick-tick* of the Moviola. When Reynolds appeared, a bit more hair and a bit less padding around the waist but unmistakable, Jerome sucked in a breath. I kept my eyes on my shoes, my attention turned away from the flickering campfire inside the Moviola, but I couldn't help myself. I glanced over at the screen as Reynolds's face contorted with anger, his hands reached out, Lola's body flew back—

Jerome spat out a swear and a moment later the screen went black.

"What are you going to do with this?" he asked.

"It's what *you're* going to do with it. Play it tonight at the premiere. Instead of my movie."

Another swear, which at least was better than him throwing me out.

"Why would I do that? Why, when it would all but guarantee the end of my career? Not to mention the end of *your* career. You think the critics are going to stick around to see *Train Car*? You think anyone's going to go see a single Silver Wing film once this gets out? Is this worth it?"

"You mean telling the truth about an innocent girl's murder?"

My response seemed to stun him silent. Then he shook his head.

"Damned righteous youth," he muttered, and he reached over to the spooled-up film, took it between his hands, sighed. "Did you know...I met her?"

A shiver went down my spine. "I had a hunch. You waxed plenty poetic about the silent days."

Carefully, he dropped the film into its canister and brushed his fingers along the lid. "Just the once. They had me over for dinner. The way Fay looked at her...She was something."

"Will it be hard to do?"

He gave me a sharp look, a mountain's worth of protest welling up inside him, but then, as his eyes searched my face, he softened. Maybe he was seeing another girl sitting in front of him, with smooth, round cheeks and a lovely, lyrical laugh and someone who still loved and missed her.

"No, darlin'," he said. "No, it won't be hard. I make a copy of the film, I splice it to the beginning of your movie, I give the reels to the projectionist."

"Put it after the opening credits. I don't want anyone to miss it."

"Shame to be out in the lobby buying peanuts and popcorn when this studio bursts into flames."

I reached over and planted a kiss on his cheek. "Just make sure you stick around for whatever rises from the ashes."

CHAPTER FORTY
DECLAN

"I didn't know. I'm sorry. It was stupid, and…I was just looking out for you, I swear it. Duke, you're my best friend. I wouldn't do anything—"

His words were like waves, flowing into my ears without meaning, while I tried to make sense of things:

> Pep had given me up to Mulvey
> He was the reason Mulvey went after us
> He was the reason Mulvey nearly killed Henrietta
> He took our letters, the girls' stories, the best shot we
> had at taking Silver Wing down, and put them right
> into Reynolds's hands

My *best friend* did this. I didn't know whether to cry or kill him.

"Duke, I…You know I wouldn't do anything— I never thought— Mr. Mulvey was always decent to me. Mr. Reynolds even stopped by my desk one day. He wanted to hear about the Mission and Mamá. He told me I was a credit to my family, my name, that he'd look out for me…"

Angry as I was, I knew that Reynolds had a gift for telling people exactly what they needed to hear, getting them to do what he wanted. Pep just wanted to protect me and make a good name for himself; Reynolds and Mulvey showed him how.

"I know." The words came out of me automatically, but the second they hung in the air, I could feel how much I meant them. When I put out a hand, Pep stared at it, uncertain, before taking it. I pulled him to his feet and didn't think, just threw my arms around him. I'd always been taller than him, but this was the first time I felt bigger, felt how fragile my best friend was. He wanted the best for me. He wanted the best for himself. He wanted to believe in the people who were decent to him.

"I'm sorry, too," I said. "If I'd been honest with you...I told myself I was keeping you safe, but really...I worried you'd be mad at me for getting in your way."

"Getting in my..." Pep shook his head. "You think I care about any job more than you?" He pulled me close in for another hug. When we broke apart, he kept his hands on my shoulders, a shadow of a smile on his face. "You're family, Duke. You're my brother."

His words sank into me, like an anchor, rooting me to the ground, helping me to stand taller, firmer, and I didn't know what to say in response. I just nodded, my throat closed, and Pep squeezed my shoulders.

"Listen, I can get those letters back," he said, a determined look in his eyes. "I can break in—"

"Don't bother. Reynolds must have them by now. If he knew Mulvey was chasing us, he's probably also figured out we were behind them."

"Then what else can I do? I'm going to help you stop him."

I let out a sigh. "The letters were confessions from Mulvey. We put everything he'd done in there, all the things he did at Reynolds's order.

Now that Reynolds knows how much we know, that premiere isn't going to be safe for Henrietta. I was nervous enough about it just on account of that hate mail—and she didn't write it, I'm certain. Whoever sent the letter knows what happened to Miriam Powell. She didn't leave town. She's dead, and the person who wrote that letter was probably involved."

"No premiere," Pep said, nodding. "Got it."

"Well..." I dragged a hand through my hair, sighing. "Much as I'd love to believe I could convince Henrietta to skip her own premiere... something tells me not even the threat of death would keep her from stepping onto that red carpet. There'll be hundreds of fans, a theater full of people who want to get close to her. I need you, Pep. Come tonight. Help me keep her safe."

"Yeah, yeah, of course," Pep said; then he studied me. "You really care about this girl, don't you? It's not just some job. I've never heard you talk about anyone like that." He laughed, soft. "And here I thought she was driving you crazy."

"She sort of was. But...I don't know. I got to know her better, and..." I shook my head. "It doesn't matter. After tonight, we're over. She's going to be a big star. She doesn't need me anymore."

"Big stars don't need nice boys who care about them?"

"She doesn't think about me like that. She...She thinks I'm in love with someone else."

"Who?"

"Um. My...mother." I grimaced as Pep's eyebrows shot up, and I told him how Henrietta had found Mam's photo, how she'd jumped to conclusions, how she seemed so relieved that I didn't bother correcting her.

"It's fine. It's better like this. She wants a real career in Hollywood. I'd only hold her back. After the premiere, I won't see her again."

"Then you've gotta say something to her," Pep said, and he reached out to straighten my tie. "Tonight."

"Why would that be a good time to tell her the truth?"

"I don't know, Duke. Sounds perfect to me."

CHAPTER FORTY-ONE
HENRIETTA

"He's la-ate," Irma sang.

"Don't be a brat." Jet swatted her with a beautiful bone-inlay fan. The girls, in solidarity, had gotten dressed up, too. High-necked pale blue taffeta and white silk gloves for Lola; Jet in a spangly black gown that would have made my flapper older sister absolutely expire from envy; golden fringe and a cascade of blooming gardenias for Tressie; and an explosively pink number on Irma that I recognized from the Academy Awards red carpet a few years ago. Even Midge had turned up in elegant navy blue, fluttery sleeves waving in some ghostly breeze.

"Nervous?" she asked me, and then we both burst into only-slightly-hysterical laughter.

"The question is: What am I more nervous about? The premiere, the threatening letter, Fay's film, or..."

"Waving toodle-dee-doo to your boyfriend," Irma said, summing it up as usual.

What did it say about me that the thing that really sent my stomach swooping with nerves was knowing that tonight was the last time Declan would take me out somewhere, hold my hand, pull me close?

"We're just friends," I said to the girls, to myself, too, and when I was met with five all-too-innocent looks, I added, "Really."

"Henny—" Midge started, but I cut her off.

"It doesn't matter. He's in love with someone else. It doesn't matter."

Irma, balanced on one edge of the sofa, made a tutting noise. "Take it from a dead girl: kiss the boy."

When a knock echoed through my apartment, they each gave me last smiles of encouragement before fading away, so that by the time I opened my door to see Declan there, we were truly, completely alone.

All right, but did he have to look so *handsome*?

Maybe it was the months of exposure to Hollywood glamor, finally working its magic, but he looked right out of a magazine, his dark hair slicked back and shining, a black tuxedo cut slim to his tall frame. I would've thought Declan Collins might take to a tuxedo with the same affection and ease as prison stripes, but I'd never seen anything fit a body so perfectly, like he'd been born to live in elegance and had just come home.

Damn, this was going to be hard.

For a moment, we stared at each other—his eyes sweeping up and down before settling on my face—and then he recovered first.

"You look…," he began, and I jumped in with a nervous laugh, turning to fetch my wrap.

"Don't get me started. I know. *Such* a cliché, the starlet off to her flashy premiere. The studio sent this over, I'm not keeping it."

"Beautiful," Declan finished. "You look beautiful."

I froze, my back to him, my hands on my sequined cape. Last month, the studio had sent me dozens of sketches of gowns to choose from, something the Henny of yesteryear would have turned into a project as vast and all-consuming as the building of the pyramids, but in the wake of . . . everything, I'd put it off for so long that I eventually panicked and picked the simplest one. At first, I'd been glad of my indecision, because if this evening went the way I'd planned, the last thing I wanted was to swan in on the red carpet in some feathered, jeweled, voluminous extravaganza. Then the dress arrived, and I wondered if I'd lost my damned mind.

It was simple, sure. All it did was skim over my body as closely as a second, shimmering layer of skin. Pure silver, it flowed like water, the delicate V at my chest held up by straps so thin they seemed to float over my shoulders, the back dipping low enough that I felt every waft of air down my spine. I'd never worn anything that made me feel so absolutely, completely like a star, like something burning and rare, but when I saw myself in the mirror for the first time, I wanted to rip the whole thing off. Why did everything have to fall in place just as I had to leave it behind forever?

Speaking of . . .

"You're waiting until our last outing to be nice?" I asked, teasing, my back still to Declan, my fingers shaking as they tipped my lipstick—fiery red—into a tiny purse.

"About that." Declan had stepped inside and, after a moment's hesitation, closed the door behind him, setting my heart hammering. "I'm . . . sorry. For giving you a hard time. You didn't deserve it."

"Don't apologize." I turned around with a warm smile, hoping he couldn't tell how nervous I felt. "You were honest with me. In this city, it's easy to lose track of who you are. You never let me forget."

A smile pulled at the corner of his mouth, and I felt my insides turn into warm gold. Why did he have to make this so hard?

"Yeah, well. I know everyone is supposed to fall for Etta Hart, but I think I prefer Henrietta."

"Henny."

He gave me a confused look, and my cheeks went pink.

"It's just—my friends call me Henny. I only hear *Henrietta* when someone's annoyed at me...so...probably it fit, you calling me that, given how we started, but now, well, you're my friend, and, if you'd like, I'd...like you to call me Henny." My voice had gone so much softer than I'd planned.

Get ahold of yourself! I turned back to the table, tidying up the newspaper I'd torn apart earlier this afternoon, and before I knew it, my mouth had kicked my brain right out of the director's chair and taken over: "I know, it's ridiculous—it was all my sister, my twin, Genevieve. Although really, how could anyone expect a pair of two-year-olds *not* to mangle *Henrietta and Genevieve*? We were always Henny and Genny, Genny and Henny—drove Mama crazy, she'd sooner die than have anyone think she gave her twins names that *rhymed*, but—"

What was I even SAYING—but when I turned to face Declan, he was watching me with a smile.

"What? We can't all be 'the distinguished and eminent Mr. Declan Collins.'"

He cleared his throat. "My, uh, my mam...she called me Dee-Dee."

"Dee-Dee!" A thrill went through me, but Declan's smile had faded, his expression growing unreadable. "Oh. You don't...like to talk about her, do you?"

"She, uh...She..." He drew in a breath, and I was ready to jump in, change the subject, when he kept talking. "She was a dancer. A chorus girl. Always wanted to be famous. Ran off to Hollywood when I was eight, and..." He seemed to be turning something over in his mind, deciding something, and then he put a hand in his pocket.

"Do you want to see her picture?"

CHAPTER FORTY-TWO
DECLAN

My heart couldn't stop pounding. I knew we should get going—Henrietta's premiere would begin soon, and she needed to take her star turn on the red carpet—but seeing her here in front of me, in that dress, I didn't want to leave. After tonight, she wouldn't be Henrietta—Henny—anymore. No one would be able to forget her after they saw her film. She would transform into Etta Hart, for always and forever, and Henny would just be some trivia, something from her past. A past that now included...me.

I realized what Pep had meant. If I wanted to be honest with her, I had to do it right now.

"Oh." Henny smiled at me. "Yes. Of course."

I always kept it in my pocket these days, the photo of Mam, and I pulled it out and handed it to Henny, watching her reaction. Her eyes went round, recognition flickering across her face.

"But this..."

"You wanted to know why I came to Hollywood. Mam's the reason. I only agreed to come out here because I wanted to find her. That's why I started working with Sam, too—she disappeared while working on a Silver Wing movie, and I thought she was one of their lost girls. Even roughed up Lloyd Rodger when I heard he'd been sniffing around her right before she went missing," I said, and Henny raised an eyebrow. "But I couldn't find any proof of anything." I rubbed at the back of my neck. "Listen, there never was any other girl. No long-lost love. I should've told you right away…"

Henny stared at the photograph, her expression hard to make out.

"Anyway. I figured I should say something. Now. Before…you know."

"Before what?" she asked, looking up at me.

I searched everywhere for the right words. "Before we have to say goodbye."

"You act like you're never going to see me again."

"Maybe…I won't. After tonight, everyone will see you as Etta Hart. Even without some flashy contract—you're going to be a star, Henny. Your whole life is going to change. You'll have your pick of whatever handsome, wealthy, famous fella you want. And I already decided I'm getting out of this business. This isn't the life for me. In a year, no one is going to remember a thing about me, and you're going to be the most recognizable girl in the world."

A strange smile had come across her face, almost rueful, and when she let out a laugh, it sounded like cover for a sob.

"No," she said. "That's not happening."

"I know the tabloids have been harsh, but when real reporters see your picture—"

"The theater isn't going to show *One Night in a Train Car*," she said, her eyes welling with tears but a determined smile on her face. "I gave an editor friend Fay's film, and he cut it into mine. Right in the beginning, where no one can miss it."

I stared at her, stunned. "But—But—"

"There will be reporters in the audience," Henny continued. "And I contacted the Motion Picture Review Board. Told them, anonymously, that Mr. Reynolds had snuck an indecent shot into the second reel. I was in the publicity office when the request for four tickets came in. As soon as everyone sees that footage of Reynolds...he'll be done for."

Reynolds, Silver Wing, and also...Henny. *One Night in a Train Car* would go the way of whatever unfortunate play Abe Lincoln was watching when he had his run-in with John Wilkes Booth. Even if Silver Wing survived the pain the federal government had in store, it was hard to imagine anyone looking at Etta Hart and not thinking about the downfall of Hollywood.

"You're sacrificing your own career?"

Henny had a funny kind of smile on her face, as though exploding all her hopes and dreams was just an unfortunate consequence.

"Well," she said, lifting her shoulders in a shrug. "I needed to guarantee as many eyes as possible, especially since Mulvey's confession hasn't popped up yet."

"About that," I said, with a wince, and I told her about Pep, how the letters were probably with Reynolds right now. She looked drained when I was done.

"And you said...this is a friend of yours?" She sounded suspicious—fair enough.

"He's a good person. Reynolds and Mulvey used him, like they used so many others. But I trust him. He wants to help us. He's going to be at the premiere tonight, keeping an eye on things. Unless I can convince you it's a good idea to skip the whole thing, since Reynolds probably knows we wrote those confessions."

"*Ha,*" she said with a wry smile. "As if I'd miss the last night of my career."

"You shouldn't quit," I said, forcefully enough that Henny lifted an eyebrow in surprise.

"What—quitting's good enough for you, but not me?"

I shook my head. "It's not about that. I've seen dozens of actors on sets. You're different, Henny. You're *good*. I should've said something weeks ago. The way you move, the way you speak…There's no one else doing what you do." I stepped closer to her, until I could really see her, her eyes bright. "I don't care that it's acting. I'd tell you the exact same thing if you happened to be a world-class jockey or champion knitter or whatever. I *see* you, Henny, and you were made for this. Whatever happens—it's not fair for you to give up your dreams to make them pay."

"A lot of unfair things happen in this city," she said, and then she pulled on a battered smile. "Anyway, I thought you'd be happy. Another heartless starlet, out of the business."

I wanted to reach back in time to the kid who walked into that screen test all those months ago and wring his neck.

"I can't believe I called you that," I said. "Henny. You've got more heart than anyone I know. It's what sets you apart from everybody else."

I was so close that to look me in the eyes, she had to tilt her face up. The studio makeup artists had heavy hands, and I'd gotten used to the overdrawn, dramatic looks they gave her for evenings out, but Henny must've done her own makeup tonight. She was there, the girl underneath the movie-star glamor; the lipstick and rouge and shadow only bringing more of her out. I'd always thought she was beautiful, but now that I knew her, seen her bravery and strength and the joy that burned inside her like a meteor, she was radiant.

"You're really not in love with anybody?" she asked me, her voice quiet, and I couldn't help it—my mouth pulled into a crooked smile as I stepped even closer, her staring up at me in that incredible dress.

"I...don't know if I'd say that."

When I reached up a hand to tuck a strand of hair behind her ear, she went still, watching me. She reminded me of the girl who stood in my arms at the screen test, looking into my face, a little bit question, a little bit answer.

My touch wandered down her neck, shoulder, running the length of her arm to her hand. I felt her fingers flex before wrapping around mine, twisting to hold me tight, pulling me in so that nothing could have slipped between us. I'd seen what that dress had shown off, but I wanted to feel it myself, and I brought my other hand to her back, running my fingers over her skin.

"No cameras here," Henny said, closing her eyes, and I grinned.

"Nope." One impossibly slender strap ran over her shoulder, and I tilted my head down, touched my lips to that spot.

"Is this...real?" she asked, breathless, and I pulled away, because I wanted her to see me.

"For me, it's been real since the second I laid eyes on you."

The spell broke—she let out a snort of laughter. "The *second*?"

"Well...okay. Maybe it took a little longer than that," I said, grinning, and a smile bloomed on her face, until she beamed like a tiny, perfect sun.

"Idiot," she mumbled, and she rose up on her toes and kissed me.

What's it like to kiss the prettiest girl in Hollywood?

So many people had asked me some version of that question. The truth was, kissing Etta Hart never felt like much. Usually there were flashes of light around us, or at least eyes watching, and the assurance that I'd see this kiss in a magazine. Kissing Etta Hart felt like a barber giving me a trim or a makeup artist brushing powder across my cheeks—professional, lasting only as long as necessary. But kissing Henny...

She was liquid against my skin. The hand holding mine twitched and tightened, and the other reached up to my neck, slid into my hair. I could feel her smile in her kiss, and it made me smile back. I couldn't stop smiling, which complicated things, because I also couldn't stop kissing her, and it was surprisingly tricky to do both at the same time. But I was determined to figure it out.

Then she ran her fingertips down my neck, over the muscles of my arm, and it was like everywhere she touched, she left trails of sparks, lighting me up. My whole life, nothing had *really* touched me. Nothing got underneath the surface of my impenetrable skin. Yet here was Henny, slipping in so easily, leaving her fingerprints all over me. She could shatter me, this girl, this starlet, but I didn't care. I'd been the incredible, unbreakable boy long enough; I'd never understood how much strength you needed to be fragile.

So what was it like to kiss this girl? Like realizing after nineteen years you were a creature who needed to breathe oxygen. I pulled her closer to me, feeling her melt into me, her hair spilling over my fingers, her mouth—

"Oh, *damn!*" She pulled away so quickly, I almost lost my balance and had to grab for the wall.

"Wh-What is it?" I'd sort of forgotten how to speak.

"Honestly. You *would* do this at the worst possible time." When I just stared at her, she threw her arms up in the air. "The premiere! We have to go!"

"Do we?" I pulled her closer and she swatted at my arm.

"Stop being so adorable. Couldn't you have gotten here an hour earlier?!"

"You're arguing with me, right now?" I asked, more impressed than anything, and she grinned and landed another kiss on my lips that made my insides go as incandescent as anything lit up on a screen.

"It's part of my charm," she said. When she smiled, her nose wrinkled in a way that was, yeah, absolutely pretty charming, and definitely made me want to kiss her again, premiere be damned, but this time, she pushed me away with a firm "Nope!" She spun around to grab her purse and cape off the table before beelining for the door.

"No time for kisses! We've got to go blow up the movie industry."

CHAPTER FORTY-THREE
HENRIETTA

Though the Knickerbocker sat only a handful of blocks from Grauman's Chinese Theatre, the studio couldn't have their star arriving on foot, so they'd sent a car for the occasion. With traffic, the five-minute drive stretched into twenty, every second of which Declan and I took full advantage of, the unflappable driver looking straight ahead.

"Lipstick check," I said to him as the theater came into view, and Declan pulled away, catching his breath.

"Looks good to me."

I pulled a compact from my purse and held it up for him.

"I was talking about *you*." I reached over to rub the red from his lips, and Declan caught my hand.

"Who cares?"

"We're supposed to be on the rocks," I said, laughing, and he kissed the inside of my wrist.

"Again: Who cares?"

Happy shivers ran over my skin, and I practically swooned. "I guess you're right. After tonight, no one's going to be talking about us."

"Hallelujah," Declan murmured against my skin, and I pulled my arm away as the car slowed to a stop. A swarm of flashing photographers jockeyed for position at the edges of the narrow red canopy that led into the theater's outdoor courtyard. Silver Wing had erected massive bleachers lining the sidewalk, and they were full of people, some who looked like they had been waiting there for hours. Declan glanced at the scene, unimpressed, and then leaned over the front seat to talk to the driver. "I'll give you a twenty to keep driving."

"Don't you dare." I peered at myself in the compact. "I want to see Reynolds's face when this thing blows up. How do I look?"

Declan dropped back against the seat and pulled me close, resting his forehead against mine, lips curled into a smile.

"Perfect."

With a flush on my cheeks unparalleled by anything dreamt up by the makeup department, I stepped from the car and out into what would be, in all likelihood, my first and only red-carpet premiere. Night turned to day as dozens of cameras exploded around me, flashes of lights like fireworks, but I felt like the brightest thing there, glowing with Declan's attentions and heart pounding with anticipation.

"Miss Hart! Miss Hart! Etta!" They shouted for me, called my name, and I smiled and posed and slipped my arm through Declan's. Declan was trying his best to maintain his usual stoniness but seemed to have a hard time not breaking into a grin.

"Keep this up, and they'll think you actually enjoy it," I said to him out of the corner of my mouth, and just the thought of that must've been enough to put a damper on his mood, as he pulled on a frown.

"Etta Hart, Declan Collins! Welcome to the Chinese Theatre!" At the end of the red carpet, where it spilled into the famous cement-paved courtyard, an older woman with the grand voice of a duchess gestured for us to join her at a microphone. "The public has anxiously been awaiting your arrival, nearly as much as we have been looking forward to this picture! Miss Hart, do you have a message for our listeners?"

My publicity team had prepared me for this. The radio message would go out live to hundreds of thousands of listeners across the country, and the list of approved responses ran through tepid variations of "It's a thrill to be here tonight and I do hope everyone enjoys the picture!"

But when had I ever done what someone told me?

"It's going to be nothing anyone expected," I said with a smile. "I just hope everyone's ready for what's coming."

The radio host blinked at me in polite confusion. "Well! How exciting. Oh, look! Here comes—" And we were ushered away, probably before I could open my mouth again.

"That sounded like a threat," Declan muttered.

"The sooner they get used to it, the better."

This theater didn't have a lobby, the mingling kept to the open-air courtyard, decorated with lush palm trees and a large, gurgling fountain. Protected from the screaming crowd by sturdy barricades, the Hollywood elite chatted in tails and gowns under the dark sky. Above, the stars were dimmed by the megawattage of flashing signs and spinning spotlights.

I spotted Jack, chatting with a mass of admirers, arm around a wide-eyed girl in ostentatious purple—no doubt the *next* next big thing. But strangely, I didn't feel any jabs of disappointment at seeing the baton passed to a shiny new girl. For her sake, I hoped she had a Declan in her life to keep her feet on the ground.

Standing near the doors to the theater, looking anxious to get to their seats, four men in boring gray suits regarded the Hollywood glitter with silent suspicion. They had to be the members of the Motion Picture Review Board, and my stomach gave a nervous jitter. Since Declan had told me about losing Mulvey's confessions, I didn't know how we'd find justice for the girls. But we could still take Reynolds down. As I watched, Reynolds walked over to them and shook their hands. He had the air of a gracious host at a busy party, checking in with everyone from the young usherettes, dressed in embroidered silk costumes, to Silver Wing's flashiest producers, all of them hanging on his every word.

Enjoy it while you can, I wanted to say to him. *They won't look at you like that much longer.*

While I shook hands and kissed cheeks, Declan wouldn't stop fidgeting, glowering at anyone who approached.

"I don't think you need to worry about Little Mary Maples," I whispered to him, after the pint-sized star darted away. "It's not like that tutu conceals a knife."

"The person who sent you that letter is here tonight, I'd bet on it." He scanned the courtyard. "Where's— Ah!" The tension in his expression broke as he nodded to a shadowy alcove, where a young man with dark hair and a brown suit stood with his hands behind his back, watching the crowd. "That's Pep." Declan let out a breath. "Good. But I'll feel better getting you out of the open. Come on."

He squeezed my hand and led me through one of the painted double doors, underneath the large, dramatic red pagoda, lit up tonight with flickering candles. Inside, the foyer stretched high, the walls dancing with colorful hand-painted landscapes stretching from floor to ceiling, but the space was narrow—less of a lobby than a pause. My heels sank into the thick carpeting, and I put out a hand to catch myself on a carved wooden chair resting against a wall. I'd never been in such a beautiful theater. Not a single detail seemed to have been spared: even the brass push bar on the door to the forecourt had been designed to look like a length of bamboo.

"Should we sit down?" Declan asked.

One of the usherettes opened a black lacquer door to the theater, the hundreds of tiny embedded mirrors in her costume catching the light, but I shook my head.

"Wherever Silver Wing put me, it's probably next to Jack and Reynolds, and I just can't stomach that. Let's wait a minute, go in at the very end."

It didn't take long. A moment later, the lights flickered, and Declan and I watched from the side as the crowd filed through the foyer into the theater.

When the last people had entered, Declan turned to me, his hand wrapped around mine.

"Ready?"

In spite of my nerves, I couldn't help letting out a small gasp when we stepped inside the auditorium. I knew it was a big theater, about two thousand red-leather seats sloping down to the screen, but it put the rinky-dink picture houses of Chicago to shame. This was a veritable *cathedral* to movies, a place so grand it felt holy. As soon as we stepped out from under the overhang, I turned and looked up: Golden figures like angels perched high above, facing the screen as though they couldn't wait for the picture to start, either. Over our heads, the chandelier, shaped like a massive Chinese lantern, hung from an intricate golden sunburst made of carved pieces of wood and stretching nearly the width of the room. Even the air had a richness to it, a sweet and cedary perfume that seemed to come from the walls themselves. Up front, the heavy fire curtain still hung across the screen: trees and pagodas and birds and flowers picked out in gold, set against a sky-blue background.

Chills ran over my skin, and I had to fight the tears that filled my eyes.

"Are you all right?" Declan whispered to me, but how could I possibly answer that? Instead, I found two seats on the aisle near the back of the theater and sank into the velour cushions as the lights turned low.

Silver Wing had sprung for the full package, and at the front of the theater, a tuxedo-clad orchestra began playing, light and bright, surrounded by dozens of glowing paper lanterns. It should have been a beautiful moment, a transition from the bustle of the courtyard to the dream world of the film, but I couldn't sit still, my knee jumping under my silver gown, my hands tearing at the program I'd accepted from an usherette.

Then the music stopped. Every light went dark. There we were.

That moment.

My favorite moment of any movie, the anticipation coiled up in darkness so solid you could almost reach out and feel it. I'd always wondered what it would be like to sit in a theater knowing it would be *me* up there, that the vision of light and heat and love and brightness would be my body and face and voice, leading people out of darkness into somewhere new.

Tonight, it felt like jumping off a building and not knowing how I'd fall, what I'd hit. It felt like throwing myself into a void.

The screen lit up with the title card, *One Night in a Train Car,* the orchestral music swelling, and I leaned forward so far my knees knocked against the seat back in front of me. Declan pried my stiff fingers from where I'd been gripping the armrest and held my ice-cold hand between both of his. I could make out some of the heads in the crowd, glowing in the darkness, silhouettes of the audience shifting, smiling, leaning over to whisper to companions.

By the time I glanced back up at the screen, I'd missed my own name—which wasn't even my name, of course. The credits continued and my heart pounded so hard I could almost hear it thump over the music, until—

The screen went black.

A jump.

A jagged cut.

My fingers wrapped around Declan tight enough to cut my rings into my skin, but I didn't care, I couldn't look away, I couldn't—

"Oh, shopgirl! Can you tell me if you have these in brown?"

Interior, shoe store, New York City, cut away to reveal Virginia Leigh, buried in a pile of shoe boxes.

What?

Where was Fay's film?

I turned to Declan, who was watching me with a confused expression.

"Where is it?" I whispered to him, and he shook his head. Around us, the audience chuckled right on cue. The scene rolled along, but I wasn't listening; I stood up and hurried out of the auditorium.

"Wait—" Declan's warning followed me out to the foyer, where I spun around, breathing hard, searching.

"The projectionist's booth," I said to Declan as he joined me in the foyer. "How do I get there?"

"Miss Hart."

We both turned to see—who else?—Reynolds, standing in the East Foyer like he'd been waiting for me.

"You won't find what you're looking for here," he said, his voice calm. "One of the members of the Motion Picture Review Board contacted me this morning to ask if I was attempting to sneak an unapproved cut of the film into tonight's premiere. Naturally, I had to review the film myself, privately, earlier this evening, which was when I noticed something odd about the first reel. Thank goodness I was able to correct it." Reynolds stepped closer to me. "Miss Hart, let's take a walk. We have some things to discuss."

"I don't have anything to say to you," I spat, and Reynolds smiled.

"I think you'll want to hear what I have to say."

"She's not going anywhere alone," Declan said, but Reynolds didn't look surprised.

"Of course. This concerns you, too."

He walked deeper into the East Foyer, toward a stairway that showed a sign pointing down a level: MEN'S LOUNGE. But then he turned to an inconspicuous set of stairs going up, narrow and darker than anything else in this glittering jewel box of a theater, and began to climb, leaving me and Declan to give each other equally baffled looks.

I went for the stairs, but Declan caught my wrist.

"You don't have to go up there," he said, and I slipped my hand free, biting back a scowl.

"I came here to take him *down*," I said, following Reynolds up into the dark. "I'm not leaving until he's dust."

CHAPTER FORTY-FOUR
DECLAN

The stairs led to a small landing and a hallway, stretching the width of the theater and studded with black lacquer doors, inlaid with intricate gold designs. Henny and I, her hand in mine, walked behind Reynolds's dark figure until we reached a door at the end of the hallway, which Reynolds opened to reveal a small but handsome office, L-shaped, with a set of stacked windows that looked out to the courtyard below.

Reynolds didn't bother turning on the lights; so much spilled from the neon flashes outside the window that the whole room was bathed in a dim glow, Henny beside me luminous in her silver gown.

"You can't hide anymore," Henny said, and Reynolds turned to regard her.

"I believe you were the one hiding things, Miss Hart. You and your investigation."

"It's too late."

"Is it? Do you have more traps to spring on me, after the film, after your letters?" He opened a drawer in the heavy oak desk at the back of the office and removed a long, thin envelope. "In spite of the signature, the Richard Mulvey I knew did not write this. How did you come to invent these fabulous claims?" Reynolds sounded so polite, so cool, like he stood at the head of a meeting, running down the agenda. He folded his hands behind his back, weight balanced solidly on the balls of his feet.

"I didn't have to invent a thing," Henny spat out. "You know it's all true."

"Oh? Let's take them one by one." He cleared his throat and began pacing before us. "Georgette Jewell. You say she died from complications of a medical procedure I forced her to undergo. Yet we have testimony from the doctor who treated Miss Jewell, verifying that she died from appendicitis. Her death certificate states the same."

"How much did you pay that doctor? The coroner?"

"Irma Van Pelt. Drowned as a result of negligence on the part of Donald Anderson. But the truth is that Miss Van Pelt had grown dangerously infatuated with Mr. Anderson, a married man. When Miss Van Pelt went missing, we attempted to locate her. Our investigators couldn't prove anything, but their findings strongly suggested that Miss Van Pelt took her own life, by drowning, after Mr. Anderson rejected her advances."

"You know that's not what happened!"

"We tried to explain this to the Van Pelts—I called them personally to give them the news," Reynolds continued in his mild, professorial voice, "but I'm afraid they were unwilling to accept the truth. Should I go on?"

"If we're going to be acting, let's just go back down into the theater— I'd rather watch myself up on the screen instead of you."

"Ah," Reynolds said, as though speaking to a particularly bright student, "but that's it exactly, Miss Hart! We are storytellers, aren't we? Here are the stories we tell. This letter says the studio used, exploited, and failed to protect these young women, but we have a different story. You claim Tressie Washington was taken advantage of, her vocal recordings used against her wishes, but it's standard practice for singers to be paid a flat rate for a day's recording—"

"Her whole catalogue! That you used, uncredited!"

"Standard practice."

"What about Gussy Cob? Standard practice for studio executives to put their girlfriends into the hospital?"

"Miss Cob died of an overdose after years of addiction, along with a history of dramatic stunts designed to boost a flagging career. You have no proof how she received her injuries."

"You want to talk about proof?" Henny asked, eyes glittering. "I saw you. I saw you push Lola Rosado to her death. *I saw it.*"

"And who will believe you? The clip you asked Jerome Calhoun to insert into the *Train Car* print has been removed and destroyed, along with the original, which we found at Mr. Calhoun's home. What's more, our investigators uncovered illegal material suggesting Mr. Calhoun engages in outrageously indecent behavior with his male roommate. He has been arrested; anything he says about the studio's practices is simply a desperate attempt to save his own reputation."

"No!" Henny looked like she was going to rush at him, claws out, and I grabbed her by the arm, keeping her at my side. She yanked at me, trying to get free, and then burst into angry tears. "You're a monster! A monster and a murderer!"

"I'm telling a story, Miss Hart. The story about Delores Rose's death has always been a tragic accident. Do you know what people say about Fay Fairfax? That years ago, an actress she was in love with died, and it broke her. She wanted someone to blame, and she started saying someone had pushed Miss Rose."

"*You.*"

"No. The way the story goes, first she accused the director. Then she suggested it was the fault of another actor. Did she mention my name?

301

That's a new one, I hadn't heard that before." He said it all so smoothly, as fine as any actor he employed. "No, the truth is, Delores Rose died in a car accident. Miss Fairfax was the driver. Mr. Argent, meaning to be kind, covered it up. He told the papers that Miss Rose was alone in that car. He worried Miss Fairfax simply wouldn't survive the ordeal of a trial.

"The studio offered to keep her on, if only to look out for her, but the guilt got to be too much. She came up with that story about Miss Rose dying on a picture set. She accused countless people of being at fault. Even me. But if you only knew what I did for her... still do for her. Did you wonder how she could pay the rent on that house in Pasadena? I've been taking care of her for years."

"You're *awful*," Henny muttered, shaking her head.

"I know the value of a good story. Let me tell you another one. I noticed a few names missing from your list. Orla Collins."

My grip on Henny's arm tightened as the floor seemed to tilt under my feet, and she turned to me with an uncertain glance.

"What happened to her?" I asked, not sure I'd believe anything he said.

"Nothing. As far as we know," Reynolds replied. "Mr. Mulvey told me you believed the studio had something to do with your mother's disappearance. That was a surprise even to me, so I checked our records. We did employ an Orla Collins for several features, ending in May 1926 when she failed to show up to set."

Was he lying? Did he know more? I wanted to scream at him, lunge at him, but all I could do was listen.

"I can't tell you what happened to her after that, but I can tell you that a few weeks later payroll received a request to forward Orla Collins's last check to an Orla Lee in Irvine, California."

Mam—in Irvine? Maybe...alive? I shook it off. "Why should I believe you?"

"That's up to you," he said with a shrug, before turning his attention back to Henny. "There was another name I was surprised was omitted. Miriam Powell. She was your friend, wasn't she? You never learned how she died?"

Henny stared at him, fierce, like she wished he would burst into flames. "So you admit she died? She never went home to New York."

"No," Reynolds agreed. "No, she did not. I am sorry to say, Miss Hart, that Miriam Powell was a troubled girl. She had her struggles. Addiction. We tried to help her, brought her to doctors, professionals, but I am afraid it was not enough. I'm sorry," he added as Henny began trembling. "She was a lovely young woman. Much loved. Much missed. The news was a shock to her family. They begged me to keep the details quiet. Perhaps it was wrong to lie, but..." He paused. "You know, I have daughters, Miss Hart. I understand."

It was an incredible performance. Award-worthy. But then I glanced at Henny and saw the turmoil spinning through her, and I wondered... Could any of it be...true?

Henny had never learned the facts of Midge's death. Even Midge couldn't—or wouldn't—remember. All we knew about Miriam Powell, the living girl, was that she was kind, quiet, didn't have any friends, and her family knew she had died but wouldn't admit it.

Reynolds smiled. A small smile, but it twisted in my gut.

"You see, Miss Hart? You know you shouldn't trust me, but even you can't deny: it's a compelling story."

"I wouldn't trust you to tell me the weather," she said, but there was a shiver in her voice.

"All right." Reynolds folded his hands behind his back again, posture straight, addressing his classroom. "In that case, why don't we work on the next story together? I'll give you the choice, and you can decide which we go with." When Henny stayed silent, he nodded.

"Right now, on the other side of that wall, something miraculous is happening. The birth of a new star. You, Miss Hart. In just under an hour, the doors of this theater will open, and you will be the only thing anyone can talk about. The papers will fall all over you, fans will clamor for your next picture. And you will deliver, Miss Hart. You will sign a new contract with Silver Wing—not one as lucrative as I first offered, I am afraid to say, but handsome enough—and you will go on to make many wonderful pictures. You will win awards, you will travel the world, your pictures will be treasured by generations. And the only thing I ask is that you never speak about any of these girls ever again."

"That's not going to happen," Henny responded, but Reynolds held up a hand.

"Now, hold on, Miss Hart. I told you, you would have a choice. Here is your other story. You continue your investigation. You contact reporters, politicians. You write another note to the Motion Picture Review Board. Let's say, in fact, you project anything less than absolute joy and contentment with your position at Silver Wing. In that case, I shall be forced to release incriminating footage of Mr. Collins here, showing that he is something other than human."

A gasp slipped from Henny's mouth, and fire leaped through me.

"How did you get—"

"We've had it for some time now. It seems your manager and I ran into the same problem when we were caught in compromising positions on film: we failed to locate the original before any copies were made.

When Mr. Perez paid two thousand dollars for footage of you trampled under that wagon, the director had already made a copy for himself, just in case. I've seen it." Reynolds was staring at me, the force of his attention almost knocking me off my feet. This was a man who didn't need to touch me to break me in half.

"I was happy to ignore it, Mr. Collins, as long as you kept up your end of our bargain, but now…I imagine there are scientists who would like to find out just exactly what you are. Perhaps there would even be some legal implications—proof that you were involved in Mr. Mulvey's death. Or other deaths, other accidents. In any case, whatever you are, you cannot be allowed to walk free." Reynolds turned back to Henny, whose eyes glittered with tears.

"What will happen to Etta Hart when the news breaks about her sweetheart? I don't think people would look favorably on her, especially if it was suggested she somehow assisted Mr. Collins in his crimes. Certainly, she would no longer be a box office draw. No one would be surprised if her film contract was quietly dissolved. She's erratic, ranting, raving, showing up late to set, throwing fits, unable to learn or recite her lines. Etta Hart would fade away to nothing, and Declan Collins would remain locked up in an institution.

"So." He stood still, looking Henny in the eyes. "Which story do you want to tell?"

CHAPTER FORTY-FIVE
HENRIETTA

Light swirled through the office windows, the spotlights swinging their beams into the sky. I could hear the buzz of the crowds outside, waiting until the picture ended and the actors emerged, along with the muffled music from the auditorium, vibrating through the soles of my shoes. Reynolds watched me with dispassion—just another girl making trouble, another mess he needed to wipe away.

How many times had he done this? How many times had he held an axe over someone's head to make them obedient? If it hadn't been Declan, he would have found something else. He would have figured out a way to get at my parents, my sisters. He would have dug up some ex-boyfriend to spill salacious, extraordinary stories. He would have trapped me in a compromising position and held on to the evidence. Or maybe he wouldn't have bothered with any of that. He was a man who could say or print or manufacture whatever he imagined. He owned a dream factory. Spinning reality was his specialty.

But just because I could see through it didn't mean I could beat it. I looked over at Declan, and he took my hand, twining his fingers through mine.

"I'll be fine," he said, strong and clear. "Don't worry about me."

I didn't know what to do. It wasn't just that the thought of Declan picked apart by cold-faced scientists made something inside me wrench so hard I felt broken. Reynolds was right. We had no proof. The girls had already been silenced, and I couldn't speak for them.

"That's not true."

I turned to see Midge, standing beside me in her premiere finery, like she'd been there all along.

"You've kept our stories alive," she said, "and you can keep doing it."

"I don't know how," I whispered, and from across the room, I could feel Reynolds's puzzlement. "I can't do it on my own."

"On your own?" Jet stepped forward from nothing, the beads on her dress twinkling in the dark. "When have you ever been on your own?"

"Makes a girl feel like mincemeat," Irma said, from behind me, so I had to twist around to see her, rearranging the cloud of pink tulle exploding around her shoulders. "You should know we're always here."

"Miss Hart? Do you have an answer for me?" Reynolds sounded a tick impatient.

"Blah, blah, blah!" Irma swept past, standing two inches from Reynolds's face. "Don't you ever get sick of hearing your own stupid voice?"

Lola floated through the window to join us.

"I want him to see us." She stared at him, her expression hard. "I want him to hear us."

"But how?" I asked, and Reynolds stepped forward, passing right through Irma, who let out a noise of disgust and swept her hands down her body, shuddering.

"What was that, Miss Hart?"

"You know what to do, darling," Midge said.

No, I didn't know. Even if I repeated every word they said, I was only one girl. Who would listen to me?

A low, beautiful noise filled my ears, raising shivers over my skin, and I turned to see Tressie, eyes closed, mouth open, pouring into the air a song with no words that hung and shimmered like a blanket of stardust. It sank into me, kindling a fire in my chest, and I glanced over at Declan. He heard it, too, his eyes on Tressie, he—

Of course. He could see them. He could *still* see them. Whatever had tipped from me into him when he and Gussy touched me—it hadn't gone away.

I looked over at Midge, her eyes bright, nodding.

She was right. I knew exactly what to do.

"Mr. Reynolds?" I dropped Declan's hand and took a step closer to Reynolds, who watched me, unruffled. Around us, the girls glittered, a beautiful and burning constellation of souls, and slowly, as if called by Tressie's song, even more ghost girls winked into the room, candle flames bursting into light.

"Do you know why I wanted to be an actress, Mr. Reynolds?" My eyes drifted over the girls' faces. "It wasn't because of the fame or the glamor. I didn't care about the money. I never dreamed that everyone in this country would know my name. I wanted to be an actress because the movies made my life into something brighter and more beautiful than it had been. I wanted to be the thing that did that, for other people. I wanted to be a star, Mr. Reynolds, so I could fill people up with light."

He was so well-mannered, even as he waited to crush everything good in my life. I could feel his impatience, but he didn't say a word.

"This city makes that *so* difficult." Slowly, I walked closer to him. "Did you ever consider that maybe you'd make more money and have more success if, instead of coddling drunks and abusers and covering up for bad behavior, you simply let brilliant people shine? If instead of treating girls like me as pawns or playthings or disposable toys, you saw us as people? We can do amazing things, Mr. Reynolds, if only men like you would let us. And maybe we would have been generous enough to share."

An arm's length away, Reynolds shifted his weight.

"We have our stories, you know." Out of the corner of my vision I saw Midge hold out a hand for Tressie, humming now beside her. The moment they touched, Tressie stretched her other hand to Jet, who linked up with Gussy, and then all the girls reached for one another, hand in hand in hand, until Declan, Reynolds, and I stood inside a shining loop of spirits.

"You can try to rewrite them. You can try to silence them. You can try to shout over them. But they are always there, because they are true. You know it. They're a part of your story, too, even if you want to ignore them."

The polite mask Reynolds wore was beginning to strain at the edges, impatience simmering underneath.

"I'm afraid I'm going to have to reject your offers, Mr. Reynolds," I said, and I made sure my voice was smooth and strong. "Instead, I'm going to make you another one.

"As soon as we leave this theater, you get to work. Hand over Declan's footage to us, along with any other copies, because I'm sure they're out there. Next, you get Jerome out of jail and give him back his job—with a nice raise, and throw in, oh, a bottle of the finest whiskey you can buy, with your apologies."

Reynolds looked amused, and Irma let out a small *hiss*.

"Every man on that list—" I pointed to the envelope with Mulvey's confession, sitting on the desk, "they lose their jobs. In fact, any man at Silver Wing who engaged in indecent behavior and swans along like nothing happened will be fired, immediately. And maybe consider filling a few of those vacancies with a different kind of person. When you're done cleaning up Silver Wing, you will announce your resignation."

By now a bright look of surprise had appeared on Reynolds's face, patronizing delight, as though a four-year-old had just walked into the living room and declared supper was ready. But I had more to say.

"Whatever wealth you've got—and I'm not just talking *cash*, Mr. Reynolds, but the whole kit and kaboodle—you put it into a trust, payable to the families of the girls on that list, plus any others I want included."

Behind me, Lola delicately cleared her throat, and I added, "You can make Lola's checks out to Fay Fairfax. Once that's all taken care of, you turn yourself in for Lola's murder. Oh! And I'd like that first contract back, thank you, but I'll have my sister take a closer look—I doubt it's to my advantage."

"Is that all?" Reynolds let out a laugh. "Miss Hart. Why would I agree to any of that?"

"Oh, I don't know," I said with a shrug. "It's the right thing to do, after all, and you should have done it from the beginning. Plus, if I've learned anything from you, Mr. Reynolds, it's to follow up the carrot with a stick. So: you can agree to do it yourself, out of whatever scrap of dignity is in there. Or you can be made to do it, but I don't think it'll be pleasant for you. Do we have a deal?"

He stared at me. "Miss Hart, I believe you're under some kind of delusion, if you think—"

"Is that a no, then?"

The smile slid from his face. "No deal, Miss Hart."

I nodded. "In that case, Mr. Reynolds, I don't think we have anything else to say to each other. Good luck. I think you'll need it." I put out my hand, and for a moment, I wondered if he wouldn't take it, if I was banking too much on the story he told himself, that he was a gentleman, a fatherly figure, that I was a fragile actress who could never hurt him. But the stories hardest to change were the ones we told about ourselves.

He took my hand, his skin cool and soft.

"Now!" I shouted, digging my nails into the back of his hand as Midge grabbed onto my shoulder. I felt her spirit slip inside me as though I was being filled up like a balloon—less backseat driver, more like we shared the same beautiful dress. I felt her senses sharpen through my eyes, my ears, my skin, and from far away, I was aware of Reynolds's hand attached to mine, glued with an electric current, his wide-open eyes and shocked mouth faded and blurry.

It was his scream that brought me back into my own body, Midge delicately slipping away. Reynolds, white as a sheet, pulled free and scrambled backward, eyes shooting from girl to girl to girl, all of them watching him like crouched lionesses.

"How— How are you— What kind of stunt is this?!" He took another step, lost his balance, landed on his rear.

"No stunts here," Tressie said clearly, in her musical voice. Reynolds crawled back like a crab.

"We're as real as can be," Irma added. I noticed that her pink dress had been replaced with something long and velvety black, her nails glittering with varnish. "We always have been. Real. Here. Watching you. Hearing you."

"And now," Lola said, a smile curling the corners of her Cupid's-bow lips, "it's your turn to listen."

CHAPTER FORTY-SIX
 DECLAN

I couldn't tear my eyes away from Reynolds, shrieking, hidden behind a cloud of angry girls, and it took a second to realize that Henny was swaying on her feet. I caught her just as she started to fall, her eyes fluttering closed.

"Hey! Henny?" Her skin had gone grayish, her hands cold and clammy where she tried to hold on to my arms. "Henny!"

"Get her out of here." Midge appeared at my side, but I threw a glance back at Reynolds. Had more girls materialized? Would they tear him apart?

"It'll be all right," she said. "He's got too much to do. They won't drive him over the edge."

"What's the matter with Henny?" I scooped her up and made for the hallway.

"I'm— I'm just—" Her voice was weak, but her eyes had opened. "That took…"

"Don't talk. Let me get you out of here."

The hallway ran right, but I took a chance and opened the door on my left, breathing out a sigh of relief to see a set of concrete stairs leading down to the courtyard. It was dark and deserted but still surrounded by hundreds of star-crazy fans, and as we reached the bottom of the stairs, I looked desperately around for another exit.

"Duke?"

Pep emerged from the shadows, staring at me and Henny, pale in my arms.

"What happened?"

"We need another exit, Pep, and a taxi—right now."

He nodded, and then tossed his head to the lacquer door to the foyer.

"Wait inside, I'll be back soon."

He took off, and I heard Henny say, her voice weak, "I think...I can walk. Just hold on to me."

"Yes, ma'am," I said, and she looked over at me with a smile, the tiniest bit of color back in her cheeks. I led her to the doors and pushed one open.

"Pep said he'd—" But the words died in my throat when I stepped inside and saw Jack Huxley, standing in the West Foyer, looking bored as hell with a cigarette dangling from his lips. I considered pulling Henny right outside again, but they'd spotted each other; Jack yanked out the cigarette and dropped it to the floor, grinding it into the lush golden carpet.

"*You*," Henny said, pushing past me, and Jack gave her a dry look.

"Couldn't stand to see that garbage, either?" he asked, jerking his head toward the closed doors of the auditorium. "Almost lost my dinner. Good news is, we seem to be the only ones who aren't fans. Make sure you stick around for the applause. We can go up there together, give the people what they want, a preview of *Salty Waters*."

"I have no idea what you mean," Henny said, her voice sharp now.

"Didn't you hear? We start shooting in three weeks, Huxley and Hart, together again!" He stretched out his arms as though hanging some invisible billboard. "'They fell in love by train; now watch them set sail!' Or whatever they come up with. This time, they want the romance to jump off the screen, so it looks like we'll be seeing a lot of each other! Parties, dinners, dates—you already know."

"A romance? With you?" Henny was breathing heavily, holding on to the wall for support. "Try to kiss me again and you'll get more than a knee in your groin."

"Come on, let's put that nasty stuff behind us," Jack said, smiling his million-dollar smile. "We each did things we regret: you attacking me, me sending you that letter..."

The air suddenly vanished from the room.

"That was *you*?" I asked, but Jack waved it away.

"Happens to me all the time: I have a few drinks and pick up my poison pen," he said. "What did it say? I don't even remember."

What little color Henny had regained vanished. "It was about Midge. My friend." The words came out in a whisper. She'd gone still, staring at something in the Main Foyer, and when I followed her gaze I saw...

Midge. Standing pale as a wisp of smoke, her dark hair loose from its elaborate hairdo and now streaming over her shoulders.

"Really? Huh. That's funny—I don't know a Midge."

"That's not true," I said. "Henny said you had final say over your costar in *One Night in a Train Car*. You cast Miriam Powell—before Henny."

Henny gave me a look of surprise; then we both looked over at Midge. She had an expression on her face like she'd been slapped, shock shuddering through her before she turned on Jack with narrowed eyes.

"Oh, right," he said, looking absently into the distance. "Maybe we met, once or twice." Something nervous twitched through him, and he swept a hand through his sleek blond hair as Midge crept closer. She'd always seemed so gentle, steady, calm, but now, her face had curdled with some emotion I couldn't completely figure out—rage or disgust or betrayal. It radiated off her in hot, uncomfortable waves. "Well, whatever was in that letter couldn't've been too important."

"You told me to leave the city, or I'd end up just like Midge." Henny had lifted her chin, staring Jack in the eye. "But she's dead, Jack, and not many people knew that. How did *you*?" The silence hung in the air, Jack's smug smile smooth as glass as Henny took a step closer to him, her voice harsh: "*What did you do to her?*"

Something in Jack's smooth veneer cracked. It happened so fast: he lunged at Henny, I leaped in between them, every hair on my arms standing on edge, my lungs scrambling to breathe, while around us...

Midge had grown bigger, blacker, swelling like a poisonous cloud, filling the beautiful bright foyer with an oily blackness.

"*What did you do?*" Henny's voice was a deep rasp, and Jack took a hasty step back, bumping hard into the wall.

"Nothing!"

Midge's lips curled in disgust, and everything in my body went heavy, invisible magnets pulling at my bones, pinning me—and Jack—in place.

"*Don't LIE!*" A blend of Henny's and Midge's voices spilled from Henny's lips, and I tried to reach for her, but I couldn't move. Was Midge controlling Henny now? How much more could she stand?

"I—I didn't...," Jack panted, small and weak, and then he burst out, "It was an accident! A stupid accident! She got the part, she wanted to celebrate..." An electric charge snapped through the air like an invisible whip, and Jack winced, his hands balled into fists. "All right! I invited her out, we got—*I* got drunk, and we, I..."

Henny and Midge made gasping noises, and the theater disappeared, dropped away, leaving the four of us inside our own private auditorium, a screen stretched high above, flickering with a silent scene: Midge, pretty and alive, and Jack, all his smoothness sticky with alcohol, walking the studio lot together, late, Jack pulling her arm, laughing, having fun, not noticing or not caring about Midge's discomfort. The scene shifted to... an opera house? No—not a real opera house but the inside of Stage 6, the biggest soundstage on the Silver Wing lot, eighty feet high with a full-scale theater and stage, and there was Midge, and there was Jack, stumbling badly, pulling her up the stairs to the very top of the theater, to the catwalks hung with elaborate lighting rigs. Jack had his hands on Midge now, and she was trying to get away, pinned between his arms, pushed up against the thin iron railing of the catwalk.

Close-up shot, Jack and Midge, Midge fighting silently, tears down her cheeks. She pushed, she slapped, she ran, he grabbed her, pulled her too hard or pushed her too fast, and she...went over.

The film stopped, rewound, played the scene again, faster this time: the studio lot, Stage 6, the catwalk, Midge's fall. Again, and again, and again, an endless loop, until Jack, curled up in whatever strange space we'd fallen into, screamed, "Stop it! STOP IT! Enough!"

"You killed her!"

"No! I didn't—" Jack's words were cut off by a whimper. Everything had gone dark, the silence of the picture replaced by a wild, mad *click-click-click* of rushing film, loud enough that I pressed my hands to my ears, but it didn't help. The noise seemed to come from inside my own head.

"It was your fault!" I couldn't tell who was speaking now, Henny or Midge, and when I tried to open my eyes, everything had gone hazy, fizzing with sparks. I could just make out Jack, moaning on the floor, and the

flickering images of Jack, Midge, up on a screen that seemed to be growing bigger, bigger, bigger—but Henny—*Henny*...

Her skin had gone completely bloodless, her platinum hair limp, her eyes pure white, her face a mask of rage. Midge was pouring herself into Henny. Her fury was taking over, and it wanted to swallow up Jack but it would take Henny first.

"Stop! Stop it!" I tried to move, only my body felt a thousand pounds too heavy. Henny needed me, I had to reach her, had to help her...

"*TELL THE TRUTH!*" It exploded out of her, exploded *through* her, nearly knocking me off my feet. The thought of Henny, her spirit, her fire going dark—I couldn't bear it. I reached for her, pulling every bit of my strength, and the moment I touched her—

I'd been set on fire.

Fallen from buildings.

Dragged by horses.

Beaten. Hit. Shot.

But even if any of those things could have hurt me, they wouldn't come close to this. I felt Midge's agony at losing her life. Her anger that Jack had gotten away with it. The grief of never getting to experience another kiss or touch or sunshine warmth. Midge's pain rolled through me, and I felt my skin burst into flames, my nerves lit up with lightning, my shocked lungs struggling for air. It seemed to flow from Midge, through Henny, to me, and it was endless, bottomless, a chasm that Midge couldn't carry alone anymore but had to pour into us. I wanted to drop to my knees, but Henny was in my arms now, limp, and I shouted, "Midge! Midge, you have to stop! It's Henny!"

It was like trying to pull back a tidal wave, Midge's spirit flowing around us, filling the air, and I screamed, again, "MIDGE!" and finally, she turned her attention to the girl in my arms. There was a pop, and the world righted itself so fast I felt dizzy, my body buzzing, but Henny didn't wake up, her skin pale and cold, her eyes half closed.

"Henny?" I shook her, held her tight, smoothed the hair from her forehead as I gulped for air. "Henny, it's Declan. Can you hear me?"

I babbled without even knowing what I was saying: "Henny, come on—you need to wake up, don't do this—you want to break my heart someday, sure, fine, go marry a millionaire or move to Siberia. Don't do it like this! Come on, starlet, stay with me, stay—"

A weak whistling, she sucked in a breath, and my heart leaped. Her eyelashes fluttered, her eyes wild and unfocused until they found my face and everything in my world shifted back into its proper place. Her mouth twitched into a smile so beautiful I could've sworn the sun skipped its regular routine and popped into the theater just to shine on the two of us. Everything went blurry and for a second I worried we'd slipped back into Midge's nightmare theater until I realized I was crying, and I let out a laugh, wiping the tears with the back of my wrist.

I kissed her, I kissed her, her lips, her cheeks, her forehead, like kissing her was as necessary as air, which felt pretty accurate. She touched a hand to my cheek, and in between the laughing and the kissing it took me a second to hear the noise behind us. Jack, rolling on the floor like a cockroach, moaning.

"J-Jack?" Henny's voice croaked, and he sat up, wide-eyed, frantic.

"All right!" he screamed. "All right! I did it! I killed Midge Powell! It was my fault! *It was my fault!*"

CHAPTER FORTY-SEVEN
HENRIETTA

I woke up feeling as though my soul had been wrung out of my body and then halfway poured back in. Sunlight filled the room—my room, back in my hotel suite. Through an open window, I could hear birds singing, could smell the fresh, cool air, could see the electric blue of a perfectly clear sky, and the combination of all those things alone made me feel about twenty percent better.

The duvet had been pulled up over my shoulders, and beneath, I still wore my glamorous, slinky dress—no shoes, but so many hairpins poked into my scalp my pillow might've been swapped for a hedgehog. Someone had gotten me home and tucked me in—and there he was, curled up at the end of my bed like a giant, friendly dog, snoring softly.

I smiled, watching Declan's chest rise and fall. He'd taken off his tuxedo jacket and button-down and wore a clean white undershirt with black pants. I spotted his shoes in a pile by my door and I craned to check that—yes!—he was in his socks, one tiny toe poking from one tiny hole.

Everything in me ached, but I managed to bend toward his face, taking it in like the world's best close-up. Sleeping, he looked about ten years younger, aside from the shadow of stubble running down his cheeks. The pomade in his hair had lost its hold and heavy locks fell across his forehead; I reached out and brushed them back. His eyebrows furrowed, he let out a gruff-snort that set off an explosion of happiness inside my chest, and I ran my eyes over the lines of his incredible body.

So much had happened in the last few days, I'd hardly had a moment to think about just *how* incredible his body was. How could it be possible that he never got hurt? That he could survive anything? Why was he the way he was? On the other hand, why could *I* speak to spirits? Were there more people like us out there? WHAT DID IT MEAN?? Thinking about it made my head spin, mysteries I wanted to untangle, but I decided that, at least right this second, the "why" was less important than the "what." I could talk to the dead, and Declan could never be broken. What would we do with these gifts? What would we do now that we'd found each other?

Declan gave a stretch, took a deep breath, and his eyes opened, finding my face with a smile.

"You're awake," he said, his voice thick with exhaustion, taking my hand. "Finally."

"Finally? What time is it?"

He squinted down at his wristwatch. "Three in the afternoon. You've been asleep...seventeen hours."

"Seventeen hours!" I sat up and stretched, feeling my muscles pull and strain like dried-out rubber. "That must be why I want to eat a bear."

"Let me see what you've got—didn't look too promising last night."

"No," I said, and I rubbed at my cheeks. "I want. A bear."

Declan rolled off my bed and onto his feet. "I think I saw some eggs in the icebox."

Before he left my room, he grabbed my robe from its hook by the door and tossed it at me. I was grateful—as lovely as this dress was, I didn't think I could stand to wear it another second. Just looking at it brought everything from last night pouring back. My movie, and Reynolds, disappearing behind a cloud of girls, and—Jack? Did something happen with Jack? And Midge? A quiver of nerves ran through me, and I hurried out of my dress, into my robe, and toward my suite's doll-sized kitchenette, where I noticed a lot of banging and some discouraging smells.

"How about...bread?" Declan asked, running a blackened pan under water, and, quick, I shoved open the window.

"Good lord, just give it up! The Knickerbocker's got room service." Honestly, I could've eaten a block of wood sprinkled with salt and pepper, but, for now at least, Silver Wing still covered my hotel bill, and frankly, I deserved a feast on their dime. While we waited for it to arrive, Declan watched over me as though worried I'd shatter into a million pieces.

"I'm *fine*," I said. "Really."

"It's just...Last night..."

"What happened? I'm not sure I remember the end. We'd finished with Reynolds, and then Jack was there...Midge...She was so angry..." The memories flickered through me. "He killed her." I dropped my face in my hands. It seemed so unreal.

"I'm glad Midge got the truth. But I'm worried about what it did to you," Declan said, and I stared at him, surprised, until he explained it all to me. "I've never felt anything like it before."

"You've never felt *any* pain," I joked.

But he didn't smile back. "I felt that. If I wasn't what I am..." His voice trailed off, and he shook his head. "I'm not sure either of us would still be here right now."

"Then I guess we're pretty lucky to have met each other," I said, reaching across the table to give his hand a squeeze. "What happened to Midge? And Jack, I guess."

"Midge faded away. Said she'd be back later, but I haven't seen her. I don't know about Jack. I was more worried about getting you home. Pep showed up, hurried us out a back exit to a cab. I could've kissed him."

"And Reynolds? The girls didn't...Well. He's still in one piece, isn't he?"

"Irma showed up here in the middle of the night. She was light on the details but she said not to worry, they'd handle him. Speaking of Reynolds, you had a message delivered this morning." Declan reached into his pocket and handed me a telegram. In neat, blocky type, I read, *Free as a bird, sorry the film didn't work out, talk more soon. —J.*

"Looks like Reynolds can make quick amends when he wants," Declan said, and I set the telegram down with a sigh.

"I hope so. We've got a lot to do and no time to waste."

"There's more," Declan said, his expression unreadable.

"Oh, lord. What did I forget?"

In answer, he walked into the sitting room and retrieved a newspaper from the side table. I braced myself for whatever was waiting for me in those pages, as he folded the paper and set it down.

It was...me.

A full-length shot of me from *Train Car*'s premiere last night, smiling and waving in my silvery dress. Above, a headline an inch tall marched out: *ETTA HART ELECTRIC IN ONE NIGHT IN A TRAIN CAR; A MUST-SEE!*

"Miss Hart has arrived." Declan gazed down at my photo, a strange look on his face.

"What? Hoping for a pan?"

"The studio wouldn't stop calling the suite. They have a new contract they want you to sign. Interviews. Photos. A whole promotional tour. Twelve cities in two weeks, but you'll have to juggle it with filming, because they want you to get started with another picture right away—not the one with Jack, something else. They rang up so much I had to yank out the telephone cord."

I took a peek—Declan had pulled out a chunk of the wall, too.

"I'll fix it," he muttered, and I laughed.

"What is it you're worried about? You look sick to your stomach."

He ran a hand through his hair and sat down across from me. "You know I'm quitting acting."

"Sure. You shouldn't be stuck doing anything you don't want to do. I'll get the girls to poke Reynolds and let you out of your contract, and that'll be that."

"So, Etta Hart steps out with . . . unemployed ex–stunt man, ex-actor?" He waved a hand at the papers.

"Excuse me, did you think my opinion of you had changed since the last time we were alone in this suite?" I'd hoped my words would put the memory back into Declan's mind, and, judging by the pink on his cheeks, it'd worked. "Who *should* I step out with? Someone like Jack Huxley? Since when have I ever done anything just because it was expected of me?" I pushed the newspaper off the table, the pages fluttering down to the floor. "I don't want another Jack Huxley. I don't want another actor. I want *you*. Declan Collins, unemployed ex–stunt man, ex-actor."

He watched me, and then the tiniest smile appeared at the corner of his mouth, and I absolutely would not rest until I kissed it.

"I mean," I continued, "I can't believe it myself, and probably I'll regret it, and I'll have to hire a cook, I guess, because you're just hopeless—"

"Hopeless! I think those eggs were hatched sometime during the Civil War. I'd like to see the cook who could—"

"See? I'm regretting this already," I said with a grin, and I leaned closer, elbows on the table, until I was inches away from that adorable, impossible face. "I've got plenty of people to fawn over Etta Hart, but there's only one person in this city who looks at me and sees Henny."

"Joke's on them," Declan said, his breaths coming out ragged. "Etta Hart in some fancy dress isn't too bad, but she's got nothing on Henny Newhouse in a robe and slippers."

"Stop talking," I mumbled, leaning in to brush my lips against his, and he pulled back with a grin.

"Make me."

It was one of the few moments in my life I happily took a direct order. No cameras, no crowds, no expectations, just Declan Collins, perfect and maddening. How many times had we kissed before? Enough to have gotten used to it, but Etta Hart and her featured-player beau apparently hadn't had a clue what they were doing, because I felt sure we'd reinvented the whole thing right there, right then at my table.

Declan pulled me into his arms, which seemed like just about the greatest place in the world a girl could find herself. If I had learned anything about this boy kissing me right now, it was that he didn't hold much to his heart, but what he did, he kept safe, not just with his body that couldn't be broken but with his soul, his spirit, the thing that wouldn't let him be anything other than exactly who he was.

I felt lighter than air, like something precious held with great care and attention, I felt like a star had burst inside my body, filled it with bright, beautiful, warm sparkles, and in between kisses, I mumbled "Oh, *damn*."

Declan pulled away with a question on his face. "What's wrong? You didn't just remember another movie premiere you have to rush off to, did you?"

"No," I said, and cross my heart, I couldn't've stopped smiling if someone offered me a million dollars. "But I think I'm falling in love with you, and there's not a thing I can do about it."

He looked at me, surprised, and then a smile crept over his face, and I couldn't help it—if I didn't kiss him right then and there I would go mad.

Knock, knock.

"GO. AWAY," Declan said, not even bothering to open his eyes.

"It's breakfast!" I slipped out of his arms.

"More like lunch," he grumbled. "*Late* lunch."

Laughing, I ran to the door and threw it open. A man I'd never seen before stood in the hallway, tall and large in a long, dust-colored trench coat, a crumpled fedora in his hands. His eyes looked bloodshot, his face whiskery and shiny with exhaustion, but he had a pleased look on his face.

"Sam? Come in!" Declan appeared behind me, and when I turned to look at him he said, "Henny, this is Sam, the private investigator who got me involved. Sam, this is Etta—"

"*You're* Sam!" I threw my arms around his neck and planted a kiss on his cheek, which glowed pink. When I let him go, Sam gave me a warm smile.

"If I'd known this was the reward for all this hard work...," he started, and Declan, closing the door behind him, cleared his throat. "Right! Well, it's a pleasure, miss, to meet you, something to tell the grandkids about someday. Heard your movie went off like a house on fire."

"Did you have something for us?" Declan asked—a little impatiently, to be honest, but I couldn't blame him. Sam nodded, an excited glow in his eyes.

"Last night, Donald Anderson turned himself in for his role in the death of Irma Van Pelt. They booked him this morning, after he made a full confession. Not even his fancy lawyers can do anything to help him now. We won."

I thought the news would make me feel a rush of joy, and I was surprised when my eyes filled with tears.

"Winning would've been Irma still alive," Declan said, slipping his hand around mine.

"Well…" Sam frowned and nodded. "You're not wrong about that, kid, but given the circumstances, I'm gonna take it."

"Her family?" I asked. "Her parents?"

"I called them right after I got the news. Those talks are never easy, but they've at least got an answer." He was quiet, and then he gave us a funny look. "Rumors are that it was Reynolds himself who ordered Anderson to go to the cops. He's cleaning house. Every junior executive and frisky director in a hundred-mile radius is quaking in his boots. Even heard a little bird say Jack Huxley was a sobbing mess outside Grauman's last night; lit out for Europe at first light." He paused. "What the hell happened? Did you make some kind of deal with the devil to pull this off?

I glanced at Declan, then shrugged. "More like a few angels."

CHAPTER FORTY-EIGHT
DECLAN

"One more thing." Sam cleared his throat. "I've got an update, about, you know, our other business. If you'd like to talk pri—"

"Henny can hear whatever you have to say," I said, and when she glanced at me, I explained: "It's about my mother." My blood felt fizzy, my head light, as I looked at Sam. "Did you find her?"

He was quiet, quiet for too long, and then he frowned.

"Maybe."

"*Maybe?*"

"I don't know, kid." He shook his head, held his hat lightly in his hands. "I followed that information you gave me last night, the new name, and I found her apartment in Irvine. I traced her through Southern California until her last address, Long Beach, in 1932. That's all I could find out."

"Long Beach…" Henny frowned. "I don't know many cities in California. Why do I know that name?"

"Because," I said, "last year it was hit by an earthquake that killed dozens of people."

Sam nodded. "At least a hundred and twenty."

It had happened too far south of San Francisco to feel the rumbles,

327

but my city still lived with the scars of the quake of 1906, and for days, the events in Long Beach were all anyone could talk about. I'd never been to Long Beach, before or since the quake, but I remembered the pictures in the paper, the small city a mess of rubble and debris, crumbled buildings, crushed bodies...

"Was she...Did she..." I couldn't get the words out.

"I don't know," Sam said again. "There was no record of any death, no one reported her missing, but then, there never was an exact count of dead. People I talked to remembered her living there when the building went down. Was she in it when it happened? Was she somewhere else in the city? I don't know. There are bodies that were never identified, there might've been people who died whose bodies were never found. Or maybe she made it through and decided to change her name again, start over somewhere new. I don't know."

I had my gaze on the ground, and as Sam's words filtered through me, it was like my body dissolved. I was an empty shell, nodding blankly while two stories unspooled around me.

In one story, Mam escaped. She survived, shook up but unbroken. She lost everything, but she kept going. A new home, another new name. Somewhere, somewhere out there, she was alive, making coffee in the morning, washing her hands, laughing with a friend, fishing through her purse for streetcar fare. Alive.

And in the other story: she was dead.

Which story was true?

"I thought you'd like to know," Sam said, his voice quiet. I couldn't speak. "If anything comes up, I'll tell you, you know that, right?" Sam placed a hand on my shoulder, kept it there until I tipped my eyes up to meet his. I nodded. "I wish I had more for you. I'm sorry, kid."

Another nod, and when I still didn't say anything, Henny leaned over to take Sam's hand. "Thank you. Thank you for everything."

"Seems like I should be thanking you, miss."

Dimly, I was aware of Henny walking Sam to the door, saying goodbye, but I couldn't seem to bring myself back to the present. I just shifted, back and forth, between those two stories: Mam alive, Mam dead. And I understood what Sam had meant about the Van Pelts, about knowing, how the truth could be so painful but it was solid, something to build on, push off from.

"I could try to find her."

My head snapped up to see Henny, standing in her robe.

"What? What do you mean?"

"If your mother is dead, if her spirit is out there, somewhere, I could try to find her."

I blinked, the words not making any sense. "I didn't think it worked like that. I thought the girls just appeared to you, when they wanted to."

"I've talked to Midge about it. She said there's something about me— she said it was like a moth and a flame, like everything had been dark before me, and then when I tried to find her, when I called her name, the candle was lit. She felt drawn to me. If your mother's spirit is out there...I don't know what will happen, but I can try."

My throat felt dry, and even when I swallowed, I couldn't get the words out without a few tries. "W-will I be able...to see her?"

"I don't know. Maybe." She paused. "You don't have to decide right—"

"I want to do it. I want to try," I said, fast. Just like jumping off that building—do it before I thought it over too much.

Henny nodded. "Take a seat," she said, gesturing at the sofa. My legs felt wobbly as I made my way over, and she went to the windows, drawing the curtains closed. When she sat down by my side, the room had grown dark, everything shadowy and indistinct.

"Do you still have her photo?"

I pulled it out from my pocket and set it on the low table in front of me.

"What should I call her? Miss Collins? Mrs. Collins?" Henny asked.

"Orla." My voice came out so small and scared that it surprised me. Henny took my hand between hers.

"It's going to be all right. I'm right here."

She closed her eyes, and I suddenly wanted to tell her *No. Wait. I'm not ready for this,* but she had already started.

"Orla? Can you hear me?"

I could almost feel her voice, quiet but strong, cutting through the darkness like a beam of sunshine.

"I'm here with Declan. Your son. He wants to talk to you."

Do I? All these years, whenever I'd thought about Mam, it was in the past. An eight-year-old me, waiting for her to come through the door. An eighteen-year-old me, looking for her in every lineup of chorus girls and backup dancers. I'd closed the door on her for so long, I couldn't picture her in front of me, now. I didn't know what I needed to say to her.

"This was a mistake." I pulled my hand out of Henny's to sweep up the photo. "I'm sorry, I shouldn't have—" I stood up, and—it was Mam. Standing at Henny's door like she'd just stepped in but wasn't sure if she was invited. Two impossible thoughts ran through my mind: *She's dead* and *There she is.*

"M-Mam?"

She didn't say anything. Her gaze went from me to Henny and back again. She looked so much older than the photo in my hand. Not a beauty from the chorus or a washed-up actress kicked around the block too long, but a nice-looking woman in a nice dress, dark, patterned with flowers, sensible shoes, flat-topped hat.

Behind me, Henny stood up.

"Orla?"

"Oh," she said, and then she looked at me and said it again. *"Oh."*

"Orla, do you know where you are? Do you know what's happening?"

Mam blinked at Henny, and then looked back at me. Her face seemed to ripple like a reflection on a pool of water, years falling off her, her clothes brightening, hair going darker, curlier, until the figure who stood in front of me looked like the woman I remembered from my childhood, bringing me along with her from dance hall to dance hall.

"Of course," she said, her voice young again. "I'm putting my boy to bed."

I gave Henny an uncertain glance but she just nodded, urging me on.

"Mam?" I looked back at her, and the shock that went through me—I almost wouldn't have been surprised to look down and see I'd fallen back in time, too, five years old in my old, threadbare nightshirt.

"It's been such a long day," she said.

"I..." I didn't know what to say. "You went away. You left me."

"It's just for a little bit, Dee-Dee, I promise. I need to make a bit more money. Everything's so expensive here, and the schools are no good, but when I have enough, I'm going to get you."

"No, Mam—you didn't come back. You left, and..."

Confusion darkened her face. She shook her head, and Henny stepped to my side, placing a hand on my shoulder until I let out a breath.

"Mam, can you try to remember? You came here, to Hollywood, and then you went away. Do you remember why?"

She was silent, her lips pressed together.

"Orla?" Henny's voice was warm, friendly, like she was speaking to a girl her own age. "You were working on a picture when you left the city... Did something happen? Something to make you leave? This is a hard city for a young woman, I know."

Mam didn't say anything, her eyes dull as she studied Henrietta's face.

"Something did happen," Henny said after a moment, her expression falling. "Something you can't even speak of. Was it Lloyd Rodger?"

An electric shock flickered through my mother's body, disgust flinching across her face.

"He was out of town when my mother didn't show up for work," I said to Henny, but she ignored me.

"He hurt you," she said, and she leaned closer to Mam. "You didn't tell anyone, because you knew they wouldn't do anything, or—no. You did tell someone, but they didn't do a thing. Not even Reynolds heard about it. You knew they'd never get rid of Lloyd. So you left instead."

Mam still hadn't said a thing, but as Henrietta spoke, tears filled her eyes.

"But why didn't you come back?" I said to Mam, and my voice came out broken and pleading like I was a kid again. "You could've come back, but you forgot about me, and I tried to find you, but you...you..." The words choked off as my throat closed. Tears burned at my eyes, hot and fierce, and I swiped them away quickly, but more appeared, Mam staring at me behind a blurry veil.

"Oh," she said. "Oh, my darling..." She reached out a hand and pressed it to my cheek and I shivered. She was cold, but it was more than that. The way skin touching skin passed warmth or comfort, my mother's spirit passed into me a tangle of emotions and memories, matted together like a heavy, thick, wet blanket, weighing her down—how did she carry it all? I tried to pull it apart, to make sense, but then I felt a sharp prick of pain, as though buried inside those knots was a thicket of thorns, memories like a million small needles: the sudden strangeness of her own body, the aches in her joints, the end of her career, the shame of giving up. She'd failed as a dancer, as an actress, as a mother, she was no good, worthless, her boy didn't need her anymore, he was better off without her—

"That's not true," I said, the words bursting out of me. "You were a good mother. You were, you…" But I could hear, now, the phone call to the house on Valencia Street, Pep's bright, high voice: "No, he doesn't talk about you, miss. Yes, he's happy here, my mother takes very good care of him."

"If you'd just come back," I begged, "you would have seen…I missed you, Mam. I wanted you back, every single second…"

I reached out, took her hand, bracing myself for the thorns, the weight. I wanted to find something else, wanted *her* to find something else. There was so much muck inside her, thick and matted as seaweed, spiny stinging needles, choking and heavy and wet. I tried to fight it, the black tangles, and it wasn't until I was exhausted by it, stopped fighting and let myself relax, that I realized it was only a layer floating on top of water, endlessly deep. Underneath it was miles and miles of…

Love.

Love?

As soon as I felt it, just a trickle, it was like a dam bursting open, the whole thing crashing over me, overwhelming me, leaving me breathless. It didn't make any sense. It was just there, as undeniable and huge as the ocean.

"Do you feel that?" I asked her, because I wasn't sure she did; maybe she'd spent so much time carrying her weights that she forgot she was more than them. And then I wondered: If she could push her memories into me, what could I send back?

It seemed impossible at first, my skin too impenetrable, my unbreakable body a cage that couldn't let anything out, but I could feel Henny beside me, her warmth, the parts of her that showed me how to crack open.

Mam let out a gasp, her eyes widening, and she grew older again, the woman who first appeared in Henny's apartment. Her eyelashes fluttered, her gaze going unsteady before settling on my face, and I knew she could feel it now, my own quiet ocean. She could see me as I was just at this moment: not a lost little boy, but grown, tall, with a girl beside me who I loved.

"Yes," she said, soft. "I understand. Yes."

"I miss you. You can't leave me again, not now, not after I've found you."

She nodded. "I'm not going anywhere."

But a moment later, she disappeared, and that old little-boy anger flared through me until I realized: she was right.

EPILOGUE

Six Months Later

"Miss Hart?" My assistant, an absolute peach of a girl, poked her head into my dressing room. "Your family's arrived at the station. The driver just phoned to say it'll be about half an hour."

"Thanks," I said, not looking up from the letter I was writing. "I'll meet them down at the Main Gate." The moment I heard the door close behind me, I continued.

"Oh! You said you have a little sister, right? Anything you'd like to tell her?"

The girl sitting on the cozy love seat across from me tucked a piece of her dark bob behind her ear. "Mui mui," she said, nodding. "I kept all my playbills from the Mandarin in an old shoe box in the back of my closet. I want her to have them."

I nodded, adding that to the letter, and a moment later, when I showed it to her, she let out a breath, the relief washing over her like something unexpected.

"Thank you," she said, just before she disappeared.

"You got her address this time?" Declan stood up from the chair in the corner of the room and picked up the letter from where it had fallen to the floor. "You always forget to ask them."

"Actually, I *did*, thank you very much," I said, taking the letter from his hands.

"*I* got it," Midge added. She was perched on a corner of the vanity, ankles delicately crossed. "Save myself the trip chasing after the poor girl later."

"It's not fair when you two team up against me." I pushed back from my chair with a sigh. "You know, usually when a movie star takes up a hobby, it's something fun like yachting or marrying princes." But they'd already moved on, Midge reciting the address of the spirit who'd come to me, Declan printing it on the envelope.

"Secretary to the dead" wasn't ever something I expected to add to my résumé, but I didn't mind the work. It could be hard, and it felt depressingly unending—it seemed the world would never quit throwing away their girls. But once I started, I couldn't stop. Though these girls were gone, their stories were still there. How could I not tell them? I could help them, let them say one last time, *Here I am, I mattered, I was important and valuable and funny and precious and brave.*

They found me, either by accident or because I went looking for them or they got nudged along by Midge and the other girls, and I explained it all: I could write down their story, I could send a letter for them, I could drop some clues to police or investigators. Usually, they didn't have much that would solve any crimes—and sometimes there weren't crimes at all, just tragedies, misfortunes, bad decisions—but anything concrete went to Declan. After he'd dissolved his contract with Silver Wing, he'd flailed around for a bit, unsure of what to do next, until Sam had appeared one day, annoyed, wondering why Declan had never called to ask for a job.

It didn't pay much, but luckily Declan happened to be attached to one of the biggest stars in Hollywood, who was more than happy to bankroll Cranston & Collins, Private Investigators—secretly, of course, because we agreed Etta Hart, movie star, didn't need any more publicity.

The last six months had felt a bit like jumping onto the hood of a speeding convertible and trying to keep my balance, while tap dancing, blindfolded. *Train Car* had done well, although maybe not quite reaching the sky-high expectations piled on it after Jack Huxley abruptly announced—from London—that he was quitting Hollywood forever. The wave of intrigue over what had led to this decision threatened to drown our movie, but it seemed like most people still wanted to see Jack's suave smile on full display one last time—although they walked out of the theater dazzled by Etta Hart.

It turned out some dampened returns were a good thing, in the end. For my next picture, the studio decided against romance and went for a cat-and-mouse mystery without a single kiss, and audiences ate it up. Right now, I was halfway through shooting my first drama and quickly establishing myself as a nimble actress able to handle just about anything (except musicals—not even Silver Wing's illustrious instructors could get this songbird to squawk).

I'd worried how Midge would take the news about Jack, rushing off to Europe to escape justice, and I'd even asked her if she wanted me to try to find him to make him confess. But she'd said no.

"Vengeance almost destroyed me once," she'd said. "I've got enough to take care of right here."

She wasn't wrong about that. For a while, every day I woke up to another news story, another badly behaved man out of a job, reports of assault, abuse, exploitation, consequences. But what had started as a flood dribbled to a trickle as the public moved on to other stories, and after a few months, most of those once-vilified men had showed up in other offices on other studios or tucked away in different departments, as though nothing had changed.

There were a few victories: Donald Anderson went to prison for Irma's death. Jerome got hired back, with a promotion. Tressie's catalogue, with full credits, burned up the radio airwaves, royalties paid out to her family in Harlem. Declan's friend Pep got a plum sales position in an office on the Silver Wing lot that had previously only welcomed in someone with the last name Perez to sweep the floors. My sister Ruby slashed-and-burned the contract Silver Wing had handed to me, going over everything line by line before declaring, "This thing says they can decide practically everything about your career, what pictures you make, how long you work, where you work, for *seven years,* and if you don't like it, you get time added, as punishment! How brave do you feel? Because I'm pretty sure that's illegal."

Bravery I had in spades—time in my schedule was the problem, so I told Ruby to come up with something she could live with and we'd fight more battles another day. She grumbled for a bit but finally drew up a contract that gave me unprecedented control over my own career and earnings. Reynolds, as promised, agreed.

The girls didn't give him a moment's peace, always there to remind him of the next step to take, of the things he had done. But maybe we'd underestimated Reynolds's capacity to ignore what didn't suit him: after a few months of firings, after the creation of a reasonably sized—but by no means big enough—trust, Reynolds quietly announced his retirement and within a few weeks died of a heart attack on a golf course in Florida. Or at least, that was what the papers said. The girls told me different, that Reynolds had made his own ending, unable to tell the full story.

It had been too much, too hard, too sudden. The good work Reynolds had done—had been *forced* to do, certainly, but had still done—began to unravel. His widow and daughters scrabbled for ownership of the trust. Fired executives appealed for, and won back, their jobs. The turning of the tide slammed back to the way things had been.

In the wake of it all, I decided to contact a reporter. June St. James, sympathetic but formidable, was happy to sit down for a full interview. I told her everything: Reynolds and the girls' disappearances, Mulvey and what he'd done for the studio. I figured either I had gotten big enough for my voice to actually matter, or June would blab to the studio and they'd send me to the firing squad. But what ran in the paper was something I hardly recognized: a milquetoast account from "Screen Siren Etta Hart" about how dangerous Hollywood could be for a young girl. My ensuing "must-follow safety tips" apparently included: "Be sure to walk everywhere in pairs, politely reject any offers of liquor, and never get into a car with a stranger."

I never knew if June St. James refused to run my original account, or if her editors stopped her, or the studios, or what. She wouldn't return my calls. But I hoped, somewhere, those notes existed. And just in case they didn't, I wrote them down myself.

"Are you sure this isn't a waste of time?" Midge would ask me when I'd finish a long day at the studio by sitting up at my desk, scrawling away until my hand cramped.

"If I don't write it down, it'll just burst out. Anyway, it could come in handy someday."

She gave the papers a doubtful look. "Sometimes it feels like we're screaming all this into nothing."

"Well," I said, tapping the pile into a neat stack. "Maybe if we scream it loud enough, my grandchildren will hear."

"Too bad we can't deliver these in person," Declan said as he folded up the girl's letter and slid it into the envelope. "Chinatown's less than three miles from the Mission."

No return address—that was the rule. The girls got to send one letter, supposedly written by a friend or a roommate or landlady or whoever, who had known the girl in life and wanted to express condolences, wanted to pass along a few things the girl had mentioned about her family, her friends. I wasn't sure how the families took these last messages. Well, I hoped.

Fay had certainly taken it well. Before he retired, Reynolds offered Fay a job at the studio—head of story development—but to our surprise, she declined. She'd gotten in touch with one of Lola's cousins, in Mexico, and accepted his invitation to visit. Her last letter had included a snapshot of her, smiling in the sunshine, surrounded by laughing blurs of dark-haired children.

Declan...I wasn't so sure. My beautiful, unbreakable boy didn't have much experience with healing. But it seemed he was learning that things mended more easily in the light. At night, alone, he would tell me stories, his childhood, his mother, slowly piecing the memories together until the whole thing left him tired, mumbling in his sleep, but every morning he seemed to wake more whole.

I wasn't able to contact Orla anymore. I wasn't able to contact a lot of the girls anymore—not Irma, not Jet, Gussy, Tressie. I'd wondered if I'd lost my touch until the new spirits arrived and I realized that there was another step beyond this way station, a place not even I could reach.

"I've known about it for a long time," Midge whispered to me one night, in the dark, both our heads on my pillow. "I can feel it, out there. Like a place between air. Sometimes, I can feel it pulling at me."

"Does it scare you?" I asked, because the way she described it scared *me,* but Midge thought for a moment and shook her head.

"I think it's almost like going to sleep after a long day. Like letting yourself drift away and become something…new. It's peaceful, I think. It's good."

"Then someday, you'll…," I started, but I couldn't get any more words out. Midge had become like a sister to me over the last few months, but I couldn't hold on to her, if she wanted to go.

"Someday." She was quiet while I tried not to breathe, tears rolling down my cheeks, and then I felt her cool hand on mine. "But not for a long time. I'm not quite done with life just yet."

"Will I get to meet your family?" Midge asked, hopping down from the vanity with a smile. "Your sisters?"

"Sister," I said, standing up. "Just Ruby. Genny wrote, quote, 'I am far too busy with too many important things to bother taking a vacation right now,' end quote. I guess if she doesn't blow up the world, I'll see her next Christmas. But no. No, today's lunch is strictly for the living. Sorry, darling, but if I told my family what I could do, I think my mother would pass out—and Ruby! Miss Practical, she'd probably hand me over to her fiancé doctor to be dissected."

"Pity," Midge sniffed, and she winked out, leaving me and Declan alone.

"Fiancé doctor?" He stepped closer and wrapped his arms around my waist. "How will they handle one of their daughters dating an ex-actor, ex–stunt man private detective?"

"Oh, you'll be a huge disappointment," I said, snuggling into him. "Especially compared with Peter—he's so polite, and *handsome,* and—"

Something in his expression made me stop, the smile slipping from my lips, and I remembered that Declan hadn't really felt part of a family for years. I took his face between my hands and kissed him.

"You don't have a thing to worry about."

"They're not going to wish I was a doctor?"

"No more than they wish I was a lawyer." I leaned my forehead against his, looked into his eyes. "They're going to love you, because I love you. *And* they're going to love you because you love me. My sister's biggest fear was that I'd come out here and get eaten alive. When she sees I found you instead, she's going to be doing backflips."

I gave him another kiss, and he looked at me with a lopsided smile that made my heart do a few backflips of its own.

"Can't say I blame her," Declan said, and I raised an eyebrow.

"For loving you?"

"For not wanting you to come out to Los Angeles. Ever since I moved here, I've been trying to get out, but you know what?" He shook his head, laughing. "It'll never be the Mission, but with you . . . it might be home."

"You're just saying that because you moved off Hollywood Boulevard."

He laughed again. "Rent's cheaper in Boyle Heights. Anyway, we can't all be as tough as you, Henny Newhouse. You beat the odds. You're a star." He said it like he always said it, with just *the lightest* touch of teasing, but he couldn't hide the pride in there, too, and after another kiss, he turned and gathered his things while I thought it over.

What kind of odds had I beat? It was something that had gnawed at me for a while now. I wasn't any better an actress than Midge had been. I couldn't tell stories like Tressie, who'd had her voice stolen away. I wasn't more self-possessed than Jet, hadn't been more confident than Irma, or more championed by powerful people than Lola. It'd been luck, maybe, that got me to where I was, that had helped me manage to avoid the things that had taken the rest of them down—certainly, there wasn't anything about me that deserved it more than them. What was a star anyway but a pretty girl with a lot of press clippings? But when I voiced that to Declan, as he slipped on his jacket, he shook his head.

"That's not what I mean, Henny. I don't care about stuff like that." Declan swept a hand at the messy piles on my vanity—posters, signed photos, press clippings, fan mail. He reached into his pocket and pulled out the letter I'd written for the ghost girl—Esther was her name. "I mean this. You hear these things and you carry them around with you and I worry they weigh you down but…instead you help those girls, just by being willing to listen to them. You hold them, and you can still smile and laugh and dream of a better world."

"You don't think that makes me a terrible person? To be happy after knowing everything I know?"

"Are you kidding? You think Midge or Irma or any of them—you think they would rather you shut yourself up in some cave? What does your misery buy them? You know," he said, leaning in close to me, "the things that brought down those girls are still out there, and they want you to fail, they want you to be beaten down and broken, but you don't let them. You swing joy around like a sword, and it's just about the best damn thing in the world to watch. And *that's* what makes you a star, Henrietta Newhouse. I could care less about your ticket sales."

He held out his hand, and I took it. His words seemed to slip inside me, rolling and warm, and for once, I didn't have anything else to say.

We left my dressing room, walked outside to the January sunshine, the studio lot busy with knights in armor and girls in mermaid tails, with twenty-foot-tall trees and shining ships loaded onto the backs of trucks, musicians, magicians, creators, innovators, a dream world made of painted plywood and thick makeup and flattering lighting. Etta Hart fit in here, gallons of ink spilled about her and her life and most of it several miles off from reality, but that didn't mean there wasn't a place for Henny, too.

Why had I wanted to be a star? I wanted to be bright and beautiful. I wanted to fill up everyone who saw me with light. To shine. To *burn*. Declan worried that those girls' stories weighed me down as heavy as lead, but truthfully, I'd never seen them like that. They were like diamonds, precious and valuable. They were like gunpowder, filling me with fire. They were the things that kept me grounded while I tilted my face to the sky.

And they changed me. Showed me how to stand up for myself. To stand up for my friends. To kiss the boy. To take all the buried things and nurture them, grow them into beautiful flowers. To live in the sunshine, holding on to someone who loved me, introducing my family to this wonderland.

Thinking about it made me smile, and it must've been a special kind of smile, because Declan had turned his attention to me, beaming, lit up with happiness. A memory came back to me, one of my very first times ever in a movie theater: I'd been sitting in the front, caught up in the magic, when something had made me turn around. And there, stretched out before me, dozens of faces tipped up to the light of the screen, smiling and dreamy in the darkness. It gave me a secret thrill of delight, like I'd looked out through the screen at them.

That was the first time I'd decided I wanted to be up there, to be the thing that made people glow with happiness, and now here was this boy, my beautiful boy, smiling back at me with that same glow.

"Like what you see?" I asked. He sighed, his hand tightened around mine in a way that made my heart leap.

"Henny, I could watch you forever."

And I turned to him with a grin. "Promise?"

ACKNOWLEDGMENTS

Some books come together in a struggle; others fall into place so easily and joyfully it feels like a dream. *A Starlet's Secret* was one of those happy books, but I was only able to have such a smooth path because of the hard work, dedication, and care of these people.

This book would have about half the heart and eighty percent more adverbs if not for the brilliant eye of my editor, Sally Morgridge. She has been the hugest supporter of this book, and her insight and thoughtful comments have shaped this story into something I am so proud of.

Thank you to my agent, Sara Crowe, and all the folks at Pippin Properties for always being there to guide me and my career.

The entire Holiday House team has been such a treat to work with. Thank you all for your kindness, humor, creativity, and support. I feel so lucky to have found such a wonderful home for my books.

I am still in awe of the absolutely incredible artists who lent their talents to my books. Thank you to Corey Brickley (and the entire Holiday House design team) for the drop-dead gorgeous covers—I never could have imagined the worlds I created could be captured so beautifully. And thank you to my *Modern Girl* audiobook narrators, Valerie Rose Lohman and Max Meyers (and the whole Penguin Random House Audio crew), for bringing my flirty flapper and shy science boy so brilliantly to life.

Thank you to all my friends (the writing crew, the Cambridge parents, my '07 fam) for keeping me sane and indulging an introvert who goes over the top planning get-togethers.

Thank you, as usual, to Mackenzi Lee, even though you strongly encouraged me to skip writing these acknowledgments. I love you, and I don't know what I would do without your support and guidance through all life's darkest moments (by which I mean season two of *Love Is Blind*).

This book was, among other things, a love letter to movies and movie-making, the stories and performances that continue to change and inspire us, and especially the female, POC, and LGBTQ+ pioneers who helped create and establish the form. It was also an excellent excuse to visit my favorite local theaters for "research." Thank you to the Brattle Theatre, the Harvard Film Archive, the Coolidge Corner Theatre, the Somerville Theatre, and Kendall Square Cinema for keeping alive a love of independent and classic film.

So much of this book was inspired by the real activists, whistleblowers, truth-tellers, and courageous survivors who spoke up about the injustices of the Hollywood system, many of whom faced in response intimidation, retaliation, further abuse, and attacks on their credibility and character. Your bravery, hope for change, and dedication to equality, fairness, and justice push us all to work harder and do better.

Thank you to my local indie bookstores, especially Brookline Booksmith, Porter Square Books, Trident Booksellers, and Harvard Book Store, for continuing to give my books a home on your shelves. And thank you to my local cafes, especially 1369 Coffee House, for keeping space for writers and creators to work in community.

My daughters' teachers and caregivers granted me both the time to write this book and the comfort of knowing my girls were always happy, safe, and beautifully taken care of. Thank you for everything you have done for my family.

Thank you to the Toniattis, O'Rourkes, Michaels, and Kennys, for your continued enthusiasm, gentle pestering of your local libraries and bookstores, and supportive text messages.

Sloan and Gahyee, I miss you both and wish you lived up on our third floor forever. Thank you for your love and for crossing the ocean to spend time with us.

To Dave, Iris, Flora, and Abby (the dog): I know I rhapsodized...frequently...about the rare stretches of alone time I took to write this book, but the truth is I would be nothing without your joyful distractions and endless cheerleading. You are my best successes and my proudest accomplishments, and I am endlessly thankful I get to call you mine. I love you.

My mom and dad, Keith and Denise Kulper, have shown me nothing but unwavering support while I go off and pursue some deeply unusual careers. You introduced a love of reading, sent me to writing camps, encouraged me when I wanted to leave behind a stable job for the wild world of publishing, and have provided the best childcare (and grown-up care) imaginable. I have never doubted what I could accomplish because you have always believed I'm capable of anything, and every day I realize even more what a truly powerful gift that is. I will never be able to put into words how grateful I am to you both, but here's a book.